ABOUT THE AUTHOR

JP lives in Western Sydney with his family, and an army of dogs.

Before his writing debut novel 'The Invisible Tether', JP focused on writing songs for the melancholy masses and in complete contrast, also developed vibrant and catchy children's songs.

He has worked in a variety of fields but is often dreaming of other wordly adventures and experiences.

You can find him posting bookish parody videos on social media, planting native bush foods in his backyard and chasing the sun through rivers and national park trails.

Jpmcdonald.com.au

THE GEMARINE CHRONICLES 2

BEYOND THE BOUNDS OF TIME

JP MCDONALD

Cover Art by Jennifer Rackham
Gemarine Logo by Jennifer Rackham
Edited by Lauren Humphries-Brooks
Developmental Editing by Emmie Hamilton
Internal by Daiana M (@daianav)
Comic art by Iaioart
Character art by @Graph_desinglit
Title designs by Upklayak @ freepik

NOTE TO THE READER

Gemarine has been built to be tolerant and non-judgmental, but there are several considerations I'd like you to take into account before reading this piece of work. I apologise if by some chance, you are offended by anything listed below and strongly advise you consider your wellbeing if the following pieces of content may in fact, become a trigger for you.

Depictions of, and references to death, violent conflict, genocide, recollections of war, extreme violence, gore, trauma, abuse, torture, animal/creature abuse and death, graphic sex scenes, kink scenes, group sex scenes, substance abuse, adult language, and manipulation.

If you are put off by graphic sex scenes then it would be best to avoid Chapter 20 and Chapter 29.

Otherwise, make yourself at home on Gemarine.

ALSO BY JP MCDONALD

THE INVISIBLE TETHER
BEYOND FORSAKEN WORLDS

DEDICATION

For the members of various marginalised communities who often do not feel safe and comfortable being who they are. Gemarine will always be a safe place for you.

CHAPTER 1

Threads of time writhed like tentacles emerging from the quantum sea, dragging the *Attenborough* through the groaning portal gate. Kaleidoscopic light filtered through the rectangular viewports and glowed bright with nuclear bursts. The inside of the ship warped as they navigated through the portal, bending with the pressure of fragmenting reality.

Xan clung to the grates in the boronium floor with his dominant hand as his body buckled from the force. Juniper had reached across with her strong exoarm and held tight to his shaking left hand.

Did he need her physical strength to help keep him balanced? No. But he needed her presence for far greater things that lay within him.

Her cold metallic appendage locked like supporting metal struts for his internal walls. The ones that contained the emotional butterflies fluttering with tensile wings as the hint of love echoed throughout its chambers. The ones that trapped the fear burning with sulphuric acid in the pit of his gut, churning with each desperate moment. The ones that contained his gigantic heart, weeping with indignation at every injustice, but beating in a rhythm that showed an unyielding desire to fight.

The *Attenborough* shuddered as the faces of the tired crew melted into silent screams. Their entire essence was torn and thrown to the wolves of the universe.

Pressure built inside Xan's chest, like his rib cage was expanding to combat his heart, swelling in protection of his crew mates; Lilianna, Ryker, Massy, Dallis, Juniper and Qilin. He had coaxed them here, promising salvation and some sort of heroic penance.

But what did they need to be absolved from?

They were following him into the murky bowels of time to fix a mistake by a genocidal maniac: Madame Bleu, with her snake-like face, angular nose always upturned to the observant stars as if she were bright enough to walk among them. Xan wanted to rip that puffy head of faded blue hair off her scalp and feed her to the *rhinovaders* in the Wilds of Gemarine. Instead, he and the rest of his crew wore her mistake on their chests like a badge of dishonour.

After uniting the three celestial crystals together, they were all immersed in a vision of a galaxy broken by Madame Bleu's disruptive hand. They had just ventured into the portal on a course to repair the destruction. Important markers were placed in time on three separate planets and their mission was to set the right course as salvation beckoned them all.

The fabric of time frayed around them. Stitches pinged off the ship and dissolved into the blackness. Desperately, they held onto threads of one another to create a constant. The constant was the quaint home each of them recognised within the company of the crew. A home that was stronger than any structure; a home that time couldn't touch with its tarred brush.

At once the warping ceased, and out they catapulted from the mouth of the wormhole into Sytheria's atmosphere.

MASSY
25 YEARS OLD

It took a moment for Massy to understand where he was and what the shit was going on...aside from his brain feeling like it had been urinated on then launched out of a cannon blaster. With trembling hands, he took control of the yoke as they shot out into the bluest of skies at supersonic speeds.

At ground level the sound alone would have been catastrophic. The poor little Sytheracts would be terrified it was a bomb blast. He chuckled, thinking about the panic it would cause, but reacted quickly, switching cloak mode on the dash as he swung across skies with barren land below.

"Switch cloak mode on, Massy," croaked Xan from behind him.

Other crew members groaned, while a splatter of vomit slapped against the floor. This was often followed by the tip-tapping of Qilin's paws as she sought a fresh meal.

"Already done, sir," he quipped, pride blossoming. "I'm a true professional."

Cloaking mode was often thought to be a simple aesthetic change. Massy was astounded when Lilianna approached him a year ago about how they might stay hidden on Borgoloth when the cloaking of the ship would not disguise the sounds of supersonic travel.

Massy laughed. "Girl, the day has arrived when the teacher has become the student."

Lilianna's cheeks flushed with embarrassment. Those honest cheeks brandished the correct reaction because she should have known, being a sexy little wannabe scientist and all.

"*Well, my dense little friend,*" Massy began, *straightening his suit while Lilianna crossed her arms in a sulky disposition.* "*Get this—they cloak the sound also.*"

Massy pointed his gnarled finger at her, producing a wink. But as she unfolded her arms and her lips curled upwards in a daring smile, he feared he had hit a snag.

"*But how?*"

Massy gulped, knowing he could not answer. The 'Massy way' was to feign until one could not feign anymore. "*Research, my dear student, it's all about research. I recommend you do some before talking about these sorts of really intelligent things with me. At least you'll be on my level.*"

And off he went before she could protest and discover that he had no idea how anything really worked. With his head held high, he knew that the piloting skills he possessed were way more important than knowing how cloaking worked.

They were all still too high up to see what was down below, but according to the map, they were a long way from crashing into the city. He allowed the *Attenborough* to slow naturally.

The city skyline stood tall in the distance. Elongated towers bled with neon signs and darting lasers. Surrounding buildings looked like serpents digesting a rat, swollen at the throat and sleek at the tail. Pixelated advertisements flashed and flared, but they were too far away to discern the content. Hovercrafts, robots, and Sytheracts sped among the buildings like weaving birds in a dense forest.

Ryker volunteered to check the maintenance hub to ensure the ship hadn't been damaged in the reality fucking they had just endured by Periah's pulsing portal penis. Dallis followed him like a drunk dimwit in need of a chaperone. The others crowded around Massy in stunned silence, watching the wondrous sprawl of a bustling alien city out of the viewport.

There were endless reasons for Massy to be nervous, but he swallowed them all as he sailed across the unknown skies. It was imperative to bestow calm upon his crew mates. Keeping them at ease was paramount.

CHAPTER 2

LOCATION: SYTHERIA
YEAR: 2505
LILIANNA – 22 YEARS OLD

Lilianna felt ill. Not just because they made it through the thorny bushes of time, fresh cuts grimacing with oxygen-rich blood, but because she was on her home planet for the first time since she had been taken. Worse yet, she was about to meet the Sytheract soulbond she had effectively abandoned. That life was dead to her, or at least she thought it was. She had spent a blissful night in the embrace of not just Xan, but Juniper too. Since then, confusing thoughts were muddled with the intense feelings, feelings that swarmed like a furiously busy *philix* around a pollen-filled flower.

Maybe this was a chance to find someone who would truly love her. Someone who would choose her and only her every single time.

Lilianna's mouth fell wide open as the skyline came into view. Small transpo-like ships zoomed across the cityscape, robots flew with Sytheracts on jet packs from one building to another, braving dizzying heights.

"Lilianna!" yelled Massy.

She succumbed to the desperation in his voice and moved her eyes in his direction, the orbs of gold wide and rheumy after being awestruck. "Girl, I've been trying to get your attention."

Qilin sidled up to Lilianna, using her forked tongue to stimulate her senses. The same tongue that lapped up someone's vomit a moment before. Lilianna yanked her outstretched hand away in disgust while Qilin's mouth curled into a goofy smirk.

Xan squeezed her shoulder. "Are you okay?" The concern in his stare was a jolt to her heart. Thoughts of another "someone" a second ago dissipated as she stared into eyes of grey smoke that billowed across a starless eve.

Would his charm ever wear off?

The song of her soul was a dissonant lament of unrequited love. Love—the defect of her soul. At least on Gemarine it was considered a defect. Clans were formed as part of necessity. Seldom did they form because one Sytheract stared with lustful intent into the eyes of an attractive Human, with whom their consummated love would shake the foundations of several worlds combined. Sure, she knew a handful of clans that contained an odd coupling or two, but was it the same kind of love she desired? In the arms of both Juniper and Xan, she had felt a special and endearing connection. Did she love them both equally? And more importantly, could they ever give that back to her?

Xan roused Lilianna out of her complicated thoughts. "Massy wants to know where it's best to land."

Taking a moment to consider what district they were in, she searched across the city, trying to recall anything mildly familiar.

"There is a central nature reserve across from the government headquarters." Lilianna swallowed. "The island in the middle of a circular moat will be big enough to house the ship while we take a look around...I think."

"'I think' doesn't sound so promising," Massy teased.

Juniper whacked him on the back of the head. "Your face isn't promising."

Massy winced. "What the fuck does that even mean?"

"You're ugly," Juniper said flatly, "in your soul."

"Yeah, okay, and I'm also trying to land this ship on a planet none of us have ever been to, so I'd recommend, you know, not hitting me on the head."

Lilianna breathed in deep and smiled as Juniper gave her a wink. Even Juniper could understand that Lilianna was emotional, shaken and ridiculously freaked the fluff out. Xan stepped forward with his hand at her back and whispered, "Are you sure? Take your time." Her two protectors – one with the soothing aura of a crooner and the other as gentle as a pin prick in the cornea.

The Sytheract native gathered courage from both of them, standing up taller and clearing her throat to confirm with Massy. "The island will work, I'm sure of it."

"Nice to know sugarti—"

Juniper slapped him on the head once more. "I hope you weren't going to call her sugar tits, because that type of misogyny in my company is unacceptable and I swear to Starlord I will de-ball you."

Massy didn't rub his head this time, preferring to cup his nether regions. "I was going to say sugar tin! Because she is…sweet like sugar… and it's…uh…all contained in that…body of hers," he spluttered, all the while still managing to steer the ship's course to where Lilianna had suggested.

Juniper started toward the back of the ship, flicking the exoblades back to regular fingers, and murmured, "Mmmm unlucky. I was craving a bit of Aranther testicle soup."

Massy's face lit up. "Well, you can sample these anytime you—"

Lilianna yelled at Massy, "Stop! Before she murders you, you idiot!" This time *she* slapped the back of his head as Xan laughed at Massy's insolence.

XAN
24 YEARS OLD

In the style of an operatic tenor, Massy stood with one arm aloft and the other clutching at his chest. "What a landing, what a landing, what a la - a - an - dingggggg."

Qilin's ears flicked downward as she placed her paws atop her head to muffle the sound. Xan nodded at her in agreement, looking queasy at the lack of pleasant tonal quality from Massy's completed melody.

Massy unclipped and strode forward, the air of royalty putrid in his canter. "They call you King of the Wilds, but they call me Lord of the Skies." He stopped in his tracks and waited for kudos.

Xan gave him the only reply filled with sarcasm befitting of such a king. "We could never be worthy in your presence, oh, dominant Lord of Otherworldly Skies. I bow to thee."

"Go on, then." Massy waited for Xan to kneel, but instead Xan scoffed, "Bad knees buddy ol' pal. I'll take a rain check."

Walking over to the pilot bay storage closet, he stuffed some spare A3 chews into his pack, along with a medkit and other knickknacks. Qilin leapt up and swiped at her favourite little toy, knocking it to the ground, then clasped it in her jaws and dumped it into Xan's palm.

"Really?" Xan said, inspecting the mythical Tianlong, the celestial dragon who was known in Chinese culture to guard the dwelling of the gods.

Her tail wagged and her forked tongue searched for a section of Xan's skin to lather in saliva. She found it.

"You really want to play now, Qilin?"

She jumped up and down furtively, so he threw the Tianlong across the ship for her to fetch.

"Alright Massy, you can come with—"

"Look, sir." Massy fiddled with a knob and swung the squeaky chair around to face Xan. "I think I'm going to chill on the ship. You don't need the lot of us waltzing around being like, 'Sup Sytheracts—we're an alien all sorts gang, but we come in peace. Blah blah, don't shoot me, blah blah.'" Massy waved his hand dismissively.

Xan considered for a moment. "Massy bringing the logic! And they said you weren't all there."

Qilin had returned the saliva bathed Tianlong and Xan threw it once more toward the back of the ship, where her galloping paws sounded like metallic rain.

"Wait, who said that?" The circular black and yellow birthmarks on Massy's forehead creased with concern.

Juniper stepped in front of Xan. "I said it! You brain dead bongo." Juniper flashed her middle finger in between his eyes as the hatch door hissed closed behind her. The wound on her bicep obtained from Periah had been smoothed over with regen gel.

"Oh, if it isn't Murderous Marge."

Long eyelashes batted with glee. "That is such a lovely compliment, Massy." She leant forward and kissed him on the cheek. "It's so nice when the people you protect with necessary violent actions give you kudos." Juniper sauntered off, her bulging ego swinging from side to side, as Qilin bullied her into participating in just one game of fetch.

Massy started, "That's not what I—" His shoulders sunk. Juniper had already made her way to another part of the ship.

Xan put a hand on Massy's deflated shoulder. "I've been through this many a time. We can't win."

"Oh, I'll win one of these days."

Xan started to walk off thinking that Massy would need to dedicate his whole life to getting a win against Juniper. Whenever there was battle, whether it was signed in blood with a flesh eaten finger, or lightly sketched with a feather quill—she would fight to the death in order to come out on top.

The Tianlong dropped at Xan's feet. He smiled with sadness at Qilin, because he knew she wasn't going to like what came next. Xan knelt down and ran his hands across Qilin's fur. Her ears went from acute and weary to relaxed, smoothed down and draped across the nape of her short neck. "Alright girl, you need to stay on the ship—can't have you running around freaking out the poor Sytheracts." She turned her head away, abandoning the Tianlong toy, and whimpered with bitter disappointment.

She always seems to understand what I'm saying. After all this, I wonder if there is a way I can find someone to develop a piece of tech that will allow me to actually understand her?

"I know, I know." He soothed her by rubbing just underneath her chin and allowed their foreheads to rest against one another in the way that he often did. It made him feel comforted, like they were in sync. In that gesture, in their touch, there was a deep love that no one else in the galaxy would know.

Xan opened his eyes and caught Ryker watching them wearily from across the other side of the ship. He looked haggard, afraid either about what was to come or the harrowing adventure he had just endured. The Cryptoborgs chasing after them, the red eyes of Qilin atop the ship as Juniper fought off the alien slug…it was more than the shy kid had ever endured, but he *had* endured. Through all the craziness that wound its way around him, he remained still in the face of peril.

Although he didn't think himself a hero, Xan could see that Ryker was growing into one. Heroes don't exhibit strength in bulges rippling across a tight space suit. Heroes quell the fear with the welling of love; love that spurs action, that dims doubt; love not for self-preservation, but for the lasting legacy of family. Although Xan and the crew weren't tethered by blood lineage, choice was far thicker, and there was no doubt in Xan's mind that Ryker had chosen them.

A stifled smile etched across Xan's face. "Look after them."

Ryker flinched. "Are you talking to me or Qilin?"

Xan laughed. "To you, mainly."

Ryker tousled his fringe and covered part of his vision. "What am I going to do? I'm the weakest link in this entire chain."

Xan took for granted that people needed positive reinforcement. He often went about his day yelling directions at Lilianna, telling Massy where to fly them. Maybe it was growing up with Juniper, who didn't need that reassurance, but it appeared as though he should dish out more positivity.

He settled for: "C'mon, buddy, I wouldn't ask you if I didn't think you were capable."

That was okay, wasn't it?

Ryker smiled as much as Ryker could muster a smile, and replied without gusto, "You got it, boss."

He walked out, leaving Xan looking at Qilin. Qilin snorted and turned away.

Yeah, I guess it was a measly attempt.

"I'll work on it, girl."

She turned back around and held eye contact for a few moments and seemed to smirk, as if she were saying, "Sure you will, mate. Sure you will."

Xan stood at the edge of the ramp with Juniper and Lilianna about to head out into the city. The moat water masked the pleasant fragrance of the melaleuca trees, producing a musty scent with a mild dash of sulphur. Three hoverboards usually stored on the *Attenborough* were tucked under his arm in order to take them across the body of water.

Juniper pulled the hood over her head, stray spiral curls fighting against containment. Noxious jade eyes glowed through shadow, searching him.

"So, fearless time travel explorer—can you remind me what we are actually doing again?" She frowned mockingly. "'Cause little bitty Juniper is too dumb to comprehend quantum time and multiverse theory, so give it to me in simple terms." A pout materialised on her plump lips, while she jiggled various assets in his direction, playing the part of ditzy warrior princess.

As intelligent as Xan was, repairing a broken timeline was a whole new level in the game of quantum theory. But he did his best to explain it and declined to invest in such assets presented in Juniper's portfolio.

"As far as I can gather, there is Timeline A—which is our present life on Gemarine. Once we have travelled through the portal and changed what we are meant to—Timeline B will be created." He tried to recall how he synthesised information in the ancient text to explain it to Juniper and Lilianna. "Once we are finished creating different branches on the time tree, if you will."

Juniper clapped. "Oh, very nice."

Xan bowed and continued. "Then we emerge from the portal and basically press the button to unite all timelines together, thus rendering Madame Bleu's catastrophic actions obsolete."

The water lapped against the moat walls thick with moss. The island was raised slightly higher than ground level, containing a dense population of eucalyptus tree variants surrounding the ship. Hardy native grasses tickled their ankles as they walked off the ramp onto the surface of Sytheria.

"Okay, so we have four important events to make right, so four 'timetree' branches to prune." Lilianna spoke with a soft voice, her brow sheened with sweat. "We need to set the course right as if we were in these timelines all along. Here in Sytheria, the most important thing is locating that fuel source."

"Mainly so the planet doesn't mine itself to death," Xan finished, adjusting his hood to make sure it covered his ears. Sytheracts usually wore hooded cloaks walking through the city streets, so the disguise would ensure they blended in.

"What about the other events on all the other planets?" Juniper asked, swatting away an insect as she walked between two youthful trees swaying in the early morning breeze. The sun had only just risen, coating them in golden shards fragmented by the canopy of intimidating skyrises.

"Let's brief one another before each different planet so we can just concentrate on one at a time."

"Alright, alright—dumb Juniper strikes again. But wait, don't we need to find Lilianna's soulbond?" Juniper grinned and raised her eyebrows as if the thought of such awkwardness elated her.

Lilianna avoided both their gazes, tucking a strand of blonde hair behind her cuspated ear. She said in a small voice, "The soulbond and I discovered the fuel source together in the alternate timeline, so it's the most...likely place to start I suppose." She breathed in deeply, scratching her elbow and biting her bottom lip as she referenced the shared vision brought to them by the crystals on the ship.

In the whirlwind of their mission, the importance of righting the galaxy's wrongs, Xan had forgotten to publicly acknowledge the emotion attached to each situation.

Lilianna's was quite possibly the most emotionally charged. It was worse, Xan thought, because of who she was. She could never quite let go of her idea of love – monogamous and all-consuming love. There was a distinct possibility that in a moment of weakness she could turn to regret, as if walking blindfolded in a garden of the most exquisite flora, haemorrhaging vibrant colours. The sorrow of not seeing this would drive anyone mad.

Xan pitied her but decided at the same time that he needed to be ultra-aware of her emotions. If she needed a shoulder to cry on, he'd have a tissue dispenser that discharged out of the elbow just in case. Comets above knew that Juniper would never have been *that* perceptive.

As if on cue, Juniper's mischievous smile faded, and she placed a solemn arm around Lilianna. "I know this might be tough, but lucky you have us two if you need anything."

Xan was struck speechless, staring like a halfwit neanderthal.

Lilianna looked at him expectantly. Her golden eyes twinkled with fear, arrayed by the glassy sheen of fragile hope. But Xan fumbled and in his hurried attempt to shatter the silence, his comment fell insincere. "Ah, of course. We always have your back."

What is wrong with me today? Pull yourself together, man!

Juniper clapped her hands decisively, and Lilianna jumped. "Alright team, our first family holiday. C'mon, Daddy, show us the way."

Xan groaned a wordless reply as he continued to the edge of the moat wall, searching for and locating a slick set of stairs suitable for the hoverboards to launch across the water. He looked at Lilianna expectantly and handed her the smallest one.

She nodded. "It's been a while but it's just like riding a bike. Some things you just don't forget."

CHAPTER 3

LOCATION: SYTHERIA
YEAR: 2494
LILIANNA – 9 YEARS OLD

Dusk was a curtain draped across the capital city of Sytheria. The low clouds pregnant with rain waddled close to the tops of skyscrapers so sharp they could puncture them. Fluorescent globes fixed to the front of hovercars lit up the sky in dazzling colours, piercing the pupils of onlookers who dined at skyline restaurants.

Evolution did wondrous things over millions of years: bestowed abilities that saw the landscape of Sytheria change from lush valleys and housing confined to the canopies, to a beaming city filled with flashing lights, aircraft, and robotic companions. Much like Humans or Aranthers, Sytheracts went from hunched ape-like creatures to walking tall and proud—and from foraging in the wilderness to devouring manufactured goods from vending robots who flew to your door.

But some things lay dormant, triggered by fear, waiting for the moment to transport a race back in time. When the primitive blended with the modern and consumed the rational mind.

Lilianna shouted out to Arcadie, her sister's faithful robot companion in Sytheria, "Why would you let her do this?" A pulse visible beneath her pale skin as fear beat the drum within.

Arcadie was always hovering to counteract having no legs. Did small thruster jets as legs count? The thrusters were the size of two children's backpacks. The gleaming coils of his retractable arms lulled beside him. His outer casing was off-white like forlorn feathers buried in snow. The pixelated circular eyes snapped to an underscored line on his face plate. That was his worry showing.

His tone was even; some might say it ached with monotony. But his words were rapid, as if time demanded action rather than accuracy. "She insisted that she would be able to succeed in her quest."

A calculating mind like his should have known of the peril that awaited Fleurah, Lilianna's older sister, but without a literal backbone, it appeared that trust claimed victory over intelligence.

"You are meant to be a wise guide? You should have stopped her," Lilianna grumbled, not for the first time wondering whether his experimental programming was worth the hassle.

"I'm still an infant!" he screeched, digital sine waves disrupting his usually levelled voice.

He, of course, was right. Arcadie was younger than them. Although he was connected to the cloud of information, there were branches of Sytheract social nuance that needed further exploration.

Fleurah had slipped off a rafter one hundred and seventeen floors above the city as the sun sought refuge from the illuminating toil of the day. Fleurah's quest had been one of maximum stupidity: break into the construction zone of the Sawtech building and get Arcadie to take a holo of her as she posed mid handstand on the edge of the metallic beam. Lilianna had been playing in the juvenile corner two levels down, when Arcadie dialled her commbud installed in her inner ear.

This was the first time that the colour had drained from Lilianna's face, her stomach fell, and the primal call of being a sibling echoed between her ears. Her fight or flight mechanism kicked in with rapid delivery.

Fleurah had her arms outstretched on the beam, clinging on with everything a child could muster. The sprawling city with its neon crowns glinted sharp rubies and soothing sapphires. Large holographic letters danced across the tops of buildings—consumerism ravaging the eyes of anyone who looked skyward. On street level, Sytheracts walked unaware, clad in sturdy dark hooded cloaks, awaiting the evening cleanse—a daily downpour of rain as night vanquished the day.

Arcadie's jets spluttered, hovering around her. The exclamations of "oh no" repeated over and over in that vaguely Sytheract way, but with the emotional nuance of a glass bottle. There would've been hilarity in the moment had it not been for Lilianna's sister straining on the precipice of death.

Fleurah shrieked—tales of unbridled horror told with just one scream.

Lilianna shouted again, "Just hold on, I'm nearly there."

She raced up more sets of mechanical stairs, traversing the space in double the time as if she let herself be moved. Reaching the open door, she noticed it had been wrenched ajar by Arcadie's dexterous pincers.

Lilianna crawled out on the metallic beam, peering down at the street below. A gasp fell from her mouth, and she hoped desperately that was the only thing that fell. Steadying her breath, she ignored the salty taste in her mouth and the smell of ground down metal shards that hung in the air of the active construction site.

"Arcadie, instead of flitting around like a useless gust of wind, please get underneath her and support her weight." She threw a pointed finger at Fleurah's dangling feet.

"Lil, help me please, I can't hold on for much longer," Fleurah cried, high pitched and doused in manic fear.

Lilianna shuffled across the beam support to where Fleurah hung like an uncoiled rope, looped into a noose for the shadow dwellers. Her muscles were not developed enough yet to pull herself up. Lilianna locked her own legs around the beam for support and grabbed Fleurah's forearms with sweaty hands. Arcadie was beneath Fleurah now, providing a rickety base from which to push up toward Lilianna.

"When I give the signal, Arcadie will give you a little push up toward me. Use his push to get a better grip on my body."

"I'm scared!" Fleurah cried. Her eyes were glass that could shatter with the lightest tap.

"Don't be. I'm here. Just grab onto my body and you'll be fine." Lilianna pursed her lips in concentration, her hands shaking with the uncontrollable dominance of adrenalin. "Now!" she yelled.

Arcadie thrust upwards, his head connecting with the bottom of Fleurah's feet so it boosted her, as momentum pushed her on top of Lilianna. The momentum was excessive, so to counteract the gravity threatening to transform her into a splattered piece of art on the sidewalk, Fleurah's fingernails dug into Lilianna's cloak. Arcadie's thrusters pulsed with mint-green vapour, speeding toward Fleurah as she struggled across the beam. The robot gently nudged her so that she could climb across Lilianna's back with more stability, sliding down her sister's legs and across the beam to safety. Lilianna couldn't see her, so she called out, "Now crawl across the beam—be careful and take your time."

Arcadie gave a whoop sound as Fleurah reached the other side, bobbing up and down like a buoy in the ocean celebrating the passing of a storm. As Lilianna scampered backwards across the beam, she closed the door behind them and hugged Fleurah in a tight embrace. The adrenalin within her subsided as her family member was restored. Sanity crawled across the empty space of desperation and Lilianna snapped back into herself.

"Why do you do these things?" she lambasted, separating herself from the warm hug wound tight seconds before.

Silence was an ancient tree and Fleurah climbed its trunk, nestling into its branches as if its strong arms could protect her from anything. Her small feet shuffled, her shoulders squeezed in tight, gaze focused on the floor.

Finally, she murmured, "I wanted more."

Lilianna crinkled her brow. "What does that mean?"

"I just…feel…invisible." Her lips were quivering as she fought the tears that levelled fists against those glass eyes, splintered and cracked, giving way.

Lilianna placed her palm on Fleurah's cheek. "I'm with you all the time, I—"

"Being with me is different than seeing me."

Lilianna thought for a moment. *How can she say that? I look after her when our parents are concentrating on other matters. I'm doing everything I can to raise her properly.*

"I don't understand," Lilianna admitted.

Fleurah swallowed, letting some kind of resignation pass across her stare.

"It's ok, I'm sorry for doing that. It won't happen again." She came forward in a stiff hug. Her eyes were shut tight and her cheek grazed Lilianna's shoulder. "Thank you for saving me."

Lilianna rested her chin on her sister's strawberry hair. "That's what sisters do. They're always there for one another."

Except that they weren't, because two years later Lilianna had been taken to Gemarine.

CHAPTER 4

LOCATION: SYTHERIA
YEAR: 2505
JUNIPER – 24 YEARS OLD

Juniper, Xan, and Lilianna walked through the streets bustling with Sytheracts. Even in the early morning hustle, the ground-level neon burnt and fizzed like a lit cigar. Flying vehicles, hovering robots, and jetpacked Sytheracts darted in and out of bulbous buildings above them. Skyscrapers stretched toward crafty clouds that crept in long before the rain was due.

"It just rains every day when the sun goes down?" Xan said, astonished.

"Yes, the evening cleanse. It has something to do with the whole cycle of evaporation here. There is more solar energy, kind of like what happens in tropical regions. Then it'll feel humid in the daytime."

That's why I feel so sweaty and gross. This whole planet is an armpit.

"Fascinating." Xan thumbed his chin, as the street vendors in their loose hooded cloaks barked about some latest knock off technology they were desperate to sell. Wafts of skewered meat sticks on charcoal reached

Juniper's nostrils, making her stomach crave some real food as opposed to the bland A3 chews.

She was less impressed with meteorology. "I'd rather be soulbonded to one of these losers for an eternity than talk about weather any longer." She scowled at the many said losers who passed her with different iterations of hopeful serenity scrawled across their faces, advertisements and logos beaming from the shop corners reflected in their pupils.

Juniper felt uneasy still. Although she had done her best to eliminate all the Cryptoborgs waiting for them on Periah, who knew if a select few were just biding their time until the portal opened upon their return?

That is a long way off. We need to take each mission one by one before Cryptoborgs become a concern.

The issue of betrayal still nagged at her. Someone within their own crew was working against them, she knew, but had no evidence to prove it. There were enough apparent coincidences that didn't add up. But here on planet loserface, searching for a disgusting soulbond, she couldn't dedicate enough investigative power to figure it out.

Gemarine was built on rebellious Sytheracts who had wanted to break free of societal bonds – begin non-judgmental copulation, liberate bodies and minds from the tyranny of society. Even Juniper realised she was all too quick in her judgment of this species who craved the company of another singular being. It wasn't necessarily that fact, just the pompous way in which the soulbond was described as the pinnacle of existence. Just like all the things she'd read about marriage. It was a good little experiment for five years, but one person could never satisfy every desire, need, or requirement of one's being, could they?

She'd known nothing but a clan, but to her that was the most logical solution. If someone's personality was too dramatic for one member of the clan, converse more with another member who was chill. *Why try to be something you're not? Why try to invent all these extensions of yourself all for waning love – when in actual fact we are all whole, we are all good enough? That kind of mentality makes us feel like we aren't.*

Juniper turned to Xan. "You know the city itself isn't that bad? I like that it's got a gritty, tech vibe going on."

Xan looked around at the cobalt-blue buildings with black tar trimmings as they rounded the pavement into an area where laser lights pulsed and the voice of the neon signs were croaky with sickness. "I don't mind it, but I feel like I'm blinded by capitalism. All these advertisements... I wonder what *Sawtech* is about – that shit is everywhere."

Juniper nodded. That was one aspect she didn't particularly like. Advertisements beaming constantly meant that branded messages became subliminal desires in the depths of the subconscious mind. Luckily, she wasn't epileptic—otherwise the only way forward would be through kinetic convulsions.

Juniper was unable to see Lilianna's face as she walked ahead of them. The tone of Lilianna's voice was an A3 chew—a bland, chalky paste of nothingness. "Sawtech was the company that revolutionised most of Sytheria. Every family was assigned a bot to assist with everyday life. Sawtech provides the bot." Street vendors were behind them now. As they walked through the decrepit arcade strip, it felt like they were wandering into the bad side of town. Robots and hover vehicles zoomed high above them still, chirping like migratory birds working the skies.

"Sounds pleasant enough." Xan shrugged.

Juniper wasn't so sure. She played it out in her mind.

I am the president of Sawtech—here, have an expensive-ass robot for free and we expect nothing at all in return.

Another Sawtech advertisement flashed up beside her like a flamboyant acquaintance she was trying to avoid, waving their hands, desperate for her to notice them.

"My dad actually used to work for them. He sort of messed around with developing different AIs. We had a prototype in our family that basically became like a brother to me – well, to...us." Her gaze trailed toward the overcast sky as if recalling a memory tangled inside the emotion of her departure from the planet.

"How the fuck did you know it was a he? Did it have some dangly wire between its thrusters?" Juniper laughed.

That seemed to soften Lilianna a little. "Well, no. I think my dad modelled him off one of his good male friends. So when we switched him on, that was it, I guess."

"Don't worry. If we meet him, I'll stick a strap-on where his dick should be and bam, no surgery needed. Erect member equals yet another male idiot."

Lilianna's look was quizzical, as if she were unsure whether she needed to be worried about Juniper actually following through.

Juniper sighed. "Don't worry, I don't need to make sex robots." Lilianna sighed with relief. "I've got my own fuckbot right here." She slapped Xan on the muscled bicep, and he grimaced.

"Robots don't move with the agility of these hips." He began a thrust or two in the direction of both Lilianna and Juniper, who ran away from him, giggling. They moved further up the street where the neon insects didn't buzz beside their eardrums or feast upon their pupils with a colourful hunger. The Sytheract crowds had been sucked into the black hole of suburbia as the trio walked toward the apartment block in an unimpressive complex. A small glowing sign beamed the name of the suburb, "Quaxia."

"Quaxia, is this a village for a horde of ducks?" chirped Juniper.

Xan turned toward her, his face grave. "*Attempted* humour doesn't look good on you."

"Um, that wasn't *attempted* humour, that joke definitely stuck the landing."

Xan snorted. "You've been led astray at some stage in your life if you thought *that* was good."

There was a quiet calm in the street as they approached the blinking sign. Trees lined the sidewalk, planted in dead straight rows. Even nature couldn't stand by, minding its own business, without a little Sytheract interference. A stationary robot next to the Quaxia sign grinned as they approached, launching into some jerky dance movements as it touted, "Welcome friends," several times over.

Hearty laughs bounced off the walls. It had been a harrowing week and a robot's funky fresh dance moves provided a surprising smile for them all.

Lilianna's face suddenly dropped as she stared at the boxy complex ahead of her on the street. It had the same slick faded blue polymer blocks as all the other homes. A marbled grey door was painted like ghoulish clouds wafting across a haunted sky. A large window on the top floor peered down onto Lilianna's small frame. She was a smooth pebble trapped beneath congregating boulders during seismic shifts.

Xan moved up behind Lilianna and put a steadying hand on her shoulder. Golden eyes cast a stifled glow onto his face. His prominent jaw clenched, eyes narrowed as if eclipsed by an empathy asteroid. That perfect idiot was doing the whole, "Imma give you strength with my handsome face, baby girl."

Lilianna's smile was a volcano erupting sticky bursts of infatuation all over that face. Juniper felt obligated to step up on the other side of her. The left arm hovered above her shoulder, considering the horror of copying Xan's warmth would cause it to spontaneously drop off. She did it anyway, and when Lilianna threw that same look of gross infatuation upon her, she nearly puked right then and there. Juniper held it together as Lilianna sucked in a breath, steadied herself and walked the pathway to the front door.

It was weird how much Juniper had resisted the warmth, resisted doing what might have been expected. But to see Lilianna walk forward into the unknown, alone, into the life that she had thought was long dead…it made her feel something. She was actually a little proud. An ember of strength that glowed in the face of hardship. She wondered whether at the right time, could Lilianna let it burn the world? Or was this only because a match was struck and discarded on a pile of tinder, fuelling a momentary flash of bravery?

LILIANNA – 22 YEARS OLD

Lilianna's heavy footsteps were caught in the coarse sands of anxiety. But still she trudged onward. The path to the front door was lined with colourful lilies bowing with grace at her long-awaited arrival. Before she reached the grey door, it swung inward. The guiding hand of fate couldn't stop her lips from parting in shock as her soulbond emerged. Lilianna's fist had frozen in the act of knocking, her face paled further, sucking in a stale breath, her heart a wild creature bounding across a desolate plain.

The slender figure of Braemar Tyllieth crept gingerly onto the porch as if waking from a dream. This was the Sytheract male they had all seen in their collective vision on the ship. The vision of the future that would have been. The future they needed to ensure *would* now come to pass.

His wide eyes were russet flecked with golden sparks. A noble chin raised in the air with a poised and defined jawline that held, as the rest of him faltered at the sight of Lilianna standing there.

The Gemarinian-Sytheract girl stood vulnerable, trembling in fear at what this might mean in the context of her current existence. Thoughts of Xan, Juniper, her former family, the potential expectations of this… male…this bond to her soul, a magnet in the threads of their DNA.

A look of horror and concurrent wonder filled Braemar. He dropped to his knees; blonde hair like ocean whitewash spilled over his eyes and he wept openly.

In the midst of the emotion, Lilianna was startled by Juniper coughing with embarrassment behind her.

"I'm going to throw up." Juniper's voice echoed inside the narrow street.

Lilianna had imagined this moment ever since she was young. The expectations of Sytheract society were grand and the promise of fulfilment would only have been a few measly years away before she was taken. As the gates of Topaz City opened, her heart closed, knowing the tethers to her bonded soul would remain frayed and billowing in the wind of regret.

But in this moment, there was a single thread, an echo of a dream gone dark. A feeling welled that she had never known before, from the pits of her stomach, spreading throughout her. The feeling was the child of happiness. It shared the same subtle smile as its mother. But an essence needed to be nurtured over time. It was a feeling she wanted to grasp, but had she changed too much? Was this second chance even real?

Lilianna recalled why she was here. Why they were all here. To set this timeline on the correct path and merge it with their own, ensuring that Sytheria would not be destroyed. Ensuring that the reversal of Madame Bleu's genocide was possible.

Once all the timelines were united—would Braemar be permitted into Gemarine? Would Xan and Juniper accept a Sytheract tradition? Or would she feel compelled to find a way back to him and give up her home? The soulbond was a part of their DNA—was it something that she could ignore?

"It's you." He stammered, "I...I...can't believe it. I have searched for you, ached for years." His voice was full of emotion, a brittle leaf crunching under footfall on a neglected forest path. Braemar had waited longer than anyone else because at his age the soulbond had usually been fulfilled. As friends around him all paired up, he would have lingered listlessly in the labyrinth of loveless fiends.

Lilianna hesitated under the weight of the moment. "I'm not sure... what to say." Anxiety raked nails over her trembling hands. Her mouth was a dry creek bed. The moment he had been waiting for, and she was worried that she was a disappointment. It was a thought that had plagued her for too long now. Wondering why she had to want more than what others could give, wondering where she actually belonged because of it.

Was it here? Braemar seemed to sense her nervousness, and immediately rose up from his knees, stifling the intensity in his eyes.

"Then don't say anything." He smiled, hiding his teeth. "Please come inside and we can take some time with one another. Just share a simple moment."

Lilianna shuffled on the spot, still finding it difficult to paint words on the blank canvas that Braemar was holding out for her.

"We shall have a warm brew of *thymel.* I'll break open the tin of sweet fern biscuits."

The last time she had tasted the herbal warmth of *thymel* was the night before she departed, sitting by Fleurah's bed as she slept, her button nose twitching as a dream took hold, knowing that in the morning Fleurah would wake to a nightmare. Blind to Lilianna's sacrifice. Blind to the impending loss of her sister.

Out of the corner of her eyes, she saw Juniper shift uncomfortably, murmuring what she imagined were jokes with Xan. She took strength from that in a bizarre way. This wasn't a joke to her. Although she had lived on Gemarine for half her life, she had read fictional tales of true love, remembering what it was to believe in bonding. It was enough to push her forward, to see what this could be.

"I mean, I'm not sure you'll be pleased about the reason we are here."

Braemar's glance shifted to Juniper and Xan as if noticing them for the first time. They were laden in their thick cloaks, lumbering and lingering in the exposed street.

"Who are they?" His eyebrows arched as a ringlet of blonde hair dangled like a hook on his forehead.

"I think, if you'll extend your invite to my friends, we can explain everything to you." She smiled reassuringly, and from the Juniper playbook, placed her hand on the inside of his arm knowing it would make him malleable.

He considered her hand for a clouded moment, then a true smile beamed across his pale face, now dancing with light. As if intuition meant more than trust earned.

Lilianna returned the smile, feigned through the veil of sadness. It wasn't like her to play on other's emotions to get what she wanted. Braemar's smile was both heart warming and heartbreaking.

She called out to Xan and Juniper shuffling on the street like spider crabs: "C'mon you two, it's time."

CHAPTER 5

The windows in the living room were covered by a heavy curtain used to block out the natural light. It was disorientating at first, until Braemar gave a quick oral command. Splashes of light dropped from the ceiling, highlighting a minimalist's dream. There was a long, navy-blue couch, a crumpled grey blanket discarded in the corner guarding an empty packet of rice crisps. A small side table with a vase of wilted flowers and a holo remote was tucked into a corner. The room broke out into the combined dining area and kitchen where bizarre robotic arms lay stiff and inert above a cooking stove and sink. The scent reminded Xan of a hospital, bitter and sterile with high-grade antiseptic.

Braemar placed his hands behind his head and breathed out deeply, pacing in front of the couch. He was a decent-looking character—composed and calm, and genuinely pleasant. Even at this early stage, Xan could understand how Braemar and Lilianna's souls might be interwoven through the fabric of fate.

Braemar blew out a gust of breath. "This is more than a lot to take in."

"I know, I know," Lilianna soothed. "It's not even the half of it."

Xan considered his reaction. Although the revelations definitely weighed on him, Braemar had absorbed it well—the time travel, the alien planet, the need for him to lend an effort to saving the galaxy.

Trying to bring them back into the moment without inducing anxiety, Xan asked, "Look, you're a geologist, right?"

Braemar nodded but pursed his lips. "Well, yes, I sort of look at different sections of geological formations. Collect what I can and try to break them down for parts."

"Parts for what?"

"I work for Evercorp. We're the major competitor to Sawtech. It's mainly for developing robots with better AI functionality."

As if on cue, a little cleaner bot collided with Xan's boot, reversed, and carried on its path on the walnut hardwood floors.

"A lot of the geological materials from Earth were mined to construct microchips and components that made up small technological devices."

Xan directed his comment mainly at Lilianna. She squinted back at him. "I know the history of Earth too, boss."

Xan didn't understand why she was getting defensive. He didn't say anything remotely problematic. Merely factual.

"Oh, you two work together?" Braemar asked with a twinkle of hopeful ignorance.

Xan was about to confirm and maybe hint at a little more, but Lilianna spoke up quickly. "We work in the field of galactic xeno biology. It's a fascinating field." Lilianna motioned to Xan with her thumb. "I'm basically his protege and he is the grumpy ol' boss," she giggled.

Braemar returned her laughter uneasily, but agreeably said, "I can see it."

Xan was dumbfounded by Lilianna's sudden change in demeanour. His scowl cut her like a knife, and her cheeks reddened. Xan hadn't encountered the feeling before, but he suddenly felt betrayed. For so long they had toed the line of co-workers, ignoring the calls of desire. He was respectful of her virtues and morals and made sure not to cross the line for fear of not being able to give her what she wanted.

But all three of them—Lilianna, Xan and Juniper – gave into temptation a few nights before. Her feelings toward him were clearly written in the way she gave herself willingly, melting into a puddle of longing in his vicinity. But now, standing in front of someone else she wanted to impress, she cast Xan into the void to appear free of his essence, free of his hold on her.

Taking a step back from his emotions, he realised maybe this was the evolution of Lilianna. The way that she would find herself and be content. He wouldn't have to worry about being anything for her, he could just *be*. Watch her find love and concentrate on doing what he did best: saving creatures lost in the galaxy and fooling around at Fusion with Juniper.

Xan focused back on the task, folding his arms as he stood next to the window shielded by the curtain, "I'm definitely a boss that gets straight to business." He glanced sideways at Lilianna, who wouldn't look him in the eye.

Juniper inched forward, putting a barrier between Braemar and them. "I'm sorry, guys, but we've been standing here by the window like awkward little nerdbots while this couch is begging for my juicy ass."

Braemar coughed. "Oh goodness, how rude of me." He started pushing the blanket to the edge of the couch and then gestured. "Please, please sit."

Juniper was the first to take up the offer. After the couch kissed her juicy ass, she turned to Braemar with a gigantic smile laced with all that naughty stuff she was famous for. "Thank you, oh gracious host."

Lilianna took a seat next to her, and Juniper poked her in the sides, eliciting stifled giggles. Xan watched on, still standing with Braemar.

"So, back to the geological stuff. We just need to consider a place on your radar you've been hoping to explore. Maybe there are geological areas that might contain higher levels of energy?"

"And you're saying we need to locate these sites with higher energy output or what, Sytheria might…die?"

Xan twisted the truth a little and didn't for once feel bad for it. "Yes. It is a grave matter." He spoke with the solemn song of a grieving tenor, daring Lilianna to interject with a dissonant cry of admonishment.

"And if we find a place worthy of exploration—we are all going to do this together?" Braemar said expectantly.

Xan nodded.

Understanding dawned in Braemar's doleful eyes, his shaking hands revealing how nervous he was about everything.

"Even you, Lilianna?" Braemar's voice was a single droplet in a gushing waterfall.

Where she sat, Lilianna reached for his hand, clasping it gently. "All of us will go."

Xan watched her hand and wondered whether he would lose her. It wasn't Earthen jealousy. It was more than that. After the other night, it became clear to him that he wanted his own clan with them. The sexual attraction was a bonus; but at the core of it, it felt like all three of them needed one another.

"I shall go then." Braemar nodded. The stoutness of his stance illuminated him in proposed glory.

Xan straightened his posture, effectively looming over the Sytheract. "Thank you, Braemar."

"Damn, I was hoping we would have to torture you with some controlled cuts along those shoulders of yours." Juniper licked her lips and arched an eyebrow at Braemar.

Xan laughed internally as the Sytheract male recoiled at the flirtation.

A flirtation from Juniper might be categorised as harassment, especially with a teeny drop of blood play.

Lilianna forced a laugh to stem the awkwardness, standing up and seizing Braemar by the elbow to lead him away from the menace into the kitchen area. "Oh, that's Juniper, always joking with inappropriate things."

Xan heard Braemar chuckle to compensate for his lack of understanding. Turning to Juniper, Xan flexed a disappointed look of fatherly distaste.

"What?" she spat aggressively with a gigantic smile on her face. "Or did you want to take his place? Your shoulders are mighty fine, also." She twirled a stray violet curl with her forefinger and bit her lip.

"You are an animal." Xan grinned and shook his head, then followed the two soulbirds flying arm in arm as Braemar gave a tour of his abode.

Juniper called out after Xan, "I'll pencil you in for later then?"

Xan and Braemar sat over a desk upstairs, scouring the topographical map holos and picking through Braemar's research. Lilianna and Juniper were in the kitchen gorging themselves on Sytheract snacks drummed up by the robotic arms. Xan only had a dense biscuit on a plate, with a warm cup of spiced *labberry* juice. It was surprisingly delicious, even if the berries had been developed in a lab.

"These three areas contain the highest levels of energy according to the canpuction read-out delivered by my own personal drone bot."

"You have a drone bot?" Xan asked, looking around the study, which was just a small room with a desk, three computers, and a holoprojection field.

"She is powered down in the ship currently."

Xan was concerned about Sawtech having eyes on them if they were to venture out, now that Braemar had a bot in his ship. He looked out the small window into the street and reached over to close the blinds.

Braemar seemed to sense Xan's hesitation. "Oh, don't worry, I work for the competitor, remember? None of our bots are on any of the

Sawtech clouds. That's part of our pull, helping people disconnect from the watchful eye of Sawtech."

Xan had his doubts. A corporation like Sawtech would be able to find ways around the little guys. But hopefully Evercorp was small enough that it didn't cause any circuitry waves in the vast ocean of the datasphere just yet.

Braemar zoomed in on one of the holomaps. "*Zaps and Zoots,*" he exhaled.

Xan wrinkled his nose, unaware of the phrase.

Braemar chuckled. "Oh, that's a little phrase like saying, 'Mmm, wow, that's crazy.'"

"Alright, well why is that so *Zap and Zoot*ed?"

"Well, this particular energy signature is nearly ten times the amount of any of these other options."

"That's it then. We need to go there." Xan stood up and started to head back downstairs. Admittedly he was thinking about what Juniper and Lilianna might be eating, feeling like he got the short end of the straw.

"Just hold on a minute." Braemar blocked his way and pointed to the holomap.

"Why? What's the problem?" Xan's stomach protested.

"Well, it's in Valinous Canyon. Here…" Braemar pulled up data on Valinous Canyon and Sawtech's logo flashed up all over it like vultures to a carcass.

"Why does Sawtech have anything to do with a canyon in the middle of nowhere?"

"I suppose that might have been why I've never gone. But this energy source must be something that they need or want…for robotic evolution perhaps?"

Xan clicked through some of the data, ignoring Braemar's deduction. "We really need to go here. This is the place."

Braemar combed his fringe through bony fingers. "I…I…just don't know if we can even…get to where the energy signature is hot enough. Look." He pointed to a spot on the map. "Here is where the energy source lies and here is where the Sawtech station is."

"Even better. We can bypass the entrance and repel down into—"

"Do you not think they will have surveillance?"

Xan knew he could be a little careless, especially if the outcome was saving a creature. In this case, the need for this energy source outweighed the potential negatives.

"You don't know what they are capable of."

"I do, Braemar. I may not have encountered a tyrannical corporation before, but I've encountered a tyrannical leader, so I can appreciate the dangers."

An alarm started blaring inside the house.

"What is that?" Xan peered through a crack in the blinds.

"One of the dangers we are worried about," Braemar said, his voice fluctuating while a camera feed showed three drones encircling his property. "Shit." He got up from the desk and ran down the stairs with Xan trailing behind.

CHAPTER 6

LOCATION: SYTHERIA
YEAR: 2505
XAN – 24 YEARS OLD

"**W**hat can we do?" Xan hissed as they entered the kitchen. It smelt of freshly baked goods and Xan's stomach grunted in frustration once again. The girls weren't near the stove or kitchen basin where the robotic arms feverishly cleaned dirty cookware and dishes.

Rummaging through the fridge, Braemar threw Xan a clear frosted pill. Xan turned it around in his fingers and saw the Evercorp logo inscription.

"What is this?"

"Take it," Braemar said flatly.

"Wait, I'm not going to take some experimental—"

"Take it – it will mask your heat signature so the drones can't detect you. Then hide!"

"Why do you have this?" Xan was hoping that Braemar was about to admit that he was a master thief.

"We have clients that don't want to be tracked by Sawtech, remember? We developed this to keep them…hidden. Now take cover!"

Braemar ran into the lounge room where Juniper and Lilianna lay dozing, full from their little feast. "Take these and hide."

"Ooooh, things are getting spicy—" Juniper started but Xan said, "No time for jokes – drones."

Juniper quickly understood and shoved the pill down Lilianna's throat, who gagged unceremoniously. She did the same with her own pill and awaited further instructions.

A blaring voice echoed in the street beyond: "Braemar Tyllieth, present yourself to the doorstep. You have T-minus ten seconds to comply."

Braemar shooed the rest of the crew into various spots in the lounge room. "If they come in, make sure you're well hidden!"

At the count of three he opened the door. "Hi folks, here I am."

"Good morrow, Sire Braemar." The drone hovered just outside the patio, a large screen visible with a Sytheract plastered on it. "I am a representative from Sawtech Corporation. We have received an alert that you were accessing sensitive information."

"Oh, really? I was just continuing my research into geological energy anomalies."

The drone's metallic arms and legs tensed, hovering like a winged spider about to pounce. "Since you work for Evercorp—a frankly inferior facsimile of Sawtech—we need to monitor when our interests are being, shall we say…*compromised*."

"Your interests?"

"Sawtech owns everything in the Valinous Canyon, so whatever you're searching for simply *cannot* be in there."

Braemar started to object once more, clearly unaware of the implicated threat. The Sawtech drone shot forward aggressively, nose to nose with the sweating Sytheract. "I suggest you move on to another area." It was no longer an earnest hand, guiding him into a perfect garden with climbing roses, adorning trellises in fists of vibrant colour. A second drone with an armoured cannon flattened cold steel against his chest, pushing Braemar to the edge of a precipice where the echoes of hope faded into the horizon.

Juniper had her exohand primed and ready to send the blade fingers slashing at dazzling speeds. But Xan placed his hand on hers and forcibly lowered the blades of death against her thighs.

She gave him a look that suggested carelessness, but he silenced her with a stern shake of his head.

Braemar, initially startled, appeared to wrestle back a sense of feigned calm. "Oh, my mistake." He stepped back, allowing a comfortable distance to return. "Would you tell those good fellas at Sawtech that I shan't be bothering them again?"

The representative appeared to scoff, "A wise choice, Master Tyllieth. Farewell."

Braemar went to close the door, hand trembling on the handle.

"Just a moment. The drones need to do a sweep of the property. There was a minor heat signature discrepancy upon initial assessment. You won't mind, will you?"

He gulped. "Not at all."

Lilianna was lying flat under the couch, but Juniper and Xan were gathered together, observing the interaction out of eyesight. Both rolled into the kitchen area and searched desperately for a place to hide.

The buzz of the drones scanned inside the lounge room first. Juniper climbed into the pantry, sealing the doors.

Xan glimpsed the laundry at the last moment before the drone rushed into the kitchen.

He crashed on the floor, piling dirty clothes and blankets on top of him. The smell of wet animal encircled him, reminding him of Qilin jumping onto his newly washed sheets after galloping in the rain.

The wings of the drone beat as fast as his heart hammering in his ears. It entered the laundry. He kept as still as he could. The lurching of his heart against the cage of his chest was surely a target for the restless drone.

It flew a small arc inside of the laundry, then spun back around to join its counterpart as it explored upstairs.

"Everything sufficient?" Braemar inquired as they exited out the front door.

"You are cleared for now. Do not continue with your geological research. Good day."

Xan listened as the drones buzzed further down the street like a swarm of departing bees.

Lilianna rushed to Braemar's side to check on him. Xan and Juniper both ran to a crack in the window as the menacing Sytheract drones turned to harmless flying creatures holidaying on the belt of the horizon.

"What the fuck was that about?" Juniper said.

"I…I've never had that happen before," Braemar said. "There were rumours that Sawtech monitored data, but I mean, that was within minutes of us researching some potential areas to scope out."

Xan was reminded of a time on Earth when corporations were being accused of data mining. Somehow, this appeared more sinister and less covert.

"We're really going to have to be careful going to the Canyon now." Xan exhaled a large breath, letting his shoulders relax.

"Um, so sorry my guy, but we can't go now," said Braemar. "I told him that I wouldn't go."

Juniper squared her shoulders. "I'm not sure if you understand—we aren't really giving you a choice, young buck. We are going, and it would be so very lovely if we wouldn't have to gag your plump lips and drag you across the entirety of the canyon by your luscious blonde locks."

"Excuse me, young lady, I will not be—"

Juniper didn't let him finish before the back of her fleshed hand struck him across the cheek. Braemar stumbled back into the wooden door, then held an arm out to Lilianna for support.

Lilianna held him upright and then moved to stand in front of Juniper. "Walk it off," she warned.

"We don't have time for this—"

"Juniper, this is not the way forward here. Let me handle it." Her tone was final, almost like she expected Juniper to back down.

Juniper stood firm, looming—unsure of her next move. But Xan stepped in, taking Juniper by the arm and leading her away to the couch. She shrugged him off violently, whispering, "I can walk on my own, Mr. Chaperone Switzerland." Xan watched her plonk down on the navy-blue velvet couch, looking as though she could rip Braemar's coiffed blond hair right from his skull.

Lilianna stroked Braemar's reddening cheek. "I'm sorry, Braemar, but there is a lot at stake here. We need to do this, and we need you to help us."

Xan wondered whether this show of affection was genuine or whether she was being manipulative. He'd never seen her be anything other than who she was, and it alarmed him slightly. Had Xan encouraged this in her? Or, more likely, Juniper?

"Why does this…Human…actually care about what happens to Sytheria? Not just the galaxy…but Sytheria specifically?" He craned his neck in the direction of Juniper who was cleaning the dirt from her real fingernails with the exo finger blades.

"There are grave consequences for other worlds. It's not Sytheria alone."

"Oh, so you're all just pretending to care about *this* world."

"No, not at all. There are all different species here together. Humans, Sytheracts, and others to fight against a very large extinction event. It affects each one of us!"

Braemar's eyes were cast downward.

"You must understand, the passion she has, that we all have, is because we not only want to save the world—a big feat in itself—but also to put things right for the entire galaxy."

Braemar swallowed and looked at Juniper, who gave him the fakest of smiles that might have ever graced her face. He turned to Xan, seated next to her, with his best genuine smile rimmed with overgrown stubble. Xan nodded with reverence in hopes that consensual help would be forthcoming, and the Juniper method would remain locked away. Braemar finally searched the glowing, golden eyes of his soulbond, standing, pleading for him to rise to the challenge.

Xan knew what Braemar would do. If he said no, the hope of developing a connection with Lilianna would be lost to him. If he said yes, it meant that he would pry seeds from the grasp of time, allowing love to germinate in the garden of his hope.

There wasn't even a hesitation as he sprinkled fertiliser across the soil and smiled, hoping that spring was in Lilianna's heart.

For such a well-put-together guy, the inside of Braemar's miniship was in disarray.

They had to wait outside the ship while he gathered up tins, bottles, and dirty cloaks and tossed them into the corner of the garage, shouting careless apologies more than once. Juniper and Xan filed into the miniship, squishing together in the back. Braemar took out his drone bot and tucked it inside the garage under a pile of unwashed cloaks so that Lilianna had space to sit.

It didn't take long to get to the botanical gardens. They parked the miniship in an extended parking bay, as if paying the gardens a visit. They strode out past the fern fairyland, the autumnal tunnel, where a carpet of deciduous leaves crunched underfoot through a conical shaft. They saw the island up ahead with the cloaked ship sitting idle in the middle and crept toward the row of dense bushes, where they concealed the hoverboards. As inconspicuously as they could, Lilianna and Xan dug around the roots until they located the bulky frames. They would need them to take turns getting across the moat to the *Attenborough*.

The sharp zap of an electrical force startled them both, and they spun around instantly, sensing danger. The bodies of Juniper and Braemar were already motionless upon the ground. Two figures must have been hiding in the bushes. A robot hovered in the air, looming down over them with a meek look of pixelated satisfaction on its faceplate. A stocky figure in a grey hooded cloak held a small sapphire laser pistol. Xan stared down its stout barrel. It winked at him with sardonic pleasure, clicking as it opened its mouth, ready to disrupt the relative composure of the garden setting. Lilianna caught her breath as she cowered behind Xan. Small hands gripped his shoulders in fear. He did everything that he could to stand tall, to shield her from harm.

"If you move—a bolt of electricity goes through you, too," the hooded figure remarked. It was a voice like split glass, raspy but with an air of refinement.

Xan held his hands up in submission as he stared once more at the comatose bodies of half his company on the ground. Before the rage overtook him and he repeated the same slaughter-first mentality that eradicated a ship full of Valkors, he glimpsed Juniper's chest rise and fall. She was stunned and not dead.

The pearly white robot with timid patches of rust gathering on its left shoulder, stared with large, pixelated eyes. Small pixels turned inward in random flickers around the edges, making it appear angry. But Xan did not see anger or aggression, he saw curiosity, a timid sense of wonder that was difficult to contain.

The hooded figure said, through gnashed teeth, "I want some answers, alien. You don't belong here."

Over his shoulder, Lilianna took a sharp intake of breath as if pierced by an arrow.

CHAPTER 7

LOCATION: SYTHERIA
YEAR: 2505
LILIANNA – 22 YEARS OLD

It wasn't the voice that gave the two assailants away. Lilianna didn't know that voice.

But the *way* they spoke held in the air at dusk, a shadow of someone she left behind. It pained her that in one version of this reality she would have known its timbre, would have harmonised with its melody until the song was wrapped in a satisfying cadence.

But as she recognised Arcadie, a little rusted and a little faded, she knew that underneath the hood of the menacing figure, her sister, Fleurah, would be staring at them, too many questions in her sandstorm eyes.

How would Lilianna explain being here now?

How had fate placed her sister here in front of her – real enough to touch, to hold close, as if a whispered wish uttered to an ashen sky had power enough to change reality?

Lilianna stepped forward in front of Xan, who flinched at her movement. She shook her head at him and turned to face the family member that she had abandoned for the first time in an age.

Arcadie lost the scowl, and his cybernetic eyes grew wide in surprise. His mouth formed a perfect rectangle giving the impression it was agape.

"Fleurah, is that you?" Lilianna's small voice was an insect caught in a rushing storm.

The trembling arm of the hooded figure dropped to its side. Arcadie spun twice in the air with spluttering thrusters, exclaiming, "Oh my goodness, Oh my goodness."

The grey hood fell back and there she was, her older sibling betrayed by the memories locked inside Lilianna's mind. The strawberry-blonde hair was now knotted in dreadlocks; one long scar was sliced from forehead across one eye to the base of her left cheek; a part of her tapered ear looked like it had been chewed off. Time hadn't caressed Fleurah gently as she searched for answers; it had treated her with utter contempt.

As Lilianna stepped forward to embrace her, Fleurah flinched. Each hopeful dream of seeing her sister again, each hardship she had endured had given birth to this very moment. The stark reality thrust upon her so suddenly was maybe more than she could bear. A welling of emotion took hold of her. The lengthy scar and the dishevelled nature of her older sister confirmed her deepest fears—abandonment had sent Fleurah over the edge. It wasn't a stretch to think that her life had been consumed by a question that ravages all people who are abandoned: why?

Lilianna fought with guilt—the feeling of butterflies twisting in her gut, the taste of salt on her tongue. It was all just a speculative consideration, of course, but if Fleurah's life had been doused in rose petals and soulbond kisses then there would be nothing more to see than fulfilment and happiness. A tear slid down her own cheek as she fought against everything to stay strong, to show her sister love rather than pity.

"Fleurah please." Her voice quivered.

"How is this possible?" Fleurah finally let out.

Lilianna's shoulders sagged. "There is just so much to tell you, I don't even know where to begin."

Xan stepped forward. "I'm sorry to break up the reunion, but your robot just tasered our friends into oblivion. Help us at least get them back on to the ship for some medical treatment."

"The ship," Fleurah grunted. "What ship?"

"It's over there." Xan pointed across the dark water slick with the reflection of a crescent moon. "The cloaking sheen is activated right now to remain hidden."

"Of course it's cloaked," she sighed. "That's how you've been able to conceal everything."

"How *did* you find us?" Lilianna inquired.

"Let me take this one, Fleurah dearest." The rust bucket that used to be pristine property, Arcadie, hovered forward, his thrusters coughing like an ill patient sprinkled with grey hairs and sagging skin.

"I have been programmed to recognise the seismic activity similar to the night of Lilianna's departure. We have been researching and building toward this moment, trying desperately to figure out when it might happen again. Finally, I picked up similar readings early this morning. I then followed the energy signatures to here." His retractable arms extended, and three clawed fingers stroked his metallic chin. "I really should have switched to infra-red mode to allow for better detection. Darn it, I wasted time."

Xan looked at Lilianna. "What the fuck is this programming it has?"

Lilianna was exasperated and a little taken aback by Xan's anger. "My dad tinkered with…things at Sawtech—I think Arcadie is a prototype, but I'm not sure what's happened over the years."

"Isn't that the truth?" Fleurah relayed bitterly. Silence came upon them fast like whistling wind through the sheer walls of a canyon.

Lilianna's emotions were at their pinnacle, gazing out across the horizon from a height so dizzying she could barely stand. Her sister, her robot brother, her soulbond, her lover or lovers. The intensity of it made it difficult to breathe normally.

"Well, are you going to enlighten us?" Xan said impatiently as insects in the botanical gardens chirped into the evening sky.

Fleurah rolled her eyes. "Yeah, he's a prototype – the most intelligent AI you'll ever find. The closest to regulating Sytheract emotional capabilities, learning from experiences, and building upon an already wide knowledge base."

Arcadie interjected, "In fact, it is probably the widest knowledge base of an AI because I can access *any* data sphere, within a specific range of course, as well as learning the depth and breadth of emotions over time."

"So you *have* changed then?" Lilianna squeaked, as if time itself squeezed against her throat. The loss of years wreaked havoc on her both physically and mentally.

"I am pleased to report, my long-lost sister, that I am indeed quite a lot better at discerning dangers…and recognising emotions better too. But I need to continue to get better. There is still so much more I need to grasp."

Lilianna felt a pang of regret. In fact, many pangs gathered into a horde of pangs and their pack mentality overcame her.

"I'm very proud of you then," she said softly. "I knew you'd look after Fleurah in my absence."

"I never forget a promise."

"Yes, yes, Arcadie. You literally can't forget. Your programming means you retain everything. So don't go bragging about shit like that. It's like saying, hey, how great am I 'cause I have a mouth. You just have one." Fleurah knocked him on the back of the head, causing a dense metallic ring like a hefty brass bell. Bat-like creatures sprung from the trees at the sound and flew over the small island where the ship sat cloaked.

Arcadie blinked several times and rubbed his head. Turning to Lilianna, he said, "Well, as you can see, *other* Sytheracts have changed, too."

Lilianna smiled with the song of sadness playing in her ears. Legato notes lamented an absence of rhythmic stability, lost in tritone dissonance. Strength was more than swallowing sadness; it was being able to cope with changes despite their severity.

"Did you get my sarcasm? I was actually talking about Fleurah!" He bobbed around excitedly, believing it to be a big reveal.

"Enough of this farcical reunion," Xan snapped. "Help me bring our friends to the ship and get them in the regen chamber." Shifting close to Fleurah and levelling a finger in her direction, Xan said, "You better have one hell of an apology planned for when they wake up or you'll be getting the life beat out of you."

Fleurah scoffed, "I'd like to see them try."

Xan lunged at her unexpectedly and grabbed her throat just fiercely enough to alter his scowl into an open-mouthed grimace. She was pinned against the rigid striped trunk of a zebra tree. Xan lowered his voice an octave. The tone was sinister, like the rumble of thunder before sheets of lightning coated the sky. "Just because you're Lilianna's sister doesn't mean you can treat any of us with disrespect or apathy. Watch yourself and work on being contrite, you little shit."

Lilianna faltered in the defence of her sister. A moment of shock hit her. She tried to come forward, but an unknown force stopped her from interfering.

This time, rather than turning away from Xan's darkness, she let it float; she wanted to see if she could swim in the same waters and glide to shore.

Xan let go abruptly and Fleurah gripped the tree trunk, straightening herself against it. The fear escaped Fleurah's eyes, replaced by a sort of bashful awe.

"You *will* form an apology when these two wake up and you *will* start to talk to your sister with some form of respect. Understood?"

The sparse sound of evening fauna twinkled around them as Fleurah stared at the ground.

"Answer me," he growled, his anger reverberating off those cavernous walls.

"Yes. Okay." She tried to raise her voice, but the defiance had evaporated when met with the heat of Xan's protective nature.

Lilianna felt a hot flush rise to her cheeks as she felt the embodiment of Xan's love shower her. She could see now that his rage, his wrath, his dominance and protection came solely from love.

Qilin had once been taken from him, and it was as if he himself had been taken along with her. Now, in the face of disrespect and defiance against members of his found family – his crew – he made a stand to ensure that no one fucked with them. It had taken Lilianna a lot of her own growth to recognise what this was, but the more she stared, the more she was taken by the view.

"You and Lilianna take the male, and I'll take Juniper with Arcadie." Xan's eyes were now dark shades of grey.

Fleurah nodded, with a feeble apology escaping her lips.

Lilianna and Xan picked up the hoverboards. He frowned, looking out at the island. "How the fuck are we going to take them across?"

"Allow me, good sir." Arcadie zoomed forward, nearly knocking into Xan with his excitement. "I believe this act of strength I exhibit might prompt forgiveness perhaps?"

Xan leant on the hoverboard, vertically digging into the soft ground covered in wispy reeds. "What act of strength?"

Arcadie scooped up Juniper and Braemar as if collecting polished stones at the water's edge. Extending his loopy arms out around the bodies, he squeezed them in tight to his panels and lifted up from the ground. The thrusters strained momentarily, making the little robot wobble. But he steadied, flipping around to show a smug, satisfied look written in pixels. He zoomed backwards across the moat, maintaining eye contact. "See, I'm better than a body build—"

The ship was still invisible so when Arcadie was too busy bragging and not slowing down, Lilianna yelled, "Stop, you're going—"

He backed into the ship with a clank and lost his balance. The robot tipped to the left with Braemar's greater weight, and the Sytheract started to slip through. At the last moment the three-clawed hand seized Braemar's undershirt before he fell into the water. Arcadie righted him and hovered in the air. "Oh, I'm terribly sorry, but ah what shall I do now?"

Lilianna hid her giggle from Xan as the handsome but ill-tempered man huffed and puffed getting on the hoverboard. "Just don't drop them! I'm coming now to get you into the ship."

CHAPTER 8

LOCATION: SYTHERIA
YEAR: 2505
RYKER – 21 YEARS OLD

Ryker had just finished servicing the compressor while Dallis watched over his shoulder. The ship's internal lights provided enough illumination upon the area in question, but Dallis was an everlasting eclipse. It didn't matter how many times Ryker tried telling the immovable mountain to hang back; his natural curiosity always got the better of him. Ryker was effectively performing a surgery in blinking darkness. Accepting his fate, he did his best to appease Dallis, showing him how to service the particular parts he had an interest in.

"Well, thank you kindly for providing me with such knowledge." Dallis's weathered skin creased as he grinned like a child. An auburn curl swung across his forehead.

Ryker couldn't make his mind up about the Valkor male. He was naturally good looking, extremely helpful and doting, speaking with incredible refinement. But it was hard to take him seriously. His inability to discern the nuances of the Gemarinian interactions caused a certain level of ridiculousness that couldn't be ignored.

Adding to the Dallis eclipse, Massy had some horrible music turned up to maximum volume and was leaping and dancing around the ship. His muddy boots thudded into the metal grates as he twirled in the air, flicking dots of dirt wherever he moved.

Qilin, confined to the ship, growled whenever Massy came too close.

Not for the first time, Ryker wondered how Massy could be so frivolous, so unassuming and carefree, when all around them chaos reigned. But then again, wasn't it his endearing trait? The thing that made him bearable?

One thing was for certain: Ryker was surrounded by idiots.

As Ryker finished cleaning just a small part of Massy's mud signature near the maintenance hub, he noticed on the camera display that there was a commotion on the ramp of the ship. On the feed, Xan waved frantically at the cameras. Juniper lay at his feet unconscious while Lilianna and someone he didn't recognise had just laid down another body next to her. Ryker coughed reflexively as he spotted a robot floating over the bodies as if checking their vitals.

What is this about?

Ryker pulled down the lever and the *Attenborough's* hatch opened slowly.

Xan rushed in, the cracks of thunder starting to tear across the sky as the sudden rain pelted the ship. "Regen chamber," he called, as he bustled past Ryker with Juniper in his arms. A Sytheract girl followed Xan into the ship with the robot carrying Lilianna's soulbond. The robot had formed a stack of pixels on the end of a thin line that appeared to be its mouth.

Was it trying to smile at me?

Ryker didn't say a thing as Lilianna climbed aboard and closed the hatch. She shrugged with an unusual sadness. "It's a long story," she said, then turned away and trudged after them, her wet hair sulking from the downpour.

Aside from actually looking forward to hearing the bonkers story of what had just happened, he reconsidered Lilianna for a moment.

The sadness might be mainly…annoyance or frustration. But over the course of the last few days there was definitely something weighing on her.

Ryker watched them disappear down the corridor as Dallis found his usual spot over his shoulder plunging him into perpetual shadow.

"Do you know what happened?" His sapphire eyes glowed expectantly.

Ryker shook his head but didn't say a word. He caught a glimpse of some Massy mud splatter that had been missed and knelt down to eradicate it from his section of ship, cursing messy Massy.

His thoughts returned to the weight of sadness.

Can sadness be redeemed by heroism? Will I be redeemed by an act of colossal bravery? A moment when I'll stand while others cower, a moment where I'll be more than a figure draped in shadow cleaning stains off the floor?

The light returned as Dallis moved down the corridor to satisfy his overzealous curiosity. Ryker squinted as he realised that some people worked better in the darkness, for in the darkness one could tinker away without prying eyes.

LILIANNA
22 YEARS OLD

As Xan placed Juniper carefully in the chamber and set the regeneration course to run for a full cycle, Fleurah caught Lilianna's attention and gestured toward Xan as he set the dials, grumbling to himself.

"So, who is grumpy pants to you exactly?" She swept waterlogged dreadlocks of hair across her shoulder.

"He is my…well…" Lilianna struggled to define their relationship. In the presence of Braemar, she had stupidly categorised Xan as just her boss and immediately saw it sting him the way it used to sting her. She didn't know why she did that really. The pressure of meeting her soulbond, of being in Sytheria—all played havoc on her emotions.

There were so many things that happened within just one week with Xan that she could no longer say boss as easily as she used to.

"He is like…a boss friend, I guess," she spluttered, scratching her neck.

"A boss friend? First time I've heard of that," Fleurah snickered.

"Well, it's complicated, I guess." Her cheeks gained colour as she scrambled for footing at the end of the noose.

"Wow, Lilianna the soulbond connoisseur going for complicated. Who'd have thought?" She laughed properly for the first time. It was nice.

A flash of memory hit Lilianna with force—the feeling of rain soaking into skin, the sky streaked with sunset blood, sisters' hands clasped together, smiles like a rainbow arching from one beautiful moment to the next.

Lilianna blinked and eradicated the memory. "Who cares about me— where is *your* soulbond?" Lilianna took off her wet cloak and hung it on the edge of the first bed in the shared quarters.

A brief moment of silence fell as Fleurah shifted her pack, letting it hit the floor haphazardly, next to the second bed. "I fell out of the customs a long time ago, sister." Fleurah scratched at the inside of her eye and then sniffed whatever fluid had leaked onto her finger, looking out a circular viewport as the kamikaze rain made sacrifices on the windowpane.

"You did?" Lilianna couldn't hide her disappointment.

And Fleurah didn't hide her contempt. "It's a bit hard to dedicate one's life to finding a soulbond when my best friend robot and I are trying to locate my long lost sister, isn't it?" She cast off her coat into the corner, underneath a shelf with melted candles and holoframes displaying expedition memories. Glowing tattoos trailed up both her arms like a bioluminescent rash intersected by deep scars.

Lilianna's face dropped. That confirmed her initial thoughts as to why Fleurah appeared unkempt and downtrodden. Where there had once been a loving sister, a wound of absence festered for all to see. But it wasn't only the absence – the nature of Lilianna's departure changed the course of Fleurah's entire life. The germinating guilt in the pit of her stomach sprouted in bursts of regret. Roots wound throughout the connective tissue of her body, digging into funnels of flesh until they were a part of her.

Guilt would become a stoic tree within, watching weaker emotional empires fall. As ages passed by, it would remain until the last leaf wilted and she was no more.

"Excuse me for a moment." Lilianna left the room as Fleurah eyed the spread of alien food resting upon the table, oblivious to another emotional empire rising inside her sister.

RYKER
21 YEARS OLD

In the common room, Ryker watched Massy swagger forward, smoothing the birthmarks on his forehead.

"Well, well, well, delighted to meet your acquaintance." Massy stooped low, kissing the new female Sytheract's hand.

Ryker ran his fingers through his own hair in embarrassment, just wanting to look away but fixated on the carnage ahead of him. A new piece of meat and Massy flocked to her side with a knife and fork, ready to tear in.

She recoiled but looked capable of reining in any hatred in earnest. "That's a hell of a lot of 'wells,' but yes, thanks." Yanking back her hand, she stared after Lilianna who had vacated the room a moment before.

Arcadie presented his dangling three-clawed dominant appendage to Massy. "Would you like to do the same to my hand, kind-souled alien?"

Massy thought for a moment, shrugged, and kissed cool metal. Arcadie giggled with glee, his eyes turning to slits and returning to circles in quick succession.

Xan stepped forward. "You know me well enough by now, despite being acquainted in regrettable circumstances." His intense gaze scolded Arcadie and Fleurah. "I should explain – this is my ship, the *Attenborough*. I am essentially the commander of this vessel and Massy here is my pilot, one of the best I've seen. Ryker is equally skilled in maintenance. Dallis is over there." Dallis gave a bizarre gesture, where he craned his neck to the side and curtseyed low, dangling his hands at his feet and wiggling his fingers. "Giving you a weird bow or something. Braemar—the unconscious Sytheract we have developed a working relationship with and Juniper our soldier warrior who you decided to taser into oblivion."

The grubby young Sytheract looked overwhelmed at the faces around her, and Ryker wondered why she had been brought onto the ship if she had caused such chaos.

"Who is this fine specimen?" Arcadie hovered near Qilin, who was sniffing with increased fervour in the robot's direction.

"Qilin. She is my Mika Tikaani companion. You should tread carefully, she—"

Qilin started to lick Arcadie's claws, and he squealed in delight. The more he did it the more she thought it was a game, and in the end Qilin chased Arcadie around the common area, knocking packets of chews on the floor. Xan looked embarrassed.

"Listen, I do apologise for how it all went down. My name is Fleurah," she gestured to the group, "and this is my robot brother, Arcadie."

Ryker breathed in deep. He briefly recognised the name but couldn't place it.

Massy is going to enjoy a new potential plaything. Finally, someone living and breathing might be interested in him. If not, there is always the robot, I suppose.

"Oh my, oh my," Massy sung. "This is a plot twist."

Dallis's head shot up, eyes wide with helpful intent. "Did you need me to fix a twist in the engine parts? Ryker has been a great tutor."

Massy ignored him and continued, placing an arm around Fleurah's shoulder. "The esteemed sister of our dear Lilianna. How wondrously fate filled."

That's where Ryker recognised the name. It was Lilianna's biological sister, of whom he had heard her tell short tales about.

"It seems the reunion didn't go so well." Massy chuckled, looking for someone to take pleasure in their pain but finding no one well versed in the art of schadenfreude.

"Alright, alright enough with this." Xan's grumbling voice shot out like a cannon blaster.

Massy pulled back his arm as if shot.

"Let's just focus on letting Juniper recover and put energy into planning our journey to the Valinous Canyon." He pointed at the robot and his companion. "Fleurah and Arcadie, you might be able to assist if you know the terrain."

They looked at one another and nodded.

"I cannot lie Master Xan, but you should be aware that our knowledge of the terrain is rudimentary at best. Sawtech does not permit us to venture often into territories such as those."

"Look, I appreciate your honesty," Xan said, warmth returning.

Arcadie's faceplate cheeks flashed with red dots, as if he were pleased with himself for pleasing Xan.

Xan continued. "…but I'd much rather have local guides wherever possible. Besides, a robot on our side might come in handy."

"How so?" Arcadie thrusted closer to Xan, a little bit more comfortable now that Xan had shed his grumpy winter coat. Qilin trotted after him, watching with those big amber eyes, her tail peaked upwards in curiosity.

"You can hack networks and data clouds, right?"

"In mere seconds, Master."

"Well, looks like we are going to be good friends." Xan winked at the robot.

Eyes lit up in yellow flashes. "I've never had a real friend before!"

Ryker smiled.

It's not like Xan to befriend some weird ass alien…thing.

He looked around at the crew gathered there and realised they were all weird ass aliens. Him included.

CHAPTER 9

LOCATION: SYTHERIA
YEAR: 2505
JUNIPER – 24 YEARS OLD

Juniper awoke groggy and alone. The lights in the med bay had been dimmed. The regen chamber in front of her had just powered down. She sat up gingerly and rubbed her temples, stimulating the blood in and around her head. Opening her mouth wide, she cracked her neck, turning it to the left and to the right, feeling a nerve cry out as she did so. Juniper tasted metal as if she had deep throated a big robot dick.

Robot dick! Some robot was *a dick.*

She recalled the sneak attack from the robot in question, certainly not one that she had performed her famous fellatio technique upon.

I'm going to give it an organic heart just so I can rip it to shreds inside its body. Now where the fuck is it?

Her head lolled from one side to the next and she stared out of one eye feeling like she'd had thirteen *bundle of delight* cocktails at Fusion bar when she first started attending. Gooseflesh crept with stealth across her skin, exposed to the constant purring of the recycled air.

Instead of being bound on a Sytheract ship emblazoned with the Sawtech logo, she was back in the comforting embrace of the *Attenborough*. She was confused. If she had been captured by a Sawtech spy, then she would be in Sawtech custody, but here she was – fresh faced and as sexy as the day she came of Fusion-age, on Xan's funky little ship.

Juniper steadied herself briefly on the edge of the regen chamber before sliding her bare feet across the floor to the sink. It was like the march of the elderly queuing for a buffet breakfast.

Who am I kidding? I won't see these purple curls turn to grey ice with time's wintery breath. I'll bleed out on a battlefield cursing the asshole who finally got the best of me.

Filling up a glass and swigging desperately, she quenched her parched mouth. As she slammed the empty vessel on the table, something unnatural caught her eye. It was a colourful liquid she had seen time after time splattered across the face of her comrades in the middle of war. Something she had scrubbed off her body at the end of each pillage of Cryptoborg territory. A coughing fit ensued. Ragged breaths accompanied vivid tears that streaked her vision, like murderous rain attacking a window pane. Shaking hands gripped the benchtop to steady herself. A presence loomed behind her. Juniper spun around and nearly lost her balance, managing to flick her exofingers to blades without keeling over. She stopped just before plunging the blades into its jugular.

Xan held her arm in a strong grip and slowly pried it toward her side. He gathered her into his embrace.

"You fucking dipshit," Juniper hissed. "You know better than to sneak up on…well me…a deadly, unhinged psychopath warrior."

Xan ignored her remark, looking very Xan-like. Concerned, as if she were the last creature on earth with a flesh eating wound in the middle of her forehead. "Are you okay?" he whispered.

Juniper gathered her composure briefly. "Yeah. I…I'm sorry about nearly…decapitating you. We all know how much I enjoy lopping off heads."

Xan pulled back, put his hands on both of Juniper's cheeks, bent his head to examine her, then kissed her softly on the lips. She let herself fall into the kiss, a weightless dive off a granite cliff into the rushing waves of the ocean.

As they parted, Juniper recalled why she was so on edge a moment before and shook off the zap of lust.

"Shit, Xan, I have to show you this…" She pointed to the blue flecks of blood on the edge of the sink. Tiny droplets formed a circular path of treachery. A confirmation that a dirty Cryptoborg had somehow found its way onto the ship.

"How is that possible?" Xan searched the room frantically, craning his neck to the corners, inspecting the ceiling as if the Cryptoborg had morphed into an arachnid spinning silky webs off the roof.

"They must have got in right before we went through the portal. I don't know." Juniper trailed off, annoyed that she hadn't killed them all. It was her fault that there was a breach. A famous warrior, a former leader of the army. It was unacceptable that she'd let the enemy cross over into their territory. Then and there, she assigned herself the role of exterminator. Rolling her shoulders, she set off to where her suit lay on the floor of the regen chamber. She caught a glance of Braemar peacefully dozing in the other bed and scoffed.

Taken down in the same way as that absolute egg.

Juniper was embarrassed and enraged at being felled along with a civilian Sytheract who had as much strength as a fallen twig on the path of a charging army. She zipped up the body suit.

"Is everyone else accounted for?" Juniper had tucked every ounce of humour away now. She had to make up for looking like a fairy-winged princess and start snarling like the ravenous animal she truly was.

"Ryker, Massy, Dallis and Arcadie are all on the deck. Lilianna went to her quarters, and I think Fleurah is there eating every last crumb of food we have on the ship."

Juniper stopped manically pumping herself up and slackened her shoulders along with her jaw. "Have I been asleep for seventeen years? Half of these fuckbags I've never heard of?"

"It's a long story." Xan scratched the back of his head.

"I mean, if we have turned into an orphanage overnight and now I'm Mummy Juniper—just shoot me in the face." Juniper pushed the Cranston ray gun into Xan's hand.

Xan smirked as he brushed the gun away. "Well, you call me Daddy enough, so…"

"I'm not even letting you finish that shit joke. Besides, we have a Cryptoborg crawling around in the ducts like John Maclean at Christmas and you're all yippy ki-yaying like a cowboy."

"You know who John Maclean is?"

"I watch movies! Especially ones with Die and Hard in it."

"Alright, let's discuss classic movies later."

"Indeed," Juniper agreed. "Let's go visit Lilianna's quarters and you can catch me up on all these new characters and what the fuck actually happened to me."

CHAPTER 10

LOCATION: SYTHERIA
YEAR: 2505
LILIANNA – 22 YEARS OLD

Lilianna sat in the shared quarters space on the edge of the bed, chin resting on open palms, elbows digging into her knees. Qilin was curled up on Lilianna's pillow, twitching into a peaceful dream.

Fleurah lay on one of the beds snoring, half a butter bread pastry hanging out of her mouth. The glowing cosme-tatts rolling up her arms had dimmed while the body rested.

Lilianna wondered how long it had been since she'd had her parents around to look after her, or at least someone other than the equivalent of a teenage robot as her sole companion.

There was a loud clang, metal on metal. It startled her and Qilin. They both jumped off the bed. Lilianna's fists clenched to her chest, while Qilin's tail unfurled her spikes, preparing a defence.

"Whoops," Arcadie managed at a lower volume. "I was trying to connect to the techno signature of some of your devices in order to pry into your…alien world. Some interesting tech you have."

"You can't just sit stationary?" Lilianna exhaled loudly and bent down to pat Qilin back into submission.

"Look, little sis, I've got megatons worth of excitability pulsing throughout my circuits. Forgive me!"

Lilianna laughed; she had missed the little guy. His innocence, his exuberance and thirst for knowledge. She sat down again and positioned herself on the bed, staring up at the ceiling vents blowing cool recycled air into the quarters. Even though she missed a lot of things on Sytheria, she also missed being on Gemarine. Hardly anyone had the experience of growing up on two completely different worlds, having to adapt to two different cultures and somehow retain their own identity. She felt the pull of one in the same way as the other.

At that moment, though, she longed to be with Xan, exploring worlds and saving creatures. Somehow the security of him being there with her and keeping to a schedule was calming. This mission of jumping around through time and different planets was an absolute stress fest. No wonder she was on edge.

The door burst open and for the second time in a few minutes she was sent reeling back.

"Are you okay?" Xan spoke forcefully.

Fleurah spat out the pastry across the floor and shouted sleepily, "What's happened?"

Qilin leapt up for the second time, but because it was Xan immediately became glued to his side.

"I was okay, but I might not be now!" Lilianna huffed. "Why are you bursting through here without any—"

Juniper had snuck into the room and placed a hand over Lilianna's mouth. Searching the vents, straining with an ear all around.

Arcadie broke the silence, "Madame Juniper, might I extend my apologies on behalf of—"

"Shut the fuck up, slinky," she growled, tense with the Cranston ray gun in her grasp.

"Oh my! That is rude beyond anything I've ever—"

Xan provided the calm voice of reason. "Arcadie, please, there might be an enemy aboard the ship."

Lilianna's voice came through, muffled by Juniper's hand. "An enemy, what?"

"A Cryptoborg somehow got onto this ship." Juniper took her hand away from Lilianna's mouth.

"What is a Cryptoborg?" Fleurah asked.

Juniper narrowed her stare. "You're lucky I'm trying to find this stowaway otherwise I'd bitch slap you halfway across this room, you little cunt."

"Oh my." Arcadie whimpered like a wounded doe.

Fleurah gasped, shrinking back into the mattress.

Everyone in the room slipped into silence. Muscles tensed as they listened for any sound out of place. The rain clattered on the shell of the *Attenborough*. It disguised the thumping of collective hearts. But it also meant that discerning between creaking in the vents and the hammering of rain was almost impossible.

Lilianna quickly redirected their efforts to the stowaway Cryptoborg. "Arcadie, you said you can log into the data clouds and other tech on the ship. Could you access the cameras or even display a heat signature map?"

"Great idea," confirmed Xan.

Lilianna smiled, feeling heat swell her cheeks at the thought of pleasing him.

Arcadie stopped for a second, "Nothing to report via the cameras, but hold on. Heat signature in the maintenance hub."

"That's Ryker."

"Heat signature walking away from the maintenance hub. Heat signature heading toward the maintenance hub from the other side—"

"Wait? That's not right."

"Is there a heat signature in the cockpit?"

"Yes, there is one there."

"Ryker!" Xan and Juniper shouted.

RYKER
21 YEARS OLD

Ryker was finally alone. Dallis had shuffled off to another part of the ship and it was bliss.

Having an extra pair of very…large hands had been helpful of course, but the constant questions combined with the pressure of filler conversation was too much for Ryker to endure for a long period of time. He liked the cold caress of solitude. The dim light of the maintenance hub where he could tinker, twist, and tussle with nothing but his aching thoughts. The ones where he sometimes imagined sickening things, macabre and masochistic, imagined worlds where Lambastian wasn't exiled and they got to experience Fusion together, imagined not lying underneath the couch as Marauder's dying eyes screamed betrayal.

Ryker sat on his rickety stool and checked the comfort level on the first antigravity chamber. He brushed off gathering dust. Flecks of red took flight, settling on his scuffed boots. He clicked the formula into place. The metallic clang of the anti-gravity tube rang out as he knocked it with his elbow.

"Bitch," he whispered with broken glass in his throat, rubbing it to stem the sudden burst of pain.

A muffled click of something hard against the metallic floor pinged close by. He shuffled, trying to see if he'd dropped a screwdriver. No. Nothing lost from his grasp. A click, like a purposeful footstep. Ryker acknowledged the sound from just over his shoulder.

Confusion masks terror and it enhances denial in the face of an intuitive spike of the senses. There are only so many distractions one can give priority to, before the fear receptors engage and the body is in charge, discarding the mind's frivolous delusions.

Ryker's mind had its dance in a sunny meadow, but the meadow was now a wasteland.

A large female Cryptoborg towered above him, her helmet forged in plated gold discarded on the floor of the ship. A fresh wound tore her face in two; peels of flesh wilted as bubbling blue blood blossomed like a cluster of rancid florets. A nightmare made real, her shimmering mauve skin rippled under the piercing halogen globes, neck craned to the side, eyes like orbs of gloom scanning across Ryker's terrified face.

Ryker struck out reflexively, swatting at the ooze of blood on her face. A quick deflection left him panting as he tried with the other hand. Just as fast as before, she parried his attempted strikes and waited, watching him to see what came next. Was she playing with him? When she was bored, would she crush him with a single blow to the skull?

He didn't want to die on his knees, smiling in submission at his killer. He also didn't want to die on his feet. Reaching backwards, he wrapped his hands on an electron starter. It was used to flood batteries or bezels with electrons for an emergency charge. This *was* an emergency. Gripping the electron starter, he slammed it upwards toward the Cryptoborg's jugular, but as she deflected it caught her on the wrist, sending electrons pulsing through her. In the act of being electrocuted her dark eyes flickered to white, but she maintained enough composure to swat the charger across the small maintenance hub and push Ryker into the wall away from her.

Ryker swallowed as he looked up at her mangled face.

I might not die on my knees, but I'll die on my ass it seems.

CHAPTER 11

Juniper led the charge. She didn't bother with stealth. She bulldozed ancient elms, felled an entire enchanted forest, slick with sweat and the tears of the dismayed inhabitants. Clanging sounds on the boronium floor rang out in the ship like an alarm.

The Cryptoborg towering over Ryker in the maintenance hub spun around quickly. The damage to her face was severe, and it would make a hideous scar as the years wore on. Those years would not be permitted to glorify the battle wound. Juniper would not allow it. The Cryptoborg's black eyes widened at the sight of the warrior who had come for her.

It wasn't what she expected. Juniper felt like it was a letdown. She went for a flying kick to the Cryptoborg's face. The cheek depressed and the body crunched into a wall lined with brightly coloured knobs and switches. A fistful of sparks flew as she dropped to the floor. Juniper flipped her around straddling her, seconds away from pounding her face in, but Xan grabbed her arm.

Blue blood trickled out of the side of the Cryptoborg's mouth. Craning her head, Juniper realised she was trying to smile at her.

"The fuck you smiling about?"

"We are the hands of fate. Right the wrongs."

"Hand of fate? More like fist of fate." She readied her fist to bring it down upon the already mangled face of the Cryptoborg soldier.

Xan tightened the grip on her arm. "No, Juniper. We need information."

Rage was a swelling crescendo in a symphony of malice. She wanted nothing more than to add another number to the seemingly endless list of kills, but in the quiet of her sane mind, Xan had a point. They needed to know how the Cryptoborgs had ambushed them on Periah, and what this one had been doing stowed away on the *Attenborough*.

Juniper relented and yanked the rag doll Cryptoborg up so they were face to face. "You've heard of me, haven't you?"

She nodded with a lolling motion, desperately hanging onto consciousness.

"Then you'd know if my hunger for killing isn't satisfied, I'll drink down torture like it's a sweet smoothie. I'm about to fire up the blender."

RYKER
21 YEARS OLD

Ryker had long since tried to speak as the Cryptoborg stared at him in the midst of being dragged away. Ryker couldn't understand why his heart had not been wrenched from his chest and crushed on the floor of the maintenance hub. After they had interrogated the Cryptoborg, he needed to see her again and try to understand what had just happened.

CHAPTER 12

There was a makeshift cell in the *Attenborough*, used mainly for dangerous beasts or creatures capable of flying, often a little larger than the average *Truntalisk*.

The Cryptoborg's faded mauve hands were bound with a rope fixed to the ceiling.

"I'm not here to fuck around." Juniper slapped her with the back of her real hand, and blue blood sprayed on the bioplastic walls. "Tell me why the fuck you're here."

The Cryptoborg breathed in deeply, savouring the pain as if it were a badge of honour. "I'm here to ensure that fate is realised. That the galaxy does not fall at the mercy of Gemarine."

"Look, let's not go as big as the galaxy, shall we? I want to know what you were doing on Periah." Juniper turned to face the back wall of the cell, making eye contact with Xan, who sat in the corner, hands in his lap like some little voyeur secretly touching himself.

The Cryptoborg sighed. "We had known of the portal planet for generations. There was always a presence, a group that sat waiting for the moment of arrival. It was sheer circumstance that it would be Gemarinians that united the three celestial crystals."

They knew about crystals and the portal planet. So they were secretly just a whole race of nerds like Xan. Interesting.

"Okay, so far what you're telling me is you weren't intent on killing anyone from Gemarine, but this is all just some cosmic coincidence?"

"We don't deal in coincidence, we deal in fate." The female winced with each intake of breath.

Juniper slapped the Cryptoborg's cheek. The wound opened further, weeping blue. "That was for being all pious about fate. I deal in facts, not bullshit, so how about you just keep it real with me?"

"You aren't the person I can divulge secrets to."

"Oh, why is that?" Juniper was devoid of virtue, so patience never stood a chance.

"Trust is a two way street and right now you're beating me senseless. Regardless of what you do to me, Cryptoborg secrets don't belong to you."

Exoblades flipped out like the fangs of a cobra. Xan called, "Juniper." His tone was of warning.

He's so full of righteousness. Did I stop him when he was wasting a whole ship of Valkors? Juniper remembered calling out to him before he dealt a final blow to Dallis. *Well, maybe I did. But this is different.*

Xan whined like the fun police. "Ryker seems to think that she didn't want to harm him. Maybe there is something more to this."

"Ryker wouldn't know an enemy if it bit him on the ass." She turned to the Cryptoborg, "In fact, did you try to bite—"

Xan said, "Stop being an idiot."

"Make up your mind!" She flipped around to face the pretentious twat. "Shall I behave like the court jester, your highness, or do you want me to get answers the only way I know how, huh?"

"Just don't get all crazy warrior…ah…princess and keep your head."

"We all know the only princess in this room is you." She flicked her hair in his face. "By the way I do love it when you *try* and tell me what to do."

Xan rolled his eyes. "After you're done here, we'll see how good you really are at taking instruction."

Juniper swallowed hard. She felt deprived, and it had only been a day or so. She threw him a look they both knew well, indicating that no matter what, she wanted her thirst quenched by a fresh Xan milkshake.

She swung back around to face the Cryptoborg. "What will you give me then, huh? Your name? Your purpose? Why did you jump on this ship? What did you hope to achieve?"

"My name is Sythkin. All that the Cryptoborg's want is to ensure that the crystals are used in the right ways. If your mission disrupted the flow of what was meant to be then I would have acted."

"What would you have done?"

"Whatever I had to."

Juniper was already bored of this and would've rather lopped off her silly little head and be done with it, but there was something here, she knew it. A pocket of information that might help them. She just needed to find a way to pry that information from that hideous mouth.

"Alright, well I have some other pressing matters to attend to." She looked back longingly at Xan.

"But maybe a little bit of time to think will do you well."

RYKER
21 YEARS OLD

Ryker had to know. He knew that he shouldn't, but curiosity was a nail and he was the hammer.

In playing over moments in his head he considered that quite possibly the Cryptoborg wasn't toying with him. A beast in the Wilds letting the prey hop along until a weighted paw crushed the spine. Maybe she didn't want to inflict pain upon him. Even though their dark eyes made it difficult to discern their intent, he was almost certain that if that Cryptoborg wanted him dead, he would be dead.

The ropes were flaccid on the ground but still fixed around her hands. Gloom surrounded her like winged demons, malignant and malicious. Horror was written in her hollow eyes, in her body – slumped on the floor of the cell. In the dim light, her mauve skin looked faded and worn. Droplets of blood trickled down her cheeks from the facial wound like morning rain on a bleary window.

"It is you." Her voice was a splitting atom.

Ryker had a short moment where he was fearful of what to say but like the electron starter, he found the energy.

"Why didn't you kill me?"

The Cryptoborg sighed, eyes still focused on the floor of the cell. "Because I'm not the bad guy." A smile writhed, serpent-like across her face. "And something tells me you aren't either."

CHAPTER 13

LOCATION: SYTHERIA
YEAR: 2505
XAN – 24 YEARS OLD

Xan raised his eyebrow in Massy's direction. "Are you sure you're okay to stay and guard the Cryptoborg?"

"Look, my forte is flying, not hiking. You're doing me a favour giving me this job." Massy flicked his wrist dismissively.

Xan tried to thank him, but Massy leant forward and placed his forefinger on Xan's cracked lips. "Shhh."

Xan hit him across the head playfully and backed away. "Behave yourself!"

Massy stood with his hands on his hips like a superhero and yelled, "Never!"

Qilin stayed close, brushing up against Xan's legs, letting her tail unfurl and wrap around his wrist protectively. They both walked down the corridor, with Xan preparing to brief everyone about what to expect in Valinous Canyon.

The highly guarded entrance to the canyon was a long way behind them now. After much deliberation, it wasn't feasible to enter the canyon trying to skirt around the Sawtech guards. Braemar and Xan worked out an entry point over one hundred kilometres in, identified by the topography of the holomaps. They would spend some time monitoring the patrols from the cloaked ship across the length of the canyon and then the team would abseil down from that key point when it was safe. It was as close as they could get to the energy source before the canyon became too narrow and dangerous for the *Attenborough* to drop them in. Braemar was adamant that they would need to be extra vigilant to watch for drones or sentinel robots capable of exposing them as they went further into the canyon.

"This is the problem, we haven't taken the time to scope out how these sentinel bots work," Braemar complained, magnetised to Lilianna as he shuffled forward, saffron dust rising with each footfall.

Xan nodded. Braemar was talking sense. His instincts were usually to plan with meticulous thought, to plan for every contingency. Recently he abandoned that method. When in dire circumstances, plans were often forgotten for actionable solutions. For better or worse, this mission had prepared him to accept the presence of fate, that chance cannot be measured and often succumbing to the moment was all one could do. Still, it unnerved him.

"I understand, Braemar, but again we don't have a choice," he muttered gravely, squinting into the blaring sun.

"You make it sound like you're willing to die for this?" Fleurah asked. Her glowing arms pulsed. A sapphire pistol swung in her right hand.

Xan thought carefully and looked around at the crew gathered before him. They each stared back with a collective nervousness bound by sweating palms and trembling hands.

"We know the risks, but we also know what happens if we are apathetic," Lilianna began before Xan could utter a word. "The gravity of inaction is more severe than leading with hope."

Fleurah crossed her tattooed arms across her chest and nodded. "I don't know when you developed this whole rebellious streak, but I'm all for it."

A smile of satisfaction, of pride, slid across Lilianna's face. She quickly concealed it.

Juniper walked ahead but turned back to address them. "Let's just be smart about this. Dallis and Ryker are at the back as our sentries searching the skies for anything from Sawtech, and the rest of us will stick to the cliff walls where we will get shade about the size of a bird's dick."

It wasn't the heat that was an issue; the cloud cover subdued the intensity of the sun. It was the possibility of prying eyes—from satellites, drones, surveillance ships. If anything was true about Sytheria, it's that there was a constant presence of a technological eye, narrowing its gaze and narrowing the gap between citizen liberty and management. Braemar had each given of them the drug that effectively made them invisible on infrared, but that was only one small victory in a list of potential catastrophic failures.

Qilin stuck to Xan's heels; it reminded him a little of their time hiking in the Wilds. The whole scope however, was different, surrounded by so many members of his crew who had become a safety net on Gemarine. They were now in a different time, a different world, but the feelings were the same. Where Qilin had once tread the path beside Xan, providing companionship and motivation—the first brick in the structure that would become so strong on Gemarine – was being laid across time and space as if it were nothing.

It just goes to show that a home is not a physical place. It is the intangible essence of what others evoke; a togetherness, a union of souls.

The monotony of the hike spurred them into acquiescence. The rhythm of foot and paw, under crumbling rock.

Dallis broke the silence. "Ahoy! Ahoy!"

If Xan hadn't taken that to mean that there was a sentinel approaching, then he would have burst out laughing at the odd alert. Having a Valkor in the crew and learning about them throughout these interactions made Xan incredibly thankful. Anthropological studies couldn't prepare him for the social differences of the Valkors and Gemarinians, but instead of it being awkward, it just added a spark of humour to the seriousness of their situation.

Heeding Dallis's warning, Xan flattened himself out against the walls of the cliff while others chose to crouch behind boulders. A sparkling gemstone hovered above them. The thrumming of its thrusters was like the stampede of magnificent beasts in the wasteland of the sky. A cyclonic eye panned, scanning for any disturbance below.

Suddenly, Arcadie exploded out from beneath the cliff, rose up quickly with a burst of energy and extended his arms out toward the sentinel. He shot a bolt of electricity at its bulky frame. It swerved, evading the bolt in a graceful shift of its metallic body, and started off quickly back in the direction of where it came. It whipped back to fire at Arcadie with a red-beamed laser bolt shot from its bulbous eye. The robot seemed to have bitten off more than he could chew although it really couldn't chew. It whimpered as the pulverising beam flashed over its shoulder, severing a bank of granite cliff face above Lilianna and Fleurah.

Qilin pounced, abandoning Xan's side as she recognised Lilianna's plight. It was as if her paws split universal atoms, breaking apart relativity and gravity.

Hailstones of rock rained down from above, peppering the ground below. Fleurah dove across the ground, sheltering herself underneath an overhang of discarded rock undisturbed for thousands of years. She called desperately to Lilianna, "Come to me!"

Lilianna rocked on her heels, too afraid to risk moving through the downpour of stones. Her darting eyes were polarising ions, distorting her ability to decide. Qilin dove on top of her, chest to chest, paws wrapped tight around her. As chunks of granite splintered around them, Qilin hit the dusty path on her shoulder, rolling with the force and propelling them in the direction of the rock tunnel Fleurah had taken as her refuge. A huge boulder separated from the top of the cliff and began to tumble end over end.

An object falling slowly is an ode to finality. One recognises that in the midst of descent, obliteration is imminent. Xan watched the revolutions of the object, as graceful as stardust sprinkled across the raven sky.

He considered that often the most beautiful scenes are the most severe. The curved crest of a tsunami before it crashes down, eager embers smouldering on the forest floor before the entirety is felled, the energetic wagging of a comet's tail before plummeting onto a pristine surface.

As the boulder crashed on top of the rock overhang, Xan cried out in agony like a creature who had lost its young. The three of them disappeared from view under rubble and dust.

Meanwhile, Arcadie had zoomed upwards through bursts of laser fire from the sentinel's arm cannon. Darting in between the falling fire of fury, Arcadie showed refined grace combined with tremendous speed extending upwards to the source of concern. Claws clasped the body of the sentinel, and in haste tore it in half with a determined digital screech. The crumpled metallic remains spun out of control and crashed into the middle of the canyon path, fizzing away the last of its mechanical breath.

Arcadie could've hovered to survey the damage he caused, splitting a rusted grin across weathered panels, but he sped back, joining Xan as they arrived at the cracked boulder. Dust was a fog sweeping across a vaulted crypt.

Juniper had also arrived, tugging at larger pieces of rock that had shattered upon collision with the ground. Tossing them behind her, she called Lilianna and Qilin's names, forsaking the presence of Fleurah amidst the chaos.

The rest of the party joined in, hauling rocks to get to what lay beneath.

They heard a muted whimper. Xan tried to register if it was Qilin or someone else, but eventually he discerned Fleurah's ragged voice calling out. "We're all alive."

"Alive, how do you know? Is my beautiful soulbond still here with us in the world of the living?!" Braemar cried on his knees, his blond hair strewn in sticky pieces across his forehead.

Xan was desperate and nauseous at the thought of Lilianna and Qilin being injured or dead, but he couldn't help but roll his eyes at Braemar's dramatics. *Why make this a performance? It's not about you—it's about them. Too often we see a bad situation turn putrid with the need to have reactions validated. See to the sufferers first and then have your meltdown.* Xan wished desperately that he could scold the histrionic Sytheract but severed the connection between mind and tongue.

"Lilianna is breathing and Qilin…she….seems to be digging around trying to find a way out." A huge coughing fit ensued from Fleurah.

She chose an incredibly bad place to take a pause.

Xan wiped the sweat from his forehead and swallowed the worry so that it would fuel him for the rescue efforts. Xan turned to Arcadie hovering beside him, eyes moving from lines to hexagons for some reason.

"Why did you do that? Kill that sentinel and give away our position?"

"I hacked its vision cloud and could identify what it was capturing. It had located each of us through motion detection. Luckily, it was not a live feed, otherwise Sawtech would be here now. As it was, I've bought us approximately thirty minutes," Arcadie relayed.

Xan's shoulders seemed to diminish. "Fuck!" He screamed through the canyon. His frustration bouncing across the walls and slapping them all across the face several times. They were able to pick up motion as well as heat signatures.

Ryker stepped around Xan, avoiding his grumpy boss. "So, when we spot them it's best to just…stay still?"

"As a matter of fact," said Arcadie, "yes—become a statue." He proceeded to freeze, not shifting a circuit.

Dallis tapped Arcadie on the forehead. "Hello, hello—do you need to be oiled perhaps?"

Arcadie sprang to life and circled Dallis, laughing. "My example of becoming a statue worked!"

"You were incredibly convincing! I am impressed," Dallis conceded.

Xan blinked. *I'm all for collecting interesting crew members from different cultures, but I need the team IQ to remain at a level that will allow me to operate. I feel stupider just having been privy to that interaction.*

"How far to go…to find that energy source?" Ryker asked, his raven hair streaked with saffron strands of dust.

Xan pointed. "The cave system is up ahead, if we can bring out a couple of bags of samples that should be enough to set Braemar on his future path."

"What's my future path again?" Braemar looked up at Xan as he knelt in the dust.

Xan peered at the boyishly good-looking Sytheract and shook his head.

How is this fool going to be the keeper of the most potent source of energy this galaxy has ever seen?

"Braemar, you will have the energy source in your possession. Evercorp will take control of it and there will no longer be a shortage of power, so Sytheria will not plunge into a dark age. We've been through this!" Xan was exasperated, throwing his hands in the air.

"Sorry, it's just…a lot of pressure," he stammered.

Juniper clicked her fingers getting them to focus on the task. "You'll need to jog the rest of the way to the energy source!" She growled through fixed teeth as she shifted large stones with Ryker's attempted assistance.

Dallis stepped forward. "I shall accompany you! My thighs are strong and my speed is swift."

Without a second thought, Xan nodded. "Alright Dallis—show me those strong thighs."

The Valkor started to unzip his suit, but Ryker slapped an open palm across his wrist before he indecently exposed himself. "No," he said firmly, more so than what he usually would have, but the situation called for haste without humour.

Dallis shrugged his broad shoulders and sprinted off down into the canyon accompanied by a looming shadow of dust.

Xan turned to Juniper. "You focus on getting the girls out and making sure you can defend this territory. We'll be back as soon as we can."

He looked at her, worry and nervousness encroaching upon their exchange. Confidence in Juniper was at an all-time high, while the stocks of his other crewmates plummeted. But still, he hated not being there, not being in control of getting Qilin and Lilianna to safety.

Trust is a rope wound together by measly threads, but it creates something that could do so much more. Hoists us higher, into the territory where dreams coalesced with solitary stars. Holds us up when our will is strained, to rejuvenate. Binds us together, like tears to tragedy, so we never feel alone.

Juniper winked at Xan, confirming all the lingering doubts he had were completely ridiculous. "I got this, babe."

"Arcadie, follow me." Arcadie was about to set off an actual alarm of happiness when Ryker shook his head as if to say, *"Not the right time."* Instead, he hovered next to Xan with a pixel-eating grin on his face.

Xan readjusted the pack and jogged after Dallis, doubling his strides to get closer to the runaway Valkor.

CHAPTER 14

Lilianna awoke to darkness. She coughed. A swarm of dust burrowed into the crevices in her lungs. She coughed again. A rough hand squeezed hers. Several pin pricks of light spilled into the cave-like space.

Qilin scratched at the pile of rocks ahead of them, while outside she could hear muted grunts and shouts of concern.

Before darkness engulfed them, she recalled being dragged under the rock shelf by Fleurah just before a boulder crashed down.

"Lilianna, are you alright?" Fleurah sounded worried.

"I'm...I'm okay I think." Lilianna rose up into a crouch, feeling queasy.

Fleurah placed her hands on Lilianna's cheeks and bent forward to pull her close.

Lilianna felt a well of regret. The feeling of a blood relative. The feeling of a bond that just hit different. The soulbond pull was confusing to her; an anxiety gnawing at the pit of her stomach, soothed only when Braemar was near. But it hadn't changed any of her feelings. The sister bond was a natural longing satiated. Her arms curled around Fleurah, and tears started to flow from Lilianna's eyes exposing the emotions she had tried to repress not just over the last few days, but for years on Gemarine.

"It's okay, Lili. I see you."

In those simple words, the bottled tension between them was released, dissipating like storm clouds after being bullied by the sun. She didn't feel misunderstood or alone with Fleurah; after all, they were cut from the same cloth. There was hope now that they would be able to stitch something together again, patched and mangled as it might be.

"C'mon, let's push against the rocks and try t'get out of here." Fleurah pulled back and began kicking against the structure in front of them.

"No," Lilianna yelled, which seemed to startle even her. "We need to take the rocks from the top first one by one so that they don't collapse on top of us."

"What was that?" Juniper called from behind the rock wall.

"I said, take rocks from the top and get a big enough gap and then we'll be able to get out."

"Ryker, you weak bitch, put your back into it." Juniper's voice was muffled but clear enough to hear the sizzle as it scalded poor Ryker.

Lilianna was worried that Juniper had a head full of steam and didn't quite comprehend the requirements of physics over brute force. "Juniper, did you hear—"

"Yes, Lilianna. I got you. I'm just trying desperately to manage these useless douche canoes."

XAN
24 YEARS OLD

The canyon walls were orange satin sheets billowing in the winds of time. Stretching out for miles, curving like cresting waves, the canyons dazzled with warm hues. In the bright flash of the sun, they would glow golden; a treasure in plain sight. In pockets of shade, scarlet grooves carved by torrid seas of the past entwined with deep purple, leaving them breathless; not just because of its length or narrow passageways, but because nature always held such beauty in hidden places.

Arcadie seemed nervous as they strode deeper into the canyon, his eyes darting away each time Xan caught him staring.

"Is everything okay, buddy?" Xan tilted his head to the side.

"I suppose it depends on whether we find what we are looking for in this canyon of certain death." The little robot fell silent again; the sound of his thrusters echoed doom in a minor key off the canyon walls.

"No, I mean you seem like you want to ask me something."

"Well, I feel as though I should admit to a secret," Arcadie blurted sheepishly, clasping his hand over his pixelated mouth grate. "I connected to your available data scrolls on the multipurpose devices without your permission and I discovered a lot about you."

"Well, that isn't fair." Xan laughed. "You know a lot about me, but I know nothing about you."

"I apologise if I crossed a line. I sometimes find it difficult to know what is acceptable to search through and where to stop because there are no literal lines to contain me." His pipe-like arms drooped in disappointment. "You can compute that statement?"

Dallis had dropped back, allowing for Arcadie and Xan to catch up to him. The Valkor wasn't breaking a sweat, even under the horned bronze helmet he had decided to wear on the hike. Xan on the other hand, felt the heat despite being in relative shade in the slot canyon. Beads of perspiration were sluggish tears that framed his face in the tell-tale signs of coming exhaustion.

"I'm an open book most of the time, so it's okay," Xan explained, his gaze reaching to the sky for potential onlookers.

He immediately regretted the statement, as Dallis laughed without restraint. "You're a book? Oh goodness, so many funny jokes from this guy." Dallis thumbed toward Xan with a sparkling smile, his sapphire eyes wet with joy. "He's actually a Human though, not a book."

Xan had rolled his eyes enough at Dallis since getting to know him, but instead of accentuating his oddness, petitioned Arcadie to ignore him with a swat of his hand and the shake of his head. "Look, how about we even the playing field and you tell me about yourself then?"

"Lilianna's father created me in the image of a best friend that passed on. Her father developed an AI program with self-learning capabilities, retention deposits and ethos coding."

Although Xan was hyper intelligent, this kind of computer speak was not one of his strengths. Arcadie picked up on Xan's struggle. "Essentially I'll learn, I'll remember, and I'll try to form a way in which it means something to me and how I might view Sytheria."

"And what happened to Lilianna's parents then?"

Arcadie looked downcast. "It's difficult to recall painful memories. But there was an accident in the Sawtech facility. Both parents passed on only a couple of years ago. Since then, it's only been Fleurah and I."

"I'm sorry to hear that."

"Fleurah has had it tough, so you must…go easy on her. You seemed to forgive me quickly but have a higher expectation for her."

Arcadie was right. For some reason, Xan had been extremely hard on Fleurah. He just didn't appreciate anyone who stepped over the people he loved. She did that in a very unapologetic way, and he felt the need to teach her the error in her ways. The absence of parents, a sister, learning how to contextualise her own existence with a damn robot must have been quite hard.

"Often people get off to a bad start, but we all deserve forgiveness and a chance to make amends, right?" Dallis smiled at Xan and roughly patted him on the shoulder.

Xan conceded that he might have been a little too hasty in his judgment of Fleurah. He would try to do more.

"So, what have you learnt over the years?" Dallis asked as he repositioned one of the dark hexagonal plates of armour across his chest.

"I'm very keen on learning many things. I want to know more and more to give me better…awareness of *everything*, rather than just being able to narrow down on specific formulae or reciting moments in history. If that makes sense."

"You sound like you're well on your way to being considered sapient!" Xan teased. "Displeased with incremental advances, insatiable for the grand destination without actually enduring the stresses of the journey."

"Like Xan is experiencing now, with his flimsy Human body," Dallis said with no hint of a joke in his tone.

Xan nodded, wiping more sweat from his brow. "I mean, you do have a point."

Arcadie continued. "I deduce that I require more than mediocrity."

Xan pondered a reply. He had considered for a long while that often the search for deeper meaning was a double-edged sword. On one hand it gave purpose to seemingly insipid actions, but if such actions weren't categorised as meaningful, then the bow positioning the arrows of life would soon let them fly askew from the target.

"I've read it somewhere that 'Discontent is the folly of our spirit,'" Xan began. "It makes us strive, and search for more. But it also makes us aware of our limitations. Like, despite how hard we try, we can never truly scale the heights we want to reach."

"So why attempt to reach so high then?" Arcadie inquired.

"Because if your eye becomes attuned to a certain palette, even the slightest deviation in hue can evoke something within. It can create a ripple of change in the lake of tedium," Xan explained. "It's hope that allows us to do this, to push past discontent as an obstacle and use it as a tool to enact change."

Arcadie's eyes flickered on his faceplate. "It appears as though you're saying that I would need to live a long time before I could comprehend this completely. I do not see in colours, I do not know if I feel deeply or profoundly yet, but I may have the ability to do so as a result of the experiences I endure."

"Exactly." Xan almost yelled it. It bounced off the slot canyon walls to reach the trio again and again. "The breadth of what you could learn is endless. Usually, time can aid *our* development until the cells in our body cannot sustain us. But you, you will see lifetimes. You will grow with each generation. As long as you heed warnings, and you seek to eradicate the discontent programming, and rewrite it as 'hope' then maybe AIs will actually be the best of us."

Arcadie pondered that for a moment and finally laughed. "Maybe we will develop some kind of deeper and more enlightened persona than you all, but line us up with a rusty bucket and a pile of beautiful skin, and we will see who chooses what!"

Laughter travelled through the canyon for the first time in centuries.

Xan and Dallis could hear Arcadie yelling at them from up ahead, pointing down into a narrow cave. "Here it is, hurry, hurry!"

"Alright, alright—not all of us have thrusters, okay?" Xan was hunched over, sucking in giant breaths.

Arcadie beamed a spotlight of powerful light into the mouth of the cave,

"Onward we go!" yelled Dallis, yet to break a sweat.

This guy's stamina is insane. Juniper would go crazy for him at Fusion.

Arcadie turned to Xan. "Is he…how do you say it…satisfactory…in the head?"

Even a robot was baffled by Dallis. It wasn't so much that he was simple, rather an excitable character with a nubile sense of wonder. It was actually endearing. As the skin became less supple, more withered and creased, aesthetic beauty wasn't the only thing destroyed. Innocence departed, hope appeared less obtainable, and all of a sudden, the difficulty to smile in the face of adversity became a strain.

When our bodies are lost in the perpetual motion of existence, so too is our sense of wonder. Wouldn't it be nice to look at the world with fresh eyes—to feel the breeze and let one's heart soar, liberated and weightless?

He stared hard at Arcadie, "It's worth taking note that sometimes we learn the most from those who are wired differently." Xan pointed to an exposed wire. "You should know that more than anyone." He winked and sped off after Dallis.

Arcadie blinked for a moment and shouted after him, "I feel like I still have a lot to learn."

"Learning is endless, Arcadie," Xan shouted back.

JUNIPER
24 YEARS OLD

Juniper pulled Lilianna through the small gap, and she tumbled down the gathering of rocks like a weighted stone into an idle well.

Scratched and caked in fine dirt she looked even paler than she normally did. Before Juniper could wrap her arms around her, Braemar shouldered himself into the fray, stealing the tenderness Juniper was poised to give. Tenderness was the pinnacle of a sinister mountain— seldom reached, seldom given, so to take that away meant that Juniper sunk deeper inside the wall of rocks that she had built around her own core.

Qilin crawled out next, stopped before she progressed any further and shook off the dust in a hazy plume of particles. Her fur stood on ends for a moment, before it relaxed and clung to her body, joyous at its new found cleanliness. Juniper knelt down and Qilin gave her the chance to redeem that tender gesture lost to the soulbonded idiots, as she galloped to Juniper's outstretched arms, tongue dangling, lips curled in a smile. They both fell to the floor as Qilin's forked tongue trailed up and down her cheek in a slobbering display of affection.

I've had a lot worse. She laughed inside her head, recalling all types of Fusion related mishaps where she endured petty moments of mistaken tongue related sexy time.

More than once a female Aranther or an overzealous Human male had purred across her neck and licked her from cheek to cheek. Without a second thought, she'd grab the limp tongue in her exofingers, and declare, "You're banned." After pushing them off, she'd wait for the next hunk of junk to crawl into her presence, quietly hoping for a prince or princess of pleasure.

Fleurah scampered out of the small hole, grumbling,

"Cheers for the help," she said to Juniper. Strawberry blonde dreadlock strands obscured part of her flustered face, as Ryker's flimsy arms faltered with assistance.

Juniper slowly stood up, letting Qilin flit around her ankles. "Oh well, since we're on the subject, cheers for the bolt of electricity to my fucking head."

Fleurah gave a wry smile. "Fair point—how about even, then?" She held her palm out, upturned.

"Mmmm, not just yet." Juniper turned away from her, as Fleurah mithered in annoyance.

Keep her wanting my approval. Manipulate some of those buried daddy issues.

Mmmmm. Daddy issues do taste so damn good though.

Ryker scrambled like a crustacean, spindly and awkward as he raced after Juniper. "Juniper, aren't Sawtech going to come soon? What the fuck are we going to do?"

Juniper assessed their surroundings. They *were* quite exposed; the only place to hide was around the boulders or back inside that pseudo mini cave. Their heat signatures were concealed for now, so maybe hiding would buy them some time.

Juniper considered the contents in her backpack, then flashed her gaze in Fleurah's direction. "What's in your backpack? Anything to defend ourselves with?"

"As a matter of fact, yes."

"Alright then, troops, it's time to prepare for battle."

Ryker looked like he'd just atomically soiled himself.

CHAPTER 15

LOCATION: SYTHERIA
YEAR: 2505
XAN – 24 YEARS OLD

They didn't need Arcadie's beam of light. A pale orange glow from the energy source trailed up the slick walls of the cave. Droplets of moisture fell with careless grace down miniature rivulets carved by the coarse chisel of secret years. Stalactites dangled precariously from height like vertical cannons waiting patiently for the reload.

Nothing sweet lingered in the air; just the smell of sweat trapped in old fibres, and rancid bones left to fester in shallow ponds. Beetles the size of a Human fist crawled mindlessly across the ground. The feeling when one traversed across the boots or when there was a crunch underfoot made Xan shudder in repose.

The energy source had a nearly imperceptible buzz that thrummed at regular intervals – the heartbeat of a strong planet. It would need to remain strong to save the sentient species from facing their end.

"Arcadie, can you give us a reading of whether this is safe to touch?" Xan knelt down, inspecting the source without touching it.

"Radiation levels appear to be contained at surface level; however, I believe a Human won't be able to handle these without burning yourself severely."

Xan flexed gloves over his hands and approached the energy source. They looked like crisp bone fragments with a glowing violet core: jagged, elongated and mostly cylindrical with the occasional piercing barb, like the antlers of a long dead majestic deer. Each energy crystal was surrounded by petals of closely cushioned scarlet globes.

"Dallis appears to have a higher body temperature so he would handle this substance better than you." Arcadie's monotone voice was like auditory ripples in the great cave.

Dallis strode forward next to Xan, bent down, and placed his pointer finger against the crystalline substance. "Warm, but not scorching." As he rose up, he stumbled and knocked one of the red globes to the floor. "Oops."

"Just be careful and pack as much as you can into the elemental resistant packs, and we can get moving out into the open to signal Massy."

"Where is Massy going to meet us?" Dallis inquired.

"He'll have to land atop the cliff, drop us a rope, and we'll have to climb up."

"With a whole load of weight in our packs?"

"We don't have any other choice." Xan felt a wry smile approach. "Dallis, I've never seen you turn away from a task."

Dallis straightened his posture. "I am unworthy! You're right. I will abolish the negative thoughts and I will accomplish this task with gusto."

Xan laughed. "That's more like it."

As Dallis bent down, continuing to jam as much of the energy source as he could into the pack, he suddenly raked his arm back. "What the hell?"

A scuttling spider-like creature the size of a palm flared up on back legs, spitting venom in Dallis's direction.

Arcadie didn't hesitate and shot a burst of electricity into the creature, electrocuting it.

Xan often felt bad when having to kill alien creatures, especially not knowing why they attacked, but Dallis's heavy breathing was concerning. "Did it bite you?"

"I think so." He rubbed at the red mark on his wrist.

Xan inspected it and clearly discerned a pulsing red bite mark. His concern changed to alarm. An unknown alien creature in a relatively unknown canyon. Not good at all.

"Arcadie, have you seen one of them before?"

"I can't actually access any information on them, but no, I've never seen that creature."

"I'm fine you two, it's just a little scratch. Let's keep this going." Dallis's cheeks were starting to pale.

Xan turned to his pack and pulled out the Firstaider 5000 gun. Spinning through the functions he found the ven-no-more setting, placed the barrel onto the bite mark, and pulled the trigger.

"Ouch, what does that do?" Dallis yanked the hand back, grimacing.

"There is now a nanobot blockage placed within a ten-centimetre radius to stop the venom from entering any other parts of your system. If there are any nasties in that venom it will at least contain it to one area." Xan shrugged. "Now be careful with the red globes from now on."

Dallis nodded his appreciation.

"Listen Arcadie." Xan turned to face the robot. "You've done enough for us here. There's no point twiddling your thumbs."

Arcadie looked at his metallic pincer-like claws to confirm the presence of a thumb. Sadly, one could not be found.

"You should speed off down the canyon and help the rest of the crew." Xan pointed toward the narrow rock waves that encased the trio. "I'm worried about what they'll encounter."

"Are you certain?"

"Get moving, buddy, we've got this."

Arcadie zoomed out of the cave system preparing for the unknown force ahead.

LOCATION: SYTHERIA
YEAR: 2505
LILIANNA – 22 YEARS OLD

Braemar was still fussing over Lilianna. His fingers brushed strands of straight blonde hair behind her ears as he inspected her grazed cheeks, concern rife in his blue eyes. He puffed a large strand of his own wavy hair away so that his vision was no longer clouded.

It feels nice to be fussed over.

The delicacy of his caress trailed down her neck. The stark chill of winter spawned frost down her sides, sparking a bitter pleasure as he lightly dusted the soil from her shoulders.

Braemar's voice was pure thermal energy. "Zaps and Zoots, I thought I'd lost you, even before I'd truly found you." A puff of air escaped his lips. "Maybe you don't understand?"

Lilianna understood. She understood that look, his yearning touch, his wavering voice. The way he couldn't keep his hands off her, the sickness he undoubtedly felt at not being able to protect her.

She knew it well. She had seen it mostly in dreams and only briefly in another males' smoky eyes. A male so smitten with his own quest that the promise of something more between them had been muted.

Lilianna had always battled with the conflicted call of the heart and the call of her body. Now, more than ever, she felt the undeniable call of her soul screaming in violent rage, desperate for her to heed the path to its contentment so it could rest. But there was something in her that didn't allow the eager sun to warm and cultivate the soul. Eager sometimes meant recklessness and a reckless sun could scorch, could decimate.

Lilianna scoffed, "I do understand," and her heart broke at the way his eyes lit up as if all his unanswered lonely cries swallowed by the moon had been validated by her pitying words. "Although I fear the Sytheract within me has been…tainted." She shook her head. "I'd rather not use that word because in a deep, profound way—I've come to appreciate what I am. Maybe changed is the right word."

Braemar appeared confused. "This hasn't been like it was in my dreams, that can't be denied. But I see you Lilianna. All of you, and I like what I see."

Her smile was demure. It fit the moment like the wrinkled hands of soulbonds, clasping in their final hour. But she knew he couldn't see *everything*, hadn't come to know even half of who she was, the alien she had become. Lilianna wondered whether if he knew the whole truth—would he still kneel before her, clasping her hand as if it were a rare and precious stone?

An amplified voice echoed off the narrow canyon walls. Crumbling stones took issue and finally relented to toppling to the ground after their strength waned holding on for so long.

"We know you are there." The voice then used silence as its ally to compound fear. "I have four warriorbots, two drone sentinels and when I command it—they can find you in mere seconds. I don't know why you're here. I don't care." The calculating cold in his voice was clear now. "The Sawtech Corporation does not take kindly to trespassing, thieving, or the plain disregard of Sytheract safety."

Lilianna poked her head around the rock to get a view of what opposed them: four Sytheracts heavily armed, four warriorbots poised in front of them as shields, two drone sentinels hovering high above.

The thoughts that encircled her a moment ago were trivial now. Love, purpose, hearts, souls. It would mean nothing when that very heart was wrenched from an exposed chest as it blossomed with regret. Rancid petals settled with tears on the rusted floor of the canyon.

Lilianna reeled back around.

Braemar clutched her hand, his chest heaving. "What the zonk are we going to do?"

A sphere glinted in the distance. A minted coin in the sky grew with each second. Limbs tucked tight inside his body, he slammed into one of the hovering sentinels, smashing it into pieces against the canyon wall. Extending arms emerged and he screamed, "I've disabled all motion sensors." The other drone squeaked as Arcadie plunged his fists into each side of its domed head. The warrior bots aimed their turrets at him as he zoomed high across the rocky outcrops.

CHAPTER 16

LOCATION: SYTHERIA
YEAR: 2505
JUNIPER – 24 YEARS OLD

Juniper crawled across the dirt to the left-hand side, creeping in stealth mode as the bots and Sytheract Sawtech minions concentrated on tracking Arcadie's movements. Qilin stalked low to the right-hand side. The main Sytheract army rat who had called them out in the canyon was the same male from the vidlink interaction at Braemar's house. He probably thought he was hot shit in his prime, with a square jaw and long wavy hair. But the longer Juniper stared at the black beady eyes set in his pale face and the nose like a twisted carrot, the more he reminded her of a melting snowman.

She waited behind the rock for an opening. They turned upwards to fire on Arcadie and that was the cue.

Action, fuckers.

Juniper's exohand extended and widened. She let those sexy nimble finger blades fly like hornets, readying the final venomous sting for her target. The male shouted, "Forget the robot, focus on the Sytheracts." It was the last thing he ever said. The blades tore across his throat, burying inside his skin, perforating his larynx, ripping forth and flinging it across the canyon floor. A shocking force of blood discharged in a gruesome, wet splatter. He dropped to his knees, eyes hazy, bewilderment written on his face. Hands clasped at the wound on his throat attempting to stem the flow, but the blood coursed through the gaps in his fingers like a bursting dam, cracking bricks—brittle and useless. Consciousness was a cracked shell in the sprawling tide, lost in the dark. He flopped to the ground like a wet towel.

As the female Sytheract caught sight of her esteemed commander dying on his knees, Juniper appeared at her side. Her thin lips twisted in a mute scream, and Juniper seized that moment to stab the laser sword into her open mouth. The sound of climactic terror exhaled from Juniper's blade only. The boronium exohand pushed the dying Sytheract female aside.

Juniper fixed her murderous intent on those who remained. Qilin came from opposite her, bathed in splashes of blood from a previous kill. They charged toward the remaining male Sytheract at the same time and together, in their pursuit of annihilation, created a team of cute little slayers.

"What the fuck!" he cried, readying himself in a battle stance. Qilin pounced and he reflexively raised his arm. She bit down with a snarl of malice, and he screamed, levelling a knee into her side. Qilin's jaw loosened with the force of the kick; she rolled through the dust end over end, taking a flesh souvenir, as if a succulent fruit from a prized tree. Skidding to a stop, she crouched low again, shaking her fur as the last male Sytheract pointed his gun at Juniper.

He fired.

Juniper twirled in mid-air as if this dance were hers. A spotlight shone in the midst of a somersault. The choreography conceived in the womb of battle, born into life's ultimate war. Spectator breath stifled in suspense.

The laser shot met the canyon wall in a crumble of dust. Her blade sliced across his chest, but at the last moment evaded as much as he could. The wound was fickle. Qilin leapt over her shoulder and crunched down on the hand that held the laser. The shriek tore through the canyon, and he immediately dropped the weapon, trying to rid himself of the pain.

One of the larger robots had loomed up behind Juniper. Before she realised what was happening, Fleurah had become its sentient shadow, ripping at exposed wires where its shoulder met the neck. Sparks of gold reflected in her manic eyes. Juniper recognised that look well. She'd seen it on the faces of comrades rushing with weapons drawn to a bloody end. It was a face that marked a strong heart, a resilient being that would fight for their cause and defend with honour.

Looks like she has made it up for her previous shittiness after all.

Turning her attention back to the fight, Juniper saw Qilin gnawing the fingers from the Sytheract's mangled hand, while the cacophony of his cries made a threnodic choral cluster appear weak. Juniper quipped, "Oh Qilin darling, let me help you with that." She sliced downward at the wrist, and Qilin stumbled back with the entire severed hand nestled in her jaw. She crunched through bone, smiled through the ripping of flesh. Blood dripped down the sides of her mouth as she gulped down her handy dessert.

Juniper winked at Qilin, as she heard a satisfied burp of approval. The Gemarinian soldier in beast battle mode turned back to face the male now sprawled in the dirt, wailing with a resignation that appalled her.

"Get up, you weak fucking bitch." Her voice was a sturdy boot crushing pebbles of porous rock.

"Have mercy, have mercy," he pleaded through the screen of sobs.

"Do you know who I am?" Juniper loomed over him.

She answered her own question before his quivering voice found aim, "I guess not." Juniper tapped her chin with a boronium finger and pursed her full lips. "I know! I'm basically an alien warlord to you. That should give you some context." Flexing a fist menacingly, she continued. "And as an alien warlord – you probably couldn't fathom the amount of pain I can conjure into your putrid bag of skin and bone."

She surveyed at the scene around her. Fleurah and Arcadie were making their way towards them as Qilin waited for a signal to attack.

Juniper then knelt down, squeezing his cheeks between a forefinger and thumb.

"But right now, I will spare you all that terrible, unimaginable pain if you just…stop…crying." Juniper whispered the words close to his face as she stroked his scalp, speckled with light blonde hair.

He took some deep breaths and Juniper let go, reclining slightly.

"Tell me, when does the backup get here?"

"Backup?"

"Remember pain and the alien warlord thing? Don't make me go there. It will end terribly for you."

He swallowed the last of his pride in one unceremonious gulp. "We were positioned at the gateway to the canyon, this is it. Unless…"

"Unless what?"

"The robots were transmitting a distress call."

"Okay, well let's say they were."

"The time it takes to send a transmission and for someone to respond to a distress call is…. around… fifteen minutes."

A rumbling sounded overhead in the distance behind them.

Fleurah stepped forward. "It's time to end him."

The Sytheract male started shouting again, pleading for his life. Juniper was about to reason with Fleurah when she stepped forward and thrust a short, sharp knife into his jugular.

He stopped screaming. His vocal cords severed. The pleading mercy in his eyes trailed off with the realisation that fortune had faded.

"Freedom isn't afforded to those who attempt to wield control. In the end, the one with control holds the sharper knife and the higher ground." Her boot thumped into the dying Sytheract's chest as blood pooled in the wake of his last gurgling breath. "Mercy is death, and I'm as merciful as a massacre," Fleurah trumpeted.

The blade retreated into its sheath. Fleurah turned with her eyes still burning, her powerful words lingering in the rapid breathing expanding her chest. Lilianna stood there, shock etched onto her face. Braemar flanked Lilianna, their hands clasped.

Juniper shook her head, thinking of the weakness she saw in Lilianna. Cowering behind rocks with her soulbond while the rest of them spilled blood, then to have the gall to stand there, mouth agape while her older sibling did the necessary protective dirty work.

It was putrid behaviour.

The shimmering glow of fucking her was certainly waning right about now.

As far as I'm concerned, that bitch still has a lot to learn about the art of sacrificing the self for the betterment of others.

Juniper remembered the soldier code and realised all too suddenly that whatever had transpired in the last few weeks had rattled the code, the fabric of her own values, to the core.

Now that I'm no longer a soldier, I guess I need to find whatever code will apply to this mess of a warrior I've become. What the fuck am I actually so desperate to protect?

But the answer was so obvious it didn't need to be uttered in the hallways of her mind. She sighed, hoping maybe one day a new code could be forged and inscribed somewhere for her to refer to as a tether to the person she was growing into, as well as from where she had come.

That's if somehow I manage to stay alive. Maybe I'll encounter another alien slug that will just digest my ass.

Well, at least it's a tasty ass.

Juniper turned to Fleurah, who looked ill, put a hand on her shoulder and said, "You did good, kid."

Fleurah brushed the rust in her soiled hair, exposing timid freckles in braille across the bridge of her nose.

"You were something else," Juniper continued.

Maybe I fucked the wrong sister.

CHAPTER 17

LOCATION: SYTHERIA
YEAR: 2505
XAN – 24 YEARS OLD

Xan regretted dismissing Arcadie, regretted volunteering to be the one to explore the caves, regretted anything to do with the fucking space spiders. Was there a better and more biological name he could come up with? *Sure.* But space spiders they'd hence be known forever more.

After they had packed all the energy crystals they could, the Valkor and the Human began the short, hopefully relaxing stroll out of the cave.

It was not to be.

The horrible hatching sounds would haunt him forever. Subtle cracks, a moist discharge deflected by mossy rock, the pitter patter of tiny legs on a hard surface, squeaks of predatory cognisance.

Xan's head turned slowly, hoping with all that was good in the galaxy that nothing sinister lurked behind them. But each of the red globes that had accompanied the energy crystals now lay broken on the ground, bearing the gift of new life to the space spiders that crawled menacingly up the side of the cave beside the two fleeing thieves.

The energy crystals' warmth was most likely keeping the larvae contained within their birth chamber. As soon as the warmth was gone, they came searching for a tasty treat.

Xan shot the Cranston ray gun at the ground army advancing on his body weighed down by the energy crystals in his pack. It felt like he was running in waist-deep sand. Dallis shot at the sides of the cave; any spiders that jumped on him, he crushed with bare hands or tore to hairy shreds.

They exited the darkened cave and burst out onto the canyon floor, Pied Pipers with their songs of terror, chased by a swarm of space spiders.

MASSY
25 YEARS OLD

Massy yawned, watching the clock as he waited on the ship and throwing empty packets of A4 chews into the trash chute as a secondary exercise.

How hard is it to walk a dusty path and grab some energy rocks?

Massy had scanned the topographical holo map and floated out of range from potential sentinels, bobbing in the cloaked ship and watching for anything below. He was far enough from where Braemar and Xan believed the energy source was. On the cliff's top was a forest so dense, any hope of landing near there was blown away.

But he'd found a nice pocket of nubile seedlings that he'd bulldozed with the *Attenborough* so he overlooked the canyon in a slightly wider berth. A Darshan tribe folk song played on the audipod; it reminded him of his childhood. So why the fuck did he continue to play those songs? His dad was a cock nugget, and his brothers were shit stains. But some of the Darshan Aranthers on Gemarine were okay, and they played it in bars, dancing on tables as if the leaves of the *dillayla* plant were altering their minds.

The camera feeds alerted him to movement down on the canyon floor. He switched off the audipod and concentrated on the video feed. Initially, he laughed out loud. Dallis and Xan streamed down the canyon path, shock and terror beaming from both faces like they'd just been rammed by giant centaur dicks. The curved canyon walls were swollen with a horde of spiders, snapping with furry fangs and glaring with thousands of evil, red eyes.

Massy laughed until his sides hurt and then finally crept into action. He inched out with the ship and dropped a rope for them to escape from the demon spiders.

Dallis zoomed up the mechanical rope first, heroic in his Valkor armour, a ridiculous horned helmet gleaming in bronze. Massy shot spiders that clung to the outside of the canyon walls and launched themselves at Dallis as he climbed. Xan was on the ground kicking, clawing, getting jizzed on with spider web, who actually knew?

Dallis flopped onto the ship. "Fly!"

"What do you mean fly?"

"I mean get away from the walls of the canyon!"

"Alright, alright! You feed down the mechanical rope for Xan and I'll do what I do best and fly."

XAN
24 YEARS OLD

Xan grabbed desperately to the mechanical rope. As he ascended, he kicked out at the last remaining space spiders, fangs bared waiting to sink into his flesh. As it was, he counted himself beyond lucky that he had escaped a bite. Fangs had tried to puncture his suit, but the nanobot microfibres protected him. As the rope carried him higher into the air, he felt angelic, but the scent of heaven was putrid on him. The pearly gates were elusive. The mechanical rope shorted out with only a few metres left between him and the safety of the ship.

The *Attenborough* hovered on autopilot in the middle of the canyon. To an onlooker it would seem like Xan was suspended in the middle of a wider part of the canyon climbing to nowhere.

Massy and Dallis yelled at him to keep climbing.

The space spiders' army was thinned out now, but they stared out from the rock walls, daring him to fall. Xan craned his neck to look down at an ocean of the gangly creatures rocking to and fro, like listless waves moved by tidal gods.

Xan realised all too suddenly as he looked into the faces of a former foe and a questionable pilot that each thread in life was like the rope he dangled from. Often tenuous connections spawned unlikely relationships in the natural world, creating a symbiosis that benefitted each species. On earth, a drongo will usually signal a distress call across the savannah. Meerkats use that warning to hide from potential predators. Xan needed all of his crew to keep him from losing his mind, and in this case, losing his life. His muscles screamed at the torture, and he grunted in frustration, seemingly at the end of his own physical tether.

Dallis peered down at him with bright, sapphire eyes, auburn hair blowing with the thruster wind. "You can do it!" he cried, extending his large hand.

Xan bent his head, tucking his neck into his chest and swearing under his breath. If Dallis wasn't so nice and helpful, he'd just be annoying. Xan appreciated genuinely supportive people, but for some reason, a perpetual positive disposition aggravated him. He recalled young Gemarinians recognising him at the biobase and constantly sucking up trying to get holographs with Qilin to post on the MPD feeds. Having such recollections didn't help while Dallis recited motivational phrases above him. "Pain is but a blight on the pleasure you will feel when you conquer this mountain."

Xan was now straining, biceps bulging, teeth clenched. Dallis stretched out to him as Massy laughed over his shoulder and echoed certain sentiments in Dallis's words. "I believe in you," Massy yelled with feigned encouragement. A wolfish smile spanned his face.

Xan grabbed hold of Dallis's gigantic hand and was yanked up with a single arm, the bored bicep yawning.

He marvelled at the strength of the Valkor and wondered how he had nearly bested Dallis such a long time ago now after rescuing Qilin, Lilianna, and Juniper from General Heronicus. The onset of rage and the burning temperature of vengeance proved more than an ember of strength. It scorched and blackened all it touched. An inferno that made a wasteland of the heart. Or did the love for Qilin fuel his strength? Did love ensure he would continue to create wastelands upon the terrain of the enemy when threatened?

He knew he had been changed. In some ways was it really that bad that he was willing to kill and maim for the ones he loved?

Dallis embraced him and Xan felt like jelly in his arms, malleable to his will. "You made it," he whispered excitedly.

Xan was more relieved when Dallis let go. Relieved to be on the ship as much as out of his bear-like grip.

Massy clasped him on the shoulder and smirked. "Well done, slugger."

"You wouldn't have made it a quarter up the rope with arms like overcooked noodles," Xan spat without any real saliva left.

"Yeah, no, I'm totally not saying I would have. But gosh it was great to…cheer you on." Massy provided a stiff thumbs up in Xan's face. Xan went cross eyed focusing on the thumb, then swatted it away to see Massy's white grin, the protrusion of fangs peering out from his lips.

"Yes, I bet it was," Xan grumbled. "Now let's get the fuck out of here and find the others."

CHAPTER 18

LOCATION: SYTHERIA
YEAR: 2505
MASSY – 25 YEARS OLD

"Holy shitdick," Massy whispered as they peered into the canyon from high above.

Machine parts were scattered like tired tombstones in a quaint cemetery. Deep puddles of blood formed halos around deathly devout Sytheracts affixed to fresh graves.

Dallis pushed forward, wedged in between Xan and Massy, searching the ground, eager to learn.

"Is a shitdick worthy of being praised?"

Xan ignored him and probably wished Massy did too. "Well, I would work with it and try to make it a praiseworthy dick, but my advice is— sometimes you have to worship anyone who might be ready to go."

Xan slapped him on the back of the head. "Focus on finding somewhere to land, you div." He then turned to Dallis, speaking solemnly, "Please do not take any lessons from Massy."

Dallis seemed extremely confused with the interaction and slunk back from peering out the window. Figures below waved energetically, and the robot zoomed up to the unopened hatch. Massy lowered the *Attenborough* and steadied on an even plane to allow Arcadie access through.

At first glance it was almost as if the rust on the robot's body had spread, creeping like frost at the midnight peak of chill. But it was blood and oil. Lots of blood.

"This is a concerning picture." Massy waved his hands at Arcadie.

"What happened?" Xan's voice wavered.

The poor lad was probably wondering if the blood belonged to any number of his precious little bum buddies Qilin, Lilianna, and Juniper firstly and then to the recent additions to the crew. He supposed that Juniper, Fleurah and Qilin could handle themselves to an extent. But Braemar, for better or worse, needed to stay alive and bring the energy source into the public domain. And sweet Lilianna – the idea of her wielding an instrument of death for self-defence wasn't even conceivable. She had come a long way, but not that far.

One thing was for certain, that robot needed a shower or whatever the fuck you did to clean robots splashed in the blood of their enemies.

XAN
24 YEARS OLD

"Well, let me tell you Master Xan." Arcadie hovered up and down excitedly, his arms jangling as he entwined his metallic fingers together in front of him. "That warrior woman Juniper—golly Gorgoth, she is amazing at slaying enemies."

Xan stepped forward reflexively, becoming stern. "Don't ever joke about the taking of a life, Arcadie," he scolded. Arcadie let his arms dangle by his sides, his faceplate shiny with shame.

Xan was deeply concerned that he hadn't even considered what rules the robot adhered to. He knew he was timid, still open to learning and understanding life, but would this be an important lesson in his development? To value life, not take pleasure in bloodshed?

"There is no pleasure in ending someone's life. Because it's not just the end of their essence, but it disrupts the emotional stability of their crew, family, clan. And love is what binds us all. If you refuse to acknowledge even the slightest bit of empathy, you are a monster."

"Master Xan, I apologise profusely. I am simply pleased that we survived."

Xan turned away and saw Dallis staring at him. In the Valkor's eyes, he still saw the reflection of the monster he became, so consumed with hate he was willing to end someone just for being an associate of his enemy.

The change in Xan was monstrous. He knew he would never be the same. As he uttered the words to Arcadie, he did so to ensure that he would value life in a way that had passed Xan by. Maybe he would measure it better than slaughtering a ship full of innocent crew members next time.

LILIANNA
22 YEARS OLD

Lilianna was petrified, standing on the canyon floor, circles of blood spatter surrounding her. Everyone else had boarded the ship, and she waited for the robot angel of mercy to carry her to safety. Arcadie's thrusters exhaled loudly with a plume of smoky discharge, floating down, readying her for the "piggyback" to the ship. She was mere metres from the *Attenborough's* open hatch when a laser cannon singed the ends of her blonde hair, the flag of surrender rippling in the wind.

"Star bursts from hell!" she cried as Arcadie zoomed at maximum speed, slamming both of them across the metallic floor of the ship's hull. To the sentinels, they would have disappeared, but Arcadie knew better.

"Massy, you must depart," Arcadie screeched. "They can sense your presence, the motion of the ship," he relayed as desperately as a robot could. His arm spiral was bent, and he nursed it while giving the command.

Lilianna was sore all over, but she stumbled up past Braemar and Ryker, who strapped themselves into the emergency restraints affixed to the ship's boronium wall.

"Where the fuck do I go?" Massy yelled.

As Lilianna clamoured into the seat beside him, she quickly buckled in and pointed skyward. "Floor it."

There was a dangerous gleam in his eye that she never liked, but it was what made him so valuable in the air. A laser shot thumped into the back of the *Attenborough*, prompting him to push the throttle down. The thrusters engaged, the new fuel took hold and whiplash struck them all, pushing them back against their restraints as Massy flew upward.

The aim was to get high into the upper part of the atmosphere called the exosphere, so that the bots would begin to malfunction. Lilianna's father had taught her that Sawtech bots couldn't reach that high because solar winds would cause havoc on their systems. That was where they needed to go.

Other bots converged upon them from various angles, pursuing them into sodden rain clouds that crackled with angry thunder and erupted with blue bolts of lightning.

The *Attenborough's* speed was too great, and they shot through the atmosphere, flames flaring across both wings. Space was around them again, and it was oddly comforting. A dark cosy blanket in front of a fire. But Massy cranked a switch and the groans of the ship fell immediately silent while it hovered in the air. Massy then positioned the yoke so that they engaged free-fall. Spiralling down, he yelled, "Engage weapons!"

Juniper was at the helm of the pulse chargers, which were smaller grav bombs that packed nowhere near the punch, but to a pesky little robot it would be instant explosive death.

Juniper armed the chargers and sent them after the bots. As the chargers dove beneath the cover of cloud, the bots exploded as each bomb decimated their metallic bodies, raining twinkling shards of shrapnel from the skies to the ground below. Massy re-engaged the thrusters flying level with the clouds, parting them as if he were the Lord of the Skies.

"I'm detecting a lack of AI presence," said Arcadie.

"Are you sure?" Dallis put his large hand on Arcadie's smooth shoulder. "Did your circuits get scrambled?"

Lilianna giggled, unstrapped herself, and ran to both their sides. Her hand found Dallis's back, and he tensed all his muscles like her touch was a cryogenic blast. He blushed underneath the auburn frame of his fringe. She remembered that to a Valkor, touch was something sacred.

Arcadie laughed with defined beats of *ha ha ha ha*. The capability of his social nuances expected that Dallis was joking.

"Oh sweetheart, he means are the other AI signatures are all gone? To ascertain whether we have evaded danger."

"Of course, of course."

Lilianna saw Ryker shake his head in disbelief, unzip, and head off toward the shared quarters. It appeared as though he needed some alone time away from the troupe of additional crazies who now felt like very much a part of the crew to Lilianna.

Braemar watched from the back too; he shifted uncomfortably, catching a glimpse of where her hand rested against Dallis, presumably too long for his liking.

She wasn't really used to jealousy. She didn't particularly love it. There used to be a part of her that wanted Xan to be protective of her, but she realised he already was. He just wasn't possessive or controlling. He was the best of both worlds in that sense.

Lilianna just wanted Xan to give her a glimpse of anything more than friendship; a tiny bit of love like a fleck of gold in a river of rich minerals.

Juniper sidled up to Braemar. "Alright, old chap. Your work here is done." He looked to Lilianna in desperation, as if he didn't want to believe their path was at its divergence.

"Well," Xan chuckled, easing the tension by putting a hand on his other shoulder. "I've got to debrief you and provide instructions for how you'll become the undisputed King of Energy."

Braemar wouldn't take his eyes off Lilianna, as Xan coaxed him, biceps straining, toward the captain's quarters. "C'mon, let's have that chat and a quick goodbye drink before you have to head back home."

They vanished around the bend, Braemar's huge eyes slick with sadness sending a quake throughout her soul. Lilianna couldn't hear them any longer. Her soulbond by blood and the man she loved, walking away from her and her confused little heart.

CHAPTER 19

LOCATION: SYTHERIA
YEAR: 2505
LILIANNA – 22 YEARS OLD

It was evening as they arrived at the Botanical Park so that Braemar could get back into his miniship. Lilianna walked him down to the ship parking bay, trying to fill the space with conversation. Droplets of rain caressed her cheeks like a tender lover. The evening cleanse was upon them, washing more than the stains from their skin.

"So, Xan told you what to do?"

"Yeah, he told me that I have to take the substance to Evercorp and make sure to synthesise it. Then go through testing phases until it is acceptable to reveal to the public. Finally, give Sytheria a free energy source so that the planet isn't driven into the ground by a greedy corporation. That about sums it up right?" He flashed an uneasy smile with perfect teeth, his wet blonde fringe stuck to his forehead.

"I'm worried about Sawtech." Lilianna walked down a path as lush, manicured bushes stared lovingly with empty eyes.

"I am too, but Xan seemed to have everything thought out. Find the influential politicians with bottomless credits, get their backing then reveal it at the latest Techcore Fest. Once that happens, the politicians will push the free energy bill through congress until Evercorp is too big to be brushed aside by Sawtech. Then we will strike some sort of partnership that enables an energy efficient solution."

"Well, I guess it sounds—"

He cut her off. "Too good to be true." Braemar turned to face her, silky skin lit by the reticent glow of a single moon. "Is this really going to fix Sytheria? Is it going to matter *that* much?"

Puddles formed around them like two islands separated by a gulf of longing.

Lilianna was wondering where he was going with this. "Wouldn't you want to save the world if you could? Wouldn't you believe in the possibility that if you didn't act then it would all be lost?"

"Can we just...I don't know..." He trailed off. The vulnerability seemed difficult for him. "I'm not expecting instant love but can we just...run away and try?"

Braemar's request was terribly selfish, something that Xan would never have contemplated. That was all it took for her to put four webbed walls of tendons and sinew around her heart. Not just to shield it from him, but to prevent her from contracting the same selfishness as he.

But she hid her disgust behind eyes that trembled with regret. "You know I can't abandon this mission."

"Not even for love? For soulbonded love?" Tears welled in the cracks of his destined path.

"Sometimes you must sacrifice one for the greater good of all." As soon as she said it, she felt Juniper there next to her—no, within her. She knew more about the galaxy in that moment than she ever had before.

The hardships of others were laid bare. In their vulnerability, they seemed all the more impressive, beautiful even. The sunlight was selfish. It absorbed energy, and distributed warmth but as evening spread across the skies did the moon ever receive the praise? The moon deserved it. Although pale in comparison, the moon gave the impression of hope when all was dark and forlorn.

Hope drives us to strive for more.

It was bizarre that the bleak moments often gave the most clarity. She knew then that although the idea of a soulbond sounded like everything she ever dreamed of, sometimes when we opened our eyes and the dream was real, the colours were not as vibrant as we'd hoped. The realisation comes too late that we only craved the fantasy.

Lilianna leant forward and kissed him with cracked lips parted. She felt him mould into her and fate let them have one moment; that deep connection across space and time. But moments were fleeting and the ethos within oneself was eternal. Pity was all she felt now as she whispered goodbye to her severed soulbond and turned away. She felt the separation tear at her insides, the chemicals within her blood making her sick, making her need his presence. But she moved away fast, letting the rain devour all of yesterday's dreams. Reborn into tomorrow, where the future beckoned, painted in golden light.

CHAPTER 20

LOCATION: SYTHERIA
YEAR: 2505
LILIANNA – 22 YEARS OLD

Lilianna leant against the wall in the common area of the ship. She was drained physically, emotionally and spiritually. It was painful to give Braemar back to the stars, though she knew it was the right thing for them both.

Dallis sat opposite her, scratching at the bite mark on his arm. His time in the regen chamber reduced the swelling, at least. He held a glass filled with pale brown liquid and stared into its contents like a shaman possessed. The two of them were silent, lost in their thoughts.

Juniper bustled in and looked at them both. "Jeez, you two are a sad and sorry sight."

Dallis straightened his back and extended his wrist to Juniper to show her the result of his time in the regen chamber. "Just celebrating surviving, madam."

Juniper squeezed in next to Lilianna, the scent of her momentarily distracting the Sytheract from the loss she'd just endured. Lilianna felt a hot flush creep over her pale skin. Her emotions betrayed her so easily, their loyalty floating away like dispirited sighs.

"Well, little lady, it's all over. Half the ship is knocked the fuck out from exhaustion, and you have completed the big bad mission for the soul of Sytheria." Juniper nudged Lilianna. "How are you feeling?"

Juniper hadn't mentioned the state of Lilianna's soul, but it was all that consumed her thoughts. Sytheria was safe, yes, and she felt as though that burden had lessened, but she found a lot more to carry internally than she thought she could manage. Lilianna knew that the miracle of a soulbond wasn't for her now. Too much had changed within her. She could no longer fight the betrayal of her emotions and the way in which they exacerbated the call of her body to certain individuals.

Tonight, she'd decided, was not a night for compounding thoughts or emotions. She just wanted to let go. "I'm tired, Juniper," she finally answered. "I'm really tired."

"You know what cures tiredness?"

Lilianna was almost afraid to answer when Juniper gave her a devious look and said, "Sucking down an alcoholic beverage!" Juniper stood and hot tailed it to the pressurised cupboard. She pushed a button and watched as premium alcoholic choices slid out. She smiled wide at the inventory. "Any preferences, Lili? Dallis?"

Lilianna shared a look of concern with the Valkor. "Maybe something that I can handle."

Juniper assessed the labels, speaking mindlessly as she bent down to look through the bottles. "Oh, we know you can handle the ah…good stuff." She peered over her shoulder at Lilianna and winked.

Lilianna felt her flush deepen as blood rushed to other parts of her body, remembering the night she shared with Juniper and Xan. If that look Juniper just gave her was any indication of her thoughts, Lilianna suspected they were on the same wavelength.

She giggled, letting Juniper change her cloudy mood into glorious sunshine. "Let's go with my favourite botanical—gin of course fused with the *Ullolu* berry. Little touch of sweetness with a beautiful mind-altering kick."

Xan chose that moment to walk into the room, took one look between the two females, and smiled wryly. "Oh no, what have we got here?"

"It's party time, big boy," Juniper purred at him. "Pull up a seat and let's have a drink."

"After the day we've had, I'm *very* willing and able." Xan plonked down next to Dallis, and they shared an *I can't believe what we just went through* look.

Juniper slid drinks in front of everyone and raised her own glass. "Let's celebrate our first complete mission, regardless of how fucked it was."

Lilianna laughed and sipped her drink, sighing as the effects of the berry took over.

XAN
24 YEARS OLD

Empty bottles rolled across the floor of the ship. A card game that Xan had learnt in Brooderus with the Warfastions was splayed out on the floor in front of them. Juniper had the idea to make a strip version of it, and Xan watched with amusement as she flung her second boot to the other side of the common room, her suit pants rolled up.

Dallis sat beside Xan with the hexagonal armour covering his naked flesh, wearing his spiked bronze helmet as an additional item of clothing. Xan was in a similar predicament, having abated Juniper's calls to zip his suit down to the waist. Dallis drew next and lost another round. "I hardly have any garments left," he said as he looked down at himself.

"Wait, wait," Juniper exclaimed, giving Lilianna the side eye. Xan's interest piqued as he understood Juniper was up to something. "Have Lilianna choose something to take off you."

Lilianna rose unsteadily and walked behind Dallis, dragging her fingers across his chest. "Hmm, definitely keep the helmet on. I want this part of armour gone, I think." Dallis paled as Lilianna continued to touch him lazily across his body, leaning into him for extra stability.

Xan sensed the sexual energy in the room increase. He could feel his own playfulness start to rise as he thought about what to do next. Luckily, he had a winning hand, and it was the perfect opportunity to change the rules. "Instead of removing an item of clothing, can I propose that whoever wins gets to choose someone to complete a dare?"

"You know I'm game, babe," Juniper said. "C'mon, Lili."

"I'm game." Lilianna gave Xan a sultry smile.

Xan smiled triumphantly and threw his winning hand down. "Lilianna, kiss Juniper for ten seconds."

Lilianna raised her eyebrow at Xan then turned to Juniper with a ravenous look. She didn't miss a beat as she slammed her lips against Juniper's, kissing her enthusiastically in front of both males.

"Does this not make you feel anything?" Xan questioned Dallis as he reached over and pulled down Lilianna's zipper. She broke apart from Juniper and gave him a look. He had come to know that look well. A look of liberty. A look that informed him that when she'd farewelled her soulbond, she decided to leave something else behind. It made her more beautiful in his eyes; seeing yearning written on her eager face, in her playful smile, in the saliva that glistened on her thin lips. It was the look of desire. Desire that she wanted to take for herself and not simply give to another.

Juniper took advantage of Lilianna's exposed skin and enthusiastically devoured every inch available to her. Xan stroked Juniper's hair as her tongue flicked across Lilianna's peaked nipples. Lilianna moaned and shuddered with excitement, and Xan watched as she moved her fingers down to feel the slick desire pouring from her. He glanced over at Dallis, who stared wide-eyed at the two females.

"Juniper," Xan commanded, "crawl over to Dallis and see if he is… responding." Dallis's eyes were search beams on a ship, wide and wanting more, but he was nervous, hesitant.

Juniper arrived on her knees and reached for the bulge in his pants. She stroked across the material of his pants softly. "Oh, he's ready...but I think this reaction might be for someone else." Juniper followed Dallis's line of sight to Lilianna. Xan noticed his ragged breathing the longer Dallis stared at her.

"You want Lili, do you?" Xan teased. Dallis said nothing, simply watched Lilianna with an ardent stare.

"Lili, open your mouth," Xan commanded as he zipped out of his suit.

Lilianna was on her knees in an instant as Xan recognised her desire to please, her desire to be free. She gazed up at him, her golden eyes twinkling with hunger. She started touching herself in anticipation while at the same time, obeying his command to open her mouth. The zipper came down, her free hand gripping him instantly. She slowly lathered Xan's length with saliva. Xan let her enjoy herself while he watched Dallis stare intently at Lilianna, no doubt wishing she was at his knees instead.

Juniper released Dallis from his suit, taking him deep into her mouth and he responded with an ecstasy-laden groan. His eyes were still focused on Lilianna.

After Juniper had given Dallis a small taste, Xan called to her, "Juniper, come here now."

She let go of Dallis and shrugged her shoulders, crawling her way back over to Lilianna and Xan. "Do you mind if I share this tasty treat?" Juniper's smirk changed as Lilianna's tongue licked Xan from base to tip, keeping eye contact with her the entire time.

Xan watched his two lovers share him, groaning and praising them as they did. "Good girls, both of you."

Xan looked at Dallis, who was practically salivating. He addressed Lilianna: "Do you want to show Dallis how much of a good girl *you* are?"

Lilianna released him from her mouth, wiping the corner of her lip as she did so. "Yes."

His hand gripped her hair as he demanded, "Yes what?"

"Yes sir," she answered, almost breathlessly.

Satisfied, Xan looked at Dallis. "If you want her, come and claim her."

Dallis rose instantly and walked forward holding himself for Lilianna. Xan moved her head toward what Dallis offered and she took it with joy and hunger, her golden eyes shining with sexual menace.

After some time, Lilianna laid back and spread herself open. "C'mon Dallis, I'm all yours." Xan had never seen her so confident, so willing to take pleasure for herself. Dallis adjusted himself and entered her slowly, arching his head back and sighing as if a long-awaited moment had been fulfilled. Lilianna caught her breath as he leant forward to place his lips upon hers to capture moans of ecstasy.

Juniper smiled with the devil burning in her eyes, crawling forward to lick Lilianna's firm nipples slowly from one part of the areola to the end, flicking her tongue to carry her beneath the undertow in a vortex of force.

Xan positioned himself behind Juniper, inching inside her until he heard that groan of satisfaction that always galvanised him, turned him to granite. Muscles flexed as he deepened the thrust inside her, and Juniper turned around for him. Their tongues were lashing whips on glistening skin. Xan pushed Juniper's head downward to Lilianna again, and her golden eyes found his. Although she was currently filled, he knew that the craving in her eyes was for him. Even if others occupied her body, he owned her. He would make sure at the end of this she knew that; she *felt* that inside of her.

But for now—have fun, be free.

"Dallis, put your hands around Lili's throat," Xan commanded.

Dallis looked at him, uncertain, so Xan released Juniper and walked around behind Dallis, grabbing his arms and showing him the way to push down on Lilianna's throat.

"Now, fuck her again like you mean it. She wants to lose herself." He looked down at Lilianna. "Don't you?" She nodded, biting her lip and closing her eyes.

Dallis seemed to find an energy; the animal within spurned him on as his hands remained fixed to her throat, his hips pushing harder and faster into her. Xan reached down and massaged Lilianna's clit as Dallis thrust into her. Lilianna's golden eyes were lost to ecstasy and after a few moments, her legs shuddered against Dallis and she let out a deep moan.

Lilianna rolled across the floor, holding herself and breathing hard.

Juniper moved to Dallis, who was watching Lilianna recover with a look of awe. She pushed him to the ground, not giving him a minute's worth of appreciating his handy work, "Are you ready for me, big boy?" He grunted a barely audible reply, but it was enough for her to lower herself onto him. Xan appeared beside her, grabbing her throat and bending down to feel her wet tongue against his again—crashing against restless waves.

"Xan, I want you too," she groaned, motioning him behind her.

"Lilianna, I need you over here." Lilianna crawled over to Xan after having recovered from her own pleasure. She lathered spit onto his cock, readying to occupy Juniper's second vacancy.

Juniper stopped grinding on Dallis, allowing Xan to take his time behind her so it was a gradual increase in pleasure. He pushed inside Juniper, only a little at first. She groaned loudly, with a deep growl that spanned the confines of pain and pleasure. He pushed deeper as she eased up on Dallis. He gripped her left breast with a careless hand and his other cupped her throat, and the three of them moved in sync, primal sounds filling the air.

After Juniper had spasmed on both Dallis and Xan, Dallis warned, "I'm going to release soon."

"Give it to Lilianna," Juniper said breathlessly, as they disembarked. She turned back quickly cleaning them with an antiinfex wipe. "Both of you give it to her."

Lilianna watched as the two males came towards her. Xan could see her glistening, ready for them to take control of her insatiable body again. He knew she'd never had two at the same time before and wanted to make it good for her. Her pleasure, her freedom was his focus.

Xan pushed himself inside her slick opening as she opened her mouth for Dallis. He stroked himself above her. His lips twisted as he jerked with strength, yearning for his climax. Juniper was behind him, whispering into his ear and letting her tongue say all the words he needed. Xan reached out, forcing Lilianna's mouth open and she obliged by sticking out her tongue, with her golden eyes burning with passion and hunger.

Still, each thrust that Xan made was to feed her pleasure. Focusing on her sensations, listening to the subtle shifts in her body so that rapture wasn't just a marking on a map, it was a tangible treasure glinting with gold. Lilianna responded to Xan, her hands gripping the back of his legs. It was getting more and more difficult not to lose control, but he concentrated on giving everything to her. All of a sudden, Dallis let out a stifled scream, releasing into her open mouth, splattering across her lips and coating her tongue. Juniper bent down, licked off the excess, and said in a low tone, "Mmm, good girl, Lilianna."

Lilianna smiled at the praise, but immediately opened her mouth in an involuntary moan, closing her eyes and allowing herself to concentrate on the sensation of Xan inside of her. "Own me boss, own me." she cried, opening her eyes and allowing him to read her true desires.

"You are mine, baby girl."

Xan watched Juniper push down on Lilianna's sensitive spot with enough force that sent Lilianna reeling again as her eyes rolled to the back of her head. Xan picked up the pace, pounding against her, gripping her hips and slamming her back into him. The combination of Xan and Juniper pushed Lilianna to the edge.

"Fill me now," she begged. "Fucking fill me with everything you have."

Xan pressed his forehead to hers, grabbed the back of her neck with his right hand and dug his fingers into her thigh with the other. Her body gave way and she screamed, a rough, dirty, distorted scream. Knowing she was satisfied, Xan then released everything he had deep inside her, pushing deeper until it leaked out and coated the floor around them both.

CHAPTER 21

LOCATION: SYTHERIA
YEAR: 2505
XAN – 24 YEARS OLD

Everyone on the ship slept in, though whether from embarrassment or actual exhaustion, no one bothered to admit.

Qilin jumped on Xan, who was well and truly passed out in a sea of other naked bodies. It certainly woke him up and stirred others around him to open bleary eyes and search for a morsel or two of fabric to counter the skin on display.

Juniper was the only one content to rest on the floor of the ship using her suit as a pillow. Her ass poked out for anyone who wanted a morning continuation of the previous night.

After cleaning, showering, taking their pillprotex—the Gemarine form of contraception and infection prevention—they got ready to assemble for a meeting with the other less hungover crew members.

Their mission on Sytheria was complete. The path was now laid for Braemar's Evercorp to dominate the field of natural energy. Instead of

Sawtech mining Sytheria's core for minerals to fuel the planet, leading to annihilation, they had a sustainable way to survive.

Before going back to Periah to reset the portal and merge the splintered timelines, it was imperative to focus on fixing the Earth first. Moving from one timeline to another meant using the crystal remote to open up a wormhole back to Periah and then reprogramming the next destination.

Gathered in the common area, scrubbed clean of all the bodily fluids from fusing, the crew deliberated on the best way forward.

"Why do we have to split up?" Lilianna protested, folding her arms across her chest with the scowl of a delinquent. The crew sat at the round table watching Xan as he leant on the countertop. Unopened packets of chews were stacked behind him; a hydration spout like a silver flamingo dripped liquid into the sink sporadically.

"We will be able to get things done quicker," Xan reasoned calmly. "The two separate tasks that are going to be conducted on Earth seem pretty straightforward." He shrugged, then massaged his temples to stem the ache in his head.

"I'll take Lilianna and Ryker and be a tour guide of my little future dystopian Earth." Juniper leant back, arms adorning the back of her head. Ryker shifted uncomfortably on his seat, letting the raven fringe cover his eyes to hide the embarrassment of being mentioned.

"But wait, why wouldn't Xan and the professor's climate change formula fix everything on Earth further into the future? Why is it a dystopia?" Lilianna asked.

Qilin emerged from underneath the table and sat beneath Arcadie, who kept shifting his eyes toward her in distrust, unsure of whether she might lick him rusty or crunch his pixels with her sharp teeth.

"Well, the dystopia doesn't eventuate from climate change per se. We all saw the same vision, and it was essentially Human error. Religion and politics, just eating up society. A whole cycle of shit that started as far back as the Crusades that evidently repeats," Xan informed them.

"You've done research on Earthen history—you know they're all, or rather, *we* are all plagues on poor Mother Earth," said Juniper.

Qilin started to swat her paws at one of Arcadie's exposed wires underneath his buttox panel. Eyebrows creased his faceplate as he tried desperately to shift away from her without causing a ruckus in the middle of the meeting.

Sitting in between Fleurah and Arcadie, Dallis put a finger in the air and cleared his throat. "Ahem, if we are going to help Mother Earth, is there a Father Earth that also needs assistance?"

Massy, who had been quiet this whole time, called out with a deadpan face, "It's called Daddy Earth, Dallis. And yes, I'll take you there one day." He leant back and clasped his hands, pouting at Dallis.

"Daddy Earth sounds great." Dallis rolled his large shoulders in an excited, dance-like movement and flashed his pearly teeth in a childish smile.

Massy covered his mouth to stem a chuckle, as Xan shook his head condemning Massy's immaturity.

Lilianna glared at Massy while Dallis appeared genuinely baffled. She resumed the conversation, "Anyway, I do know about Earth history, but I view it from afar. Because we aren't in the action—it doesn't seem as potent."

Xan sighed deeply and tapped his leg so that Qilin would stop bothering Arcadie and come over for a pat. "The effort that any dominating species has on the environment can be extremely severe. We both know that more than anyone."

Lilianna nodded as if recalling the trip to the Khulor Quadrant or even Gorblact. The devastation had brought them both to tears. Entire ecosystems replaced by blackened wastelands; crisp corpses of creatures fleeing had been caught in the destructive sweep of flame.

Xan took a sip of water and eyed the *hungfree* pills on the table next to the sink, considering whether the hangover was potent enough to use them. The main side effect was chronic constipation.

"Look, I'll take Fleurah and Arcadie with me. Massy, you can pilot us first to our destination and then use the crystal remote to set coordinates for the others afterwards."

Massy masticated on an A3 chew and shrugged like he didn't care either way, then adjusted the clasp in his knotted hair.

"How are you going to get Dallis to blend in with people from your time on Earth? With his size, not to mention the sparkling sapphire eyes and...all that other stuff," Ryker finished quickly, careful not to highlight the Valkor's protruding forehead or hook-like nose.

"I shall go with Lilianna's crew." Dallis stood at once, shaping a sprinting stance at the start of a race.

Xan felt like rolling his eyes, but he stood and patted Dallis on the shoulders forcefully enough that he sat back down. "Yeah, okay, you big oaf."

His smile was ridiculously wide, but the scar on his cheek halted Xan's joyous interactions. It winked at him with the secret it held; the secret of Xan's unhinged, untameable wrath.

"Cool, so I have to babysit Dingus McGee, Skinny McGinny and Cassie Nova, while you get mildly useful bitch and robocock?" Juniper quipped, crossing her legs and cleaning the dried blood from her exofingers.

Fleurah folded her arms and scowled across at Juniper. Her hood was peaked, and her strawberry-blonde dreadlocks hung loosely down her chest.

"Cassie Nova? That's a stretch," Massy laughed.

"Not my best, but hey, you understood it."

Lilianna sulked, tapping her fingers against her petite biceps.

"Anyway, stop complaining, Captain Gemarine. You've got a nice trainee crew that you can mould into little Juniper clones," Xan said.

Juniper stood upright. "Challenge accepted, fuckstick." She started moving toward Xan's quarters. "If I'm captain—I'm taking your quarters to get ready for this jump, then. Make sure you get acquainted with your new sister-in-law." She winked and was gone, yelling for the rest of her small crew to follow her. Dallis went eagerly, followed meekly by Ryker and finally by Lilianna who stopped just before she vanished to throw an expectant gaze at Xan.

Instead of giving her a small piece of his tired heart, he gave her silence.

Enraptured in blowing off steam the night before, their chemistry sizzled, reacted in ways that complimentary elements do. But he was hesitant to divulge an emotion. It was easier to give the prize of his body, rather than give over his heart. Xan was afraid of Lilianna's expectant gaze, of it being too much—more than he could give, so he swallowed his silence, knowing it might make him cold. But he'd rather be cold than set Lilianna ablaze with a dishonest flame.

"What did Juniper mean, sister-in-law? Are you and Lilianna like…an item? Did something go on while I was in the regen chamber last night?" asked Fleurah.

Xan turned away from her, concentrating on packing his bag and adjusting his suit. "It's complicated."

"Damn dude, you're banging my sister?"

"Banging sister, banging sister," Arcadie yelled as an alarm emerged from the top of his head, blinking in red bursts.

"Would you both shut it?" Xan glared at them, his voice harsh.

They looked back at him, sheepishly. The alarm retreated from whence it was erected. Fleurah gave him a calculated look. "You're certainly not my type, but I 'spose she could've done a lot worse. Like Massy the little sex pest. He'd probably try to fuck one of Arcadie's retractable appendages."

Arcadie pushed out a small metal antenna that blinked out of the side of his head. "Is my hacking port not worthy of making love to?"

Qilin rose from the corner, ears pricked, sensing a new toy to play with.

"Put that thing away would ya?" Fleurah knocked him on one of his tubular arms.

Xan tried to forget Arcadie's appendage. "I thought Lilianna might have already told you a bit about the Gemarine ways, but I suppose in the short time you've had together there would've been other things to catch up on."

"I've heard some things, but it sounds like this trip to Earth is going to be a nice 'lil gossip session for me?" She clapped her hands.

Xan raised his brows in mock enthusiasm. "Hooray."

Qilin had prowled across the floor of the ship and pounced onto Arcadie, chewing on his hacking port while he beeped in protest. The robot's thrusters engaged, and he zipped over Xan as he ducked down. Beeps, computerised squeals, robotic arms flailed as Qilin used her claws to sink into Arcadie's body. But she could only hold on for so long and slipped off, crashing onto the table and knocking cups of water to the floor.

Xan and Fleurah met one another's gaze. A shared look of understanding regarding their ridiculous companions.

Arcadie floated near the ceiling, frazzled and muttering to himself. Qilin crawled under the table, ears flopped down, searching Xan for any form of affection or sympathy. He just shook his head as if to say, "No chance, that one is on you."

"Told you to put that thing away, buddy," Fleurah said through a malevolent grin.

It was after midnight, Earth time, and Massy cruised past the motionless skycars of Lantau Island. They sighed with exhaustion after a long day of ferrying visitors from one side to the other. The big Buddha could be seen through a frame of dismayed leaves clinging to maple trees. Snow-capped mountains jutted out of the landscape surrounding the peaceful God, highlighting the true depth of the wilderness areas still abundant in Hong Kong.

The ramp collapsed and the autumn breeze swept up inside the ship, carrying with it a floral incense from the distant temple, and the subtle breath of wild jasmine as it crept across the earth. The sights and smells had Xan reeling.

Thoughts of his former life tumbled within, like an oscillating chemical reaction. Eradicating the protective walls built to mask abandoning his parents and his friends – all for nothing. It was a lie. He had left to go to Gemarine on the foundation of a lie. A life on Earth had been squandered and for so many years he was oblivious, almost happy. Actually happy, he reminded himself. But often when building a life atop unsteady foundations, it's much harder to make running repairs when those foundations begin to crumble.

Xan stood behind Fleurah, who was attempting to farewell her sister while Arcadie gave them space, peeling into Xan's right shoulder. Although Xan and Arcadie shared a deep conversation on the last mission, he really didn't like it when people, or robots for that matter, lurked with darting eyes.

In his school on Earth, the brainless juggernauts would sit behind him and do exactly that. It didn't matter how much he huffed, puffed and tried to cover his work, they would always find a way to steal an answer or two. Although he was naturally intelligent, he did the work to maintain the muscles of the brain, studying for hours on end alone or with Chu. His elbow jutted out to shoo Arcadie away from him, citing personal space. But the sordid past tends to encroach upon the present, splitting seconds like a snarling axe biting into decaying wood.

Lilianna's eyes were tightly shut as she embraced her sister, speckled tears rolling down her sunset cheeks.

Fleurah pulled back. "Silly sis, don't cry—I'll see you soon enough!"

Lilianna wiped her tears and forced a smile, which allowed potential drama to pass by. Xan was almost certain she would internalise her emotions and pore over them later as she toiled on her lonesome.

Juniper sidled up to Lilianna with a forceful shoulder bump, tugging her close. "Don't you worry, I'll look after her." She looked down at Lilianna, and they both stared into each other's eyes. Lilianna began to laugh through the tears.

Juniper soon joined in the laughter. "I couldn't keep that ruse going. I'm a bloody mess, I can't even keep my crew mates alive, so what hope does Lilianna have?"

The laughter ceased—all except Juniper, who slowly trailed off, looking aghast. "Was that too far, too soon or something?" she asked, genuinely concerned.

"You are fucked in the head," declared Fleurah, "and I like it." Her face lit up while Lilianna shuffled uncomfortably away from the group, avoiding eye contact with Xan.

Fleurah turned on her heels, initiating the final splitting of the groups. Xan watched Lilianna put considerable distance between them all. He started to walk after her but hesitated.

Xan wanted to voice the internal truth aloud to Lilianna. Often unsaid words are the rock walls in a fast-flowing brook, diverting the current into other channels. A flood would come eventually. But today, the water trickled, taunting Xan as it moved by like a rippling cloth caught in the grip of a breeze. He watched it go past him undisturbed.

There was too much distance, too much silence now between Lilianna and Xan. The strength of water was often discounted. But in this case, the current had separated them enough that the gulf was wide, and the peaceful sandy shore was now unattainable.

They needed a private moment where they might be able to uncover the unsaid treasures buried beneath them. But in the haste of the mission, they couldn't do anything more than stare with sullen eyes.

Juniper stepped in to stem the awkwardness—yet another victim of her killing prowess. "Get going, beautiful man. Go save the world or some shit." She blew him a kiss and grabbed Lilianna to drag her further away. Lilianna looked longingly over her shoulder. She, no doubt, wanted meaningful words pried from him like a surgical extraction, but the wound was sealed shut.

Xan sighed as he stepped out onto the Wisdom path. Shrouded in darkness, Lantau Island abandoned at three in the morning.

The emotions flooded him upon his Earthly return, but he also felt the distinct loss of his crew, especially Lilianna and Juniper.

I could have said something like that to her. I could have said, I'm going to miss you because there is a gulf within me when you're not right there.

Lilianna was the type of individual who needed constant reassurance, whereas Xan didn't need to utter such words to Juniper. They both knew, felt it in their capillaries just how much they meant to each other. Maybe it was because their bond was forged with the accumulation of years, experiences and traumas vanquished.

Xan shook his head; none of it mattered now. He would see Lilianna again soon enough, and he would conjure the monsoon. Where the rain would loosen those unsaid words locked in stoic stones, scattering them across the sandy banks where Lilianna lay waiting for more than the puckered kiss of the tide rolling in.

CHAPTER 22

LOCATION: EARTH
YEAR: 2036
XAN – 24 YEARS OLD

They rode the MTR to the university station. Arcadie was stuffed in a pack, rock-hard metal digging into Xan's spine.

Fleurah had a bucket hat on to conceal her elven ears; Qilin, most ridiculously of all, was dressed in the ceremonial dragon outfit reminiscent of the Tianlong. Xan held her in his lap, encouraging onlookers to mistake her for a large dog, perhaps. Being the very first train operating, there weren't as many commuters on the way to work. Still, Xan understood the culture. Curious eyes wouldn't linger, and even if they did, aggressive voices would not be heard. It may not have been the same since he'd left, but deeply woven threads like that never quite escaped the fabric of the culture. Xan jolted in surprise.

Am I somehow manifesting that same energy with Lilianna? Do I just not want to engage because it's too hard or too real? He shook the thought away—his whole point was that Hong Kong natives would rather turn away and pretend like nothing was wrong than stand up and accuse him of harbouring an alien creature. Xan almost chuckled audibly at the ridiculousness of that statement.

Throughout the entire trip on the MTR, Xan gave Fleurah a breakdown of the Gemarine ways. She was impressed that it was founded by a group of Sytheract rebels and recalled tales of mass exile years before when Sytheracts refuted the planetary systems, departing on voyages never to be glimpsed in the atmosphere of Sytheria again. It made sense, Xan considered, that various settlements took place all over various galaxies.

"You know, I can't blame Lilianna for leaving. I'm sure she feels bad about it, but Sytheria lost its soul a while ago."

"How so?"

"The only freedom we truly have is in the open spaces that we build in our minds. We are way too closely monitored by tech corps that restrict us. They can track our every move. It's a freakin' new age of barbarism."

Xan nodded, gaze flickering to the corners of the train where cameras blinked like watchful owls camouflaged by the monotony of the morning migration. He wondered what tech giants were able to do on Earth now, years after his departure. Would facial recognition identify him or Fleurah as alien enemies? It didn't look like *that* much had changed in a decade but then again, things were never as they appeared on the surface.

Fleurah continued. "Don't get me started on soulbonds." Xan opened his posture, inviting the conversation. "Well, it meant that often Sytheracts who don't identify as heterosexual are cast aside. It sounds like on Gemarine, that's not even an issue."

"That's the thing I really like about Gemarine. It's almost like that isn't a factor. Everyone is who they are—their preferences, their genders, their species—it's all just part of the landscape. A tree is a tree—you don't cut it down because the wood grain is slightly whiter than the others or has some slight imperfections; you just admire it and continue on."

"And what about the sex thing for pleasure?" Fleurah asked, as a hint of displeasure wafted across her face.

"Yeah, well we can all be open about that without ramifications. It's just nice to listen to the call of your body and not have to repress those things with a made-up societal standard."

"When I get to Gemarine—I don't think I'd fit in with that Fusion place. Juniper had been rambling on about it. I haven't really been excited by much sexual stuff to be honest." She looked downcast. "Arcadie has tried to help me with…feeling things…but I just don't really have that… desire." Fleurah shifted on the seat, her cheeks flushing with colour.

"I haven't noticed anyone on Gemarine that has those types of feelings yet, but on Earth people would call this being asexual."

"Asexual? I thought that was when a plant…you know…was able to reproduce without any other…plant."

"Well, yes," Xan laughed, "but here, it's when you might be romantically interested in someone's personality but don't particularly have any desire to…do anything physical."

"But that is totally not Gemarine, right? Everyone there is all about that…wham bam." Fleurah slammed her fist against an open palm.

"Well, at places like Fusion it's all about the ah, wham bam, as you put it." Xan raised his eyebrows and smirked. "But Gemarine is not just a fuck fest. It's more about appreciating the call of your body and responding to that. If there isn't actually a response from your body, then it's just…I don't know…accepted as any form of consent, or non-consent rather."

She nodded and turned away muttering under her breath, "Being accepted, hey?"

Xan realised they were approaching the stop. "Let's get ready to disembark – the university is just up the road from here."

He rose up from the seat, putting Qilin on the floor in between his legs. She flopped onto her backside, trying to see out of the eye holes in the dragon head, sniffing and sneezing in discomfort. Holding onto the cold, metal rail and looking out through the window at the rushing darkness outside, Xan was transported back in time. Well, more so than he already was. Except when he looked beside him, Chu wasn't there; it was a pale elf-like alien with a clumsy creature at his feet. Never in his wildest dreams did he expect to be here again, especially with present company. He wondered where Chu would be and if they would recognise one another on the street. He doubted it. Time tended to not only alter the reality of the present but dim the radiance of beautiful memories, awash in sepia tones, detached from the emotion that had once given them life.

The train stopped moving, the doors parted, and the trio stepped onto the platform. Following the sparse migration of the morning commuters, they found their way onto the street.

Emerging from the underground they discovered it was a fresh morning. A slight chill still had the tendency to bite down onto their flesh and it did so without reprieve. Their flimsy jackets were no match for the hefty double-breasted woollen coats hugging the knees of passers-by.

The university was quiet before the commencement of classes. The odd student jogged across the gravel paths circling the campus, and a man in a beanie and trench coat hurried past them, eyes downcast. A couple sat on the edge of a garden framed by jasmine hedges, their teas swirling with steam beside them on the bench. Xan watched as they nestled into one another while taking videos.

Is that love? Broadcasting affection to the world for validation? The man lowered his phone, placing it on the wall. They kissed and the breeze swirled around them. Notes of jasmine infused with the melody of their desire, rising like bird song across the treetops.

Xan was confused. The attention seeking had been abandoned, still their intent was solely for the other. They had a place to go where they could take their sorrow, and it would be cleansed; they could take their pain and it be healed. It was within the other.

But wasn't that simplifying it too much? Weren't there things that just one person couldn't give him? Whereas in the arms of two or three or more—all needs would be attended to.

He thought of Lilianna and her love for the world, her delicate nature, calm demeanour and gentle approach to the sharpness of life. Then he thought of Juniper—the height of a tempest, lightning torturing the sky with claws of pure energy. He loved them both in equal measures.

The customs of Earth—those he adhered to previously and accepted so willingly, were now completely foreign to him. His formative years were in Gemarine, and he just couldn't go back. He saw love as a forest that could only enhance its ecosystem through its symbiotic relationships. The trees that dropped their seeds, for the birds to carry onward to a clearing, for the soil to team with insects that encourage the germination of that seed. And in the end, it sprouts to the sky, reaching with a strength made possible by the many.

Fleurah stirred Xan out of his love-addled trance by studying the directory and locating the science wing.

A restless bell chimed in the distance, sirens wailed mournfully, footsteps of a runner thumped on the concrete echoing off the buildings in the main square.

Pushing the glass doors inward into the campus's main building, they jog-walked through the halls, heads spinning to locate the stairwell. The bell tolled listlessly, as if an unattended alarm. The sirens grew louder; the roar of the lion—a warning in the urban jungle, telling all who heard that the open arc of life would soon close into a circle.

They raced up the second stairwell on the right, Qilin the dragon bounding up with them. Luckily no one delivering breakfast to this part of the university passed them, with the potential claim of an alien presence hampering their every move. They reached the fifth level and Xan bolted down the hallway followed by Qilin. Fleurah shouted, "Wait for me, you athletic bastards!"

Xan didn't know why he was running flat out. His intuition had flared as they tore up the levels, like he was absorbing a flurry of punches to the gut. The sirens wailed louder; the manic cries of a prophet with doom on their tongue. Was it the sirens? Or was it irony coming for him? Irony quietly snickering as Xan uttered the words, *"it will be simple enough"* to Lilianna on the ship. Irony stating, *do I have news for you, cocky fool.*

Panting, he reached Professor Mingyung's office door.

Professor Mingyung was Xan's mentor in their collective vision. The person that would have teamed up with Xan to discover the climate change formula and subsequently save the entire world.

An open palm thumped on the door as Xan braced himself, but it was already ajar, and it flew inward hitting the wall. After stumbling, Xan straightened, mouth slack as he and Qilin walked inside, followed by Fleurah, who came behind with heavier footsteps.

The air was dense, with a musty smell. A wooden desk stained in caramel lacquer. Maroon carpet with a pattern of golden stars, faded from the footfall in the office. The lab was at the back, cut off from the office by plexiglass, but instead of the stark white of a sterile environment, a viscous pool of blood trailed across the floor, a large slashing spatter hugged the glass in its descent. Legs in olive trousers were splayed at awkward angles. Xan pushed through, his face pressed up to the glass, and halted in horror at the professor's corpse.

"How did this happen?" Fleurah gasped.

Xan's eyes bulged. Arcadie's muffled voice came through the backpack. "What has happened? Let me see!" he pleaded.

Fleurah knelt down and unzipped her pack, allowing him to power up and extend himself. His eyes flickered, adjusting to the bright light in the room.

"Oh goodness," he murmured as he caught sight of the professor's body.

Xan couldn't believe it.

The distant sounds of sirens grew closer. Qilin the dragon paced the floor, jumped up, and scratched at Xan's thighs with her front paws, then resumed pacing. Fleurah and Arcadie were arguing. Xan turned back to the plexiglass, head resting back and closed his eyes to block out the sound.

Think.

He opened his eyes and spun around, glimpsing what he needed in the corner of the lab, winking at him. "Arcadie, can you remotely log into the camera feed? Trace the movement and find out what happened to the professor."

"Give me a minute."

Xan snapped into leader mode. "Alright, in the meantime, let's get ready to get out of here. We can head to the MTR and book accommodation via networks through Arcadie and figure out our next move from there."

Arcadie's voice crackled. "Oh my."

"Do we know what happened?" Xan asked.

Arcadie seemed to gulp, though he lacked any function to make that necessary. His makeshift fingers intertwined, and he rocked from side to side. "Oh, goodness. Oh, goodness. I know who murdered the professor. Xan, before I show you, I must say – I apologise for being the bearer of such awful news."

Xan's stomach lurched.

"Someone has betrayed you."

CHAPTER 23

On the top of the ramp, Juniper looked out across rolling dunes at dusk. There was a grace in their shape, curving in just the right places and tumbling onward into the great desolation of the desert. Wind whipped the fine grains of sand onto her cheeks, like the earth was spitting in her face from afar. The smell of dirt and burning wood rose up from the uninviting hills.

After using the crystal remote and selecting the right date and time period, they moved through the portal once more. Ryker rushed toward Juniper to inform her that Dallis had grown ill in the last few minutes.

Could the Valkor have been opposed to a little desert hike?

When she came forth to examine him, she knew that wasn't the case. The spider bite had swollen considerably on his wrist; pulsing purple blotches throbbed on the epidermis. Juniper winced, watching Ryker bandage the hand and dab Dallis's rather large forehead with a wet cloth.

Dallis will be joining me in the amputee club shortly. That wrist is gone.

She decided that Ryker and Dallis would stay behind on the ship while Lilianna and Juniper sorted out their easy little mission in dystopia land.

Let's face it—Spiderman and Mary Jane were just going to annoy the fuck out of me anyway.

Juniper watched as Lilianna stood on the edge of the ramp as the thrusters idled, with Dallis wanting to say goodbye to her. There was an awkward exchange of a back slap and a weird half hug that made her wonder how he actually fucked well the night before.

I suppose he needed a bit of encouragement before he really got going.

Massy came up behind her. "Watching little Pristine Bitch and Doofus, are we?"

"Yeah, they're the only comedic options I have right now."

"I guess you don't have a mirror to see your shit haircut then, 'cause that always makes me laugh."

Juniper ruffled her curls and let them tumble across her shoulders. "Dayum, look at you, firing shots."

He laughed. "Ah, I'm going to miss this." Massy pointed his finger back and forth, indicating them both.

"Fuck, it won't be that long." She swatted a hand. The wind had eased off a little as the fine sands skipped playfully across the rolling dunes.

"Yeah, I guess not." He looked out the window wistfully, as if he were considering the future.

Dallis shuffled past them both, looking tired. No, looking like absolute shit. "Good luck Miss Juniper—I will see you shortly."

"Cheers buddy." She held out her knuckles to clasp together, but he stared at her fist and asked, "Do you have something for me?"

She sighed. "No, just…look after yourself." Pulling back, she brandished a peace sign.

Lilianna had jumped onto the sand and was trying to get Juniper's attention to join her for a romantic stroll across a forsaken wasteland.

In the control room, Ryker engaged the thrusters and the *Attenborough* started to rise.

Juniper began walking down the ramp.

"Get to the control room, you idiot," she called to Massy.

Massy walked forward down the ramp, "Ryker can handle this part at least. I needed him to." The thrusters weren't fully engaged as the ship hovered above the shifting sands.

"Why? You trying to teach him or something? *You* of all people," Juniper scoffed.

Massy's forehead creased. "What do you mean *me* of all people?"

"You're not the most leader-y of people, or the most…teacher-y, for that matter." She laughed, turning away as she bent down to fix a strap on her boots.

"See, that was your problem," Massy scratched his cheek fiercely, his charcoal hair blowing in the wind. "You always underestimated me."

Juniper rose slowly, noticing his eyes were dark. Alarm bells rang out. Beneath the placid lake, she spotted the barbed tail of an evil monster lurking, threatening those at the surface.

Her laugh was nervous, a baby bird flapping for the first time venturing out and over the nest. "What do you mean, Massy? We love and—"

His leg kicked out straight into her gut. The force of the blow knocked the air out of her and became gravity's adversary. Tumbling as if time slowed, she saw the malicious intent in his gaze. A heavy boot came to rest on the edge of the ramp. A sickle grin, evoking malevolence at Juniper's demise. The desert floor beckoned her—a place to abscond from her failure. Detective work was clearly not her strong suit. The person who ended up betraying them was farthest from her list of suspects because he was the class clown.

Suddenly she was on her back on the searing sand. Lilianna appeared at her side, screaming into the wind.

Juniper couldn't believe it.

Fine particles blew around them as the *Attenborough* climbed higher.

"I'll always have the last laugh now, you piece of shit," he yelled at Juniper, and the ramp closed, hiding that putrid face.

Juniper stood up, her voice tearing across the skies like thunder. "I'm going to rip the fucking skin from your face, you fucking—"

A sobbing Lilianna placed a hand around the inside of her arm, a gesture of warmth and love amidst the heart wrenching act of betrayal. The shouting stopped immediately as skin braced skin. Cool water doused open flame. The boronium ramp was sealed shut and the *Attenborough* was a hovering reminder of what she was losing in that very moment. Devastation wracked her with the knowledge that Xan and Qilin were lost to her forever. In the past, long dead and buried.

Lilianna's chin came to rest on Juniper's shoulder and acted as a caveat for fragile tears to trickle onto her chest. But Juniper soon realised tears could never accept the solitary path. Tears were misery and they needed company. As Lilianna and Juniper's souls broke apart, they were forged as one by the adhesive quality of pain.

The *Attenborough's* cloak engaged, and it vanished, along with a future both females had always held onto. Lilianna and Juniper were not separate souls in grief anymore. They would be forever fused in fatal affliction.

CHAPTER 24

LOCATION: CRYPTOBORG TERRITORY
YEAR: 115
JUNIPER – 21 YEARS OLD

Blood gushed onto the ground in heaving spurts. Clouds of fog crept across her vision. Bile rose like a cobra, intent on striking out at the heart of her resilience.

Juniper's severed arm lay twitching on the ground, encased by a grove of godlike trees. Nerves screamed in the same way as her throat had, rage seizing the morsels of adrenalin stored within and violently dumping its contents so she could continue to fight.

She wheeled around with the dagger in her other hand and slashed across a mauve throat of the assassin. Blood fizzed into Juniper's eyes, and she stumbled back. The three bodies of her team were strewn across the forest path. Deciduous bodies atop deciduous leaves. Up against ten Cryptoborg assassins, they shouldn't have stood a chance. Valour and skill were all it took to honour life. They did what they could, but the sheer numbers combined with the sneak attack did it. It was a cheap trick, but cheap tricks make eyes glaze over in wonder and that is often the true measure of a magician.

Juniper, now missing an arm, had four more to overcome before she could rest. She killed for vengeance, killed in anger, killed for time, killed for the sanctity of life. But more than anything, she killed to find answers. This was not where the Cryptoborg army bases were meant to be. No one should have met them on this path. But the assassin teams tucked themselves under far reaching ferns and behind thousand-year-old trunks. Someone had betrayed her.

She would live so that *they* would suffer.

After the last Cryptoborg choked to death under a vice grip of hate, she dropped off the body and lay on emerging seedlings, now maimed. She called the Phineas system on the MPD fixed to her wrist. "Call for medihelp, I'm…fucked."

She passed out before the AI responded. The only breathing body in a killing field, lush with expired souls who floated free.

The infirmary smelt of sadness. Pitiful groans were lullabies at night. Xan didn't leave her side and took extended leave to nurse her back to health. After a week, he arranged for countless soldiers to fuck her senseless. She wanted to forget. She wanted a momentary break from losing her arm, from living life with a missing piece of her that lay rotting in a field of slain corpses. Sometimes it would be several fuckboy soldiers at once, other times they'd come and go while Xan directed them to give her everything she desired. All for a distraction.

In the second week, she was using her exoarm with more dexterity, revelling in the new features that made her even more fearsome.

As Xan departed, she began to look into that fateful mission more—trying to figure out who it was that sent her to the slaughter. Someone betrayed her—it was just a matter of who.

The leader of the Cryptoborgs had sent half the assassin horde and yet Juniper still managed to kill them all. When you send one half of something, the other remains. She needed to locate the assassin den and make the rest of them talk.

Juniper walked with Boorak on a dusty path at dusk. They kicked pinecones, while conifers and pine trees ogled them striding forward. Smoke from a campsite up ahead fluttered like extinguished fireflies.

"Is this not dangerous? We are in the heart of Cryptoborg territory. Who sanctioned this mission?" Boorak whispered, eyes darting through the trees at squirrels scurrying to the salvation of the shadows.

Juniper had a skip in her step as she admired her new exoarm, flicking her fingers to blades and back again. "I'm gonna level with you." She was deadpan serious. "This one is off the books."

"What?" Boorak stopped in his tracks. "I'm not going a step further in this—"

Juniper jogged back and linked arms with him, "Oh c'mon, buddy, it's been so long since we have been on the rampage together. Let me have this little win, yeah?" She held up her exohand and frowned, drawing his attention to her new appendage.

"Gahhh, you're so…"

"Radiant, beautiful? Shucks, I know, I know." Juniper stroked the handle of her sword.

"Manipulative. Was what I was going to say." Boorak's voice was wilted like a wildberry under a scorched sun.

They wandered out into a clearing. Boorak started to slow alongside Juniper as they took in the sight. The army camp was deserted. Not necessarily physical desertion, as blackened bodies were scattered across the campsite like lumps of sticky excrement. The docile smoke they had seen before originated here. It was an offending aroma that Juniper could taste at the back of her throat. Not because it was wood smoke but because it had that putrid nauseating scent of rancid leather and cooked meat.

Boorak backed away uneasily. "Wait, I know where we are, I know what this—"

Juniper turned before he ran away, and in a blinding movement, swiftly severed his left arm with her rusty sword.

As the blood squirted across the soil, it jarred her from the moment of triumph, enacting vengeance upon the person who betrayed her to the actual consequence of his betrayal.

A screech from her memory tore across his whimpering screams, and she dropped the sword. She continuously slapped herself on the head, trying to rid herself of the memory. The weakest moment of her life.

She heard herself laughing as she saw Boorak trying to back away on the ground.

"Where do you think you're going? I'm not done with you."

"You're crazy, you've lost your mind—"

Grabbing him by the hair with exoblade fingers, she stabbed into his scalp—sliding in like a well-lubed finger fuck. She wrenched him along the ground as he kicked frivolously at nothing. Juniper threw him up against the trunk of a sturdy young tree, pulled a rope from her pack, and started fastening Boorak to the tree as blood poured down his cheeks.

"You know, I actually love what you did to me. Now with all my enhancements I can dominate the battlefield more than I already did."

"Why are you doing this?" he cried.

She tied off the rope, satisfied that he was completely immobilised.

Squatting down face to face with the snivelling little ape, she said, "Ah yeah, that's a great fucking question. Why *did* you do it, Boorak?"

"You're insane. I *did* nothing."

"Oh no. Wrong move lying to me. You've only got a certain number of limbs and each lie means you lose one." She moved forward, and he motioned to kick. To ensure he didn't move too much, Juniper took her sword and impaled his leg to the ground through the knee.

Crack of bone. Rubbery sinew creaking. Cute little squirt of blood.

He wailed, tormented by the pain. It swelled her heart with delight. She pulled out a special bottle she had told Xan to smuggle in for her.

"This is a special Teflon container. It's the only container that can store fluoroantimonic acid. I've been saving this for you." Her tone was wrapped in sarcasm. It made her appear all the more psychotic. "This particular concoction has been modified so that the vapour is nontoxic. If poured on skin, well, that's a different story."

Boorak was still screaming, sweat gushing down his forehead while his dilated pupils spelt fear. She loved it.

"So, now, I present you with…acid burning off your leg."

She poured the canister onto his right leg with a curtsy, as if the world were a stage and this performance were her masterpiece. As soon as the acid sizzled skin, she backed away and he thrashed. Flesh bubbled, screams of agony multiplied until his voice was hoarse and useless, tear ducts depleted.

She took her sword out from the leg and hacked across his thigh so the acid didn't spread. Even after a few minutes the chemical was seeping into the ground with liquified blood and bone. It was a disgusting soupy mess.

Juniper waited patiently until he was able to talk.

"Admit it, and play time ends."

He swallowed. He wasn't himself anymore. Two limbs gone, ghostly pale, sunken eyes. Boorak was walking death.

Or maybe he was hopping death because acid had devoured his other leg. Right?

Boorak swallowed. "I did it."

"Good boy. Why?"

"Because…because of Everlaine."

Juniper's head bowed. "Emotions are like an anal sphincter. Hold 'em in for too long the more shit you get all over yourself. You, my friend, are all covered in shit now."

The limbless, useless, soon to be dickless pile of shit continued to weep.

Juniper recited the mantra of war, taught in the learning centres on Gemarine: "Sometimes, the sacrifice of one ensures the safety of many."

Boorak found his voice, cold and hoarse though it was. "That is taught by people who don't know love, who don't see the heart as anything more than an organ that feeds us life." He coughed; blood crept out the corner of his mouth. "When love finds you and you falter…falter when sacrificing them, I hope you remember this moment. Remember that you killed me because I could love, and you could not." The strength went out of him, and he slumped against the tree, sobbing pitifully.

Juniper heard his words and even considered them for a moment. But she looked at her exoarm, she remembered the pain, she remembered the bodies of her colleagues on that forest path, and she nodded to herself, knowing that this was just. Knowing that he did this to himself when he decided to seek out the enemy and leave her to the wolves.

"Let yourself believe what you want in your final moments, Boorak. If I didn't love or if I didn't feel, then I'd just hack your pathetic little prick off right now and let you squirm in your own testicle juice, but I think… you've suffered enough."

She started zipping up her pack and wiping the bloody sword across a conifer bush. "I'll collect your corpse in the morning. In ceremony, you'll be buried in your golden armour. No one will know of your betrayal. Your death will be sheathed in the glory of laying waste to the other half of the assassin horde."

"You're leaving me here to die?"

"I'm sorry, I didn't hear you say 'thank you for preserving my integrity and honour in death.'"

"Juniper, don't do this."

Juniper blocked out the sounds of mercy from the traitorous little swine, as her boots thumped back onto the path away from him. She switched on music on her MPD, a swelling clash of orchestral synths, a bass drum like a steady heartbeat and a triumphant vocal melody.

Even as she danced over fallen leaves to the energy of the song, something wasn't quite right. The feeling of victory was muted by Boorak's final words; she hated that he had gotten to her.

Love transcends the here and now. In its glassy eyes, it wouldn't recognise sacrifice. It would never point an accusatory finger. Because love is eternal, and it speaks in a language we cannot truly comprehend.

Juniper wiped a tear away and let her mind fill with images of the only beings she felt love for. Xan and Qilin jumping on her bed after an alcohol-fuelled sleep-in. Xan and Qilin skirting the edges of a lake motioning for Juniper to jump in with them. Xan and Qilin lying on the couch on her level, ready to surprise her after she returned from her first deployment. They were, instead, asleep. Finally, Xan and Qilin sitting together watching a holostream as she looked at her spot on the couch ready to join them.

Fuck that piece of shit, Boorak.

She knew about love.

CHAPTER 25

LOCATION: EARTH
YEAR: 2114
MASSY – 25 YEARS OLD

The ramp closed on Massy. He stared as if he still saw Juniper, most likely kicking, screaming, cursing his name forever more. He'd heard it plenty of times, so why was he fixed on this spot now? Because it was the end of Massy in the shadows. It was the death of mild Massy, and out of wrath's womb, he writhed and wriggled free of all the shackles, ready to make his mark.

Dallis and Ryker could be dispatched soon enough. He now had the Cryptoborg to team up with, to give him power in a pack. His own crew. The leader of something for the first time since...he shuddered. It was still painful after all these years to think of his fly buddies. The day after the Pinnacle Star Festival. After he begged Juniper for the stardust, then stayed up all night partying and fucking whatever was moving around him. The call woke him, and his buddies left for that fateful flight.

Enough of that memory bullshit. It's time to turn the screws.

Ryker called out to him, "Massy, I need you to fly this thing—I can't do this anymore."

Useless little prick. How hard is it to fly a spaceship like a legend of the galaxy? Massy almost tried to find a reflection in a piece of shiny metal so he could wink at himself, maybe even blow a kiss.

"Just set it to autohover. I'll be there in a moment."

He danced down the hallway, metal clanging from the force of his boots. He spun twice, pointing fingers to the roof and thrusting out his hips. Dallis peered at him quizzically from the chair beside the cell. "Just dancing, Dallis. It's to show you feel on top of the world."

"We are on top of *this* world, so please teach me these moves someday when I feel better." Dallis coughed. He looked like shit. Pale and bloated, holding his bandaged hand like an injured fawn.

The whole Dallis thing is endearing at the start, but if this guy takes anything literally one more time, I'm going to stuff a sock in his gob cause I'm sick of it.

"How about no, Dallis." He strained through a counterfeit smile, maybe the last he'd endure. "Now stand up like a good boy and clear out that shit in the cell."

Dallis sat there for longer than was comfortable. "I don't know why you choose to disrespect me once you are alone on the ship. I didn't think you were such an individual." He rose shaking his head, opening the cell with his good hand and shifted toward where the Cryptoborg lay, mess at her feet.

Massy shut the door tight, and Dallis spun around.

"Bye-bye now."

Massy skipped down the hall once more with Dallis shouting behind him. He entered the flight deck, Ryker staring straight out the window at the space junk in this trash heap of an atmosphere. "Why is Dallis shouting?"

Massy put his hand on Ryker's left shoulder. His eyes met Massy's.

Those are dead eyes, thought Massy, not for the first time.

The kid was a fucking weirdo. Thrust into this by royalty. The bloodline of their leader. Meant to have vision, but all he had was apathy; tinkering on little screws, sucking off inanimate objects as if they could love him back. It was a waste. Madame Bleu had actually asked him to tattle on this crew, and he had fed her bullshit. Massy knew because he was feeding her the good stuff while Ryker gave all his loyalty to Xan. Xan, that do-gooder piece of shit. It was disgusting. Ryker was given everything and accepted mediocrity. In fact, he accepted less than.

The needle at his side pulsed with a need to penetrate. It hadn't learnt over time to caress or to lick with gentle purpose. A needle penetrated hard and fast, just the way Massy liked it.

He pushed the sharp metal spike into the side of Ryker's neck, and the kid's eyes widened in horror.

Maybe there was something in him after all.

"What, what is that?"

The realisation dawned on him as Massy smiled close to his face and kissed him on the lips. "All will be clear in due time, kid—just make sure you stay on the right side this time." He slapped Ryker's face. It was mild, but Ryker still toppled to his right and couldn't straighten. The drug had taken effect immediately.

Massy stood there as he saw clarity reach Ryker. That look of betrayal made him feel powerful. He seized that look and buried it in the garden of his soul, to fuel his rise, to feed his ego. Ryker fell. Massy slid into the chair and sighed in satisfaction.

RYKER
21 YEARS OLD

Voices were muffled as if swimming underwater. Creatures in the dark remained unfocused, moving like a trail of spilt oil. Ryker heard his own cough, clearer now. Felt a large, rough hand brushing the long strands of his hair away from his face. Dallis knelt beside him—such a large thing, but gentle. The gaze of a being that could love, could nurture. A gaze that could never fall from Ryker's eyes upon another.

"Just don't move too fast," Dallis breathed out while caressing Ryker's cheek.

Ryker sat up, feeling dizzy and nauseous in one.

"We have been betrayed, Ryker," Dallis said flatly.

In annoyance, Ryker almost blurted out, *no shit.* But the look on Dallis's poor innocent face made him pity the displaced Valkor. Not to mention his blotchy skin and bandaged hand.

He'd nearly been sliced in half by Xan, bitten by a venomous space spider and watched everyone around him drown in their own blood. Pretty horrific. Now, a part of his adopted family just betrayed him. This dude needed to catch a break. Ryker decided to go with, "I figured that much, Dallis."

"Of course, of course." He sighed and looked over his shoulder at where the Cryptoborg should have been but wasn't there.

Ryker searched out of the cell, imagining Massy flying the craft and sighed. Madame Bleu had approached Ryker about a betrayal, but he couldn't bring himself to do it. Xan had won him over. He cared, truly cared about him. The first person in a long time. Sold him the dream of one big happy family just for a clown like Massy to ruin everything.

Massy. He couldn't believe it. But then Ryker recalled, Massy had always been the first to turn and run. Self-preservation. And he *never* felt bad. Ryker always felt a pang of guilt, especially when it came to this crew. But Massy was only in it for himself. He should have taken greater notice of the lack of loyalty. But what could he have done? He wasn't Juniper.

Juniper, Lilianna, and Xan are gone. Lost in time.

The realisation hit hard like a punch to the gut. Ryker found his voice. "Massy! What are you doing?" He rose shakily and pushed his face against the reinforced bioplastic. "Massy!"

The Aranther's chastising voice came over the loudspeaker. "Kiddo, nice of you to wake up. How was your sleep?" He waited a fraction of a moment as Ryker was about to yell something at him, but the voice returned, "I actually don't give a fuck. But hey, fasten your seatbelts, 'cause we will be soaring through the portal and on our way to your lovely Aunty to update her about everything!"

"Massy, what are you doing? Xan loved you." Ryker banged against the bioplastic.

Massy's voice was distorted with emotion, "Shut up, just shut up! He used me, he used all of us to get whatever the fuck he wanted. He doesn't love, he takes. You think Bleu is bad? Well Xan is *just* the same."

"That doesn't make sense!"

"You know what, I'm cool. I'm cool. Ain't nothing gonna get me down today. I've won. So you should just kick back with everyone's favourite loveable idiot and we will be back on Gemarine in no time. Over and out."

"Massy!" Ryker yelled. "Massy!"

Dallis put one of his large hands on Ryker's shoulder. The physical touch moved him. Losing his family, their predicament, losing…just losing in general. It hurt. It hurt the same way it did when his parents died, when Lambastian was exiled, and when his home had been ravaged by his tyrant aunty. Tears came heavy. He openly wept for the first time in a long time and let Dallis cradle him while he did so.

SYTHKIN
27 YEARS OLD

The Cryptoborg watched intently from the other side of the cell after Massy released her from containment. She rested her chin on cupped hands, mauve skin still crusted with dried blood from the laceration on her face. She nodded and half smiled at the two new prisoners who had replaced her in the cell. A Valkor and a half Sytheract. Both of them implored her with sad little eyes. Words were not required at the time, so she got up from her seat and strode down the hall to join Massy.

Finally, I'm on the right side of the cell. Fate is always with me.

LOCATION: SYTHERIA
YEAR: 2505
SYTHKIN – 27 YEARS OLD

Massy had informed Sythkin of his plan while they both waited for the rest of the crew to finish exploring Valinous Canyon.

"Listen Scarface, I'm going to—"

"My name is Sythkin," the Cryptoborg with the scar on her face interrupted flatly.

Massy considered this for a moment. "Hmmmm, no, I like Scarface better. Anyway, I'm going to reveal something to you right now." He paused but Sythkin remained seated, giving no indication that she cared. Massy seemed annoyed by that, starting with a grunt, "Eh, I'm actually working against these do-gooder pieces of shit, and I'm about to go back through the portal and kill some old professor."

He started to disrobe in front of her and put on a long black coat with a circular cotton hat that he squeezed onto his head, hiding the birthmarks and knots of hair. Sythkin did not respond, merely sat there observing him.

"Jeez, Scarface, do you have any reaction at all? Doesn't that mean we're on the same side? We can be partners."

Sythkin shrugged. "Anyone who is a vehicle of fate is a partner of mine."

"I take fate into my own hands." Massy adjusted black gloves and started walking toward the flight deck. "Once I've used the crystal remote and gone through the portal, done some sightseeing, and killed a professor, then I'll come back here to Sytheria to pick up these idiots and they'll be none the wiser. I'll fuck up their little plan before they're even halfway to fixing anything."

As he continued his jaunty walk with his back turned, Sythkin called out, "If we are to be partners, when are you going to release me?"

"Patience, Scarface. Let me nudge fate in the right direction first and *then* we can hold hands watching the sunset, you romantic little cutie."

He blew her a kiss and sauntered out of sight, singing operatic tunes she'd heard him sing before while she was curled up in the ship's venting systems.

Massy was an interesting character, but was he the partner Sythkin could trust with her own mission? Was he really fate's accomplice or just a fallen log on the path to the promised land?

CHAPTER 26

LOCATION: EARTH
YEAR: 2114
LILIANNA – 22 YEARS OLD

The sun kissed the hazy horizon. The sand dunes were red lips parted, sinking into evening lust.

Juniper strode ahead, treading the beaten path worn with crumbled stones sullen with the stain of time.

Shadows darted across drab buildings standing three metres high. The swirling wind carried the toxic flecks of paint shed like a winter coat. Windows were cracked like the broken Earth reflected in its panel shards.

Stooped Human shapes seemed to glide across the ground as if the coming darkness of night would envelop them. There was fear in every enervated eye that blinked under spluttering streetlamps. Lilianna felt an uneasiness about her now, but it seemed to propel her forward. Light footfall until her hand squeezed Juniper's real hand.

"Do we know where we're going?" she whispered with dread.

Juniper turned, her ears rimmed with a pale pink from the coarse sand and the pain of betrayal. "I thought I'd be able to find what we needed but I'm just…lost."

Lost.

Lost in the labyrinth of a half-ruined dystopian city. Lost in unknown questions that made Lilianna's stomach churn. She recalled Juniper's bursts of anger as they walked the sand dunes toward the town.

"I knew there was someone in the crew. I knew it!"

"When did you suspect something?"

"When I had to kill Maraudar." Juniper stopped as it dawned on her. "It was him! Massy made the call and tried to get us caught." She scratched the stubble on the shaved side of her head. "But why?"

'I can't believe it. He was our…friend" Lilianna's hair streamed behind her like a sun-streaked sky.

"Xan didn't think it was anyone. Couldn't fathom anyone betraying him. What an idiot. Look at us now."

"Hang on, did you discuss this with him?"

Juniper almost looked ashamed. "I needed him to acknowledge the possibility."

Lilianna turned away, hurt. Another instance of being on the outside.

"There was no need to bother you at—"

"Don't lie to me," Lilianna snapped. "Especially now."

"I wanted to be sure of who to trust. You were never on my radar, but I wanted to keep the circle small."

"You mean, not a circle at all."

Juniper let fly expletives. "I don't want to deal with you crying about some unimportant shit right now. If you can't keep it together at least until we find this person, then keep your mouth shut."

She stormed off.

Once united in grief, now separate in anger.

Lilianna had turned so many thoughts over in her mind. The jealousy burnt, the anger simmered in a cauldron of disbelief and the worry floated on the surface, surprisingly more potent than anything else. But she held onto Juniper as her tether to home.

She'd abruptly turned her back on her soulbond mere hours ago—a part of her life that had made her question everything on Gemarine. It had shaped who she was, what she had allowed herself to become. Maybe a drunken orgy with an impressionable Valkor last night was not her greatest moment, but shedding the shackles of who she had desperately tried to be felt liberating. The problem was, without the lasting effects of the alcohol to dim the emotions and to stave off the regrets, she was more than free, she was exposed. Maybe she could have spent some time mourning that loss instead of drenching herself in male fluid.

Juniper grunted as she led Lilianna into what appeared to be another dead end. Sheer walls enclosed them both, eclipsing the light of the moon. Two meek feathers caught in a nest of thorns.

Turning to find another way out, they were stopped in their tracks. Figures rose from speckled shadows to hulking ghouls. They weaponised themselves with flexing fists away from their sides. Sneers, glowering eyes, tongues lashing their top lips, salivating for what was on display.

Fear snaked through Lilianna, activating a thrumming pulse while stealing her stale breath. The feeling in her stomach was as if she were falling from a great height, flapping wildly and unsuccessfully.

Lilianna noticed Juniper tense beside her. The Cranston ray gun was only charged at five percent, so they'd both be relying on the exoblades to defend them.

Would that be enough against five or six assailants?

She didn't get to finish the lingering thought when a figure launched from the mighty wall behind them and crashed on top of Juniper, knocking her to the ground.

Lilianna screamed, shrill with pure terror.

The ray gun was knocked from Juniper's grasp immediately and it slid across the ground resting in a divot in the concrete. The figures ignored the weapon, pouncing on Juniper instead. Three strong Humans restrained her as she spat, swore, and flailed with determination and adrenalin. Two others came for her. She wrenched an arm free and tried to spin away. One male with a scarred cheek and bald head seized Juniper's throat. "Ooh dis one have kick." He squeezed harder. "Ya like dis, whore?"

Lilianna crawled desperately along the earth, a gangly spider inching up frosted leaves. Her shaking hand grasped the ray gun, and she flicked the charge up, hyperventilating. Two men pointed at her, "She got sumthin'."

Lilianna closed her eyes and a bolt sizzled from the weapon in her hand. An extension of her chaotic heartbeat.

Her eyes peeled open. The man had loosened the grip on Juniper's throat. A hole had eradicated his left eye, the depressed cheek torched and hollowed out. Charcoal coated the edges of the wound, and he flopped to the ground, wisps of smoke slithering like an uncoiling snake atop his head.

Juniper kicked into gear, twisting free of their grasp, finger blades embedded in a throat beside her, elbowing a nose behind her. Prompted by the flurry of action, Lilianna shot again, this time at the man with a dagger held aloft, seconds from plunging it into Juniper's guts.

Cavernous chest, incinerated heart. He dropped on top of the other body.

The remaining men started forward, but a couple of flashes ahead felled them. Two silhouettes stood. A Human and another smaller, more bizarre body. Their saviours inched into moonlight.

Lilianna gasped. She couldn't believe her eyes.

CHAPTER 27

"**M**aster Xan, I'm sorry to say this."

"Just spit it out, Arcadie!" The sirens were gathering like a murder of crows. Mock laughter from high on a thorny branch.

"Spit?" Arcadie asked.

Xan couldn't have been more frustrated. Surrounded by an alien creature who didn't speak, a robot who didn't understand colloquialisms and one who stared blankly, unable to help.

"Just tell me."

The pixels of his eyes shifted. "It was Massy. Massy killed the professor."

Xan didn't know how to react. His only thought was *how*? How was that possible?

He crouched down on the ground, sucking in huge breaths, orientating his spinning mind. Qilin pounced on top of him, licking his cheek, showing that she was there during this freakout.

"Sorry to interrupt your…ah…mental breakdown, but those sirens are getting closer." Fleurah paced nervously.

"I've hacked into the surveillance network and it looks like the police are approximately five minutes away."

Xan took a deep breath to consider his moves. "Okay. Arcadie, book a rideshare down the street. Let's run there now." He turned to run but halted, "Wait, Arcadie do your little transformer thing and get back into the bag!"

Arcadie went into ultimate conservation mode, where his head collapsed into his body and his arms retracted so he looked just like a tech cube. In this form, Fleurah stuffed him into her pack and hoisted him onto her shoulders.

They each bolted out of the office, not bothering to sanitise anything. The stairs trembled with their intent. Eyes aimed forward undeterred.

Sliding into the rideshare, the driver spoke in Cantonese. "Mon Kok area, right?"

"Yes, please."

Xan whispered into the bag, "Did you book somewhere already?"

Half of Arcadie's faceplate emerged. "I'm extremely productive." The coordinates flashed up on the screen, and Xan noted it down for when the driver dropped them off.

Police cars flashed past. Red and blue lights painted in splashes on stark skin. But they faded as the car surged through streets moving away from the dead professor and the university.

Now was the time to consider how Massy had done it. Xan realised it would've been their hike through the canyon on Sytheria that had allowed him to do it.

While Dallis and Xan collected the energy source into packs, Massy had moved forward in time and killed the professor. He came back to

Sytheria, picked them up at the canyon while being pursued by space spiders and then took them back to the exact ruined timeline on Earth. Massy wanted their mission to fail. But why? The obvious conclusion was that he was connected to Madame Bleu. What did she have over him? Or what had she promised him?

Xan would not be deterred. Yes, the professor who had a platform to the scientific world was gone, but that didn't mean all avenues were closed.

The modern apartment was fit for purpose. A barrage of white like the flash of an explosion hit them as they opened the door on the forty second floor. Each filed in and sat around the small circular table made of double paned glass. Fleurah unzipped her bag and Arcadie emerged like some man-made zombie.

"Just want to say, you did a great job getting us out of there, Arcadie."

Arcadie's cheeks flushed scarlet rectangles in embarrassment, "It was nothing." He paused. "But I did have to hack into the entire Hong Kong cloud network, reroute the—"

"This isn't the time to pause for praise, buddy." Fleurah rubbed his lower back. He looked up at her solemn expression and understood.

"We have failed the mission and we are stuck on Earth. There is no way Massy is coming back for us. Which means Lilianna, Juniper, Ryker and Dallis will most surely be either dead or displaced." Fleurah wiped a tear away.

Xan was certain that if Juniper and her cohort were lost in time, then they couldn't fail their mission. Could he bury something in a crypt that they could use? Get a message to them so that Juniper knew he tried everything he could before he died wrapped in wrinkles and thin grey strands of wispy hair.

"I know how to make sure our mission doesn't fail," Xan declared.

"How could you? The professor is dead."

"He wasn't the only way to release the climate formula."

It wasn't easy developing the formula for saving the world. Since Xan had glimpsed it in the crystal vision, he only needed Mingyung's research to put it all together. Many might have said, couldn't any scientist have thought of this? Couldn't any scientist have placed that final piece in the puzzle?

Truth be told, they *might* have been able to do it. But Xan had been studying xenobiology with advanced technology on Gemarine for years now. He had extensive experience with climate control on Germaine and an understanding of how different organisms reacted to changes in climates and atmospheric pressures. There was no one better to place that final piece.

After Arcadie played the footage of Massy murdering the professor, Xan told him to scrub all video evidence from the cloud. This included everything that captured Xan, an alien creature dressed as a dragon, and an alien and her robot hacking genius.

While Qilin and Fleurah played quietly on the lounge, watching the disturbing details of the murder as well as political riots that flared every so often, Arcadie fed Xan with the banquet of data from Professor Mingyung's archive. The research consisted of what Mingyung had been working on. The professor had explored many avenues and possible inventions that could assist the world in combating adverse climate effects. Xan was extremely proud—proud of what the professor had done and proud that he would be able to complete his legacy.

After two days of scouring the archives, finalising the patent for Mingyung's technology, completing the formula and ordering dim sum, Cheung fun, BBQ pork buns and mango pancakes to their room, Xan was ready for the final piece.

CHAPTER 28

LOCATION: EARTH
YEAR: 2036
XAN – 24 YEARS OLD

Xan sat before a crisp white wall. The Guó huà paintings that once hung proudly had been taken off the wall and placed into another room. Paintings of landscapes depicted spring, blossoming flowers on branches that dangled over miniature streams, the Huaniaohua with dancing cranes beside a lake, flush with lotus flowers and a sprawling orchid that emerged from the bottom of the scroll like an unfurling palm.

They were far from a lake now, but Xan was internally reflective instead. He was surprisingly calm knowing his broadcast would be watched by the world. The nervousness didn't plague him; he was excited to finally complete the mission. The mission that was meant to be completed by Professor Mingyung.

Xan had only come to Earth to finish the research, collaborate and let the professor take this into the future. But he had been murdered and now Xan would deliver the gift to the world.

Xan wore all white, hoping to blend in with the wall. He knew that if Juniper ever saw the broadcast, she would call him McBoringFace or something, because it wasn't extravagant enough, but he wanted his location and identity secret. He wore a red Jing mask to hide his facial features. The red mask was a specific choice. It symbolised loyalty, courage and righteousness –

all important to the overall cause that he was championing.

Arcadie was the cameraman or camera bot. He streamed the video from Professor Mingyung's social media account onto every little section of the web, bypassing any blockages erected by the government.

Xan, underneath the Jing mask, explained the legacy of Mingyung to the masses.

"The following patents and formulae are the life work of Professor Mingyung. Upon his untimely death, I was tasked to reveal the formula for combating climate change. It is a three-pronged approach that contains patented technology and bioengineering that, once enacted, will rectify issues created by Human footprint. When this approach is utilised, it will ensure the preservation of our way of life, as well as the other vulnerable species under our care."

Arcadie changed the camera angle, showing a summary of the three-pronged approach.

"Upon the screen you will see three things that can be put into place immediately. All calculations have been tested thoroughly and will prove to be successful within approximately three to five years. The first is a large network of high-level CO_2 exterminators that can be built in space. Their task will be to gather CO_2 in the atmosphere and store it through both geologic sequestration and biologic sequestration. Geologic sequestration will be carbon that we can store in porous rock formations on Mars and the moon. Biologic sequestration will be stored in vegetation and soil on Earth, thus further ensuring that carbon is neutralised through encouraging more biomass. If this is completed on a mass scale the temperature of the earth will not rise further."

The screen shifted to point number two, showing the details of a synthetic energy source code.

"The second point will contribute to the burning of fossil fuels. There is a synthetic energy source code that Mingyung has developed. If this is replicated, it provides at least 100 times the energy than all fossil fuels combined. All carbon neutral. This measure is an insurance that the planet's CO_2 emissions remain stable regardless of the CO_2 exterminator's success rate. Furthermore, there will be no need to burn fossil fuels any longer. The energy source code will enable jobs within the clean energy industry and if you transition into this industry within the first three years all your re-education will be paid for."

Arcadie changed the screen.

"The third point refers to nanobots and plastic eating enzymes deployed in the arctic. Nanobots will refreeze and stabilise unstable ice fields and then the enzymes will start to break down any plastic material found in and around the sea. This ensures the water levels remain, and ecosystems are kept in check. This point reinforces that our planet is shared and therefore anything that we implement will have a positive effect on not only Human lives, but the lives of animals that we directly affect."

The screen changed to a current satellite of the Earth spinning in orbit.

"There are things that everybody can do to lessen the effect that we all have on the environment. Find alternatives to overfishing, use biodynamic alternatives to plastic, greenify your urban environment, understand what biophilia is and maintain that connection to the natural world around us."

Xan spoke the last line with deep reverence: "Professor Mingyung believed in us to do the right thing and now we stand on the cusp of ensuring future generations will not only live on, but they will thrive in relative harmony with our environment. Do not forget that even though you are a singular being, what you do can make a lasting difference."

The camera feed went dead, replaced by a website where all the technologies were available for download. They provided information on how full funding had been made available in cryptocurrency syphoned from millions of accounts across the world, made untraceable by Arcadie. Applications would need to be filled out for Xan and Arcadie to approve which private companies would be suitable to commence the project.

The question remained – how would they have known that the projects would go as planned? How would they have been able to monitor and test whether everything would go off without a hitch? Maybe it was a blessing that they were stuck in this timeline, so they could all oversee Earth's safety.

Fleurah had just finished her fourth crispy pork bun and tossed the last one to Qilin, who gobbled it up with delight. "So now you've saved the world, oh mighty one, how the shit are we going to save my sister and the others?"

Xan was exhausted. The last week had taken its toll on him. He hadn't slept in days, evidenced by ashen, bloodshot eyes, and he hadn't actually figured out what to do past creating a time capsule care pack he could bury in the same coordinates they would be landing in 2114. But what would that matter? Put in a few knives, a gun and a little love letter. What would be the point?

"I've come up with a solution," Arcadie said, clawed fingers clasped on the table. Qilin sniffed around him hunting a dumpling on the table.

"Who would've thought a robot from Sytheria would be so influential in saving Earth!" Fleurah knocked him on the arm, which startled the robot. "I'm proud of you."

Arcadie chuckled bashfully.

Xan sat back and folded his arms. "Well, let's hear it then, buddy."

He glanced at Xan briefly, then Fleurah and an audible whimper escaped him. His eyes were squeezed down in sadness, worrying Xan. "I need to be here on Earth when Lilianna is abandoned."

"What do you mean? We don't even know if anything—"

"If they had overpowered Massy, they would have come back by now, but they haven't." Arcadie interrupted.

The silence was a scar carved by Fleurah. It lingered. It tainted supple skin. Words could blemish and maim, but in this case they remained unheard.

"Please say something." Arcadie's voice was a feathered pillow.

Fleurah turned to the window. The sunlight kissed the freckles on her nose, the blemish that trailed down her cheek, the strawberry blonde dreads that were swept across one shoulder like Lilianna always did. It kissed her, but it didn't soothe her.

Qilin slumped down at Xan's feet; her search for more food had been futile. Xan tried to take the focus away from Fleurah. "What do you propose then?"

"I need to be there in the time and place where they appear, just to make sure they're okay. I can help ferry them from the desert. You know it's the right thing to do."

Suddenly Fleurah erupted, "Why are you doing this? Everyone in my life has left me. You were the only real family I had, why would you—"

"Fleurah, I...love...you or at least you are the person that has taught me how I think love feels. But you also taught me lots of other things and one of them was that you always strive to do what is right, even if it's the most difficult thing."

Fleurah burst into tears and Qilin leapt up using her front paws to scratch her thighs lovingly, blinking concern in her whisky eyes.

Xan stood up and kissed Fleurah on the cheek, patting her shoulder. "C'mon, Qilin, let these two have a bit of one-on-one time."

Qilin dropped to the floor and crawled over to Xan as they left Arcadie and Fleurah to grieve their impending separation and share some moments together before the end.

Xan realised it was the time capsule plan in action. Arcadie would be a living time capsule helping a long-lost sister and a stranger who he knocked out with a taser bolt. To say that these actions were noble was an understatement.

This AI shows more heart than half the other aliens I know. Isn't that what sentient species are known for? Their heart, compassion, empathy? If a circuit board shows more of these emotions than we do, there is a problem that needs fixing.

CHAPTER 29

LOCATION: EARTH
YEAR: 2114
LILIANNA – 22 YEARS OLD

The crescent moon was a sickle, an omen of death, overseeing the corpses in the alleyway. The horde of dilapidated buildings watched as well; their fossilised remains haunted the present just as much as they mourned the past.

The Cranston ray gun chirped like a forsaken broodling as the battery life ebbed away. It had served its purpose. Lilianna's heart still beat furiously inside her chest; her hands were polar ice caps trembling into the sea. Bile had climbed into her throat and her eyes watered as she swallowed it down. Juniper sucked in large breaths on her hands and knees and turned to their saviours.

They inched forward so the moonlight exposed their identities. Lilianna gasped. Her eyes were surely liars.

"Arcadie!" Lilianna's voice was hoarse. Not only had the fear sucked the moisture from her mouth but so too, the exhausting walk through the desert.

"No time for pleasantries, follow us." His tone was controlled, more refined Lilianna considered, in that first, brief interaction.

The robot and a feminine figure draped in flowing silk sped off, coaxing them onwards through the dusty streets devoid of synthetic light.

Juniper held out her hand to Lilianna and she grasped it tightly. It stemmed the tremors of adrenalin still pulsing through her nervous system, but the frantic beating of her heart thumped in her ears like the soundtrack of fear.

Striking red boots the colour of anger flicked dust in the air. Arcadie and the woman moved through the mist to a walkway lined in chain linked fence. Arcadie held open a rusty door and they all piled inside with haste.

The woman in the cowboy boots slammed the door shut. Metallic clicks echoed in the room behind as locks snapped tight. The lights in the ceiling glowed like nubile fireflies and slowly filled the room.

The woman had olive skin and hazy emerald eyes, a copper hijab tied around the top of her head and neck for protection from the sun. But it had a way of framing the dainty features on her face, the tip of her nose drooping slightly; her lips were full, pursed together before she took a deep breath in. Releasing the hijab, hair like burgundy wine fell onto her back, long and messy.

"Guess it's awkward doin' proper intro's n'all, but imma Amani Ba'ashari." She nodded quickly, as if pressed for time. "Arcadie found me long ago to prep me for this mo' right now." She choked on her words. "Soz, it's just…I've been waitin' sah long."

"So long?" Lilianna spluttered. "I don't understand."

"Can 'splain if wantin'," Amani said.

Juniper stepped forward, shielding Lilianna. "I think we just need to rest and refuel. We were pretty fucking lucky to get away with…both our lives." She didn't look at anyone in particular but cast her gaze across the living quarters. In the desert, consumed by betrayal, Juniper had been beyond inconsolable, letting her anger faucet burst in Lilianna's face. She still seemed on edge but there was an unspoken apology in her recent actions. "Is there anywhere to …bed down and we can figure out everything in the morning?"

"Sure, sure." Amani waved her hand dismissively. "Arcadie, could ya help 'em to—"

"You don't have to tell me even once." He smiled in that pixelated pattern Juniper had come to understand over the few days of knowing him.

"Follow me you two!" he said cheerily, tottering on low thrusters toward an enclosed room at the back of the living space. "Please don't mind Amani's speech—language has um…well, devolved over time, so it takes a bit to comprehend."

Juniper turned to Amani before following the robot. "In the morning we'll catch up properly, but I'll just say…thanks for stepping in there at the end."

Amani didn't say anything. She bowed her head and gave a nonchalant grin as if it was all in a day's work for her.

She's not a warrior like Juniper, who washes all who are in the vicinity in a violent bath of blood, but a strength lurks within. Like a geyser, actively working below the surface until an explosion is imminent.

Lilianna settled into accepting that despite her soft tone, Amani's face was hard and within the emerald eyes sparkled a warning that said, *Don't underestimate me.*

Lilianna's heart was beating against her chest as she remembered firing the gun, watching Juniper get ambushed and feeling so helpless. It was dark inside the room, and she had just woken up, sweating under sheets that constricted her, just like her heart had been when she killed those men.

Juniper was at her side within a second. Hand on her back, pulling her in close, soothing her as she cried.

"Oh my stars," Lilianna breathed, tears welling in her eyes. "What did I do?"

Unable to process her actions in the moment, it spilled out of her now. The sheer desperation, the mindless decision to shoot. To be a saviour. Within the nightmare there was a flicker of light, of something… beautiful.

Juniper pulled back and stared at Lilianna, holding her palms in hers. "You saved me. You went against who you were and killed someone to save me. Why?"

Lilianna stared at her lips then into her eyes and recalled Juniper's tongue sliding across her skin. She immediately bit her bottom lip. The danger, the thought of losing her had evoked…desire.

"Because."

"Because why?"

Did she want to admit this?

Juniper was an intimidating figure, and Lilianna was wildly inexperienced in all facets of acting upon desire. What did it really mean to possess the courage to utter words?

Lilianna considered the many things that she had done just to get to where she was now; manipulating Zondini, travelling through time, forsaking her soulbond, allowing her body to roam free, killing in self-defence. It all paled in comparison to simply speaking.

"Because, I…couldn't live without you."

"Is that right? You *need* me?"

"Yes," she said, blonde hair falling over her face like moonlight after dusk. The silence lingered between them, as Juniper's fingers crawled like vines, entwining with Lilianna's.

"What else do you need?"

"I need…you…to…kiss me."

Before Lilianna finished, Juniper grabbed at the back of her hair, and they kissed as if the winds encircled the desert of the wilds, whipping around their faces and emblazoning them together. Their lips were pressed like rose petals in a closed fit, the perfume of passion filling them and fuelling them. Juniper's tongue flirted with Lilianna's, caressing and soft, surprisingly sensual. Time called an intermission as they flowed into one another.

Juniper's fingers curled into a squeeze at the back of her neck; the kiss became more forceful, more desperate. Lilianna climbed on top of Juniper, cupping her cheeks, wanting to taste her sweetness, craving it as if she had a nutrient deficiency. Sugar was on her lips and Lilianna licked each granule, spiking energy levels and desire. The two females moaned and sighed in a crescendo of ecstasy, each daring the other to explore the full range of what they could produce.

Juniper accepted the dare, reaching for Lilianna's zipper. The slow descent of the zipper sent chills down Lilianna's side, her stomach twisting with butterflies as her breasts were exposed to the frigid air in the ground floor room. Her nipples hardened by the kiss of air. Juniper wet her tongue with a string of saliva and licked them slowly and decisively, so Lilianna felt every tingling sensation arrest her. Juniper pulled the zipper further down with her mouth pressed against her chest. Lilianna loved the attention on her, whimpering and begging for more.

"Fuck me, Juniper. Please," Lilianna whispered to the peeling concrete on the wall, as she massaged the mess of Juniper's curly hair.

Juniper flicked a switch on her exo hand and rubbed up and down Lilianna's slit. A small vibrating sensation spread across the area, and Lilianna let out a cry and bit down on Juniper's lip.

"Oh, you like this, do you?" Juniper said, her face right up against hers, licking Lilianna's quivering bottom lip, as she slowly pushed inside her. Lilianna folded into herself like crumpled wrapping paper, her eyes flitting with the rising tingles that radiated outwards from her wetness down her twitching legs.

"How?" is all she managed to say through stifled groans, gritting her teeth against Juniper's lips, her tongue, across the valley of her neck and back to a flickering, teasing kiss.

"Being modified has its advantages." Her sensual voice spoke into Lilianna's neck.

Lilianna didn't hear her properly. The feeling of deep vibrating pulses thrumming violently and trailing off pushed through her. The intensity bubbled up from deep within, rising with each strong beat and the echoes that followed. She tried to keep herself neutral but Juniper's two fingers were surrounding her sweet spot, slowly crowding with gentle movement at the same time her other hand was working magic. The absence of pressure directly on the spot was enhancing both modes of pleasure, and she savoured Juniper's intuition to treat her to a languorous time, rather than something forceful and frantic.

As the penetrative intensity increased, and the fingers closed around Lilianna's spot, her breathing quickened, her toes started to feel numb as the potent crest of the wave inside her body threatened to break. Juniper hissed, "Let go, let it go."

Lilianna's body lost control with a strong orgasm. She convulsed from her legs to her arching back, eyes rolling into the back of her head until she collapsed forward onto Juniper, making sounds she had seldom made before.

Lilianna, panting and spent, brought her forehead to Juniper's and kissed her in vibrant bursts as she tried to catch her breath and refocus her body wracked with nerves brimming with delight.

Lilianna whispered, "I want to taste you."

"Oh you do, do you?' Juniper teased, her tongue skirting the edges of Lilianna's lips.

"I've never done it before, though."

"I'll tell you what to do." Juniper unzipped carefully. Lilianna didn't hesitate putting delicate kisses across each morsel of skin she revealed.

"Is this what you like?" Lilianna accentuated the eye contact with Juniper as she carefully licked across her exposed, hardened nipples.

"Yes, girl. Suck them and bite them."

Lilianna obeyed, giving Juniper what she wanted. In the moans of her fusing partner, she felt validated, wetter and eager to please.

She threw the rest of Juniper's suit across the floor. Lilianna knelt, looking over Juniper and feeling her attraction to this woman well deep inside of her.

JUNIPER
24 YEARS OLD

Juniper felt Lilianna's delicate hands trail over her, moving around her navel to the insides of her thighs.

Part of her wanted Lilianna's tongue and fingers to be inside of her already, but then the other part that felt the goose bumps, that gave her butterflies in her stomach, told her to wait.

Lilianna positioned herself in between her legs, giving her a long solitary lick upwards, flicking her clit. Juniper felt a sharp pang from within and let out a delicate moan. Lilianna made eye contact with her, smiling and repeating the action, this time placing one careful finger inside.

Juniper bundled the bedsheets in a white-knuckled grip. "You wanna taste me, babe, then taste me."

Lilianna moved down, extending her tongue out further with a finger still inside Juniper. She felt the wandering tongue explore and tease, then end more forcefully, pushing upwards against her clit. Another sharp echo of pleasure thumped through her. Juniper was surprised at her reaction, and at Lilianna's intuitive play.

"Is that okay?" Lilianna frowned impishly, her golden eyes prying.

"Do you like what you taste?" Juniper arrested soft strands of Lilianna's blonde hair, weaving it through her fingers.

"Yes. Can I taste more?"

She played the submissive whore well, much better than Juniper could. Juniper couldn't help but respond violently, like an internal switch flicked, changing her from sensual to slutty in an instant. She grabbed Lilianna by a knot of hair and pushed her down onto her pussy. "Show me what a good girl you can be."

"Mmmm, yes, Juniper," she tried to say, with her tongue buried deep.

The eagerness with which Lilianna pursued Juniper's pleasure was what sent her over the edge. She was attentive to Juniper's movements and her moans, and became malleable to being positioned just where Juniper liked it. When Juniper had finished and she tasted herself on Lilianna's lips with an erotic, sensual kiss, it was painfully sweet to share the moment with her.

Juniper draped an arm around Lilianna's naked body, pulling her in close. Under sheets of dusty white, they closed their eyes in a world where at least they had one another.

CHAPTER 30

LOCATION: EARTH
YEAR: 2114
JUNIPER – 24 YEARS OLD

Arcadie was busy at the small kitchenette preparing some food for Lilianna and Juniper. Amani and Juniper spoke in hushed tones about the state of all things. Although Xan's patented technology and 'formula' for reversing and stemming the effects of climate change had been successful, the deeper issues of the inhabitants of Earth had ultimately led to the demise of modern society. The disparity between classes and religion were the main causes.

Gone were the days of sitting on fences, a mild nuisance to the rectum from a wooden impaling – the left swung all the way to the end of the road and the right went so far across the barren strip of compromised ground that it was no longer tended or cared for in any way. Then, the sturdy walls of religion were erected, steeples so sharp they could cut, stained glass windows so potent they coloured the soul with tunnel vision. All of a sudden, beliefs weren't sacred anymore, they were tyrannous.

Gods conjured to unite further accentuated the divide, and before the world knew it, people with crosses adorning their necks spoke with bullets rather than sermons. Society collapsed in on itself and the world was thrown into disarray.

Amani held a high commander position in the army, the same army that served with a heavy hand to maintain decorum. At nightfall the feeling of safety diminished considerably and anyone on the street during that time was left to their own devices. Juniper and Lilianna were a perfect example.

In a few weeks, there would be a coming together of leaders across the united globe to present options for peace or compromise. This event would be where Amani would have to table the idea of the factions and the Watchers. If she didn't succeed, civilisation would commit further crime.

"Okay, this is what you need to propose." Amani shifted closer and leant forward. Juniper did the same, swaying her arms rhythmically like a conductor. Her orchestra was the future, Amani the first violinist embarking on a solo so rapid, so beautiful, so technically demanding that the crowd would shower her with applause and long-stemmed roses. But it was the conductor part that halted Juniper from a celebratory dance. She was used to participating, being the key player in that troupe, certainly not directing or watching from the sidelines. How would she become a mentor, give up control and leave it in the hands of, frankly, inferior individuals?

She swallowed her pride and regurgitated just a tiny bit of humility, letting it sit on her tongue as she recalled parts of their vision:

Red, green and grey colours distributed as totems for each faction, as far as the sun's reach.

An office door with the symbol of an eye and the text, "The Watchers" scrawled beneath.

"You need to propose factions, my dear child." Juniper added the last part for sarcasm. It felt appropriate.

The factions would allow the world to separate into different colours based on their political and spiritual ideologies. Countries, continents and cultures wouldn't matter. Each colour would be given territories to reign over and do with their land and systems as they would. The strength of unity is in shared ideals, and it would be no different here. Only unity wouldn't be shared between the entire Human race.

It was a shame that it came to this, but decades couldn't pacify the storm. Gale winds blew, bullets continued to maim or kill. The only common ground Humans have is disharmony. No idealist could deny that. So instead of sowing the seeds of tranquillity in killing fields, they'd have to build communities on common ground instead.

Red colours would represent right-wing beliefs, grey colours would represent left wing beliefs while green would encompass new ideologies that could not be categorised but had the means to coexist.

Not everyone would be easily placed into a bucket and left to live a life of perfection, which was why the Watchers were important. It wasn't an Orwell, big brother type of watcher. It was a softer approach of law enforcement that ensured various members of the factions were held accountable for their behaviour and adhering to faction policies and ideals.

This was the reason Juniper was taken from her timeline to Gemarine. Putting an end to year after year of war upon war, this would repair the world. It was a radical measure, but the world was radically declining. In desperation, Humans often made such choices to ensure their dominance persisted.

Ideals are often born from a defiant raised fist. Remedies soothe with open palms willing to clasp another. Both can repair a broken system. Both permeate flesh and bone.

"Lilianna let's—"

Arcadie zoomed over to Juniper and put a metal digit across her lips. She was about to grab his metal phalange and crush it flat with the strength of her boronium grip, but he pointed with the other hand to Lilianna curled up in the corner, dead asleep.

"Poor thing has been through so much."

Juniper considered this. Farewelling her soulbond, departing from Xan, trekking across a desert, killing a man or two, having bomb-ass sex with a female… "Fuck," she whispered. By Juniper's lofty standards, she had to admit that was a heavy couple of days.

Arcadie nodded, smiling with curved pixels as he looked wistfully at Lilianna but also most likely into the distant past through neurons weaved throughout his circuitry.

"I always admired Lilianna's strength," he mused.

Juniper's arms folded across her chest as she looked at him. "Strength, you say?" she uttered doubtfully.

If he noticed her defiance, he ignored it. "There was a time I had neglected to take better care of Fleurah when she was younger. Lilianna scolded me for it."

"Well, I suppose if you were built for a purpose and you didn't fulfill that, she was entitled to be pretty pissed."

"It was more that she put trust in me to look after her sister, and I wasn't able to understand back then how much love informs care, concern and protection."

"Well, what did she say?" Juniper let her hands rest on her thighs.

"That she would never leave me alone with Fleurah until I looked after her just like Lilianna did. It took me years, but the day before she left for good, she sat me down and said…" He searched the ceiling, recalling the moment. "'I'm proud of you for listening, for wanting to be better. I know now that if anything were to happen to me, I could count on you to look after Fleurah as I would. You're family now, Arcadie, and don't forget it.'"

Juniper nodded. "That's a…nice…thing to say." She wasn't used to talking in niceties.

"You know she isn't just *nice*," Arcadie protested. "When she stands next to you or Xan, maybe she doesn't stand as tall or flex her muscles in the same way, but there is a strength within that permeates any group hierarchy. In the important moments the ones who love hardest, will never back down."

"What does love have to do with anything?"

"By now, I'm surprised you haven't acknowledged that love is the most powerful of motivators. She loves harder than any of you. *That's* what makes her strong. Love makes you do things that defy logic, defy your own physical limitations."

"What do you know of love, Arcadie, let's be real?" As soon as she said it, she felt bad. Like she was mocking someone who had three eyes all pointing in the same direction. Being born with a limitation shouldn't elicit ridicule.

A computerised groan scrambled in the air. "I have observed two different worlds over many, many years. I've seen what brings us all to the brink, what makes us want to leap off the edge and what makes us want to turn around and fight. The more I observe, the more I learn, and the more I learn, the more I begin…to feel."

Juniper swallowed, thinking of RC-9 cleaning her level on Gemarine, smiling at the bundle of circuits and even patting it just to make it feel… worth something. Before her sat the most functional AI she had ever encountered and yet she doubted him. "I…apologise. I barely even know you. I didn't give you much of a chance—"

He cut her off. "A lot has happened in the time I've spent with Amani. But who or what would I be if I didn't evolve? I live because I learn, and the moment I stop is the moment that true death will claim me."

Juniper felt his metallic fingers reach out for hers. They clinked together in an awkward way that a screw didn't quite fit inside of a hole; as it twisted, it gripped for a moment then slipped and fell away. But there was a kinship there. Metal on metal, heart against heart.

"Just remember that your strength isn't just in squeezing those fingers of yours against mine, rather, it's in the way you use your restraint to caress gently." Arcadie tried to wink; his face plate flickered.

Juniper smiled with a warmth that felt foreign on her face, abandoning the model-worthy pout. "You don't know shit, you little rust bucket." She knocked him on the head playfully.

After initially being startled, Arcadie carefully resumed his gaze. "Please though, remember this about Lilianna if you decide to move closer to her: she won't expect you to be anything other than yourself, but if you expect her to have altered her ways for you, so too must you consider breaking part of your vulnerability to let someone in. Someone other than Xan, of course."

With that he zoomed away and left Juniper staring after him and turning back to Lilianna as she slept. The golden eyes had retreated behind the clouds of her eyelids, blonde hair swept behind her neck in the way she always did. She gave an audible exhale like a wafting autumnal breeze through a ravaged orchard, expelling expired leaves on sodden earth. Juniper crept across the concrete and bent down, brushing a single, shining strand of hair from her forehead which made her stir. "Honey, let's get to bed."

"What?" Her voice was raspy and laced with peaceful dreams.

"I can't carry you, but we should go to bed, c'mon."

Juniper was suddenly very, very tired.

Lilianna rose, her hair falling across her face as Juniper cradled her in those strong arms and slid across the ground to the room where they had bound their bodies to one another.

When loneliness collided with lust, barriers dissolved. Bodies were miscible liquid forged as one entity. When lust succumbed to something more, what became of the heart as it sought to infuse with the rational mind?

Now, as they laid down to sleep, Lilianna put her head on Juniper's shoulder, her lips resting dangerously against her neck. But Juniper only brought her arm across to pull her tight, binding their hearts and minds together.

CHAPTER 31

LOCATION: PERIAH
YEAR: 118 GTC (GEMARINE TIME CYCLE)
MASSY – 25 YEARS OLD

The shuddering ceased as they were thrust out into Periah's atmosphere. The kinetic force of the energy tipped the *Attenborough* on its port side, its wing reaching toward the sky as if waiting to be pulled from the ravenous ocean.

Massy straightened the ship and turned across the cliff top in an arc. Sythkin craned her head against the window at the scene below. Bodies of her comrades were strewn across the landscape. Blood glinted like fresh fallen snow at first light. Massy caught her glance and recognised the opportunity to drive the nail of loyalty further into her aching heart. "Don't forget it," he said, keeping his hands taut on the yoke.

She looked at him, puzzled. "What do you mean?"

"I mean, don't forget this sight. The feeling that it evokes in you. Let that anger fizz and fuel your actions now. Make the bastards pay who did this to you."

It took a while for it to register within her, but she nodded slowly. "Yes, yes I will remember."

"I'm glad we've found each other." He turned to face her and smiled. "To unite the Cryptoborgs against the one true enemy—the Valkors and all their pathetic little conspirators."

"We are the hands of fate, right the wrongs." The Cryptoborg bowed with reverence.

Massy looked at her as he was bringing the ship down upon the surface. "The fuck is that?"

"It's a Cryptoborg mantra that we live by. We are very much concerned with doing the *right* thing."

Massy unclasped his buckle. "Well, you're definitely on the right side now." He laid a hand on her shoulder and squeezed. "I honestly can't wait for Madame Bleu to see that we have the Cryptoborgs as allies now. That's crazy."

He pressed the button to open the hatch, screwing on his MPD before trudging out onto the surface of Periah. "At least I'll be able to get a signal with this fucking thing now. Time to call Madame Bleu and warn her about all this—"

His boot had only just touched down on the surface when he felt the blow to the back of his head. Stars danced in his vision—not the beautiful shining gems holding all the secrets of time, but the sinister ones who called to him like sirens in the deep ocean of space. The stars clouded his periphery like burning flames across crinkled white paper. He didn't have time for thoughts before he fell into darkness. Thoughts were not important though; the feeling was important. He felt the ever-present need for revenge roil with greater fervour than ever before.

RYKER
21 YEARS OLD

Ryker heard the ramp open and Massy's boots shatter the rocks underfoot. He expected to remain encased in his tomb until his wretched aunty plucked him from his depression and strung him up against the red cliffs of Untiqua as a spectacle. But it was Sythkin who strode toward them. She walked straight to the lock, an MPD blinking on her wrist. A pleasing beep, the door released and a gust of air exhaled, the taste of liberty fresh upon Ryker's open mouth.

"Why?" he asked.

"We are the hands of fate, right the wrongs."

Dallis, used to speaking in tongues, inched forward. "What does this mean?"

Ryker turned to Dallis. "It means that, for some reason, she is on our side."

"I will explain all shortly, but we must hasten this getaway." Although she appeared calm, Ryker was aware that this was as chaotic as she would appear. There was a solitary bead of sweat tiptoeing across the wrinkles on her mauve forehead. Her blackened eyes were pits of doom, hard to decipher and harder still to endure. They followed her, Ryker doing his best to assist Dallis, who was shivering with venom sickness. They walked past the ramp, where Ryker acknowledged Massy lying flat on his face on the surface. Shallow breaths indicated he was still alive but there was no time to consider further action.

"Close the ramp and let's fly out," Sythkin announced.

Ryker was bewildered. "Do you know how to fly this ship?"

"I learnt by studying the fool as I was manipulating him."

Dallis started clapping and then faltered with his injured wrist. "So clever," he managed.

Ryker ignored him and pressed the button to close the hatch. "That's all well and good, but where are we going?"

"We must right the wrongs."

Ryker nodded slowly. "Which wrong comes first?"

"Your captain comes first."

CHAPTER 32

LOCATION: EARTH
YEAR: 2036
XAN – 24 YEARS OLD

Arcadie and Fleurah had their arms around one another. Fleurah's tears dripped onto Arcadie's metal body with a light tap.

Xan hovered impatiently, looking at Qilin and not wanting to hurry their acceptance of what was to come, but needing to feel like they were about to move forward.

Qilin saw the dripping tears down Arcadie's exterior, and she lapped at him before they absorbed into the carpet. Arcadie noticed her tongue on him and floated away, mortified. Qilin was equally unimpressed with the salty taste of the tears.

Xan was pleased that it was enough of a distraction. "Listen, both of you. I know this is going to be so hard but let's try and figure out a plan for the future. We can't stay here long term without arousing suspicion, and we need to know how long you'll be with us—"

Arcadie suddenly bolted upright. "They're here!"

"Who's here? The police?" Xan's stomach launched in somersaults. They'd been tracked from the murder site somehow.

"No, I'm detecting the *Attenborough's* signature. It's the darndest thing, it's…"

"What is it?" Xan pushed.

"Its beacon is signalling *me* specifically. Telling me to go to particular coordinates." He stopped for a moment, his face screen showing a calculation mode with spinning shapes. After the briefest of pauses, he exclaimed, as an arm shot into the air, nearly jolting straight up Fleurah's unsuspecting nose.

"The ferry terminal. They will be landing the cloaked ship on the helipad. You must go now!"

Xan grabbed Fleurah by the arm. "C'mon you heard him."

Fleurah yanked her arm back. "Not like this!" she cried. "We were meant to have more time."

"You don't understand, Fleurah; if the *Attenborough* is here, it means we can see Arcadie again almost instantly." He turned to Arcadie seeking encouragement, and the robot nodded with confidence.

"For you, it will only be hours or days. For me…it will be…well, a very long time."

"But, but…" she cried openly. "You will be different, you might not love me anymore."

Arcadie thrust forward quickly, making Qilin leap off back toward the comfort of Xan's lap. "Love is not some fickle thing. Love is forever. And *I* will be forever. So really, love is mine and I can give it to whoever I want. I choose you."

The rideshare car was down below. Arcadie nodded to Xan. Fleurah was already out in the hallway. She ripped off the Band-Aid, knowing she would see him without much time passing. Arcadie's reassurances were enough to placate her.

Xan hesitated at the open door, Qilin mirroring his faltered step. He didn't know what to say to the little guy. The robot had agreed to monitor the climate projects from afar to ensure a successful completion. Yet, he knew that when he saw Arcadie again after years buried under a sand-encrusted tomb, he would be very different. The sacrifice he was making for them was immeasurable. Braving the unknown world in an unknown time without his sister Fleurah for years. It was cruel to ask it, yet Arcadie did not falter.

The robot smiled.

Xan thought it was tinged with sadness, but how could pixels really show that? It must have been his imagination reflecting a Human response behind the multitude of dots collected on his faceplate.

Xan slammed the door behind him, knowing that if there was a way to ensure that he and Fleurah made it to the helipad, little Arcadie would be able to manipulate through networks to make sure it would happen.

Xan carefully closed the door of the car, avoiding the suspicious gaze of the driver trying to discern what was underneath the dragon costume in Xan's lap.

They all gazed at the top of the ferry terminal. A slight distortion rippled the harbour city beyond, and although it wasn't much of a confirmation, it was enough of one to solidify their intent.

Xan wondered though: if Massy had killed Professor Mingyung and then presumably stranded Juniper in the future, why would he be back?

Unless Juniper saw it coming and took him down before he had the chance?

Xan couldn't think of any other solution; she must have fucked him up. But why had it taken so long to come back?

Oh well. That counterfeit piece of shit deserved whatever Juniper had done to him.

It was nearly nine in the morning and the streets were brimming with commuters hellbent on their destination. He didn't miss that feeling. Being caught in a wheel, spinning mindlessly, trying with all their might to slowly die in mindless jobs that made rich people richer and syphoned every ounce of energy from the rest.

Then he remembered Gemarine was born from the ashes of genocide and sheepishly retreated into his little box until he could fix that issue.

As soon as Fleurah, Qilin and Xan entered the terminal, they began searching for directions to the helipad. But less than a minute into the task they were screeching, "Where the fuck do we go?" and "I can't see shit!" A piercing alarm blared overhead. There was an audible gasp from the crowd of ferry goers. When the alarm evolved into the dulcet warning tones of an evacuation procedure, all hell broke loose.

The trio clamoured up a set of steel stairs leading toward the roof. They were about to taste liberty on cracked lips malnourished by the death of hope. But hope remained as elusive as before, a bulky iron door stood with a malicious glean in its eye halting the way.

Fleurah kicked at the door. "Fuck!" she exclaimed.

Qilin leapt into the door in solidarity, scratching with claws that made raking scars across the facade but nothing more. She stumbled into the wall with the dragon costume around her head and then craned her neck trying to get the eye slits in the perfect position so she could see. All to no avail. Conquered by the dragon, she sat on her bottom and bowed her head.

Xan was seconds from decimating the access panel with his boot, but it suddenly flashed green and swung open. Air flushed the stairwell and the hair on his head blew chaotically. Xan turned his neck at the shock. The scent of the sea tickled him. A security camera fixed on top of the door caught his eye, and it all made sense.

Arcadie was inside the network watching them, guiding them back to the *Attenborough* safely. Xan blew the camera a kiss and the trio pressed forward onto the helipad, wind spraying the essence of the ocean water around their lips. The taste of salt and sweet liberty was like a perfectly balanced dessert. The ship's ramp lowered as they ran, and out stepped the Cryptoborg. Xan's heart sank.

But the feeling didn't last long. Ryker appeared over her shoulder. Qilin ran up the ramp and dove onto Ryker, who fell back laughing, trying to shield his face from the ferocious affection of Qilin's forked tongue. Fleurah laughed and wiped a tear from the corner of her eye.

"Where's Dallis?" Xan asked.

"He's in the regen chamber. I'm worried about the venom…he isn't getting better." Ryker's voice quaked.

Xan nodded. "Once we get inside, I'll start working on a solution." He turned his attention to the Cryptoborg, smiling at her.

Sythkin bowed low with reverence.

"So why the change of heart?"

"My heart was always pure."

Xan was taken aback. At first the comment was puzzling but then it registered.

He had known all along that Madame Bleu was the bad guy. He just didn't realise that she was the bad guy throughout their little part of the galaxy.

The Cryptoborgs were most likely caught in the murderous net cast out toward neighbouring planets in Bleu's maniacal pursuit of power and control. Thousands, millions of Cryptoborgs slaughtered by Gemarinians, by Juniper, and all for a lie.

He dreaded the thought; it made him sick. But Sythkin's thin, bony hand found his shoulder. "I'm beginning to see the truth. Gemarinians are not *all* monsters."

"Unfortunately, the monster was not revealed until very recently." Xan shook his head.

"We are the hands of fate and we right the wrongs."

Xan couldn't have said it better himself, but it was recited as if Sythkin stitched this phrase across the fabric of her soul.

"Is Juniper in—"

"Have no fear for your comrades, we will go forward and find them."

"Thank you."

"Let's go, no more delays."

Xan looked out across the harbour to Macau in the distance, furrowed by smog on the horizon. The return to his former home had been fraught with chaos from the first moment. On the cusp of departure, he was relieved to move forward in time. Leave his past for good. He didn't know what would become of his family, his former loved ones. But he hoped his formula would allow them to live fruitfully in the meantime, before humanity started to turn on one another.

He saluted a camera that he could see on the edge of the helipad, hoping Arcadie would know just how much he respected his sacrifice and how thankful he was. Ryker sidled up next to him and his dark eyes found his. He wasn't smiling. Xan put a strong arm around him and brought him close to his side.

"Xan I can't believe it, I'm so—" His voice quivered with sadness. Bitter sadness. True sadness that wouldn't abate with a silly joke or an awkward arm punch.

"Ryker, turn your thoughts away from Massy. We concentrate on what we can control, and we can control our path to save our girls and unite our family."

Ryker had more to say behind the rain-streaked windows of his eyes, but instead he nodded, pulling the blinds as he shifted away from Xan to walk beside him.

Xan would have carried him further, but he recognised the kid finding his strength, wanting to stand on his own feet and walk with him rather than let himself be carried. Before him, Ryker was realising his potential, just like Xan had always believed he would.

Sythkin shouted, "Buckle up please."

Wow, so polite. That certainly was a change.

They all listened to the Cryptoborg pilot.

As the ship rose, Xan's thoughts turned darker. The thing that he had told Ryker to forget was in his mind now, an infestation of hate bacteria. *Massy.* That piece of shit would die for what he did. Xan wasn't going to regret it when he ended him.

It was one thing to leave him to rot in the entrails of time, as fermenting formaldehyde bodies forgotten in evolution's exhibit. But to abandon Juniper and Lilianna on a dystopian Earth, years in the future…

Well, he should know, no one fucks with my girls.

But then again, Massy didn't see the Valkor massacre firsthand. He had run away like the little bitch that he was.

As the *Attenborough* jerked through the clouds, shuddering in a way that Massy never allowed it to, Xan felt doubts creep in. If he killed his former brother, a part of him would die, too.

Was revenge worth killing himself for?

ARCADIE
19 ROBOT YEARS

Arcadie watched as Xan bid him farewell via the camera feed, knowing and understanding that final look. He hadn't known Xan for long at all, but he felt privileged to learn from him. He would play back the important moments so it would be absorbed completely. Arcadie wanted courage to flood his circuits, wanted all the knowledge to help with rebuilding civilisations, but most of all, he wanted empathy to surge in every connection port so that he could give love to those who deserved it. There was an air of charismatic leadership to Xan, and Arcadie wanted to use that to convince others to do the right thing, rather than letting fear fuel intent.

He opened the apartment window and sped off into the sky, where the clouds migrated, moisture laden to areas that needed rain.

Calculating the longitude and latitude, he was readying to entomb himself in the desert for several years, monitoring the climate projects via weblinks. Then finally, when they were successfully up and around, he would go into conservation mode for a long, long time.

He would miss them all, but in stasis he wouldn't feel anything.

When he awoke and befriended the high commander, would he still feel the same about them all? About Fleurah?

Arcadie's battery system was made of Quantum-Lithium and would last around one hundred years. Once he charged himself down into conservation mode, he would have plenty left over when the internal alarm awoke him.

All of this was for a cause. Saving lives, the lives of his sister and crew mates that had taken him in despite a rocky start.

That was a worthy sacrifice.

Would he finally feel alive? Would the faux life that he had previously lived finally mean something? Where he could use what he'd learnt, the love he'd tended, and spread it into the wider parts of the world for an immense purpose?

In a galaxy crawling with sentient creatures, whose hearts flapped like tired wings or thumped with the passion of a saviour, Arcadie was heartless. But anthropomorphic qualities didn't make one infallible—he firmly believed that. His heart was made from an ideal and that ideal was written on the circuits within, connected by wires and nodes, stored in the great cloud of his consciousness.

The galaxy needed a guardian. A guardian made from more than skin and bone. The boundlessness of forever called to him, and he would answer the call brimming with hope, brimming with purpose. The galaxy would not just be for ephemeral creatures, the galaxy would be shared between them all.

When we share, we assume the collective responsibility of protecting what's ours.

Arcadie, the galaxy's robot protector. He liked the sound of that.

CHAPTER 33

LOCATION: EARTH
YEAR: 2114
LILIANNA - 22 YEARS OLD

They were in Amani's house for several weeks. Lilianna had heard about Fleurah, Qilin and Xan's final moments in Hong Kong recounted from Arcadie's perspective. He never saw who was piloting the *Attenborough,* but it was safe to assume that something had happened to Massy. After his betrayal she couldn't see him turning around and saying, "Yo, it was all a big joke! Totally gotcha!"

But then on second thought, she *could* imagine him doing that.

When she giggled about that, she had to untether the anchor of her memories. She would not be shipwrecked, rust accumulating on the hull, red eyes with a stern frown. The betrayal still stung.

Why would he have turned traitor? To what purpose? When did Madame Bleu get to him?

She shook her head in disappointment, and swallowed, stemming the wasteful tears. Massy wasn't worth tears.

The time had crawled in a way that almost felt relaxing, considering that over the last few weeks they had searched for the celestial crystals, located the portal on Periah and completed their first mission on Sytheria. During the day, Juniper and Amani would lock themselves away to develop their plan for the factions, detailing strategies and designing the makeup of the Watch.

Arcadie and Lilianna focused on learning the recent history of Earth. From when Xan's patents and formula were published to when private companies and governments began to work together to combat the climate crisis. Humans were the primary beneficiaries of the climate solution, but it also meant that other species on the brink of extinction were given chances to thrive again.

The cyber world war in 2056 plunged humanity into a dark age. Twenty-five years later the 'modern crusades' ravaged the world, causing its current desolation. Several Earthen regions were declared a nuclear zone and the threat of yet another attack stung the horizon with glowering clouds.

Despite what side people found themselves on, the horrifying effects of nuclear radiation acted as a deterrent, so it was a button seldom pressed.

It had pained Lilianna to learn of all this, but she felt a welling of admiration knowing that Juniper's work here would be crucial to setting Earth on a better path.

Arcadie and Lilianna ventured out into the town only a small number of times. Safety was an obvious concern. Each time, Lilianna couldn't help but stare at the dilapidated state of the buildings, the lack of greenery, the chains linked in metallic menace.

Each pair of eyes that met theirs were full of distrust. Shaking hands wielded blunt force weapons to use at a moment's notice. Bent figures dragged their shadows along the dusty sidewalks to the small canned goods store at the centre of the town square. The store was encased inside a steel cage; robot guards with arms crossed stood like statues glinting under the sun. Frozen until an indiscretion from a passer-by, at which they would awaken, yelling "indiscretion detected" over and over.

Having grown up in Sytheria and Gemarine, it was disappointing to see Earth in this way. Part of her felt pity and the other part felt gross in that pompous "I'm better than this neighbourhood" sort of way. She had tried desperately to see "the good" in the scene before her. The cute old lady in the second-hand clothes shop, with her halo of white ringlets brimming atop her head, the skinny resident bobcat who took opportunities to nab a stale bread roll tossed by the dumpster alley, the sunshine twinkling off the murky pool in the backyard without a fence. But even optimism itself got tired of painting positivity across the drab, melancholic scene.

Most nights after strategising for hours on end, Juniper would share the bed with Lilianna and teach her something new. She wouldn't be able to take the technical learnings and apply them to moments with Xan, but the essence would apply.

Overall, though, Juniper had surprised Lilianna. Never in the most nefarious of nightmares did she think that Juniper's heart beat for more than a good dicking. There were beautiful layers to be uncovered. Juniper appeared to be an island, stoic in the face of tsunamis, self-sufficient with all manner of flora and fauna, but a destination without fanfare. But one only had to venture to the other side where frangipani flowers floated in the azure shallows, abundant wildlife frolicked undisturbed by urbanisation, white sand kissed the trunks of coconut trees.

Before, I worshipped her strength and defiance in the face of trepidation but now I feel her loyalty, her willingness to give, her protective nature, her life-force. There is something so strong within her core that pulls me in and makes me believe in more. Somehow she has made me believe that she can love, because she does love—maybe not with affection or gifts or trivial trinkets but in the meaningful small things that actually matter.

Despite seeing Juniper in a whole new light, she still ached for Xan. It wasn't in the Juniper way; licking the sweat from his chiselled chest or watching the veins in his forearms pulse as he cradled her from behind.

It was just his plain old smile.

The good morning smile as she walked into the lab, the playful smile as he tested her knowledge on the habitat of the latest creature in need of saving.

She remembered the last smile he gave her. Guarded, apprehensive. What was in that smile? Was there sadness? A lot of the time spent with Braemar, flirting with the idea of soulbonding, trying to convince herself that she could go back to those dreams of truest love, before innocence had deserted her, before innocence had told her the biggest secret: that innocence wasn't so amazing after all. It wasn't just innocence. The soulbond restricted her; it was a cage. Xan, she realised, let her be whoever she wanted to be and accepted that. Braemar looked at her as if she needed to be mended without being broken.

She longed to see that smile again, to *make* Xan smile again. As the days lengthened, the longing got worse.

The heart was a labyrinth—one moment the orientation was clear and one would expect to be free of confinement, but a sudden turn would see a ventricle door open into another twisted path to traverse. Lilianna was lost on the road to who she wanted to be. The past called to her with the voice of Braemar over her shoulder. Into the horizon hazy figures gathered, beckoning her to join. She wanted the future to come for her. She was sick of waiting.

JUNIPER
24 YEARS OLD

The day of the summit had arrived. Juniper felt confident about their roles, fixated around Amani delivering the faction solution to the delegates. The AI driven car pulled up at one of the only large functional buildings left in the city. It had taken over an hour to get there and as Juniper took in the weeds snaking through cracks in the road, nature slowly reclaiming the city, she felt two contrasting emotions—the downfall of humanity meant that nature was finding its way as the predominant force of the Earth, which was a nice thing. At the same time, she felt a great sense of duty to ensure that Humans could find their way to coexisting again. This time, in the plan proposed by Amani, Humans would live harmoniously rather than piss all over every inch of good.

"Alright my sexy little bitches, do we feel like we're going to fix the Earth today or what?" She clapped her mismatched hands.

"I did shine my metal ass today, so I am feeling sexy." Arcadie spun around in the back of the vehicle, slapping his rear plate with a ding.

They all roared with laughter until the gravity of the moment was like a stone dropped into a shallow pool. The ebb and flow of nervous laughter and dead silence was the kind of beauty in duality that one lived for.

Grave focus replaced the smiles and Juniper nodded with encouragement. "Let's do this."

CHAPTER 34

LOCATION: ALPHA CENTAURI
YEAR: 118 (GTC)
XAN – 24 YEARS OLD

Xan sat in his quarters in the *Attenborough,* pacing the halls in his mind. He was nervous about the mission, worried about Juniper and Lilianna, and considering whether meeting them at the Summit was a good idea. Qilin fed off his energy. She paced in circles, flopping down with her tail tucked under her chin, then rising again in a perpetual cycle of restlessness.

After arriving back on the ship, they hyperleapt to Alpha Centauri to gather stock of the situation. Xan turned his focus to finding a cure for Dallis. He performed tests through his data link to all known flora, fauna and synthetic material on Gemarine as he tried to find a way to neutralise the effects of the venom.

Dallis was permanently in the regen chamber to keep the effects of the venom at bay. When Xan recently examined his arm, he was taken aback. Flesh-eating necrosis surrounded the bite site, slowly devouring healthy tissue. It was revolting to look at and no doubt, unbearably painful. It was lucky that Xan had acted quickly when Dallis was first bitten. If the venom had coursed through his entire system, his whole body could resemble the festering mess of his arm. As it was, he was already sick with some of the effects and needed the *brigetwort* root from Gemarine to give him back vibrancy and health.

Ryker knocked at the door and Xan beckoned him in.

Qilin arched her head up and wagged her tail at Ryker. He smiled shyly and waved at her as he sat down, allowing his fringe to cover his eyes. The Mika Tikaani locked onto her prey and aimed to kill; death by licks.

Ryker couldn't help but laugh through gritted teeth. "Stop it, stop it," he grumbled.

"It's funny how creatures aren't hindered by embarrassment. If they feel something, they will just act on it. Sometimes I envy that."

"Do you envy *me* now? Save me then!"

Xan stood up from his desk and crept up behind Qilin. He scooped her into his arms like she was an overgrown youngling, writhing to get out of his grip. He nuzzled into her neck growling playfully with her. Jumping from his grasp, she spun around in the corner of the room, crouched low, tail wagging, spikes protruding as Xan locked eyes with her.

"You wanna fight me, huh? You reckon you can take me down?"

Her response was like a high-pitched bark.

LOCATION: PERIAH
YEAR: 118 (GTC)
RYKER – 21 YEARS OLD

Ryker watched as Xan and Qilin pounced at the same time, colliding with one another until they were wrestling on the floor of the ship. Wiping

Mika Tikaani saliva from his cheeks, Ryker considered the ridiculousness of what he was witnessing. A grown-ass adult wrestling with his pet. As he straightened his fringe and breathed in for a short moment to steady himself, he marvelled at Xan's ability to preserve his innocence. Throughout everything he endured, every path that threw an obstacle his way, there was still enough positivity in him to carry others as opposed to dragging them down.

While Qilin was in a headlock Xan looked up at Ryker, "Are you feeling okay?" It was a multilayered question. The way he asked it was playful, almost nonchalant, while he toyed with the Mika Tikaani.

Why had Ryker come? Was it to check on what Xan's solution was with Dallis? No, he knew that Xan would have something sorted. Why *had* he come?

Xan seemed to sense Ryker's uneasiness and cut short his wrestling with Qilin. He walked over and put his large hand on Ryker's shoulder.

Ryker became a silk cloth fluttering in the wind. Tears came willingly, unable to be diverted to another time or place. Xan seized him with both hands, and Ryker let himself cry into the chest of his mentor, soothed not just by the momentary strong grip of love, but by the memories of Xan's consistent appraisal.

"I couldn't do anything to stop it," Ryker heard himself say. "I would never do what he did, never!" The fury rose at what Massy had done. It had hurt him deeply to think that he might have been alone in this universe again.

Xan continued to soothe in hushed tones. "None of this is your fault. We'll find a way to stop him together. You found us and now we can make our family whole again."

Ryker felt Qilin shift against his leg. He put a palm onto her forehead, while still in the grips of Xan's fierce hug.

The anger bit behind Ryker's tears. It was more than sadness. It was one of the first times that apathy had subsided. Emotions were like a dip in the ocean; if you went too deep, you could drown.

Xan pulled back and looked at him fiercely. "You hear me, buddy? We'll finish this together."

Ryker knew that was the only way. Togetherness and unity. But there was a pale ghost haunting him in the room, reminding him that he would always be too weak to fix things himself. He wanted more than anything for that to change.

LOCATION: EARTH
YEAR: 2114
JUNIPER – 24 YEARS OLD

The summit was held in a building aptly named The Cylinder. From twenty rows up, Juniper watched the delegates shuffle into an arc, sitting behind long curved tables made from light bamboo composite. Large, tinted windows obscured the burning rays, while the flags of eradicated countries hung from twisted steel ropes pouring from the upper ceiling in some misguided memorial. Perspex fencing rimmed each circular level and gave a clear view of what was occurring below.

Amani sat down amongst the delegates. Juniper sighed.

This snore fest is going to test my resolve.

She was more than capable of observation, but it was not her strong suit. Although she had invested interest in the conclusion of the summit, sitting through the explanations from thirty-seven incompetent numb skulls was about as desirable as a male who exploded inside her on first thrust.

Yuck. At least make it to double digit thrusts please. Like, I know my pussy is a pleasure chalet, but c'mon.

Juniper was roused from her musings by the current occupier of her pleasure chalet—Lilianna.

"How is it looking?" she asked through the comms system.

"How is it looking? Really, girl." Juniper could have smacked herself on the forehead. "It's some wrinkly ass gals and dudes shifting uncomfortably on chairs. There is probably one dude I'd consider banging because his forearms are nice and defined with the veins that—"

Lilianna sighed into the comms. "Juniper, I'm not talking about who looks good enough to fuck."

"Yeah, yeah." She swatted the exohand that no one would see. "Arcadie has eyes on all the problematic areas, doesn't he?"

"I am logged into the networks and scanning all activity, so I'm certain I've got you covered," Arcadie confirmed.

"That's the spirit, ol' chum."

"You know I've picked up a lot of nuances over the years but some of the things you say, I just…can't…compute," the robot complained.

Juniper looked at the nearest camera and shrugged so Arcadie could see. "I'm unique, what can I say?"

The office spaces on Juniper's level were eerily devoid of any activity. Yellowing papers congregated in a cardboard bin, dreaming of being useful once more. Virtual reality goggles lay neglected on desks, surrounded by computer screens, leering with dead eyes.

Amani popped a finger to her ear. "Can y'all shuddup?" she whispered feverishly with a hand over her mouth. "Some of us have 'portant plans to…ya know, save the world n'all."

"I'm rolling my eyes, Amani, just for your benefit since you can't see me. Just a strong, forceful reminder that I came up with those plans, yeah? Don't forget it, you fine ass bitch."

Juniper watched Amani through the binoculars trying desperately not to show laughter behind a resolute mask.

Juniper was actually going to miss her. Over the weeks she had seen great potential—the qualities of leadership, the passion for bringing about important change. Amani revelled in the weight of responsibility. Juniper highlighted all those wonderful things about Amani, and she hadn't even fucked her once.

Arcadie interrupted her thoughts. "Juniper, we have movement on the upper rafters at three o'clock."

Juniper turned, faded binoculars with a splinter in the right lens fixed to her eyes. Two maintenance workers in grey jumpsuits were filing through onto the level above Juniper. One worker knelt down to inspect an electrical box, the other watched, toolbox in hand.

Are they serious? This is the start of a bad joke. How many useless fucks does it take to appear worthy of breathing? Spoiler alert—the answer is these two.

"They seem like harmless little reptiles basking on the rocks of incompetence," Juniper relayed, shifting from propping herself up on her elbows to relaxing flat on the floor.

"Just keep an eye on them. I think it's bizarre to have maintenance crews in the middle of an important summit," Lilianna relayed.

"I'd have to agree with you on that one. And can we just point out the person who booked this venue. The summit is on the ground floor of an ornate building, but tiers and tiers of multiple levels looking down on them. It's a nightmare for security, to be honest."

Lilianna countered, "I think it's more about being streamed—they needed somewhere aesthetically appropriate and accessible to all leaders of regions—"

"Yeah, but seriously—practicality over presentation."

"Juniper, movement at ten o'clock two levels down," Arcadie communicated.

Juniper propped herself up again tracking the movements of one individual moving briskly, sticking close to the inside wall. A duffel bag swinging in their right hand.

A duffel bag. They may as well have walked in with a neon sign flashing, "Hey it's me—famous terrorist extraordinaire. I'll sign your left breast next to your suicide bombs, just flop 'em out."

She cursed out loud.

The individual opened a maintenance closet and moved inside. After thirty seconds they re-emerged, the duffel bag no longer in their possession.

Juniper leapt up. Swearing, she sprinted to the edge of the level and climbed onto the railing. The summit was still functioning below her, queen ants and their general deliberating on the construction of the nest.

She hung suspended off the railing and dropped. Fizzing past one level, her boronium exo hand clamped down hard on the metal railing. It was like a brass bell undulating with the waves of an alert. When a bell tolled it often meant danger. Juniper was sure that danger lurked below like a shark in the pits of the world, sharpening grated jaws to strike, mangle and dismember. A small grunt escaped her, but she clenched her jaw in determination. The force made her body jolt, but it propelled her enough to swing upwards and over the railing. Sprinting toward the closet, she put her finger to the comms device. Her whisper was a rusted hacksaw grating against brittle timber. "I'm intercepting the package. Arcadie, neutralise the suspect!"

"On it," he replied. She heard Lilianna yell something indecipherable and then the sweet sound of Arcadie's thrusters fire with manic deliverance. Juniper nearly wrenched the door handle from the door frame; the groaning wood wounded as she burst inside.

The duffel bag lay discarded in the middle of the closest. A blackened block of charcoal, with the seed of catastrophic destruction germinating within. Juniper knelt down, unzipped the bag and stared at the contents. Bulging, glowing red numbers smiled wickedly, taunting with every second that she spent staring dumbfounded. Denial was so often the redeemer of hope. Perpetuating ignorance and celebrating its lethargy. But in the face of a snarling bomb, it was impossible not to feel a million feelings, each one of them validated by beads of sweat that trailed down the side of her cheek. Shaking hands hovered above numbers counting down. *3:22…3:21…3:20…* Even warriors battled the enemy of adrenalin.

This is war.

The battlefield was a million light years away from what she'd known, and on a battlefield Juniper didn't usually freeze. She twirled and unfurled, like an umbrella under summer rain. Snatching the bag, she turned and let loose, aiming for the stairs to the roof. The door clattered. She didn't care about the sound this time. Footsteps echoed in the stairwell, marching hooves thundering toward the apocalypse. She rode the levels as if her lungs didn't sting, as if her short breaths only needed to carry her on one final journey.

Onto the roof now, she ran, wind blowing curls of her hair behind like a cosmic centrefold spreading across two galaxies.

Juniper saw the roof of the adjacent building and figured she could make the jump, as well as the next one. On wings bent with the weight of heroism she would soar and save the ugly idiots—Amani and that one hot dude.

Leaping from the roof, her glorious wings spread out like a dark angel taking the apocalyptic flight.

The wind slapped against her cheeks. The bomb attracted gravity, pulling Juniper down.

Would she fall to her death here? Or would she get far enough away to save them and make her sacrifice count?

Halfway across the gap in between buildings, Juniper noticed a ripple in the air ahead of her. At the last minute, she prepared herself for the shock of cloaked boronium. But when one lands on an invisible structure, it's completely disorientating. Her foot caught on the structure, and while desperately holding onto the duffle bag, she tripped forward onto the cloaked ship, sliding her way off the panel to the ruined earth below. The ramp suddenly revealed itself and the large hand of a Valkor seized her and flung her into the ship.

XAN
24 YEARS OLD

Juniper slid across the floor of the ship, smashing into the wall. The duffel bag lay a few feet from her; potent, powerful and perilous.

"Why the fuck did you bring me in here with a bomb?"

Xan yelled to Sythkin at the controls, "Fly straight up! Go now!"

Juniper scrambled to the bag, opening it. *1:03... 1:02.... 1:01*

"You absolute douche canoe, Xan, you're going to kill us all. This is a fucking bomb." Juniper levelled an exo finger at him.

"Great to see you too, bitch," Xan yelled. He braced himself against a handrail built into the wall as the *Attenborough* climbed higher and higher.

"Kick over the bag, Miss Juniper," cried Dallis, his arms held open.

"What? Why?"

Ryker and Xan both yelled, "Just do it!"

She kicked it across the floor. Dallis grabbed hold, opened it up and cried, "Forty seconds!"

"Sythkin, now," Xan bellowed.

The *Attenborough* straightened and threw Juniper against the opposite wall with a thud. The ramp opened, and the air pressure sucked Dallis toward the opening—he grasped the railing with his injured hand and a roar so deep and fierce tore through the atmosphere. The grimace in his face, the heaving of his chest, the very last ounce of strength summoned by the Valkor to fling the bag out into the pimpled face of space. It disappeared from the ship out into the unknown.

"Go," Dallis yelled.

The *Attenborough* kicked sharply and tailed off at sonic speeds. Xan held onto Juniper's arm, preventing her from rolling across the floor again. Her jade eyes found his. For Xan, it had only been days, but Juniper been stuck in time for weeks. They stared at each other like they were young again, before their lips found home, becoming entrenched together in the cosmic echo of fate.

The explosion detonated high above the earth. A white flash filled each viewport, and Juniper fell forward into Xan. She pressed her lips to his again and he sunk into her kiss. Hungry with desire, hungry because they were alive, chalking up yet another moment where they had cheated death.

CHAPTER 35

LOCATION: EARTH
YEAR: 2114
LILIANNA – 22 YEARS OLD

Arcadie neutralised the terrorist with ease. A sleep serum was deployed into her veins, biding time until Juniper would be well enough to interrogate.

Lilianna's heart hammered. Juniper had stopped relaying information through the comms minutes ago and then a bright explosion lit up the sky. It would have been beautiful if it hadn't been so forceful and terrifying. Lilianna was at a loss as to how the bomb that Juniper had located suddenly ended up in the atmosphere. The last she heard, Juniper was tearing up the stairs to the roof. She was strong, but not strong enough to toss the bomb high into the atmosphere.

Arcadie allayed her fears instantly. "It was Xan," he said as he put his clunky hand on her shoulder. Fingers creaked as he squeezed softly.

Her face lit up with expectation. "He's here?"

"I felt the presence of the *Attenborough* not long ago, but we were a little busy." He motioned to the shackled prisoner who he had dragged into the van. They were dreaming of sheep bounding over a paddock fence, presumably.

Amani hastily blared across the comms. "Lettin' ya know we are evac'ing to the basement 'til falling space junk ain't so dang'rous'." There was a slight pause, and her whisper turned even softer. "I guess one of ya had somethin' t'do with that."

"Yep, I'm sure you can guess who it was," Lilianna replied.

"Is everyone okay?"

"We think so." Lilianna massaged her forehead and breathed in deeply.

Arcadie suddenly froze. "What's wrong?" Lilianna asked him off comms.

"Don't go to the basement," he blurted out.

"We're all gettin' ferried like cattle down 'ere now, what's up?" Amani sounded afraid.

"I...I..." Arcadie stammered. Lilianna saw slanted creases above his pixelated eyes. His fingers clanking together. "I think I'm leaving."

The silence spread across the radio waves. Tense with static.

Lilianna understood then. The poor robot had been with Amani just as long as he'd been with Fleurah and he wouldn't see her again. In the prep that Juniper had laid out, she hadn't considered Arcadie would feel a loss, or anything at all. The years that he had lived here with her, Lilianna realised, had allowed him to grow. The chip inside him that her father had created and installed had given Arcadie a flood of...emotions that he had never known before. Or couldn't compute.

But now he could.

Lilianna felt a tear gather at the bottom of the well inside of her. Buckets pulled to the surface about to spill. Finally Amani spoke, "Arcs, meet me in the foyer now." Her voice was low tide at the setting of a sombre sun.

Without a word, Arcadie exited the vehicle and zoomed off toward the front of the building. Lilianna stepped out of the van and leant against the side mirror. Behind her, the wind kicked up from thrusters she couldn't see. Mini tornadoes of dirt spun, coating the back of her neck in a flurry of stringing pin pricks. Her heart beckoned to turn around and watch the ramp descend. Xan would be standing there, a spotlight reflecting the sun from a steel beam of the building ahead. He would smile. She would smile. They would run to one another. He would sweep her into his arms and they'd twirl like flowing silk and in a kiss, the echoes of forever would encircle them.

But in just a couple of weeks, stark realism had found its way into her imaginings, like a reel of old film exposed to the sun.

Lilianna resisted the urge to turn, to let reality dilute dreams that were never truly as good. She watched Amani hold Arcadie's metal hands, tinged with rust, saw her mouth move, her lips tremble with sadness, her chest depress with a heavy loss, heaving as tears became rivers carving canyons of sadness. Arcadie's face was hidden from Lilianna, but he grasped Amani, bringing her in tight to his body.

Fleurah arrived next to Lilianna. "Hey sis," spoken as if they had only conversed an hour ago. Lilianna smiled with sadness, lolling her head onto Fleurah's shoulder.

They watched the private moment play out when better individuals might have turned away. But beauty was hard to come by even when it was wrapped in sadness. Her eyes were pleased to savour something beautiful in this broken world. Juniper waved a hand as she stood with Xan on the street. Amani returned the gesture, her cheeks red with pain. Then she turned away to save the Earth, just as Juniper would have in a different time, in a different life.

CHAPTER 36

Sythkin hyperleapt into the atmosphere of a planet within Alpha Centauri. She set the spacecraft to hover mode and bobbed there as if anchored to the bottom of a shallow reef. The water was the colour of plucked raven's feathers.

Xan, much like everyone else, wouldn't have predicted such a despondent scene. The coming together of the crew was usually filled with such positivity and love. But frowns fuelled the silence. It fuelled the smell of sweat and anxiety. Massy's betrayal had torn through the fabric that bound them. For weeks they bobbed limbless and listless in the middle of a channel at the mercy of the tide. Now washed upon the shore, they were bedraggled, soaked to their bones with self-pity and mourning the loss of what they were before this ordeal began.

They all sat in various positions in the shared living quarters. Fleurah's head was back against the wall, her knotted ropes of strawberry blonde hair drooping like starving flowers. Arcadie, with his thrusters disengaged, sat beside Fleurah, holding her hand in his silver claws. Lilianna lay in Fleurah's lap, curled so that her knees tucked into her chest, golden eyes hidden by the curtain of closed eyelids. In a wistful thought, Xan wanted her to be dreaming peacefully, of times where her view of the galaxy had not been tainted by the blinding explosions of reality.

Juniper had her arms crossed, sullen after allowing the terrorist to remain on Earth 2114, interrogated by Amani and the Watch. Leaning against a bedpost, she stared accusingly at Sythkin as if the years of battles between their races were carved into the calcium of her bones. The Cryptoborg race had been an enemy for years; she had seen them do terrible things. They had taken her arm. How could she just get rid of her perceptions immediately?

Sythkin was calm, tucked into the shadowed corner, stroking her ear lobes. According to the data scrolls, it was a soothing gesture used to rid nerves. Finally, Dallis the Valkor giant and his skinny little pal, Ryker, sat on the edge of a bed next to one another, closer than Ryker would allow most others. Dallis's wrist was bandaged in a fresh cloth wrap, but he grimaced in pain after he'd thrown the dangerous bomb into the atmosphere.

Qilin clawed at Xan, and he knelt down. She put her paws onto his shoulder while on her hind legs. He felt her long ears brush against the inside of his neck as he closed his eyes. She purred, her honey eyes blinking twice, and her lips curved into a reassuring smile, giving him strength to address the crew.

"Much like everyone here, I'm at a loss to describe the events over the last few days and weeks." He gestured to Juniper and Lilianna.

"And lifetimes." Arcadie's voice chirped from the corner trying to be funny.

Xan nodded, smiling meekly, "Lifetimes for you, my friend."

"Despite the duration of time, we all endured a certain level of... trauma that will probably scar us for years to come." He paused to compose himself, as he recalled Arcadie's sacrifice, Juniper's bomb disposal heroics in saving a world she despised, Fleurah having her robot brother altered beyond comprehension. "But despite the odds, here we stand now with the Earth safe and on the precipice of the final journey."

Ryker's voice shook with tremors in the faultline of his emotions. "Xan, I think the final journey won't be how you imagined it."

"What do you mean?" Xan asked.

Qilin shifted from Xan's side with eyes for Arcadie, but as the robot moved to object to any sort of wrestling, Qilin licked his faceplate and nuzzled into his neck. It only made Arcadie smile.

"Well, time in the portal runs slower than the outside, and chances are Massy has left Periah and arrived in Gemarine and…well, you can imagine what he's doing." Ryker shuddered as if a breeze came through the ship. He picked the skin on his lip. A droplet of blood quivered. Saliva drowned it.

"Just in case you don't have the ability to imagine," Juniper chimed in, "Massy will go dib dobbing to Madame Bleu, licking her rectal entryway, then she will go mental seeking revenge. There, I'm fucking psychic."

"Yes, Juniper," Xan said flatly. "My brain couldn't comprehend what Massy might do, but I deciphered an ancient text, united all the celestial crystals and located the portal."

"Oh yes Xan, genius extraordinaire." Juniper bowed low. "We are not worthy."

Fleurah chuckled and Juniper caught wind of it, her eyes bright with approval.

Dallis stood. "You know I don't understand all that much. This… joking when Ryker is trying to speak about important things. It's really bizarre."

Xan and Juniper both turned away sheepishly. Sythkin folded her arms in the corner, watching silently, likely fascinated by the anthropological examination of their mongrel crew.

"Ryker, what do you have to say?" Dallis asked through gritted teeth, gesturing for him to stand and deliver.

Ryker stood slowly. "I think there will be more to Dallis and I leaving for Gemarine. Of course we will need to find a solution for his pain, but also...we could start gathering an army," he finished nervously.

Xan looked at Juniper. If anyone would protest it would be her. But for once the snide objection laced with poisonous words remained stuck in her throat. Her eyes closed briefly, and she nodded at Xan as if to give her blessing. Was it because she didn't want to have to worry about another member of the crew? Or was this the only way to protect everything they'd built in Gemarine once Madame Bleu was alerted of their plot?

Ryker continued. "I don't know how many people I can gather, but there's Duffington, Ranjit and others at the biobase who will want to know what's happened and...I guess...try to help."

Qilin had enough smooching with the robot and came to lie at Xan's feet. She closed her eyes and snorted, settling in for a doze.

"What, you mean like build an army?" Fleurah asked, scratching at a spot amidst the tangle of her filthy hair.

Before anyone could answer Xan and Juniper seemed to come to the same conclusion. "The underground exiles," breathed Juniper.

"Miami," Xan said, nodding. How could he not have entertained this idea before? *I guess I was slightly preoccupied with ensuring everyone was not lost in time.*

Miami and her crew of exiled misfits that lived in the underground, abandoned dregs of Gemarine would be able to play a part. They could amass a covert army underneath Madame Bleu's nose so that when Xan and his crew returned from their final mission to fight, they would stand a chance.

Ryker's face creased in confusion, but after a moment he realised where they were going. "Wait, so the people of the underground can help us? Do you think they will?"

"They were aligned with General Heronicus's purpose, so now that the purpose is...one, I'm sure they would," Xan offered.

Dallis nudged Ryker. "I know the underground exiles. I've spoken with them on behalf of Heronicus many a time." He coughed, no exuberant fist smashing through the air while harboured by the venom sickness.

"Okay, so we go to the underground first and find who?" Ryker asked.

"Miami is their leader," Juniper said. "And then go and find Ranjit and Duffington."

Xan interjected, "By the time you've gathered everyone we will be back onboard and ready to – "

"Fuck the smugness from Madame Bleu's face with my boronium fist, then shove that same fist, lubed in the blood of Bleu into the anal cavity of Massy until he dies a horrible death."

Xan grimaced.

"You have some deep seeded trauma and I implore you to seek some help," Dallis said with a sincere look of concern on his face.

"Or..." Xan began staring at Juniper, who looked like she had candy yanked from her grasp after the first salacious taste of sugar. "Just kill her in a more sane and regular way, perhaps."

Fleurah stood, leaving Lilianna to fend for herself in the leaning-on-things department. "Damn, you're savage, girl!" she shouted with a big smile on her face. "I mean, it's clear you don't take prisoners, but literally not locking her up and just straight up killing her..." She raised her eyebrows. "...that shit is next level."

Ryker shifted uncomfortably. Xan realised that maybe a little part of him was upset at potentially losing his aunty, but he couldn't be sure. He knew, though, that Ryker's loyalty was theirs and betrayal was a distant storm fading from view.

"Look, I'm not saying that's the only solution, but I can't see her surrendering anytime soon," Xan stated.

Juniper shifted. "I don't seem to recall you mentioning how Massy will be slain."

It was true. Xan had been putting this off. From thoughts that simmered with intense wrath, to comedic, light-hearted memories that spawned guilt and disbelief. It was difficult to know just what he could manage if Massy faced off with him at the end of all things.

"Juniper, give the bravado a break for a bit," Lilianna said in a huff. "Especially when it comes to Massy. It's...difficult."

"I'm sorry—were you not there when he kicked us out into the dystopian desert of death? Or do you not remember that after such a lovely holiday?"

Lilianna stood up and placed her hands on her hips. "If you spent less time cultivating that ugly monster of hate inside you while that decent heart of yours continues to shrink, maybe you'd be happier. Monsters, masks and mania only last for so long you know—then what will you have to show for yourself?"

"Oh, thank you oh learned Lilianna. Your wisdom is only surpassed by your knowledge of the universe." Juniper bowed as Lilianna stormed out.

"Fucking child," Juniper spat.

"C'mon Juniper," Arcadie levelled. "You're better than this." His jets let out a spurt of air almost like a disappointed huff, chasing after Lilianna.

Ryker tried to get back to the task, "Listen, I'm pretty shattered and ah...everyone else is...just hanging in there. I'm going to turn in for some rest, but in the morning, Xan—I should be back on Gemarine."

He impressed Xan. With Massy's departure, Ryker was filling a huge void. Maybe it wasn't just a departure, but the *nature* of the departure. Ryker was hurt by it and instead of crawling into himself further, he used the situation like an engine to fix. He realised now that he was an integral part. Xan had always tried to cultivate this notion. The kid was finally getting it.

Xan started to make his way toward the captain's quarters but stopped by Ryker first, speaking in hushed tones. "Sounds good, I know you'll make us proud. Well, prouder than we already are."

Qilin raced after Xan and Juniper called out after them both. "Hey, why are you walking out of here?"

Xan called back without turning around, "I'm tired, leave it be."

"Do you want to fuck or—"

"Not particularly!"

"Forget it then! These loins are closed for winter, and your dick ain't hibernating anywhere near here. I will see if Dallis is ready for round two."

Xan shouted, "Leave the poor guy alone, he has been sleeping in the regen chamber!" He disappeared into the captain's quarters, leaving Juniper steaming from the ears.

JUNIPER
24 YEARS OLD

Juniper went to storm out but caught sight of Sythkin sitting in the corner with her legs crossed, studying her with intensity.

"I forgot you were even here, you little serpent. Sittin' there gathering intel huh?" accused Juniper.

"The way you treat each other is...very interesting." Sythkin said, amusement laced in her tone. "If I didn't know it, I would think you were enemies."

Juniper screwed up her face with disdain, "You're the only enemy I see."

Sythkin stood up and stretched long arms above her head eliciting a crack from her shoulders. "You're actually cute when you're cranky." She trudged off toward the flight deck smiling peacefully, leaving Juniper feeling jealous of a Cryptoborg for the first time ever.

Why the fuck is this bitch so chilled out? I want her secrets.

CHAPTER 37

LOCATION: ALPHA CENTAURI
YEAR: 118 GTC
LILIANNA – 22 YEARS OLD

Lilianna and Xan were submerged in satin sheets, drenched in the euphoria of liberty.

Her body was a prison, and his heart was the key. Parts of her that were constricted with rusted chains were unlocked.

She escaped the tangle of the sheets and tiptoed to the closest, slipping into a red kimono. It felt smooth against her pale skin.

Moving out into the hall, she headed to the common area for a drink of water. Dallis was there at the table, drinking something himself, bleary eyed and ashen faced.

"Couldn't sleep," he muttered, the exuberance in him lost to the spider venom.

"I needed a bit of hydration."

His eyes widened and he couldn't meet her gaze. "Oh goodness. Another marathon session—"

Lilianna cut him off. "No, nothing like that."

She was worried that in their little drunken tryst all that time ago she hadn't taken enough care to understand what it meant for Valkors to engage in "copulation" as he once called it. How she seduced him into something he might not have been comfortable with, like what so many folks on Gemarine had tried to do to her once upon a time.

"I thought I should say something about last time, when we, you know."

He breathed in deep and looked away, clearly uncomfortable.

"I never asked you how you were, I never considered how a Valkor might view something like…that."

"It was no secret that you were…beautiful to me, and as far as coitus went—oh, sorry. I mean fusing—I desired a physical closeness with you. I am privileged to have shared your space, shared Miss Juniper's and Mr Xan's. All of you have become so meaningful to me I would value our interaction as something special regardless of what I believe as a Valkor."

Lilianna smiled warmly as she finished filling up a glass of water, choosing to sit beside him. If every male had communicated in that exact way, then maybe she would have shared more beds on Gemarine. Dallis had a way of making her feel valued. Wasn't that what anyone wanted when they gave a piece of their body?

"What is it that you believe about fusing then?"

"It's not as freeing as the Gemarine way, but we often experiment physically with different genders until we settle upon an individual that is compatible in both regards."

"So you are kind of attracted to others and experiment with them until someone satisfies you both physically and emotionally?"

"Correct!"

"And then you have a chance to build a relationship with them?" Lilianna sat forward.

"Yes, traditionally, that's how we view things."

"I'm sorry I didn't take the time to learn about that before we, I don't know, became involved."

"Equally, if Valkors are to have a life on Gemarine, we too need to be aware of your way of life."

Lilianna realised that she was no longer as much of an outsider as she once was on Gemarine. She didn't see herself going to Fusion every week, but still, she had grown into someone with less boundaries than before. In the moment, she didn't hate that about herself. She was proud.

Dallis started to cough, and Lilianna rose, putting a hand on his back to steady him. Ryker walked sleepily into the room. "Is everything okay? I heard you coughing?"

Lilianna smiled at Ryker, and he gave her an awkward lopsided grin in return, brushing his fringe behind his ear and walking forward to put a hand on Dallis's shoulder.

Dallis looked up at Ryker and sighed. "I'm still here, my friend."

Lilianna took her hand away from Dallis's back and shifted to her lonely glass of water, sensing something more in their interaction.

"Thanks for the talk, Lilianna." Dallis pulled back his chair from the table and let Ryker shepherd him out of the common room.

She raised her glass. "Anytime."

Ryker's small hand steadied Dallis's large frame. It did nothing physically, but then again, the hand wasn't there to stop him from falling; it was there to show that someone cared for him in a way that Lilianna had not considered before.

Dallis turned around. "Can I just say that silence is easy. You chose integrity and that is loud and sometimes difficult to hear. I'm glad you spoke up. Good night."

Ryker looked confused, but focused on his chaperone duties, letting Lilianna drink the last of her water with contemplation as company.

She thought of her little spat with Juniper before and huffed into silence. Before they left for Dracia, she would speak again. She did not want to repeat mistakes that she made with the people she loved.

Xan was still sleeping but stirred when Lilianna crawled under the sheets.

"Where did you go?" he asked, barely in a language she understood.

"Hydration. You tired me out." She joked as his arms wrapped around her.

"Yeah right," he mumbled, squeezing her tight.

Lilianna stared at the slithers of blue artificial light disrupting the darkness of the void visible from the circular viewpoint. Courage was a mote of dust in the air, and she grasped it with her will, not her hands. Dallis had reminded her that silence was easy but easy rarely bolstered the fortitude of the heart. After a long time of having unspoken things between her and Xan, it was time to speak up. It was time to be strong.

"Can we talk, please?" Her voice was not as hardened by courage as she'd hoped.

"Just go to sleep love, we have all had a big—"

The dismissal would've been enough to sew her lips shut before, but the needle of his apathy was blunted by the steel inside her.

"No, I think we need to." There it was, the hard edge she had been looking for.

Xan shifted in the bed, taking his arm out from underneath her and using the dimmer remote to increase the blue light in the room.

She flipped over to face him, resting on an elbow. "Even you can admit things were awkward before we both left. We were separated for so long…I really felt the distance. It was hard."

"No, I get it." He yawned, then shuffled under the sheets with his face closer to hers. "It's just hard with us. Your expectations are something I'm not sure I can…live up to."

Lilianna's head reared back. She wrinkled her eyebrows. "What is that supposed to mean?"

Xan looked away. "Oh man, this a trap. I don't know if I can—"

"Just communicate with me, you male idiot. You're acting like you're an ape stuck in the throes of evolution."

"Alright, alright." He took a deep breath, "You expect a man on his knees in the rain, reciting a sonnet professing undying love. I'm just a practical guy. I show you that I love you with my actions and by giving you all of me. I thought that was enough."

"That's not fair to say I want all those grand gestures; I just wanted some form of acknowledgment, Xan. That this is…something more."

"Something more than what?"

"Something more than just an employee or even being a part of a clan."

"I can't be your soulbond."

"I don't want you to be my soulbond, I left him behind, remember? I want to be told I mean more than some random bitch at Fusion."

"You know you do."

"That's the thing, you have never told me—so how would I know?" She'd never seen him so uncomfortable. It made her giggle.

"I'm glad this is fun for you." He rolled his eyes. "Look, it's no secret that you and Juniper mean more than anyone else to me. Okay? I've grown up with this Gemarine mindset so it's hard for me to love the way that you want. I just hope that maybe we can find our own version perhaps."

She kissed him. "I like that we can build something that is uniquely ours. I'm not going to be coming along to Fusion anytime soon, but you and Juniper are my people. I just wanted an acknowledgment of that."

"Alright, you happy now, you fucking pain in the ass?" He took her in close. "Good luck having this convo with Juniper, by the way."

"Yeah, I was hoping you would…ah…do that on my behalf."

"Your heart has dug its own grave, girl."

They both laughed until they fell asleep in one another's arms, with an empty space that Juniper needed to fill.

CHAPTER 38

LOCATION: PERIAH
YEAR: 118 GTC
RYKER – 21 YEARS OLD

Ryker watched the *Attenborough* slip through the portal again. The glowing orb of energy swallowed the busted ship—hungry for a taste of the bitter entrails of a crew on the verge of imploding.

In the whole time of knowing Xan, Ryker had never seen him so ragged. Xan was a chain, unbroken, fastened to rungs bleeding rust. He could only stay clean for so long. Each time the chain flexed or pulled taught, the rust tainted, the rust infected.

Ryker and Dallis had entered Sythkin's former ship. She'd given them a quick demo before departing on the *Attenborough* through the portal to Dracia with the others, but Ryker was still nervous. He hated the pressure of flying and much preferred the maintenance hub where he could fiddle with cogs and gears. But that choice was gone. So much counted on him and he wondered why he had spoken up and volunteered himself to amass the underground rebels of Gemarine. It really wasn't like him. But a lot of things weren't lately.

Did a squirt of evolution help grow a tiny conscience? Or shrink the amygdala so he could indulge in risk taking behaviour without a second thought?

Before, he'd followed Massy.

Massy, who eloped with self-preservation and lived shittily ever after.

Thinking about being anything like that fuckwit made him queasy. Ryker stood up because he wanted to be nothing like Massy, even though he wasn't brave in the hero sense of the word. This was real life and bravery was about small acts that took you out of your comfort zone for the benefit of a greater ideal.

The ship hovered and he pushed forward into the atmosphere and beyond.

Ryker was brave because he recognised the importance of more than the present moment. The past, the present, the future—it all mattered, just like the boy so used to tinkering away alone in the pits of a ship thinking no one cared. Well, he mattered now. And in the small memories of everything Xan had ever said to him or did for him, he realised he always mattered.

CHAPTER 39

LOCATION: DRACIA
YEAR: 1173
JUNIPER – 24 YEARS OLD

Dracia was a land of fucking ice and blistering cold. Not the winter wonderland type with fluffy white snow like heavenly clouds. Not the cute little snowflakes that dampened cheeks, turning them a pinkish hue. Not the one where you snuggled beside a fireplace with a bear-like man, chest hair like peat moss in an expansive bog.

This was the type of ice land where you wouldn't mind sitting in a firepit burning alive just to escape the deathly cold. They were fit out in suit number seven which insulated automatically to counter the temperature outside to what the core body temperature needed, except one's face and hands were left exposed. If not for the glove on one hand and the boronium beauty of the other, Juniper's fingers would be just as forsaken as her arm.

Their final mission was to try to stop a civil war between neighbouring tribes and unite the entire race of Dracian Aranthers. Without doing so, they would tear the planet apart with their divisions, and Madame Bleu would eventually waltz in and steal core materials from the planet to power Gemarine.

World peace is super easy to achieve—it's going to be a walk in the park.

They only needed to walk a short distance to the settlement of caves in the Wyndry tribe, but each step was a feat in itself. Bones ached from the chill and skin withered with the hiemal caress. She couldn't imagine how Lilianna was going to last the entire way. Arcadie's words suddenly haunted her.

"Don't underestimate her."

Alright, alright.

After her childish outburst—she managed to stay with Xan overnight, most likely showing off the new sexy moves that I taught her. You're welcome. And then filled with a hot load of cum, she waddles out in the morning all happy and smiley.

If she wasn't such a whiny little bitch, then I'd be proud of her.

Wait, am I proud of her?

Juniper realised maybe Lilianna had been spending too much time with her, because that was such a Juniper move.

Xan hung back suddenly. "How's the weather, right?" Condensation was smoke from the heat of his mouth. The heat of those lips had scorched her many a time.

"Without these suits my nipples would be poking you in the eye right now, so real fucking cold."

"Listen I just wanted to—"

"Oh, comets above. Don't mistake me for Lilianna, please. I couldn't give a fuck about all the drama yesterday, I'm already over it." She swatted her wrist and shook her head, curls bouncing out.

"Well either way, sorry I snapped. I just—"

"Xan, I know you better than Qilin knows you." Qilin jumped up at Juniper, throwing a paw across her face. Juniper ducked and tackled Qilin into the snow and tickled her as she lay sprawled across her back. "Alright, bitch, maybe not." She tapped Qilin on the backside and she leapt up from the snow and bounded ahead, wiggling her tail as her tongue flapped out the side of her mouth like she was laughing.

"I know you're exhausted physically and emotionally. You don't have to check if I'm crying." She winked. It felt wrong on her face, and she blew out in disgust.

Xan shook his head. He reached out to her, and they embraced. "That's no excuse to be disrespectful. I'll do better."

The blizzard of white blew around them like a Shoji screen sheltering two entwining maple trees.

As they approached the mouth of the cave system, they found a wall of perpetual flame. Smoke was lost in the icy wind, but the contrast of fierce blue arctic ice with the hellish flame was a sight to behold.

Juniper felt mounting pressure at the back of her eyes. As the pressure increased, a voice like a whisper echoed inside her mind.

"Who goes there?"

Juniper stumbled, attempting to counteract the intrusion. She focused on her breathing, recalling Xan's warning about the feeling of one's mind being taken over by Aranther royalty. Xan read too many books and knew too many dumb facts, but that one was quite useful.

"I think it'll be like a plant. Although there's just one trunk or stem, multiple flowers can sprout. When a new flower sprouts off the stem, it'll be like another mind operating within your body. From what I understand, they don't have the capability to take over the body as such but there's a strong enough power to absorb thoughts, short-term memories and perhaps exert some influence over weaker minds."

An Aranther was tapping into her consciousness, and it was causing physical distress. Stomach churning, sweating pores, increased heart rate and tiny pin pricks at the base of her skull. Xan reiterated before that it was best to keep calm in the situation, to breathe and try to enhance the connection rather than fight it.

But fuck my ass and call me a donkey, it hurt.

Xan put a hand on her shoulder. "Have they reached your mind?" Qilin licked her hand in comfort.

The Aranthers on Gemarine had not been able to do this, but on Dracia something must have enabled that particular skill.

First, they'd need to understand how it was possible, then figure out how to make sure the shared consciousness was explored across all tribes, not just one, to ensure that all Aranthers could find a common ground. By putting an end to civil wars and the slow destruction of their planet, their mission would be fulfilled.

Juniper needed to let them in if they wanted to succeed. She decided to use her mind to communicate, thoroughly and carefully.

"State your person on entry into Wyndry tribe territory," the voice rumbled in her mind.

"We are aliens that seek refuge. We carry no threat, only seek an audience with your chief."

"We have received exploring aliens in our midst before, but we have never encountered species like those in your party."

"We bring news about the state of our galaxy. We want to ensure all living species understand the situation and are given the best chance of survival. Do we have your permission to enter these lands?" Juniper didn't know how to hold her breath within the mind, but the anticipation was certainly there as she waited for an answer.

"I appreciate your warnings and your honest manner. Your companions have already been searched for negative intentions and we can find none. You may enter. I look forward to conversing with you in the flesh."

The eternal flames weren't so eternal and a section of the wall stopped burning to let them through.

Xan, Qilin and Juniper inched further into the system following the guards to a structure built high into the catacombs of the cave. Fleurah, Arcadie and Lilianna trailed further behind. A male Aranther sat upon a wooden throne, carved from a large obsidian trunk, eyes closed in a meditative state. The pale blue skin rippled like vapour across a cloudless sky while his nostril slits whistled softly at the intake of breath. "I am Chief Ghanasis. Welcome Juniper, Captain of Gemarine. We are blessed to have you in our midst." The chief raised his three clawed hands in a welcoming salute.

"Oh sugar, it is us who are blessed." She turned her hands up to the domed roof of the cave, then curtsied in a way that she hoped would be misconstrued as deeply respectful.

Xan gave her a look of warning.

Oh c'mon big boy, they surely have some humour.

The royal chief of the Wyndry tribe appraised Juniper with a raised eyebrow, unsure of her intentions.

"Even though we were able to converse telepathically, please state the purpose of this visit so the royal court can listen."

"Well, we…" She stole a glance at Xan. He looked like he wished he had telepathic abilities.

Sorry, you're just a regular dude —albeit with a rather delicious cock. Juniper licked her lips. Xan was visibly embarrassed.

Whoops. Juniper conjured her best Xan impression. "Well, we are here to explain more about putting an end to the civil war. We bring tidings from worlds beyond your own."

Have I ever used the word tidings before?

Juniper hoped that they weren't prying within her mind right now."

"But what stake could you, aliens, have in our civil war?"

I'm already bored with this.

Juniper spun around toward Xan, her curly hair bouncing across the tips of her shoulders. She winked. "I present my loyal scientist to explain everything to you." Juniper looked around at the guards standing nearby. The throne room was dank and dark and not at all opulent and worthy of grandeur. A single rough stone sculpture sat in the corner. Draped casually over the top was some sort of animal hide.

Xan motioned to speak, but Juniper stepped forward with a finger in the air. "By the way, you don't by chance have an area where guards feed you grapes and fan you with large leaves?"

The chief turned to the guards, then looked back at Juniper. "What are grapes?"

"Nevermind. I shall take my leave over there." Juniper walked into the corner and plonked down, laying up against the cool rock wall of the cave. She closed her eyes but felt a large body squeeze in next to her, scraping against her shoulder.

Juniper relinquished an eyelid and glanced at the bulky frame of Sythkin, who was smiling at her. The hideous scar raked across her face, folding it like a pastry.

Gross.

"And what would *you* like?" Juniper sneered.

"Friendship, I suppose, among other things."

Juniper sighed. She had enough friends. Lilianna, Xan, possibly Ryker. That was enough. All these other lingerers like Dallis, Fleurah, Arcadie, were trying to cosy up into friendship land. It was too much work to have to care about so many people.

"You want to be friends with *me?*" She had killed more Cryptoborgs than anyone in their history. If the roles were reversed, she would have already ripped out Sythkin's eye from its socket and fed it to the chief like a grape.

That's a grape, you peasant. She thought about the chief, considering whether she would care if he were telepathically listening. *He ought to know, really.*

"I want to be the one that shows you there's more to a Cryptoborg than what you've encountered during battle." Sythkin played with her ear lobe the way Juniper saw so many Cryptoborgs do as they bled out on a battlefield, screaming for mercy or salvation.

Mercy and salvation felt akin standing at the door of death. But there was never an exchange that the reaper considered. Death was death, wasn't it? Who really cared whether you flew on magic clouds to heaven or crashed into nothingness?

Multiple scenes of bloody carnage flicked across her mind's eye like a montage of malice. It made her shudder. She shuffled away from Sythkin so their shoulders were no longer touching.

"I'm sure there is," Juniper said flatly. "But I'm not your girl."

Sythkin respected the physical gap between them but turned inward to speak. "You know, all the things you did were driven by someone else."

Juniper felt like a caged beast. "I know you think you know me, and you think it was Madame Bleu the puppeteer, tinkling with taut strings, making me do this and that."

She stood up and crouched over Sythkin, with her voice low and gravelly. "I knew what I was doing, and I fucking loved it." She didn't quite spit in her face, but she was gathering saliva behind her teeth.

"Well, I can tell you this, Juniper, Warrior Queen, lover of war and death. By the time I give my dying breath—I *will* show you. I will convince you that Cryptoborgs are not all bad and I will help you see the good in…you." Sythkin pressed her finger into Juniper's heart, then rose in one swift movement and walked to the opposite side of the cave, affording Juniper space.

What a high and mighty pain in the ass.

"I wouldn't touch my chest again, unless you want to make it worth my while, you freak," she shouted across the cave.

Those deep in conversation turned to look at her, and she remembered where she was. Juniper chuckled and shuffled back to the wall. "Yep, just a consent advocate over here giving out some free advice. Don't mind me…continue chatting away."

Juniper slumped into a darkened corner and rubbed her cheeks. If she felt embarrassed, she would've felt it then. But she was over it. Over the bullshit of trying to walk down a path lined with roses that she wasn't allowed to smell. There was always something new to learn, always another person to pretend to be.

Qilin crawled across the sparkling minerals trapped in the cave floor, the gaze of the guards following the weird alien creature. She licked Juniper's cheek just once and sat beside her. Juniper stroked behind her ears absentmindedly.

She wanted nothing more than to be on Gemarine again where she was lady liberty, dancing in the streets naked, spinning in circles, letting her hair flail behind like uncontained smoke.

But the smoke came from the flame that had burnt her world. Liberty was a lie. Her whole life was a lie.

Who was she now if not smoke? Smoke that once was thick enough to cover the sky, now only remnants of something greater, swallowed by the lie of the world.

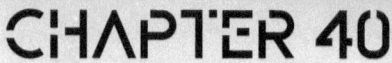

CHAPTER 40

LOCATION: DRACIA
YEAR: 1173
LILIANNA – 22 YEARS OLD

Lilianna watched Juniper sulking in the corner of the cave with Qilin while Xan played mediator with the chief.

"I can't hear a thing," Fleurah whined.

Lilianna shrugged. "Trust that they will—"

Suddenly Arcadie started broadcasting their whispers to Lilianna and Fleurah.

"Arcadie, what are you doing!" Lilianna hissed.

Fleurah lightly punched her in the arm. "Oh, shut up and listen."

Lilianna looked around to see if any of the tribesfolk were close but relented, sagging against the wall in close around Arcadie like a family in front of a fireplace.

The Wyndry chief spoke. "I understand the gravity of the situation, Xan. Our resources here are waning, sickness spreads, malnourishment is abundant. It's been horrific here. We've reached out to the Plaxxon and

Darshan tribes via mindlink but they do not seek to aid us. They move to conquer us. But what is there to conquer? This land of snow and ice is my home, but we've always relied upon other tribes to exchange crops. We cannot do this on our own."

"Where did it all go wrong?" Xan asked.

"It was greed. The keeper of the *dillayla*—the herb of the mindlink. Tribes are so protective over their lands. What is ownership of land but imaginary lines drawn? It goes to show that none of that matters— we're all the same inside. All the same." He repeated the last line, clearly exacerbated by the tensions.

"I'm sorry to hear this and I assure you that our intentions are aligned with yours. We want to unite your tribes, we want to prevent a large-scale civil war—"

The chief interrupted Xan. "Large-scale war? How do you know this is what's to come for us?

Xan hesitated. "We have…projections, calculations that we've made based on your current trajectory." Lilianna had never heard Xan lie before. "Please, as I said, our intentions are for peace—completely aligned with what you'd want."

"What do you propose?"

"A party of tribe warriors to march to the Darshan gates. There, my fellowship and I will meet with the leader."

The chief laughed wickedly. "Morcombe will never meet you. After the loss of his brother, he has become withdrawn and—"

"We must try. We must try," Xan said solemnly.

There was a pause, static crackled and Fleurah and Lilianna leant even closer to Arcadie's face plate. He giggled.

"The journey will not be for the faint of heart. Prepare your fellowship and I will brief the tribe warriors of their final attempt at peace."

Arcadie squealed in delight. Both Lillianna and Fleurah jumped away from him. The squeal echoed in the cave.

"You nonce," Fleurah hissed, then smiled sweetly to everyone who was watching.

JUNIPER
24 YEARS OLD

They stood in a courtyard surrounded by ice sculptures of past chiefs, flanked by dead trees so brittle Juniper's exhale threatened to topple them over. The mountains loomed in the distance like giant fever blisters on the lips of the horizon. The cold was a persistent annoyance, just like how when Xan returned home from one of his trips, he'd *have* to show her holos of every insect he encountered. Most of them resembled tiny rectal cavities.

Sythkin was peering at one of the sculptures. As she reached out with a clawed finger to inspect a facial feature closer, she lost her footing on the ice momentarily. Her large nail sliced into the nose of the ice chief and knocked it clean off.

After gathering it up, she feverishly licked the piece of ice and stuck it in its rightful place. Once it didn't slide off, she quickly slipped and slid her way to more compact snow and began conversing with one of the tribesfolk to hide her indiscretion.

As much as Juniper hated to admit it, the Cryptoborg would need to come along in their "fellowship."

Does Xan think he's some Tolkien scholar or something? Who the fuck says fellowship these days anyway?

The Cryptoborg spotted Juniper and was on her way to annoy the absolute dick out of her.

"Why are you grinning like you just released your bowels after days of constipation?" Juniper asked Sythkin, who wore a wide smile that made her fresh scar threaten to burst apart.

"I'm an integral part of this fellowship. Cryptoborg and Gemarinian on a quest together, against all odds." She stared off into the distance as if the stars had written this story. "I guess you couldn't wait to see how good Cryptoborgs actually are." Sythkin winked.

The audacity to wink at me.

"First, you kind of know how to handle yourself in battle, although I fucked your face up, so that isn't saying that much. Second, you are a big body and if we get some…I don't know…wonky-ass arrows shot at us, guess who I'll use as a shield?"

"I'm guessing it's me then?" The Cryptoborg pointed a long finger at herself and chuckled.

"Yes, it's fucking you, you haemorrhoid. Now go get some armour or something and prepare yourself for an arrow to the vagina." Juniper waltzed away toward Lilianna and Xan, who were sharing an intimate hug.

Eh, disgusting.

Sythkin called after her, "I'll see you soon, friend."

Juniper rolled her eyes and refused to look back.

Xan finished cuddling Lilianna. "Good luck," he said as he walked toward Sythkin, giving Juniper a curious smile as he did.

Juniper craned her neck wearily toward Lilianna. The sight of her evoked fear, far greater fear than what she'd faced on the battlefield. What was coming was an emotional punch through her love funnel into her heart.

"Please don't do this to me, Lilianna," she begged.

"What am I doing?"

"I honestly don't care about our little disagreement last night. I came to say I'm sorry we couldn't take you along."

"Xan already sat with me and let me cry into his shoulder."

"Thank the snowgods I didn't have to do—"

"That was a joke. I get it. It's dangerous and I'd be more of a liability than an asset. Staying here will keep me safe. Fleurah is *way* more annoyed." She pointed over her shoulder at Fleurah throwing stones onto a frozen lake and jumping up and down, trying to break the surface.

"I guess babysitting me isn't as appealing as participating in a tribal battle for the ages." A gust of wind blew off Fleurah's hood, while Arcadie's thrusters fought harder against the resistance.

"She does realise that by jumping up and down on a frozen lake there is a chance she could kill herself, right? A sense for dramatics runs in the family?"

Lilianna scoffed playfully. "Okay, so you've decided on being passive aggressive with me. That's fine." She shifted her stance so it was a little sassier, prompting Juniper to raise an eyebrow. "You're like… an undiscovered element. I know there is more to you and I want to reach you, but at some point you need to react to something so I can understand who you really are."

"Your nerd dirty talk don't work on me, honey. I'm not Xan."

"Just come back in one piece then, Juniper, and hopefully one day we'll speak the same language." She leant forward and kissed her on the cheek, softly. It reminded Juniper of their nights in bed on Earth 2114.

Lilianna's blonde hair swayed as she ran to Fleurah to pry her sister away from the frozen lake.

Juniper watched her go, too stubborn to acknowledge how much the time they spent together on Earth 2114 actually meant to her. It was more than physical. She had chosen to be vulnerable with someone other than Xan. Shying away from how big that was worked for a little while, but seeing Lilianna with the strength to lay it all out on the line without expecting anything in return was humbling. Arcadie had warned her of this strength and only now was she beginning to understand the weakness in herself. Standing amidst carnage, she was strong enough to rip the heart from a chest, but to let her own heart lie in an open rib cage coffin waiting to be cradled was daunting beyond all measure.

Juniper turned back around to walk and join the fellowship of the ding-dongs. Sythkin was right behind her as she spun around.

"That sounded super intense. Did you want to evaluate how that could've gone better?" Sythkin asked.

"I'm actually going to m—"

"Make me a friend? I knew it." The Cryptoborg flopped a large arm across Juniper's shoulders and practically dragged them both toward Xan, Qilin and the tribesfolk packing their bags.

Juniper let out a groan and wondered if she could join Fleurah jumping on the frozen lake in hopes that a crack would appear and all her frustrations would drown in an instant.

CHAPTER 41

LOCATION: DRACIA
YEAR: 1180
MASSY – 7 YEARS OLD

The others didn't know much about the Darshan tribe. Hell, Massy didn't even know too much anymore. Wading through the thick fog of memory took more strength than usually required. From what he remembered his father was the next in line to lead the tribe, so did that make Massy royalty?

He was treated with respect within the tribe, but in his family circle, Massy was far from the golden child.

It started out badly for him. His father reminded him every day that he killed his mother. He was no baby assassin of course, but his birth had caused her death all the same.

It wasn't like they were one another's only lovers. Massy's father's swimmers just sped through to the target like a nuclear torpedo, leaving all others dead in the water. When Massy came into the world and killed his father's favourite concubine in childbirth, he wasn't looked upon kindly.

His two half-brothers ostracised him, while his father made him feel worthless. A lovely trauma cocktail that he drank down like rancid mother's milk.

But it all turned to a new level of festering shit when a pandemic level disease ran rampant amongst the tribe. It would've been easier to have been killed, but unfortunately Massy did not perish. His older brother, however, did die. Massy was six and the entire following year of his life got worse, something he'd believed wasn't possible.

Massy often wondered what he might have been if he was taken to Gemarine earlier than seven years old. Would he harbour the same drive to be the best? Would he still disregard others because he had no one that truly loved or believed in him?

His father gave him bruises and welts that he wore like medals. He made him train with the warrior tribesfolk until he threw up on the forest floor. He made him test the natural fauna with the gatherers to find cures for disease. Massy was the product of his father's anger, grief and frustration with fate. And in the next two years anything that he didn't win was unacceptable.

Salvation came shortly after, when he was picked up in a spaceship and taken to a new planet. All the incredulous things had become his reality. Massy had sat back, watching the pilot the entire way. He was besotted. Never had he seen something so cool, felt something so exhilarating.

This was his purpose.

The pilot delivered him to a clan where he was raised with love. Quickly, he was enrolled in the learning centre where he had many opportunities to make a difference.

But he continued to want to be the best, to dominate in every field. He would not rest until it was so. Early childhood trauma was definitely a thing. When he didn't win, he'd turned to aggression and insolence until he owned the world.

But when Xan waltzed in from the Wilds flanked by a rare creature and a horde of admirers, things changed. It was no longer as easy to win because that asshole got handed everything on a platter. Despite the hard work Massy had endured, nothing trumped luck and popularity.

Massy put his head down, flew through the flight centre training courses—and ended up top of his class. He did it all himself, and it felt so good.

But Xan couldn't stop rubbing shoulders with him at the learning centre so Massy did what anyone would do. Listened to the old adage— keep those enemies close.

Finally, post his crazy fuck-up after the pinnacle star festival, on the precipice of exile, Madame Bleu handed Massy a chance at not only redemption, but to stand next to her.

At the top was where he belonged.

CHAPTER 42

LOCATION: DRACIA
YEAR: 1173
JUNIPER – 24 YEARS OLD

On the third day, the blizzards had migrated into a boisterous bluster and the snow wasn't as deep and treacherous. They had made good ground, considering the conditions, but Juniper felt sorry for Qilin. Nimble footed, she darted across the snow like a winter ninja, bolting ahead and returning with an impatient look or a snow rat she'd managed to kill for dinner.

The sunset lazily splashed the skies in pink and orange hues, reaching out and anointing the troupe of hikers as they trudged across the snow. Xan called out, running toward a thawed lake, with ocean waves winking in the distance.

Juniper arrived by Xan's side, puffing out thick streams of condensation as he pointed to the water.

"Look Juniper, it's the Dracian Narwhal!"

Sure enough, she saw a cluster of tusks or spears of some kind emerge from the water, then the whale-like body of a sea creature swimming close to the surface.

"Fuck, don't get too close, they'll poke you in the eye with that forehead spear," she joked.

"Actually, that's a long tooth. It's wrapped in a whole bunch of nerves, so they use it mainly to help them swim and navigate rather than jousting or fighting one another." His face shone with childlike wonder as he watched the scene, Qilin whimpering excitedly at his side.

Imagine having a natural weapon like that and not using it? Being a placid species must be kind of nice.

Juniper was about to tease him about being the biggest nerd, not only in this world or timeline but in the entirety of the galaxy multiverse, but he reached for her hand and squeezed it, smiling at her with tears in his stupid nerd eyes.

She couldn't help but smile back.

In many ways, he hadn't changed in the decade or so she had known him. There he was, in absolute rapture because of some swimming dickheads. After all he had been through, innocence and purity still remained.

Juniper felt both sorrow and joy at the same time. Sorrow for herself, that the innocence and purity had departed her world long ago, knowing that she couldn't find true joy in something aesthetic or seemingly trivial like this. But her joy came knowing that the person she loved most in the universe still had this in him—to feel, to ignite a heart that could easily have grown cold.

She smiled at the long-toothed swimming unicorns and embraced the moment. A moment where simple things brought more joy than any imagined details could muster.

An Aranther tribesman jogged over. "We must get moving, we have—"

"Stop." Juniper held her hand up. "Go on ahead. We'll catch up."

"But—"

"Honestly, if you ruin this moment I'll turn you into a cock cannibal," Juniper snarled out of the side of her mouth.

He immediately scrunched his face in confusion. As Juniper watched it dawn on him, he slowly backed away, palms upturned.

"Let's sit down." Juniper patted the snow beside her, and Xan did so, with Qilin falling in line beside him. Juniper put her head on his shoulder, and they watched the lake surface's crinkle like brittle paper as the Dracian Narwhals flirted in the shallows. The sky was cast in clementine segments, harbouring brilliant splashes of fuchsia to complement the gleaming glares of the somnolent sun. The sunset burnt atop the glassy lake as a moment of calm presented itself in the midst of a civil war.

From one campfire in a cave to the next, the nights began to blend together. They ate well, considering their hike through snowy terrain. Fish caught from a hand line, snow rats hunted by Qilin, and baskets of frozen wild berries gathered by some of the tribesfolk all appeared on the menu. One of the nongendered Aranthers taught Xan how to extract sap from a *bulgar tree*; it tasted like maple syrup straight from the source.

Xan and Sythkin took time to understand the Aranther mindlink and how it worked on Dracia. One of the tribe generals, Gruvian, spoke about it willingly. There was an important and potent plant called the *dillayla*. From what Juniper understood, it was very similar to hallucination-inducing toxins that opened parts of the brain. In this case, only Dracian royalty were permitted to partake in the ritual. Juniper knew that if Aranthers were to truly eradicate differences between the tribes, these laws needed to change. The entirety of the race would benefit from being at one in the mind. But it was all about the foreplay. You never start cooking main meals without oiling the pan, so to speak.

Qilin slept in between Juniper and Xan, warming one another each night. On various mornings Juniper would wake to find Sythkin spooning her, to which she replied by sending her sliding across the other end of the campsite.

"Body warmth is important," Sythkin would say with a wink topped with a cheesy smile. Juniper would just mutter under her breath while Sythkin skipped beside her in the devout pursuit of friendship.

As the hike wore on, the compacted snow and ice began to melt. On the seventh night it was still quite cold, but a lot more comfortable. The slush made it problematic for traction, and often Xan or Juniper would slip and fall on their ass, followed by a chorus of laughs and Sythkin offering a hand to help them up. Even in the midst of civil war, there were some things that were always considered hilarious.

But war is rarely civil.

During calm, calamity is never distant. Boisterous and belligerent, it hollers at the world until the calm is just a lone tear in a deluge.

A scream like tearing metal scattered the quiet. An Aranther tribeswoman dropped to her knees in the snow. A steel trap with sharpened teeth clamped around her ankle. Droplets of blood were pebbles in the snow on a path to pain. Flesh exposed, the white of the bone almost dissolved into the surroundings.

As her jaw opened for another piercing cry, an arrow found its mark. Red mist burst from her mouth. The arrow lodged at the base of her skull. She bent backwards, buried in white. There was a brief moment of *what the fuck,* as Xan's eyes widened in surprise. Qilin and Juniper saw shock take hold of his better judgement, shoving it down into a crevice, dank and dark. They dove toward him, and an arrow thumped into a tree trunk above his precious head. Mounds of snow fell from bulging branches after the impact.

Juniper dusted herself off and climbed across Xan, still in shock, sending bursts from the Cranston ray gun at figures emerging from the ground. Qilin leapt into the air, claws glinting in the light of the sun, tail spikes following her targeted destination. Juniper heard Qilin roar as she clamped onto the jugular of a soldier, tearing ferociously with her taut neck muscles until the body lay twitching on the ground. The artistry of blood spurts left a macabre mandala in the snow.

Juniper didn't see where Qilin would go next. The beautiful little beast could handle herself. The brutal grace of her murderous blow was divine, the willingness to charge toward the sharpened sickle with courage was her weapon. It was everything Juniper could only hope to be.

Dragging Xan to his feet, she spotted boulders of slick granite to their right. It was the perfect cover. "Get up you lump of shit!" she screamed, yanking Xan into action.

Xan stumbled on the slick ground in the sprawl of bodies, ducking flying arrows at head height. With a keen eye Juniper fired off shots to protect him. Approaching the rock, he finally slipped and fell flat on his face. In other circumstances she would have laughed, but as she searched the white and fell upon garnet flushes, she knew it was not the time.

Juniper stooped low to help Xan but a desperate howl from Qilin caught her attention. Her eyes followed the sound, and the world slowed. An arrow twisted through the air like a jagged asteroid in orbit. Reflectively her exoarm swiped across the arrow inches from lodging in between her eyes. Shards of wood and metal burst. Splinters and shrapnel stung her cheeks and neck. But she didn't have time to take stock of the injury.

Her jade eyes opened, Xan was crawling desperately to get behind the boulder, but a figure had emerged, charging with a long, rusted spear raised above the shoulder. There was only one outcome—plunge the spear into his back.

Xan would be no more.

Exoblades shot out, zooming like rabid hornets, but he heard them coming somehow. Without missing a stride, he swatted them away. One managed to penetrate the defences and scrape his bearded cheek. A nasty, deep gash that drew blood immediately.

Xan continued to splutter forward but he was no longer in the blade warrior's sights. The bearded man, long hair knotted down his shoulders, turned to face Juniper, and his scowl curled to a grin as if he'd already won.

That's right, you juggernaut oaf, believe it in your bones that I'll be easy.

Exofingers clasped onto their boronium slots, her Cranston ray gun nowhere to be found. She would take inspiration from Qilin and find a weapon within. They charged at the same time.

Juniper's arrogance surged as she galloped toward him. She braced her shoulder to drive into his gut. The arrogance failed her, not for the first time in life. He was twice her size, so when his shoulder met hers, she flew back as if a grenade exploded in her face.

She groaned on the ground as she watched the bearded doofus soaring in the air, spread eagled and ready to crush her. Juniper rolled quickly and he came down upon the ground instead. Vaulting atop his back she aimed her exoblades at the base of his neck. The island of a man shifted, and she dug in below his shoulder blades. Roaring like a savage bear, he swung this way and that, trying to get to her. Her exoblades were wedged so deep, she was stuck to him, flopping across his back like a fish in an evaporated rock pool. Releasing the exoblades, she was thrown across the ground again landing on the same shoulder. It was throbbing now. Her good arm was hanging limp at her side. Not so good anymore.

Is it fucking dislocated? 'Cause I can't have that.

She ran to the nearest tree and slammed her shoulder into the trunk, wrenching the shoulder back into place. "Ah fuck me!" she screamed.

When she turned around, oaf-face had already made it within striking distance despite his lumbering. The wrecking ball of his fist swung high, aiming to crush her model-worthy cheekbones. She ducked, saving her cheekbones but in the process exposing her forehead to his crunching upward knee. Her skull shook like a brass bell, and she stumbled back into the tree trunk. Vision shaking, claret cascading down her face, she brought her exoblades back to her fingers. Feeling them slide back in, she felt whole again. Her own sword pinched her hip, reminding her of its presence, and she dug it out as the enemy ran toward her. Double vision impairing her judgement, she stumble-rolled and swiped across his drawn fist. As she came up, crimson stained the snow. His arm was gone.

Welcome to the asymmetrical life my friend, it's quite uneven-tful.

Blood spurting like a fountain, pale faced and breathing heavily, he narrowed his eyes and marked her for death. He moved forward, in a relatively straight line considering the new imbalance.

Looming up once more, he swung a hefty left fist, and her block came up to protect her face. The wrist took the brunt of the hit but slammed into her own cheek and sent her sprawling across the slush.

Not the model cheekbones!

Dazed, she saw him coming again and this time launched into a kick, crunching his jaw. He stumbled back and she jumped at him, climbing two steps from the ground to his knee and grabbed a thick tuft of his beard, ripping it from his face as she focused on his remaining arm and crushed it in a boronium grip.

He roared and kicked out at her, catching her in the guts and sending her sprawling. In two gigantic steps his whole weight was on top of her. Even with one arm severed and the other completely shattered, he tried to bite down on her face. She reached up with both hands into his mouth as if tearing open a melon and with the strength of the exoarm, ripped his jaw until his face was obliterated.

Blood soaked into her vision as his body twitched with neuro detachment.

Juniper heaved off the limp corpse with a groan of exhaustion.

An explosion sounded. As she got to her feet she stumbled, searching through hazy vision toward the sound. A huge tree was in the process of collapsing. The trunk creaked with wooden groans; splinters cracked like a thunder overture. Its weight would crush her as if she were a bug under a boot.

Qilin bounded through the smoke, knocking into her and rolling away from the felled tree as it came crashing down to the graveyard of the forest floor.

Juniper took a break in the craziness of what was unfolding to bring her forehead to Qilin's after she had flapped her beautiful angelic wings. Qilin then licked her cheek and was gone a split second later. Presumably to check on Xan.

Juniper stood shakily on her two feet. She didn't usually get so dazed in a battle, but this was absolute carnage on a landscape totally foreign to her. She had to admit she was out of her depth.

The final archer must have sent the arrow from a short distance. Aranther warriors shouted when they saw it and soon after, the archer lay dead. But the arrow twirled gracefully still, splitting the air like a scarlet robin darting for prey. The air trembled at the arrow's rough touch, puncturing the expectation of gentleness. As it penetrated deeper through the dense forest of air, the compass called to it and focused its needle point toward the final destination. Juniper's eyes were glassy watching it as if she observed through a screen.

She didn't even have time to scream as it raced toward her heart. Her life would melt away like a geriatric memory lost in a chain of broken synapses. The sad smile of resignation was her own silent eulogy.

It was deafening.

CHAPTER 43

Sythkin watched Juniper's shoulders slacken as if she knew it would be over soon. The woman that never stopped fighting had given up. Fate restrained her with shackles too strong to oppose.

Sythkin saw the same arrow tear through the sky and in a split-second decision knew what fate had really planned. The moment that she pitched forward, diving into the arrow's path felt as if the past, present and future were interweaving around her, cushioning what would eventually be a deathly blow.

Sythkin packaged her life into a box of memories that she would open when the time was right. She spoke into the void, remembering what she had been through and knowing that her story was important to share in order to right the wrongs.

Innocence is the universe's gift to a child. To lose that gift at six years old was beyond tragic. As I knelt in the blood of my slaughtered mother, I felt innocence separate from my body. I shook her limp corpse, praying for comfort, praying her lullaby would touch the stars outside my window once more, praying the wails of her child would wake her.

But she was cold, even under the warmth of my wretched tears.

Grief took my innocence when a Gemarinian invasion slaughtered half my village.

Born into a broken world, I learned to fight. We fought so that we could do the breaking and not wait to be damaged any longer. Countless bodies had been shattered. The essence of who we were, decimated by genocidal intent. But we were not the only beings in the galaxy or across the universe that found one another in a desperate alliance against a potent threat.

Souls from other ravaged worlds came forth, wishing to be healed. Valkors told tales of the celestials – what they had created, their intention and how there was a way to heal the severance of plans squandered.

Suddenly there was hope.

Hope is dangerous when it's gifted so haphazardly. So easily unwrapped, its aesthetic prowess marvelled at until others bask in its shiny exterior. Hope is a plague for yearning hearts.

But our purpose became a mantra and we finally realised that we needed to fight to heal the galaxy rather than fighting to appease vengeance that bled from slain mothers or fathers. Everything could crumble around us, but if the ruin of your civilisation is inside you, nothing more will be built.

We searched for the crystals, we searched through the ancient texts and we pried against the reaches of the Gemarinian atmosphere to steal what Madame Bleu already had. But the army led by a fearless warrior Juniper, was often too overpowering, too brutal to find a way through.

For years it was the same. Toiling in the trenches while fate wanted something more for me, for us. Once I left the army and took up the post on Periah with the Oracles I felt more connected to the purpose. It might not have been action incarnate, but I found the time to think, to meditate, to read, to connect to more than violence, affirming my choice.

Every Oracle had the secrets of the timeline laid bare and that's why it was so important to be there to right the wrongs.

When the arrow sunk through Sythkin's flesh, she closed her eyes, ignoring the sharp sting. A deep breath followed to instil calm in the face of the impending slow and painful death. She reminded herself that she was fate's vehicle. The only Cryptoborg left in this cruel game to ensure that the timeline was restored.

Already she was wheezing. Already she felt the agony of the wound expand in her abdomen. The crucial organs that lay sheltered by supple skin, were now damaged and screaming at her—*Why?*

But fate silenced them.

Fate silenced *her*. For now.

As her body fell and Juniper's face filled her periphery, Sythkin motioned to smile.

"Why would you do that?" Juniper yelled into her face.

"It wasn't me." Sythkin coughed. "It was fate."

She couldn't read Juniper's expression. Maybe it was sympathy mixed with annoyance. But Juniper didn't talk; the tense boronium arm just dragged the Cryptoborg's body across the ground until she was laid out on a bed of fuzzy ferns. Through watery eyes Sythkin watched Xan and Juniper, bent over her body, feverish whispering ensued.

Sythkin closed her eyes. Consciousness was too much to bear.

XAN
24 YEARS OLD

Xan sat with his back against the wall, Qilin nuzzling into his side. Aranther warriors tended the fire. Flickering shadows were cast upon the cave walls, looming ghouls trapped in the essence of the land where they fell. Xan shuddered and Qilin moved in closer to him, making certain he felt comforted after his first glimpse of war. It had taken him by surprise. He was perturbed at how slow he was to react, how useless he felt. It was different than building rage, or even self-defence. He just wasn't used to the suddenness of it, the absolute chaos of violence that shattered the quiet calm of a hike.

He could foresee a civil war approaching on Gemarine and he silently promised he would not be caught out like that. He would prepare his mind so that his body would react accordingly.

Xan watched Juniper make Sythkin as comfortable as she could.

No one saw Juniper the way that he did. The hands that killed so easily caressed Xan so gently when she lay in his bed, tired and fulfilled. The same hands that had caused the scar on Sythkin's face. The Cryptoborg's life was at an end now, in a frozen wasteland far away from anyone she'd ever known. But yet, there was such grace in her, acting as a vehicle of fate—believing so deeply in that.

Juniper excelled at recognising who deserved her loyalty and it showed in the care she gave Sythkin in her final hours. It was easy to see that the person Xan saw in the privacy of their bond was slowly being absorbed into the entirety of who she was. In his eyes she was already perfect, but this made her divine.

Sythkin's breathing was laboured. Juniper had put a raggedy blanket on her and warmed her in the best way possible. Hours before they had inspected the wound and operated on it as best they could, suturing the laceration on the intestine with fine thread, stemming the bleeding. But without proper medical equipment the outcome would most likely be sepsis and death in a day or two.

Juniper shuffled her way over to Xan and Qilin. She scratched Qilin behind the ear, "Can you go over there and cosy up to Sythkin to warm her up, please?" Juniper pointed at the injured Cryptoborg, sweat gleaming on her mauve skin.

Qilin yawned and shifted onto her other side trying to ignore her. Juniper didn't take no for an answer, basically dragging Qilin to Sythkin's side. Unceremoniously, Qilin flopped onto the floor of the cave up against Sythkin and breathed out of her nose in an accentuated huff.

JUNIPER
24 YEARS OLD

"Yeah, yeah stop complaining you little princess," Juniper grumbled at Qilin as she turned and made her way back to Xan.

The fire light cast a glow on his chiselled cheekbones, and he smiled that smug reassuring smile as if he thought that's what she wanted. But *no buddy*. She wanted to take that smile and shove it into Qilin's anal cavity so he could taste what it was like to be a shithead. She also wanted to rage at him for being so…pathetic on the battlefield.

Juniper had splinters and metal shards embedded in her face and neck because she had to babysit little Xanny muffin.

Juniper gestured to Xan. "Walk with me."

"Where to?" He slowly rose with an old man groan.

"Further into the cave to have a more private chat." She flicked her bountiful hair and walked briskly ahead. Her muscles ached but she was all strength and poise. There was no way she would let him know how exhausted she was, and she wished that he had pride enough to do the same.

He shrugged. "Alright, we've been walking all day, but you know, let's do a bit more." The sarcastic chuckle echoed in the small space and Juniper cringed having to hear that dumb sarcasm reverberating again and again.

"You were slow as shit out there today and it nearly got you killed." She turned sharply to confront him face to face.

Xan scowled at her, "Yeah alright, I'm not a warrior queen like you, last time I checked. Go decapitate someone so you feel like you've accomplished something."

"Oh okay, shaming me for fucking protecting your ass as per usual. Ever since we were fifteen, I've had to pro—"

Xan grabbed her arm and drew her close so she could feel his stale breath on her nose. "I don't need your fucking protection."

Juniper looked at his hand, then back into his eyes, slowly. "Take your measly little hand off me."

"Or what?"

Her boronium arm came up faster than he could react, slamming him into the cave wall by the throat. Xan peeled back into the cave wall stunned.

Regaining some composure, he kicked out at her knee, and it buckled. Juniper's arm dropped to steady herself, and Xan drove her to the opposite wall. She went to knee him in the junk, but he parried it and then sent an almighty crack throughout the cave as he slapped her hard on the cheek.

They both stopped moving. Nearly stopped breathing after the echoes of the slap faded. Juniper's hand came up to her face. Xan's hand dropped by his side. "Oh shit, I'm so sorry."

But Juniper didn't hear him. She licked her lips. Her own blood, wet and delicious on her tongue. It all made sense now as she felt desire pound throughout her body. It had been a long time since she'd had Xan, and this was her way of acting out to get it. He moved forward to inspect her lips, but she launched her mouth upon his and they collided with force. Without her prompting, his hand found her throat and he squeezed. She sung raspy notes of consent in his ear, and his hand squeezed harder as he kissed her ear lobe. He was growling in her ear. She reached down and felt him. She moaned before he'd even touched her.

"Fuck me now, I can't wait any longer."

The zipper was stuck. He tore a hole. She zipped him down. His delicious cock emerged, and she gripped it as his suit fell around his ankles. Ecstasy was a groan that escaped her once more. She flipped around, pressing her cheek against the wall of the cave, Xan manhandled her ass and ripped the hole in her suit further. Lathered his tip in her wetness and slowly entered her, making sure she felt all of him filling her.

What followed was anything but sensual. It was carnal, it was rough and it was what she needed. The whack of his thrusts against her ass, the teeth clamping down on the side of her neck, the hand gripped around her throat, his words spat in her ear, "You're taking it like a good girl."

"I'm not Lilianna, Xan. I'm your slut. Now treat me like one."

He gripped her hair, pushed her cheek hard against the wall of the cave and gave her everything he had, and it was enough. He was always more than enough.

"Listen, Juniper, I want to say something."

Xan looked weighted, like he'd been considering these words for some time. "I wanted to say I'm sorry for neglecting your feelings. For not letting you break about your crew mates back then. It was selfish of me."

Juniper gazed down at her boots. She'd tried so hard to push all that down, to forget that failure, to forget those poor innocent dweebs having to die just for her to be taught a lesson about the galaxy.

"I'm not perfect, Xan. As much as you can't believe it." She smirked. "But no, I understood Qilin was the number one concern at that time. I really would never have let anything happen to her. Things were just...a little overwhelming. The whole continuing to sacrifice myself over and over."

"You will never know how much that meant to me."

"Don't get all sentimental on me now, idiot."

"No, seriously." He gripped her hand, "If we make it through this, I will spend the rest of my life giving you what you deserve. I'll always put my own concerns and needs behind yours."

She laughed with the warmth of a solar flare, her hands on his chest. "Xan, I don't need big gestures. We are more than any of that. But thank you. You can be the pretty petals on a flower, and I'll be the sturdy stem. We both need the other, just one is more valuable."

Xan perked up. "Are you implying that I'm weaker than you?"

"It wasn't an implication, it's a straight up fact." Juniper batted her eyelashes and folded her arms while turning away from him.

Xan growled, "I'll show you," as he launched at her, pinning her onto the rocky floor of the cave. Echoes of her laughter were leached from the walls and dripped onto bare glistening skin. Skin pinned to flesh writhed in serpentine coils sheathed in the darkness of their own fragility.

CHAPTER 44

LOCATION: DRACIA
YEAR: 1173
JUNIPER – 24 YEARS OLD

Imaginary scenarios were tumours growing inside the maze of the mind. Eventually the cancer would consume the host.

In the moments traversing the battlefield, sodden with the flaked tears of a mournful winter, the complaints of the body sought to be heard. The physicality of the journey was all consuming. The bitter cold, the muscle aches, the stomach pains, cracked lips bitten ravenously by frost. If one wanted a ceasefire for the ammunition of the mind, here it was.

Juniper's entire body was steeped for days in muddy trenches, her skin sagging in disgust. Xan and Qilin in their hike over the Wilds had encountered many desolate and hopeless moments. But nothing felt as grim as what they all witnessed now.

Bodies lay covered in ice, solidifying the moment of their gruesome death.

Qilin used their bodies as mounds to observe further into the horizon, sounding off a circumspect growl if anything beyond seemed awry.

After they spent days traversing the terrain, the frozen climate waned. Tufts of grass became islands in the mud paths as they left snow trails behind. Lush edible vegetation provided a nutritious snack, albeit bland. Wildflowers were plucked from their new life and steeped in boiled water. Floral tea never tasted so good after the land of ice and snow.

The forest kingdom lay ahead of them now, lush with vines that slithered up the trunks of ferns. Bold green colours were hushed by the shade of canopy giants as they walked beneath rapacious daggers of sunlight.

A negotiator guard hoisted the flag of the Wyndry tribe and marched to the vine gates, separating the forest glen and the kingdom behind. Menacing thorns stood aloft the gate like archers with sharpened arrow heads ready for deployment.

Juniper knelt beside Sythkin's body as she jerked with rasping breaths, her hand flexing with convulsions. Xan's palm rested on Juniper's shoulder, and Qilin stood by her side watching the gates vigilantly. Strangely, it was comforting to feel them beside her as she considered the next move. Sythkin's whispers transported Juniper out of her mind. "This is my time, warrior woman. You must take me there now."

Juniper closed her eyes, and whispered back, "Let's just wait and see what comes of this negotiation."

"You know this will not work. The Aranther needs to see into my mind," Sythkin said defiantly even in the grip of her final fight.

A member from the other tribe met the negotiator in the middle. The dried vine gates waited beyond the pastures of knee length grass, swaying in prayer for the planet's salvation. The two representatives from each tribe conversed for mere minutes. The negotiator of the Wyndry tribe returned panting, "It's no use. There is a flat denial from the Darshans."

Juniper wanted to collapse onto the wildflowers and crush their beautiful buds with her broken body. She wanted the scent of their perfume to exhale a mist that would allow them to hide for days. But she reminded herself of war. War was perpetual. The physical battle might last months, but the mental battles remained. War only ends with the trill of a final breath.

She whispered to Sythkin, "Are you ready? This will not be a...nice... time for you."

"I believe that the scar upon my face is nice. It is so because if our purpose is to better the galaxy, then we win. If we suffer horrors for the sake of a beautiful intention, then it is not a horror at all. A nice sacrifice."

"I'll write that on your memorial stone." Juniper sighed, then launched herself up grabbing the stretcher Sythkin lay upon and carried her onward toward the gates ahead.

"I'm glad I have at least one friend to take care of that for me." Sythkin's voice undulated with humour, as if she knew that Juniper had no choice but to accept their friendship. Sythkin had taken an arrow to the guts for her.

"You know you win by default, right? Like, it's not even a fair fight."

"I win not because of this; I win because I actually *did* start to worm my way inside your hateful little heart." Her giggle turned to a gurgle.

Juniper considered it for a moment. The little shit had been endearing in all her overt efforts to be her friend. She even made Juniper chuckle internally on several occasions in her obvious light-hearted attempt to gain her trust. Sythkin was right. It *had* been working. A pang of sadness hit Juniper as she continued to roll forward, knowing that maybe with this friendship she could've repaired the guilt she felt for being a pawn for Madame Bleu. Gestating such hate for a race when they did nothing but strive to live, while she and the Gemarinian army stomped upon their beautiful intentions for nothing more than power.

The cruel part of this fateful friendship was that it couldn't blossom, and it wouldn't heal her. It would die before the bruised skies of regret were completely eradicated by the evening umbra.

Juniper screamed Morcombe's name at the horizon, still cast in a hubris glow as dusk encroached.

She would be a stranger, an alien to him. Marvest, his twin brother, taken to Gemarine years ago, would have been a guiding light in ending the civil war. But since he was no longer on the planet, no longer a confidant of his twin brother who ruled over the Darshan tribe, the civil war would continue until Dracia met its demise.

Morcombe strode forward with an advisor or a bodyguard. It was difficult to tell from that distance. Juniper stood in the field of flowers, swaying from exhaustion but careful to exude strength in front of the ruler of the Darshan tribe.

"Nice of you to finally grace us with your presence."

He narrowed his eyes and the circular birthmarks creased with disdain. "Who do you think you are, alien?"

Juniper shuddered at his appearance, a reminder of Massy at the very sight of those birthmarks. Despite that, he looked different, with a pugnacious jawline covered by a thick coating of dark hair punctured by a swarm of greys. Long hair flowed in knotted clumps, eyes that were the colour of a spring valley appraised her. She swallowed hard and found courage enough to play her role.

"Has the Darshan tribe not heard of civility? Is this how guests are treated? My, my, how very disappointing." A playful smile was etched on her face, bathed in golden light from the sulking sun.

Morcombe's expression never wavered as he rudely snatched at the access into her mind. His brainwaves were tsunamis crashing into a meagre breakwall. Juniper recoiled with the strength of his intrusion, but she fought hard to open only the necessary doors, blocking access to the basement filled with cobwebbed tears and repressed trauma.

"So, it appears this alien is more than anything we have encountered before." Morcombe stroked his bearded chin. His tone was softer now, more curious having accessed part of Juniper's mind. "A time traveller, a warrior, a promiscuous vixen."

"I believe you're searching for the word, 'slut,' and I wear that as a badge of honour, so no harm done your…grace." She bowed mockingly but he caught it, unlike the chief of the Wyndry tribe.

"Disrespect is certainly not the way to win my acceptance of your proposal." He shook his head, but the expression remained neutral as his mane of hair billowed with the movement.

Juniper reprimanded herself within her thoughts and realised Morcombe might be able to see or hear that. He smiled knowingly, as if he'd caught her.

"As we speak, there is an approaching storm on the Wyndry tribe. You would have to do a lot to convince me to call off the strike." A shining gleam was in his dusty green eyes. She had seen it before when he was trying to be charming, but this was laced with an authority that she'd seen in only Madame Bleu.

Juniper immediately thought of Lilianna getting caught up in the madness on the other side of the snow and ice. She shook her head as if to convince herself it would be okay. But the time on earth spent with Lilianna had changed her. She liked being her protector, she liked teaching her an array of things, but most of all she admitted to simply enjoying her company.

If Juniper was a fist and Xan was an open palm, Lilianna was the arm that brought functionality without the chaos and the calm without the crazy. Where Xan and Juniper were often extremes of sorts, Lilianna allowed them to check themselves and to measure what was right. Juniper still didn't really identify with romance, but she knew that as part of a clan, they would be unstoppable.

Sythkin rose gingerly, no longer lying flat on the stretcher, and began to speak. "It's me you need to implore."

"Who are you now?" Morcombe snapped.

"I beg of you to listen. I'm going to leave my mind open to you. You must change your mind when you see, otherwise there is no hope for the galaxy. There are things I have seen…they *must* make a difference." The last line was uttered more to the universe than Morcombe. Hope was never as potent as when it came from a martyr.

Morcombe's brow furrowed as if he doubted her claim, but he closed his eyes, readying to enter her mind. Sythkin yelled, "Wait." The dying Cryptoborg turned her gaze to Juniper and smiled, beckoning her closer.

Juniper knelt down and Sythkin relaxed back onto the stretcher, holding Juniper's real hand tightly. "Make things right again, won't you?"

Juniper fought hard against the tear that eventually trailed down her cheek. She hadn't cried for many of the fallen she'd cared for in their final moments. She hadn't even wept for her own soul engulfed by a setting sun. But even the sun must rise again, and in that tear, deeper things awakened. Things that would ultimately make her stronger in that final battle.

In the end, those you are surrounded by are the ones who have given you more than they've taken. They've helped you grow, influenced you. But the key is to always let their words and actions stay with you.

Sythkin, Lilianna, Arcadie, Ryker, Qilin and Xan. It took a team of them to help Juniper. And only when she was ready did she start letting them in. But doesn't change always take a team creating a movement that spurns others to turn outward? She had turned, and she would never go back.

CHAPTER 45

LOCATION: DRACIA
YEAR: 1173
SYTHKIN 27 YEARS OLD

*B*efore adopting the post on Periah, all Cryptoborg fate oracles travelled to four destinations to reinforce how important it was to unite the celestial crystals. Earth, Dracia, Sytheria and the Senmore Section where the rubble of Ralis, the Valkors' home planet, floated in space.

We didn't just watch from afar. Ships filled with wide-eyed soldiers landed on each lifeless world.

Earth was too dangerous to land upon. It was mined to its very core, which disrupted the magnetic fields. Solar flares scorched the Earth with deadly radiation, and it was still too unpredictable to explore.

When we landed on Dracia, sunken skulls crunched beneath our boots as we walked. Spires of bones were piled high from burial pits like petrified tree trunks withered by the screeching sun.

When we landed on the capital city of Sytheria, the neon signs had long winked out, succumbing to sleep. Large spiders lurked between rotting *buildings, casting opportunistic webs across the length of alleyways. Robot parts lay dismembered and discarded like metal fungi sprouting with poisonous rusted caps.*

When extinction is all you see, it's hard to maintain the belief that hope lies beyond the horizon. But sometimes when hope can't be reached, a belief in a higher power is all you have. Whether it's a god, the presence of fate, the wondrous universe or the combined power of celestials. We needed something to push us forward.

For years I put my stock in fate. And fate brought me to you. To give you my sight, to give you my heart so that you can help piece the shattered fragments of the galaxy back together.

This is not a warning. This is not an imagined reality. This is your future if you don't do something about it now.

Morcombe, Marvest was your brother and your valued confidante. He would have been the one to initiate the coming together of the tribes. But Madame Bleu foresaw that if he was taken from the timeline, then the planet would fall to ruin, and she could extract the resvourtol *from near the planet's core to help power Gemarine.*

I have been placed in your path to warn you, to plead you to reconsider your stalwart stance on the union of the tribes. If you remain this way, then you too will contribute to the genocide of the Aranther race.

With my last dying action, I beg this of you.

MORCOMBE
36 YEARS OLD

After Sythkin had thrown her thoughts into the storm of Morcombe's mind, the rain began to ease, but the clouds remained.

Her last act was to plead with Morcombe to consider coming together. He waited for the raging internal debates, the tantrums thrown from one brainwave to the next but they never came.

Silence was horror.

Silence was absolute mortification.

It was one thing to hear her words, but flickers of Sythkin's memories perforated Morcombe's cerebral defences. He saw the desolation, the total annihilation.

Sometimes the tangible moves people. When the future was laid out before him it was hard to deny that union actually meant preservation.

CHAPTER 46

LOCATION: DRACIA
YEAR: 1173
LILIANNA – 22 YEARS OLD

The cold was more than Lilianna could take. For seven days she slept wrapped in an animal hide cocoon, trying desperately to feel a pinch of warmth. Each morning she fought hard against emerging and she certainly didn't flap with patterned wings as she evaded wispy snowfall. Her boots dragged through the cave dwellings; frosty condensation was a fleeting, misty cloud as she huffed.

Fleurah and Arcadie tried to entertain her as best as they could, but her thoughts belonged to distant hearts. She imagined Qilin, Juniper and Xan lying dead on fresh blankets of white, fine particles of vermilion dust scattered around them like petals. Not knowing was hardest to endure for those who waited.

As the sun sunk low in the sky, she felt a change in the wind. Intuition was internal and maybe the planet reacted in the same way. The changes enacted by shifting currents and changing weather patterns was like her intuition. The thump in her gut told her that trouble lay across the frozen lake. Something was coming.

Coming for them.

Robose, the chief's advisor, had been yelling commands throughout the tunnels. Tribesfolk hustled past in battle armour grunting in reply. Spears occasionally scraped the cave walls as they filed past the trio of outsiders, always glancing at Arcadie in astonishment and awe.

Lilianna raced up to Robose. "What's going on here?"

"You must protect yourselves. The Darshan tribe is advancing upon us." He turned and fled in the opposite direction, leaving Lilianna baffled.

"Did he just say, the other tribe is coming here *now*?" Fleurah asked a little too excitedly. "My boredom will be cured!"

"This is civil war on a planet we know nothing about! Why does that excite you?"

"Doesn't it make you feel alive, sis?" Fleurah grunted, clenching both her fists.

"What, staring death in the face?"

"Yes! Exactly! There isn't a time when we feel more attuned to thrumming veins, beating hearts, or circulating air—until the stare of the reaper dares us to blink."

Arcadie floated to Lilianna's side. "I'm definitely with Lilianna on this one, I must say."

"I'm going to find some armour for us all, c'mon!" She skipped off in the direction of where the tribesfolk had emerged, hooting and yahooing like a madwoman. Lilianna had no other choice but to follow her lead. That was by far the most concerning alert of the day.

Lilianna felt and looked ridiculous in the armour. She stood straight like a taller version of Arcadie, spear upright in her shaking right hand. Armour made from animal skin and metal mined from the Plaxxon region of Dracia hung loose on her body as she surveyed the field of future battle separating the break wall and the cave structure.

An icy wind came from the north with sharp teeth and an angry bite.

Horns sounded. They were close now. Lilianna glared at the opposing tribe marching in formation to the walls that appeared so strong but really could crumble in an instant.

The Wyndry tribe held their lines; archers with shaking arrows dared not let fly. Lilianna looked toward Chief Ghanasis only metres away from her to the left, and he breathed in deep, with a resolute face. He had already cried out that they must defend with honour at any cost.

The negotiator rode out with the sun rising into the morning sky, intent on meeting the Darshans on the back of a Marillidor. They were strong beasts, with a light coating of shaggy sable fur, sharpened daggers for tusks and large soulful eyes.

Frost flaked across the ground in the early hours before the reach of the sun had squeezed it senseless. Under the hooves of the strong beasts, the frost sunk deep into the ground after being crushed to liquid.

It all happened so quickly. Arrows whispered through the air and found their mark. Three lodged between creases in the armour and Wyndry soldiers fell, sliding off the Marillidor onto the ice.

A cheer rose from the other side and a cohort charged on the backs of their beasts, archers from behind sending arrows over the wall closest to the cave kingdom entryway.

The Wyndry tribe let fly their arrows in return and charged forth to meet the onslaught.

Clashes of armour ripped like a storm across the sky. Spears sunk deep into flesh, daggers found folds in the metal and betrayed their kin. Bodies lay trampled and trembling on the ground, as the Darshan tribe continued to advance.

The chief's stern cry startled Lilianna. "Bear arms and defend our land!"

He turned, pushing past Lilianna, and rushed out into the foyer to greet the attackers of his kingdom. Fleurah followed with a screech of the wild, emanating from deep within her. Arcadie motioned to follow, leaving Lilianna unsure of where to go and what to do. The spear felt foreign in her hand, and she could think of no better place than in Xan's bed, curled in his strong arms with Juniper's fingers enclosed around hers. It had happened only once. In the middle of her first experience of war she wanted to feel warm and in love, not drowning in a cesspool of hate.

Sickness spread. Nerves stung like pinpricks. It hampered everything, made her fear harder rather than keeping her alive. It was all preservation for her, and she hid behind the wall, peeping from the entrance to the cave where Arcadie electrocuted an oncoming troupe of attackers, always covering Fleurah, who was chaotic in her defence of a kingdom she barely knew.

An arrow bounced off Fleurah's armour and clattered to the ground. She was relieved and yelled in exaltation underneath a battered iron helmet. But it didn't last long. An arrow found its mark in the fleshy part of her thigh, and she dropped to the ground.

Lilianna stood up then. The fear for someone else was greater than self-preservation. She tore down stairs filled with bodies split like mitosis, others stuffing entrails back into open gashes. Swallowing bile, she focused on making it to the open mouth of the cave. The wind howled, sleet thumped into her cheeks and she shivered, creeping her way to Fleurah's side.

A large wooden bat swung across her, collecting her in the armoured chest. It launched Lilianna into the air, stealing the breath from her in an instant. Landing on her back, she slid several metres on the ice before halting. After a moment of darkness, she opened her eyes. A heathen covered in furs loomed above her with the bat.

She wanted to cry but the tears would freeze before sliding across her cheeks. The grief she felt for a future unfilled was inside her, and it hurt more than whatever the bat could do.

She farewelled that future by imagining perfect scenarios to guide her through death.

Qilin, Juniper, Xan and Lilianna sitting beside a stream on a chequered picnic blanket. The sky was bruised, punctured in beautiful violet blotches by the sun's fist. Underneath the comforting arms of treeferns, smiles were shared like freshly baked bread. Birds skimmed the surface of the water, exposing iridescent scales of colourful fish beneath. The world perpetually unveiled treasures both around them and within them.

The scenarios that she imagined were all she had now. Tears bubbled in the brook of her resignation. Her distant heart murmured, reverberating in the hollow pits of a rusted iron cage. Willing her to defibrillate with a spark of hope.

The bat was raised high, and she closed her eyes before the end came.

The spark was out.

CHAPTER 47

LOCATION: DRACIA
YEAR: 1173
JUNIPER – 24 YEARS OLD

Not even a minute had passed in the real world, after they emerged from their cerebral hibernation.

Sythkin's body fell flat, her essence ebbed away and she was gone, succumbing to her injuries. Juniper held the Cryptoborg's cold, limp hand in hers. Tears fell like shifting pebbles in the dark that tumbled down from the boulder pressed up against Juniper's heart. She thought it was immovable, but this parasitic Cryptoborg had wormed inside until Juniper could do no more than succumb to the disease. Sythkin forgave the foe who broke her world and loved her as a friend. Gifting all those broken pieces so that her foe could build anew.

Morcombe was thrown onto his backside in the field of flowers. He sat there with tears streaming down his face.

After the moments required to compose himself, he cautiously rose as if doing so too quickly could evoke a haemorrhage.

"I...I...didn't know it could be so...bad."

Juniper didn't know what he saw. But the past few days the Cryptoborg had tried to impart as much of her wisdom upon Juniper as possible, detailing atrocities spanned across the galaxy. But a few days could not compare to a lifetime, which is what Morcombe might have had access to.

Juniper suddenly felt that pang of serious concern for Lilianna in the Wyndry fortress and stammered, "Have you called off the Darshan troops in the siege at Wyndry?"

He shifted uneasily. "No, I haven't as yet. I—"

"Do it now!" yelled Juniper.

Morcombe initially recoiled at the way she spoke to him but then recalled the weight of his decisions. He closed his eyes and in a relative second declared, "It is done."

Juniper breathed out.

"My strength wanes. In order for me to preserve this telepathic connection I must consult the *dillayla*. Come, bring your fellowship inside the gates. I welcome the Wyndry tribe to Darshan land."

Juniper slowly nodded her head. From the outside looking in, others might say,

"Oh, that was easy to convince these tribal leaders to drop years of hatred and just come together."

But with the currency of an alien's life and a bleak future of absolute fuck all to look forward to, what would anyone do?

"I am permitting you to take the *dillayla*." Morcombe spoke as he extended the cup of hot liquid out to her, tea leaves wading on the surface.

Juniper started to back away. "What? Why would you offer this?"

"Because this is the cleansing of decades worth of sins, sins that would have drowned the planet in blood until..." He turned away, unable to finish.

"What did Sythkin show you?"

"She had travelled to all these broken worlds—her eyes saw Dracia barren of life, ravaged by greed and gluttony." Morcombe breathed in deep, needing to compose himself before continuing. "When you see the bones of your sons, daughters, of countless generations piled high enough that they're trees, the burnt husk of the planet that once thrived with... life, one can change dramatically."

Juniper nodded. "I know a lot about changing."

"Yes, but you are guarded still. You closed off parts of yourself so I wouldn't know you. If we are to repair this world, these connections between tribes, you must be willing to share...everything."

Juniper was good at sharing her body, but she could only think of one person who truly knew who she was and even that wasn't *everything*. She felt sick even before consuming the herbal tea.

"I don't want to lose myself forever."

Morcombe laid a hand on hers. "This transcendence is momentary, but the learnings you will gain will last a lifetime."

Juniper hesitated, watching the herbs swirl in the cup made from the dried husk of a circular fruit. Was she ready for this change? Was it that important to empathise with these Aranther tribesfolk? Enough for her to let them into the carnival of insanity that was her mind.

Morcombe moved in close to her as she stood watching the swirling tea, "Sythkin's dying wish was for you to join us."

"Why would she ask that of you?"

"She said, you would know what her answer would be."

Fate. It was always about fate with her.

Juniper looked behind her. Qilin lay on a bed of flattened flowers, while Xan watched intently, his face creased with concern. It should have been him, the man that wanted to save worlds and creatures and every fucking thing that ever hummed, tweeted or sprouted a leaf. But for some reason she was here with the tea in her hands.

"Bottoms up," she murmured.

She drank it down like a shot of *viscous vulva's* at the Fusion bar. This time though, her mind was getting fucked.

CHAPTER 48

LOCATION: DRACIA
YEAR: 1173
JUNIPER – 24 YEARS OLD

Juniper stood on the precipice of the shared plane of consciousness. After taking the *dillayla* tea she no longer felt trepidation breathing down her neck. She'd already made the choice and now it was a mission of discovery. Of the self, of an alien race, of the many fragments of the universe she needed to understand.

Spreading her arms across, she took a breath and let her mind fall. She was a cinder block tumbling from the top of a skeletal structure.

Memories burnt through her—vivid colours in the mural of her life. Her biological mother holding her tight after birth, laughter as she walked to her father for the first time, the Gemarine ship taking her in the dead of night, the learning centre, meeting Xan, her first night at Fusion covered in bodily fluids, faces of her kills haunting her, Edaline beheaded, losing her arm, discovering Boorak's betrayal, Lilianna smiling at the bar, writhing in the bed with Xan and Lilianna, Qilin licking her face.

It felt like she was back in those moments and the emotions were joining the flood, pushing against the gates, breaking containment.

The fall was brief as she was scooped into the gathering of minds. Initially, it was a blast of overwhelming energy that encircled her mind, a stinging migraine with its burst of pain so intense she squealed to contain it, but in an instant, it was gone, replaced by euphoria.

The avatars of the minds were before her. Morcombe, with his thick speckled beard and the yellowing forehead birthmarks, Chief Ghanasis of the Wyndry tribe, shimmering blue skin like arctic ice and Empress Haranthi of the Plaxxon tribe, standing tall with her shoulders bulging, green skin with silver sigils that glowed on her cheeks. They looked as they did in physical form, but all floated in a room of white.

"The discussions of the treaty will commence shortly," Morcombe explained. "I thank all of you for being here and for sharing a collective mind for the first time in a long time. In a moment I will show you the warning from our departed messenger through my memories. This is so that we can align our commitments for the future, and you can see how far we had fallen and how close we have come to the end. Firstly though, I welcome Juniper. The first outsider to be permitted into the mindlink."

A feeling of unease spread through her. The feeling was not her own, yet it invaded all her senses, nonetheless.

Haranthi spoke in a deep, regal tone, "Morcombe, this is blasphemy. It spits in the face of every tribal leader that come before us. I don't know if I can—"

"Haranthi, sister, Morcombe has seen with his own eyes what the true cost of division is. Should we not let him speak and put his case forward before rushing to condemn?" Ghanasis asked.

"Very well," Haranthi conceded, her flowing silver hair like fine threads of lichen caught in an evening breeze. "I will reserve my judgement. But the collective truth has always been sacred, and it will not be taken lightly shall this fail to heed the required result."

"If I may," Juniper began, "I apologise for the intrusion. I am here as a guest of Morcombe, but also as a representative of the departed messenger. She very much wished for me to be here. I would just like to respect her wishes."

Juniper had never tried so hard to be polite. Although Sythkin might not have been treated with as much dignity as Juniper could have given when alive, she certainly deserved respect beyond the grave.

Haranthi's scowl softened. "Very well."

"Concerns aside, I want to thank you, Juniper, for being willing to open yourself to us, so that we could see what war took from you, what Gemarine took from you, and learn how we can be better," Morcombe explained.

"I came on this journey to help repair what has been broken, so take what you need from me in order to help."

The leader of the Darshan tribe smiled. "You never came here because you truly cared about the plight of others, though, it must be said. You came here because of a duty to someone whom you love." Juniper motioned to protest, but she knew the truth deep down. If it wasn't for Xan and her desire to protect him, she would've let everything else burn.

"We will show you what we have each endured. You will feel more than you can possibly handle, but experiences that help you grow are merely notches in the expansive tree of life."

"Do you feel as though you can handle—"

"I'm willing to see everything." Her voice shook. There was no need to hide here. She feared how this might change her, but if everyone stood still, who would build a better world? She was willing to move now and be more than a puppet for a psychopath. She wanted to be forged anew, with ideals that she believed in. She wanted to atone for all the pointless lives that had been damaged by everything she had done.

I'm ready.

They were gentle, like a slow sensual fuck. In this context of a mind sharing orgy, she actually appreciated it.

In the mindlink, she was moved to tears with the heartbreak of death, swelled with pride as tribes fortified their structures and overcame adversities, trembled with anxiety with all the plights that faced them. Most of all, when Sythkin's memories were replayed to her, she felt an overwhelming sense of regret. The way she treated her, dismissed her, contributing to the slow downfall of Cryptoborgs. It sincerely broke her heart. There was no longer that pure hatred and apathy in her. She felt *everything*. She brimmed with love when it was unrefined, flaws and all. The mindlink reinforced to her, to take those mistakes and burn them with love, so new seeds will sprout from the ashes. They agreed to do the same.

Juniper was overwhelmed. When they let go, she couldn't hold on to anything but sleep. And so she faded from the mindlink, buried in blankets of hope.

XAN
24 YEARS OLD

Xan carried Juniper in his arms, following behind Morcombe and his deputy chief on their way to the accommodation. They walked a path lined with young ferns and interesting hexagonal flowers, stained with a gradual ombre of dark vibrant colours to light. Juniper's eyelids flickered, and she groaned every so often, as if struggling in a fitful dream.

"Are you sure she's okay?" Xan strained under her weight, his muscles rippling while his forehead creased with concern. Qilin pressed her little wet nose to Juniper's earlobe and tried to sniff out some kind of lifeforce within her.

"The mindlink is often exhausting for a seasoned Aranther, let alone a Human with no experience at all," Morcombe assured Xan.

A wooden hut built around a large trunk came into view. Xan craned his head to see a sprawling village of tree houses ranging from the heights of the canopy, shaded by vibrant green leaves to the forest floor. The floor was punctured by shrewd saplings, waving quillwort fingers and mounds of moss weaving through delta maidenhair plants. Mosquito-like creatures buzzed by his ear, and he couldn't wait to lather on the local insecticide to protect him from the itchy, angry welts that were sure to appear.

"I'll leave you with Jaskien, my deputy, and he will lead you to your hut." Morcombe bowed. "I can't express how thankful I am that you helped us."

Xan felt guilty, as they climbed over exposed roots and slippery rocks to get to their hut, and Qilin leapt from tree branch to tree branch just above their heads, making a little game for herself. Xan had been all gung-ho about his mission—trying to win some game of his own against Madame Bleu. But these were all real lifeforms on the ground, wiped out of existence because of her. He gazed around at the forest, as Qilin dislodged leaves that fell onto Xan's head.

This would have all been destroyed, because of selfishness, for greed, for power. Power was a rotting disease, infiltrating the very essence of who we were until buried fossils remained. Preserved only by the love we had at birth, not at all by what we became.

"Here it is, everything should be ready for you inside." Jaskien gestured to the door, but his eyes darted from Xan to a hut in the distance.

Xan noticed woodsmoke wafting across the village, dousing the damp, earthy scent that filled his nostrils.

"Thanks for your help, Jaskien. Is everything okay, by the way?"

"Oh, my concubine is pregnant and is scheduled to give birth shortly. I've left my two sons and some other tribesfolk to look after her today, but at this late stage, it's always better to be there with her." He looked away as if embarrassed.

Xan placed Juniper down onto a bed, coated in netting to ward off the mosquitos. He walked to Jaskien, placing a hand on his shoulder. "Congrats to you, my friend. That's wonderful news. I'm sure you're beyond excited."

Jaskien relaxed a little, shoulders easing. His smile was much less like a haiku of happiness and more like a grand opus.

"I am indeed."

"Do you have any names picked out?"

"Well, if it is a girl, I really like Esme."

"That's beautiful."

Qilin jumped onto the foot of the bed, curling up just a fraction beneath Juniper's feet.

"What about a boy?"

"In our language there's a word that means 'flying free.' If it's a boy, I want him to roam the tribes and bring everyone together."

"What's the word?"

"Massy," he said simply, walking to the door and opening it. A gentle wind flowed into the hut. Xan's feet felt like century-old boulders stuck in a dry creek bed.

Xan recovered as best as he could. "Ah, well I wish you the best of luck…with it all."

"Thank you, sir. Goodnight."

Xan stood looking at the back of the door until the soft evening noises of the forest became shrill cries of various creatures killing in the dark.

Time travel had already walloped him over the head in more ways than one over the course of their mission. But this hurt the most.

Juniper had said earlier in the trip, *"Time travel is the universe's way of shoving a finger up your ass without warning. It always surprises you; it hurts to even consider it and it is far from fun."*

Something so crass had never been so…right.

Now that a new timeline had been created because of their intervention, Xan couldn't help but wonder if the Massy who was about to be born would grow into the Massy he knew. Or in this timeline he would stay on to fulfil his *true* destiny?

Would he become a deputy leader like his father? Would he cure a terrible disease? Would he fight off an enemy force who tried to take over Dracia?

Whatever it was, he couldn't help but feel guilty for thinking—would it be better for the galaxy if Massy was never born?

He quickly scuppered the thought.

Pain can make meat out of yearning hearts. Flinging it at carnivorous hounds salivating for a meal. But we are more than a hearty meal for ravenous beasts. Even damaged hearts shaped by pain can grow to tame the snarling horde. All we need is time. So maybe time isn't so bad after all.

CHAPTER 49

LOCATION: DRACIA
YEAR: 1173
XAN – 24 YEARS OLD

Xan felt like he was in his own little fairy-tale. A pumpkin cart led by two majestic horses, cradling the lost slipper of a future princess in his right hand.

Instead of an actual slipper, he clasped Juniper's real hand as she lay semi-conscious, burning with delirium after consuming the *dillayla* and embarking on a journey of the mind.

The cart of sorts was constructed of malleable wood struts curved into a dome and cushioned by animal hide and rubbery sap fashioned into locks to keep everything contained and in working condition. The cart was carried by the Marillidors that had been deemed too old for battle.

Xan had yet to speak with Juniper, as she had collapsed almost immediately after the tea ceremony and had suffered with symptoms throughout the night. Once more he assumed the role of primary carer.

Although Juniper hadn't said anything, Morcombe had explained the mindlink to Xan. The three Aranther tribe leaders decided that in order to operate on a better spiritual plane they were offering the *dillayla* to more than just chieftains. They decided upon a minimum age of participating and offering it to specific council members at first. If it improved the balance of the Aranther race, then they would open the ceremonial mindlink further.

As Xan eyed Qilin asleep in the corner of the cart, he recalled the last thing Morcombe said to him.

"I must tell you, Xan, that she is not what she seems," Morcombe said.

"I know that Juniper is a deeply complex indi—"

"No, Xan." He pointed over his shoulder to Qilin who was playing with some Aranther younglings.

"That creature is not as she appears." Morcombe tapped a forefinger to his temple.

"I know. There's something deeper to her that I've never understood," Xan conceded.

"It's not something to be fearful of, at least I don't believe so."

Qilin fell back into the field of flowers after sneezing from an intake of pollen.

"But that creature is incredibly powerful," Morcombe warned, "As soon as she came close to the dwelling, I recognised intense power. I mistook that power to be emanating from you. But I have since felt your mind's presence and it is… well…normal. Hers, however, is locked tight. Not one living creature has been able to restrict access to their mind in the history of our existence, so it leads me to believe that there is, how do you say, more than meets the eye."

Xan stroked his chin and wondered about Qilin. The tests he conducted were interesting in their own right, but he'd never quite understood what that really told him about her. Were all Mika Tikaani the same or was she special? Morcombe's words made him think that she *was* different from the rest. He'd known her nearly all his life, but a part of him was deflated. He trusted her so deeply, yet she was keeping something from him. Why couldn't she somehow let him in—let him see her true self? He wouldn't turn, he wouldn't be afraid.

It's often the fear of the unknown that is worse than the revelation. The anxiety that storms, the scenarios one conjures. And being afraid often leads to acting irrationally.

Xan was seldom afraid. Only when it came to losing those he loved. But was adopting ignorance just the same? Allowing the cover across his eyes to remain just so he could perpetuate this picture of perfection?

LILIANNA
24 YEARS OLD

Lilianna posted herself just inside the Wyndry gates for days, waiting for the trio to return. Chief Ghanasis had explained that Juniper wasn't in the best of ways, which concerned Lilianna greatly. The chief, however, spoke of her with a misty reverence that people of power didn't usually give to an outsider.

As the sheet of snow lifted in the distance, figures began to materialise. Sturdy Marillidors carried several carts forward, as Lilianna stood shivering in the cold, nervous with anticipation. Matted strands of blonde hair blew across her face like raking claws. Flecks of snow were fireflies floating to land on her shoulders, coating her in the pale glow of trepidation.

Appetite had waned over the past few days. The concern for Juniper and Xan had driven her to the very edge of what she could tolerate. But wasn't that the crux of love? Vertigo inducing, altering the physiology, a maelstrom of madness swallowing us whole. If that love was true, it was *always* all consuming. But she wouldn't have it any other way. The highs were too resplendent to cast away from her aching heart. The withdrawal had lasted long enough.

The cart emerged from the screen of snow, trundling like a rusted robot on chirping wheels. Lilianna's heart swelled in her chest; the expectation of seeing them again collided with the locked box of her emotions. The lock was no more. The emotions were a swarm of wasps let loose, stinging her until the tears ached behind her eyes.

Xan stepped off the cart with Qilin at his side. His rugged beard was fuller now, the ends tipped with frost. Dark brown hair was tied in a knot atop his head and wispy strands trailed down this neck, rippling with thrumming veins. The ruggedness suited him. Lilianna felt a bashful, carnal desire to feel that beard scratch against her neck. She recalibrated herself and showed her gratitude at both Qilin and Xan looking in such good health despite the journey. Xan held his right hand out, waiting for Juniper to reach him. In the meantime, Qilin kept playfully gnawing at his fingers, circling them both and repeating. Juniper's hair was tied in a tight bun, with a large animal hide wrapped around her shoulders to keep her warm. She looked small, smaller than she had ever seemed before. Her cheeks were dusted with the pink kisses of the cold. She shuffled forward gingerly, taking Xan's offer to help.

Lilianna tore through the fresh snow, her cheeks flushed and her eyes poised to abandon their tearless vigil. Her arms extended wide as she came closer and gripped onto both Xan and Juniper with a fierceness they had seldom felt. Their arms wrapped tightly around her, and Qilin with her furry little head grazed Lilianna's outer thigh as she pressed deeper in the embraces of her chosen clan. She savoured Xan's new scent—honey and burning ash, Juniper with citrus balm, tea leaves and wild berries.

Lilianna wept uncontrollably as she let go, descending to a knee in the snow. She finally expelled the pent-up emotions of the siege, and the absolute crushing anxiety of no communication with the trio.

Qilin jumped into her lap, licking her tears as they fell. Xan came up behind Lilianna, wrapping his strong arms around her shoulders and chest. Her sobbing came hard, and she choked on the oxygen. But he held her harder, and she felt his love even if she hadn't heard that special song play on his lips.

CHAPTER 50

LOCATION: DRACIA
YEAR: 1173
XAN - 24 YEARS OLD

The thermal bathing area was awash with travertine terraces nearly as white as the snow itself. In each terrace pool, bright azure waters rich with calcium and swirling with steam beckoned tired legs and soiled skin.

Xan sought out his reflection and it was not pretty. A patchy beard had grown, and his hair curled over his ears. The Wyndry tribesfolk had seized an opportunity to tie his fringe in a knot atop his head, in a sign that they accepted him as part of Aranthern culture. Xan had never looked this rugged before nor felt so unclean. The hike itself was taxing enough, let alone being involved in a tribal battle. But he shrugged as he looked at himself. It was more important to strengthen and preserve the internal ethos rather than worry too much about the external.

They stayed another two days in the care of the Wyndry tribe to ensure Juniper was back to herself. Xan noticed that there was something a little more subdued within her, as if the weight of the past few weeks had given her an even harder edge. The tribesfolk gave her a lasting reminder of her time on Dracia: a hand poked tattoo that filled the side of her neck. It was a branch with several *dillayla* leaves. They bestowed the gift, and she cried tears of joy as they worked on her. Maybe she cried for more. Xan would never know. But Lilianna held her boronium hand while Xan held the other, and Qilin sat on her lap cleaning dirt from her paws. Their clan was taking shape in Dracia. It was a beautiful thing.

It wasn't long before they were back on the ship. Despite her newfound reverence, Juniper was backseat piloting with Arcadie at the controls.

"Just make sure you keep your claws steady on the yoke. My body is battered enough."

"Juniper, I am more than capable of keeping things steady. I'm not made of organic material, so my muscles don't really degenerate like yours will."

"Them's fighting words, buddy. I'll make sure I don't shed any tears as my muscles degenerate. Wouldn't want to increase the amount of rust across your body and all." She folded her arms across her chest and reclined in her chair.

Arcadie looked down at his body. Although it might not have been snowy white like he was when he was new, he'd held up well over a long period of time. But Juniper had made sure the barb stuck.

A small modulating groan emanated from his speakers, and he started talking to himself in frustrated little phrases that were just out of earshot.

Xan craved to be at home. But home would be a different place. Even though time outside the portal was moving slower, Xan calculated that although they lived for at least a month on all three planets, Gemarine would have experienced only about four days. He wondered about Ryker and what he would've been able to achieve in three days. Whether he had amassed the underground—whether everything on Gemarine had been turned on its head.

All in all, he was grateful to be going back to sort things out once and for all. No more wandering through different worlds, different time periods. Gemarine called him home. They were going to wrench it from the grimy, clawed fingers of Madame Bleu.

CHAPTER 51

LOCATION: GEMARINE
YEAR: 118
RYKER – 21 YEARS OLD

Ryker navigated through to Gemarine's atmosphere with about as much grace as Juniper in a room full of erections.

He spun around the length of the unexplored parts of the planet, skirting over barren landscape until he recognised artificial structures jutting out like needles in the flesh of the world.

Luckily the Cryptoborg ship had a cloaking device and he wasn't in any danger of being discovered. Arcadie had made some last-minute modifications to the technology to ensure that if Gemarine had the ability to distinguish Cryptoborg aircraft before, they certainly couldn't now.

Throughout the trip, Dallis had helped Ryker establish a connection to Miami and the underground, alerting them of their impending arrival. But his strength had waned and the sapphire glow in his eyes had turned to a dull charcoal. He hid the injured wrist under a bandage but every now and then Ryker would see a glimpse of the upper arm blotched with blackened bruising.

Ryker alerted the underground of Xan's directive to find the roots of the *brigetwort* plant. They agreed to send out a party to locate the plant and arrange for it to be given to Dallis upon arrival.

Ryker could see the discomfort in Dallis's face. It was cruel to have dragged him along so far without treatment but there was some hope that he could now rest and recover.

The underground smelt like damp clothes and dirt. It didn't help that Ryker noticed criss-crossed ropes with actual clothes drying beneath the high ceilings. Rags scrunched atop twisted sticks were driven into the sand, burning with flame. Several other members dressed in tattered robes and cloaks were scattered around. Some tended the fire with a roasting *flabber*, while a couple of others were arranging the new harvest of foraged foods.

Miami's knotted grey locks swayed as she moved forward, reliant on a sturdy walking stick. She hacked up a gross ball of flem and spat it out the side of her mouth before addressing them.

"Dallis, imma pleased to meet ya after all this time." She bowed as gracefully as her unrefined self would allow.

Dallis stumbled forward, mirroring the agility of Miami, "Likewise, but I must admit…I am not myself." He took two shaky steps forward and tried to right himself against the cave wall, but his large frame toppled to the ground. Underground members rushed around him, but he was unconscious, so Ryker took control.

"Where is the *brigetwort*?" Ryker gestured to Dallis's blackened wrist. "Give it to him now."

"You 'eard the lad," reinforced Miami.

The forager crew brought forth a mortar and pestle, with the crushed *brigetwort* root. Ryker smeared it on his fingers and shoved it into Dallis's mouth.

Ryker waited for Dallis to spring to life like it was a shot of adrenalin, but Miami put a hand on his shoulder while some of the foragers applied a wet cloth to Dallis's forehead.

"Give it an hour, and he will be on the mend," Miami declared. "But Rykie, what the fuck is this?"

She reached down, grabbed Dallis's wrist and held it up. The bandage that had covered it slipped down and what Ryker saw was incredibly disturbing. The hand was entirely black, rancid and rotting. This was gangrene times seven thousand. There was no saving that wrist.

"Ahhhh, I...hadn't noticed how bad it was."

"Ya 'adn't seen this? Shit, boy." Miami motioned to a large oaf type, "Go tell Doc Dryno to prep for amputation and um...installation."

Ryker cringed at the amputation and thought it best to speak on behalf of Dallis, "Amputation? I don't know if—"

"Trust me boy, that black wrist of death ain't gonna give no wank jobs ever again."

Ryker grimaced. "Yuck. What makes you think I want a hand job?"

Miami looked at him with utter contempt. "Take a joke, boy."

Ryker didn't feel like it was appropriate for her to mention anything sexual at a time when poor Dallis was basically comatose. Secondly, he was in no mood to joke with someone he hardly knew. This was just another part of being a leader that he avoided. Having to be nice to people, having to appease with jokey interactions that weren't even funny.

"I...am just concerned, Miami, so I want to know what's going to happen to him."

"You know that Juniper bitch and her exoarm, well think of that but...just...better."

Ryker had come to really value Dallis. In the face of venom sickness, he must have been in terrible pain, but he kept that potent positivity as well as somehow managing to save them on Earth by discarding the bomb. He had done so much hampered by injury, for a universe that sucked him in and spat him out. He tried so hard to be a part of a family led by a former enemy who had come so close to butchering him. There was a lot to respect in the forgiveness he gave the world. A lot to learn, especially for Ryker who hated most of what he saw in others.

He sighed. Ryker knew about parts. So Dallis would have an arm that Ryker could fix if required. His heart, though, was a different story. Ryker figured that he'd shown resilience before so maybe this time would be the same.

They carried Dallis off into the darkened tunnel.

Losing sight of him, Ryker suddenly felt terribly alone.

"Look, our spy in the inner circle tells us that it ain't good," Miami said. The wrinkles around her eyes sagged in dismay from the harsh light of the fire. "Massy got back yesta'day and spilled all ya secrets to Bleu."

Ryker tensed at Massy's name. The cold in the cave suddenly bit into his bones.

"So there's no need for ya to go swannin' in there tryin' to charm 'er ass, it ain't gonna do."

Helplessness was a feeling Ryker was used to—he often felt like the mouldy fruit on an abundant tree of ripened ones, but this was different. What decisions he would make now cleared a simpler path for Xan and the others when they returned. Again, he took a deep breath inward, feeling like it was all too much. But Xan was depending on him to set up a revolution so that it wasn't just a small bunch of misfits charging against Madame Bleu's army.

"Well, what am I meant to do?" he whispered, almost hoping she wouldn't hear the fragility in him.

"Boy, Xan 'ad trust in ya. You tell me tha plan," her face moved uncomfortably close to his, and she smiled with rotting teeth.

Ryker shuddered imperceptibly at the stench, backing away. "Well, I'll go and do what Xan said. Hit the lab, go warn Ranjit and Duffington at the biobase 'cause they would be in danger."

Ryker knew Madame Bleu better than anyone. Xan's most prized passion was laid out in the open. The biobase—the home of all those creatures. If she wanted to hurt him, all she had to do was burn it to the ground. It wouldn't matter that most of Gemarine loved Xan. Everyone was afraid of Madame Bleu. Fear trumped love when it came to compliance.

Ryker hadn't joined Xan's crew for the creatures but these innocent things did not deserve to burn alive. He respected life enough to refute that kind of treatment. When he thought of how crushed Xan would be if Madame Bleu managed to destroy anything, it gave him extra incentive to do *something*.

Miami flashed a disgusting smile his way. "That's the spirit lad!"

Ryker ignored the condescending remark. "What will *you* do?"

"Don't ya worry kid," She turned back to some of the exiles mulling about behind them, sharpening rusted swords and dusting off dented armour. "We gearin' up for war!"

Thankfully it took Dallis only a day to get accustomed to his new and improved appendage. It was a lot sleeker and more refined than Juniper's. It was bizarre to consider that Dryno had the resources to make something so technically superior. The recovery from the venom sickness was less swift, but he gobbled down the bitter paste of the *brigetwort* several times a day to expedite the process.

Word had come through from one of the underground spies that the biobase was currently under threat, so they needed to act fast.

Ryker and Dallis used the tunnelling system to get into the city. Lanterns lit the way through red rocks dripping with condensation.

Dallis's hooded cloak disguised as much of his Valkor-ness as he could, but if anyone with a suspicious nature happened upon them, things could turn ugly.

They emerged onto the street in front of Xan's lab and made their way into the motitube. Ryker was petrified that at any moment a member of the inner circle would swoop down upon them like a caliginous wraith. Sanity moved in closer and reassured him that the inner circle wouldn't be caught dead walking the streets, which settled his nerves.

Ranjit was at his desk, absolutely oblivious as to what had been occurring around him. There had been an added army presence on the streets, but he didn't think anything of it at first. Ryker didn't need to do much convincing. Ranjit nodded, his glasses sliding down his nose, and although he nearly soiled himself at the sight of Dallis the Valkor, he agreed to take them to the biobase.

Ranjit brought them onto the street to order a transpo. Ryker's MPD blasted off like a siren of doom.

"They're going to the biobase now." Miami's voice was wrapped in sheets of concern.

Ryker reflexively looked around the street in panic. "What? We're on our way there now!"

"Well, buckle up kid, it's 'bout to get real."

Ryker felt the constriction across his airways, as if a vengeful spirit was at his throat. He wasn't built for standing and fighting. He was built for running.

Dallis's real hand found his, trying to calm the shakes that reverberated through Ryker's body. The large fingers wrapped around his spindly ones, and he instantly felt warmed.

"Stay behind me—I'll protect you with everything I have." The sapphire eyes were shining now.

Ryker reacted without thinking. "No, stand beside me and we will... protect each other."

He was buoyed by love in a sprawling sea, the unrelenting barrage of colossal waves boxing him in. Ryker was part of a new clan, a clan he'd chosen, and the love for them gave him courage.

Maybe I wasn't built for running away. I was built for finding solutions. I'm a part of an engine and I work best if everyone around me is firing too.

CHAPTER 52

LOCATION: GEMARINE
YEAR: 118
MASSY – 25 YEARS OLD

Massy paced in the great hall. The long table used for formal dining occasions was bare, stripped of all its personality.

Madame Bleu pushed the gigantic doors inward. They creaked and cowered in fear of her frustration. "Do you want to know what I've been praising lately?" Her evenly placed footsteps echoed in the large dimly lit room.

Despite the urgency of the message he needed to deliver, he stopped pacing and allowed her to lead the exchange.

"Sure," he answered calmly.

"My sight. I've realised that sight as a sense is something to behold. A panoramic view of beauty before you, stealing a fervent glance from someone you desire…" She placed her open palms on the desk, glaring at him and leaning forward. "But you do not take for granted the beauty of sight until you have to look upon the face of pure filth and ugliness." Her cheeks sagged in disgust. "I've been spared your wretched little face for a number of days now, and you roll in here and ruin the fuck out of one of my senses!" She may as well have spat venom in his face, but Massy knew she was just swinging her dick around trying to show her supremacy. Words like that couldn't possibly be true—after all, he was a strapping stud.

"Sorry for ruining your eyes, Madame. I have something that might appeal to another of your senses though." Silence fell, as Massy prompted her to guess. Madame Bleu just glared with a pitiful scorn. "It's your hearing, you know your heari—"

"I know what it is, you fool. Get on with it."

Massy took a deep breath. After he was done, he would wait for the applause, the accolades, the bronze statue erected in this very room of him standing in all his glory.

Madame Bleu just looked angry. There was no ceremony of grandeur or even a pat on the back.

"It took this long for you to come back and tell me?" She scratched her head, and then slammed her fists on the table. "This fucking long! You incompetent piece of shit. I need my team to clean up this mess now."

Massy was taken aback. He had revealed details about the theft of her crystal, the killing of Maraudar, the spy pretending to be Maraudar, the looming presence of the Valkor. And yet here she was in a foul mood throwing all of it at him like an ape throwing shit. She had been the one that drove him into servitude after the fateful flight event and now after loyal service to her, he was treated like this. It didn't sit right.

"If it wasn't for me, you'd be at the mercy of a traitor and would have a sneak attack upon you in a matter of hours."

Her posture relaxed and she weighed his comment against her emotions.

"You know what?"

Massy braced himself for another barrage of hatred.

"You're right." Madame Bleu started to make her way around to his side.

"What are you doing?" Massy tensed.

"I'm going to apologise—I am angry, sure, but I was shooting the messenger." She grabbed his suit in a bunch. "If you want me to treat you well though, you need to…" she looked him up and down, "…treat *me* well so I can think clearly."

Massy gulped. He had always wanted to be worthy of entering her… pleasure dome.

It's time to dance.

After their dirty dance, Madame Bleu was less irritable but had focused her hatred into detailed planning. She sat at the desk beside the bed plotting various points of call on her MPD, ruminating on her plan of attack.

"What will you do with fake Maraudar, the spy?"

"I sent Zondini after him, but by the time he got to his level it had been abandoned. So, it appears as though he'd already been alerted somehow."

Massy sagged, wondering how that could've happened.

Did Scarface the Cryptoborg get to Gemarine and warn someone? Or was time in the portal a lot slower for some reason?

"I would've thought we'd caught him off guard?"

"The time crystal operates…differently. When you use it, it kind of allows regular time to move slower. You can basically do a whole lot more."

Massy grimaced. "That's confusing."

Madame Bleu was busy working away on her MPD. "To a simpleton like you maybe."

She didn't even look up or apologise. Wasn't this meant to feel better? Not just like another exchange with Juniper the mega bitch.

"Listen, I'm going to continue working on plans for the evening. Why don't you get back to your level and report here in the morning."

Massy wanted to sigh but he held it in. "Yeah, I'm pretty wasted anyway to be honest."

"Get some rest, you'll be leading your own squadron of flyers for the first time since…well, you know."

"Wait. You said I'd never be able to—"

"Don't say I never rewarded you for your service. Now, get the fuck out of my bed and don't ask for anything else."

Massy collected his boots, hastily zipped up his suit and walked out of the level, through the great hall with a gigantic smile on his face.

I'm back, baby!

The motitube took him down to the street, and he danced on light feet all the way to his own level, singing at the top of his lungs. Others on the street edged away from him warily, as they undoubtedly should have.

CHAPTER 53

LOCATION: GEMARINE
YEAR: 118
RYKER – 21 YEARS OLD

Dallis streamed ahead in the darkened tunnel; slithers of light winked like sultry stars tempting the embrace of a stellar mass. Ryker and Ranjit were doing their best to catch up, as Dallis's huge strides covered double the amount of distance in that grimy, slick pathway.

Muffled alarms stung their ears deep underground. Ryker feared the worst about the biobase, concerned with their enemies and the potential creatures facing a horrific end.

Up ahead the clang of metal rang out, and a shaft of light penetrated the darkness. Vapour poured through the hole that Dallis had created by opening the hatch.

Dallis waited at the peak of the opening, silhouette shrouded in smoke. He lifted Ranjit upwards without a grunt of exasperation, followed by Ryker, pulling him like a weed from the soil.

Ryker poked his head out just as Ranjit broke out into a swearing fit. He had never heard anything remotely negative leached from his mouth until that moment. When he gazed around, he understood why. The glow of orange flames flashed across the exhibit. Ashes floated inside the biobase from seedlings that had embarked upon life. They were ravaged by fire before they could grow to dominate their microclimate. The inferno had encircled two creatures, boxed them into a corner and then spread with burning anger, engulfing them with a gaping mouth. The two creatures were encrusted in black death, huddled in close to support one another on their way to extinction.

"I'll locate the segregaters so that the other grids won't get damaged," Ranjit yelled. "Please, just do what you can."

Ranjit ran away from the haze, but Ryker and Dallis moved toward it. They didn't run. They crept through the shroud, as if at any turn danger would spring. Dallis stayed a fraction ahead, his left arm levitating backwards to ensure Ryker never moved past him.

A piercing scream tore through the smoke. Indiscernible words were the threnody of terror, high pitched and dissonant. Even without seeing what it was, Ryker was horrified. The feeling in his gut should have prepared him for what he saw but nothing really could.

Duffington was sprawled out on the bioplastic casing of an exhibit, boronium spikes driven into both wrists and ankles. His flesh was glowing lava melting off the body, the skin liquifying and sliding off onto the floor like gold chains smelting in a pot of death.

Someone had strung him up like this, left him to burn. A slow death is the ultimate betrayal to the sanctity of life.

Ryker watched in horror as Duffington's body fought to the end, while his spirit fled, tormented by the scene.

A piercing scream parted the haze. A manic sound of torture, a desperate plea to end the pain. Eyeballs swelled with the intense heat, sunken in their sockets; his luscious hair had long departed. The Gemarinian that had been Duffington was now a skeletal mess of blackening burns.

"What happened?" Dallis asked Ryker.

But the screaming was relentless. It took on a quality of its own. Like a blaring warning siren across the beach alerting of a creature close to the shore.

Death was suspended while the flames engorged upon flesh; the soul remained fragmented in shock.

Dallis drew his Cranston ray gun and shot out a beam that found its mark between Duffington's eyes. The horrific sound ended abruptly. But the fire continued to burn through the exhibit. Ryker peered through, attempting to locate the creature before it was burnt alive like poor Duffington.

He caught sight of something or someone in one of the containment chambers, sparking another fire.

Ryker screamed, "Dallis! Through the fire."

Dallis burst through the burning bioplastic. It was faith in Ryker's word that propelled him forward into flame. He let loose ray blasts into darting figures in the adjacent chamber.

An explosion sounded and Ryker was thrown back.

A containment chamber to the left of him turned mutinous, cultivating a brewing blaze.

He lay against the wall, vision blurry, when he was seized by rough hands and thrown across the slick floor.

"Well look who it is," snarled Zondini, a member of the inner circle. "One of the ugliest creatures in this awful hell hole. Which one is your exhibit, you festering bowl of turd soup?"

Ryker coughed and spat blood on the floor. The fear had fled him.

He got to his feet. Taking the fighting stance that Juniper taught him, he tried to embody a true warrior bitch in that moment. He blew a kiss at Zondini, "Come get me, you beautiful mess."

Zondini recoiled, then his expression morphed into a predatory grin. "You're all mine."

He came forward swinging.

Ryker remembered Juniper's words. *"Sometimes it pays to observe. Take in their weakness, use it as your strength."*

Ryker evaded easily by ducking low. As Zondini stumbled forward, his torso was exposed.

A weakness.

Ryker struck hard into the kidneys as he rose upward. He then took several steps back. Zondini gasped.

"What the fuck, kid?" Zondini's purple hair not so slick now.

Ryker kept an eye on his own breathing, steadying it despite the swirling smoke invading his lungs like a cancer. Juniper's voice ringing in his memories again. *"The calculating killer will always have the upper hand, 'cause when you seek to defeat someone you call upon both intelligence and wrath in equal measures."*

Ryker waited in the battle stance with a smirk on his face, thinking of his tutor. Zondini lunged this time, tackling Ryker to the ground. He tried to react with a defensive move but the attack from Zondini was unexpected. Trying to keep Zondini in a headlock, Ryker struggled with the ascendency, rocking back and forth in an intimate dance of combat. Ryker held Zondini down for a long second, and seizing an opportunity, dug his nails into one open eye.

Zondini reared up, skimming an open palm into Ryker's throat, knocking the breath out of him. Black spots in his vision arrived, like clusters of meteors floating past the viewport of a ship. He tried to fight back, but Zondini doubled down with another four fingered jab into his neck. Ryker stumbled back this time, clutching his windpipe, tears emerging in panicked eyes.

The ghost of Maraudar appeared over Zondini's right shoulder as if to beckon Ryker into the ether.

He didn't want to die like Maraudar, but he was no match for a member of the inner circle who had been fight training for years. Through a foggy screen of tears, Ryker searched for a weakness but the ghost of Maraudar kept moving forward. A dagger now raised, biceps flexing with anticipation.

Ryker was confused. Would a ghost thrust a dagger into the side of Zondini's neck? Would a ghost watch as blood painted their skin in throbbing spurts? Would they smile as they bathed in the blood of an enemy?

CHAPTER 54

The sprinkler system kicked into gear. Ryker heard parts of the biobase seal shut. Boronium struts launched across the bioplastic outer shells, heavy set doors locking and vaulting sections so that the flame-filled breach did not penetrate further. Ranjit must have found the control room and was administering the fail-safe.

Maraudar knelt down beside Ryker, tears in his eyes despite the water droplets streaming down his face, washing Zondini's blood from his cheeks. The emotion in Maraudar's face was not something Ryker had seen before; the facial expressions were that of another boy locked away inside dead memories, festering, fuelling his famous apathy. Maraudar reached out and cupped Ryker's cheek, and the loving smile betrayed him.

No one had cupped his cheek in that way since…

"How?" Ryker managed.

"I never stopped thinking that we would reunite one day."

He bent forward, kissing Ryker with a passion that seemed lost, with love that had dwindled to a speck of ash from a timid volcano.

Ryker wanted nothing more than to wrap himself in this moment, hibernate in the warmth of a forgotten partner, but his thoughts turned to the Valkor who had been by his side through the terror of the last few weeks.

Dallis had absorbed his apathy and given him a purpose. Believed in him despite the lack of valour and presence, and who had regrown hope from a single, damaged seed in the wasteland of betrayal.

Ryker pulled away fast, "There is time to do this later, Lambastian, I need to find Dallis."

Lambastian, his former amorous partner who had been exiled and left for dead, was very much alive. But he had adopted Maraudar's disguise. It now made sense that when Ryker last saw Madame Bleu in that frenzied evening stealing the time crystal, Maraudar was in shock. It was Lambastian seeing Ryker for the first time in so very long.

Now, he looked stung for a short moment as Ryker cut their kiss short to locate the Valkor who had been his shadow for what felt like weeks, now. He swallowed and nodded, helping Ryker to his feet to find the Valkor.

They didn't have to move far. Dallis limped into the corridor, dragging a writhing body behind him, his biceps flexing with the weight. Soot covered the Valkor's face, but his sapphire eyes sparkled under the artificial light. A fringe of auburn curls threatened to shield them like an overhanging branch of autumn leaves. But he dropped the captured firestarter in between them, restrained with ropes, then brushed the hair from his face. Pearls of sweat trickled down his neck as he puffed out an aggressive exhale.

"It's quite hot in here, I think," Dallis announced.

Lambastian and Ryker shared an agreeable look hidden under bashful smirks.

Just a little warm, Dallis. Just a little warm.

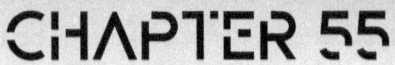

CHAPTER 55

LOCATION: GEMARINE
YEAR: 114
MASSY – 21 YEARS OLD

The morning after the pinnacle star festival Massy was still drunk, high and wrapped in the ecstasy of fucking half his squadron of pilots. He answered the MPD holo half naked with the squadron surrounding him in various positions of dishonour.

"Massy, where are you and the squadron? Your defensive shift on the eastern rim started seventeen minutes ago and not one of you has checked in." Captain Larrsen scowled at him.

"Oh, um we—"

"Spare me the bullshit and get over there now."

Massy woke the other four pilots with a quick huff of stardust and a slap on their asses. Ordering transpos to the flight deck and stumbling into their fighters with what they thought was poise and style.

On approach to the Eastern Rim there were warnings of radar anomalies, but Massy adjusted his glasses to combat the morning sun and yawned in his reply. "We are nearly there. It'll be fine."

It was anything but fine.

The stars were his and he climbed from one constellation to the next in search for true dominion. The confidence oozed from him.

They traversed from the troposphere through to the exosphere, with the ability to survey the planet from above. Massy felt like a god, leering down on defenceless ants clamouring over resources, building trivial nests in relative peace. An exertion of power from grandiose heights.

Without warning, all radars began to malfunction.

"Massy, we have radar interference on the fighter," relayed Conwar.

"Same here Massy," coughed Jezephry.

Massy's radar went batshit, spinning in chaotic circles as if possessed. He thumped the dial with a fist. "Fuck, mine is gone too. Just keep on the lookout for anything unusual. Sick of these fucking—"

Conwar's craft disintegrated in a fiery bloom of soundless destruction. The viewport speckled with a ripple of autumnal foliage in the ocean of space.

Massy watched it, unbelieving. Screams from the other three came through his comm system.

"Conwar's down! What the fuck just happened?" Wrighter squealed, her fighter darting off from their formation.

"No, fuck no!" Jezephry wailed.

Seraphina's voice trembled over the comm. "Massy help, there are some weird, ghostly figures moving ahead but—"

Massy noticed something glint like glass in the middle of the sun but reacted too late, as he had with everything that morning.

A burst of laser fire emerged from the ghost ahead, like bubbles in the deep, flowing outward to the ship beside him where Seraphina blew apart in shattered fragments. Debris cascaded into his own fighter and the viewport breached, decompressing the air in the cockpit. Wind rushed through like horny freshmen in a sex robot factory. The soundscape was filled with a blaring whoosh and the whining decline of the jet as it lost altitude in a nosedive. Warning lights burnt his retinas, and as he strained to keep his eyes open, the force of the wind peeled his cheeks back.

"Engage defence shields," he yelled at his comrades, "something is out there."

He was spiralling out in a maze of whirls. Dizzy. Slick with sweat. A silent promise was made. Massy wouldn't go down like this.

While the indistinct comm chatter was distant noise, he took a deep breath in to focus. Massy applied significant backpressure to the yoke. The elevator in the back strained to even out the tail and right the steepness of the dive. The motor was smoking so there was no use boosting any thrusters. It was about his skill to work the craft. Massy pulled back on the yoke as another aircraft burst in a hail of laser fire ahead of him. The nose was rising, and he used the wings to glide through the air. Mountains spread out before him, but he needed to focus on the horizon and find a spot of flat ground to land. Find the horizon to find the balance.

The wind still whistled in the cockpit, whispering tales of his cohorts' demise. But he kept searching for that spot of land to arrive and when it did, he slammed his fist on the dashboard. The rejoice he felt far outweighed the fear as he touched down on even ground.

As he exited the jet, he took in the sight of the spacecraft. Blackened wraiths hovered above the wings, debris punctured the outer shell, gaping holes exposed the cockpit to pressurisation and as he looked up at the skies, predatory Cryptoborg ships prowled, just waiting for him to show signs of life.

Massy was the lone survivor, as he dashed undercover to wait for a rescue team.

Massy awoke in a regen chamber, surrounded by a snowstorm of white walls. A catatonic robot with a needle stood in the corner, eyeing him with contempt. Machines beeped beside it, monitoring his heart rate. Madame Bleu sat on a clear bioplastic stool.

Her thin lips twitched. "Massy—allegedly the most promising young pilot on Gemarine." Bleu shifted her body forward and peered into the depths of his withered soul.

Massy's throat was dry and he coughed. "Ah yes, that's me, how can I—"

"*Was* the most promising pilot on Gemarine." Her hands collapsed at her sides as she leant back. "You are a disgrace to Gemarine. You flew out there high, hungover and whatever else and your squadron was obliterated by our enemies. 'Contentment through unity. Protection through peace.' It's more than a slogan."

Massy swallowed. He suddenly felt incredibly ill. He remembered when his brother died, his father would start with the same tone, but by the end he spoke only with his fists. *At least the bruises loved me.*

"Did you hear that? You let your squadron die?"

She might well have said brother and ended with, "It should have been you."

He felt small again for the first time in a long time. Tears arrived behind his eyes. Tears that had been hiding since Dracia.

Madame Bleu watched him. Her face was contorted in pure disgust.

"Such a shame that exile would claim you...unless."

The offer of hope surprised him. He looked up at her, revering her presence, revering the strength in the woman she was. But also the beauty in a second chance. He didn't want to lose his spot at the top.

"Anything to fix this, Madame. I don't want to be exiled, please."

"Do not beg, boy. That is pathetic. No one got to the top by begging to be there."

He wiped his tears and nose, straightened his shoulders and nodded, waiting for the request.

"Do you know who Xan is?"

Everyone knew Xan. "Yes, of course I do."

"I need you to befriend him, become his pilot."

"Is there a reason?"

"I need him to be watched carefully. There is something off about that boy and if he puts a foot out of line I want to know. Got me?"

"Yes, Madame, I won't let you down."

"I want weekly reports on his comings and goings. If you miss a week, or if you refuse to turn any contentious information in, you can say goodbye to flying at all. You'll be piloting his craft and nothing more. You will never lead a squadron again."

Massy didn't feel a pang of guilt for driving his mates to their death, but he would do everything that he could to redeem himself in Madame Bleu's eyes. There was still a path to the top. He would make it his everything to reach it.

CHAPTER 56

LOCATION: GEMARINE
YEAR: 118
XAN – 24 YEARS OLD

The crew kept the crystal remote safe with them on the *Attenborough*. Xan would use it to merge the timelines and cleanse Madame Bleu's disruption to the universe. But they would only do it once they had taken Gemarine out of her hands. It was too risky to leave the portal and their crystals laid bare for her to enact more damage on the galaxy should they perish.

The jump from Periah had the *Attenborough* in the Gemarine atmosphere instantly. Xan reiterated to the crew that they needed to be prepared for anything when they arrived.

They materialised with Gemarine's beauty exposed below, bright blue oceans, city lights twinkling like overzealous stars, the distant frozen tundra obstructed by heavy clouds. It was all so inviting, except for the five-winged fighters glaring with dark viewports—guard dogs of the atmosphere. Their sharp angled noses gleamed like slow orbiting spears thrown by the flexed arm of the expanse, on a spiralling collision course with the *Attenborough*.

"Fuck!" Juniper yelled.

Xan stared, mouth wide, his MPD crackling with a familiar voice.

"Look who made it back. I'm actually impressed." Massy's terrible connection couldn't mask the mocking tone.

Xan didn't say a word. In the space of a blink everything changed and once again, in the piercing jab of such a predicament he had trouble reacting decisively or with any level of potency.

Juniper kicked into action while he lay on his back legs straining for purchase like an upturned cockroach. She yelled at Fleurah to go down to the gun turrets, then relayed instructions to Arcadie with something to do with the airlock.

Shaking his head to get his mind working, he was about to ask Juniper about what he could do but she spun her chair facing him and said, "I'll take care of this. I'll see us through." She was overly confident at the best of times, but Xan hardly ever doubted her. Ever since returning from Dracia there was even less of a reason not to believe in her.

Xan took a deep breath, steadying himself and said, "Okay."

The MPD blasted again, thick with sarcasm, "Now I know you well, you're probably turning all those good memories over in your head. The especially cute ones that we shared together." Massy's voice mimicked crying now. "Thinking—how could one of my bestest buddies want to shoot my ship down in a fiery ball of death?"

Xan calmly replied, "I'm not thinking any of those things. The moment you did what you did you were dead to me." He flexed his fists and cracked his neck from one side to the other, finding a cool calmness that he didn't know he had. "We will finish you."

"Oh what, you think that love will conquer all do you? You're the saddest cunt in the galaxy if you actually believe that." Massy's tone was roiling heat in the face of melting icicles.

Qilin stood at Xan's feet. He peered down at her, stroking the fur on her head as if to laugh with love in the face of such hate.

"The problem with being a traitor is that you don't have anyone who truly has your back. You can't even trust yourself." Xan combed through his beard with gentle fingers, then adjusted the knot in his hair, remembering that he not only had the backing of his crew but also tribesfolk of different worlds, creatures who recognised him as a saviour, robots who knew deep within their circuitry that he had the entire galaxy's best interests at heart.

"I don't need anyone to watch my—"

The ship directly behind Massy exploded in a chaotic ball of fire cutting off his transmission. Massy's ship heeded the warning and whirled around out of the blast range. Juniper then engaged the propulsion and thrust forward at sonic speeds rounding the *Attenborough* in an arc across the enemy formation. Xan stumbled backwards, holding onto metal studs in the walls for purchase. Qilin slid across the floor, and Lilianna unclipped herself briefly to rein her into her embrace.

Fleurah engaged the turrets and fired off a blast of shots at the remaining four enemy ships, each of them skirting off in various directions.

Juniper yelled into the comms, "Good little boy, Arcadie, now go find another."

Arcadie had managed to sabotage a ship while Massy and Xan were conversing. Massy had severed all communication now, completely focused on evading manoeuvres until one was in a position to fire an attack.

Xan yelled as he gripped a boronium strut that helped to steady his jerking body. "Make sure you've engaged the—"

"Solu Shields are engaged, lover boy. I got this!" Juniper yelled through the second round of blasts and maniacal screams from Fleurah. One laser ray caught the wing of the fighter. It veered off hard left trying to right its course until it flared up in the atmosphere and exploded.

Fleurah cried out from the turret section like a banshee in heat.

Xan looked back checking on Qilin and Lilianna. Her blonde hair swayed as she nodded as if to say, I have her, don't worry about us.

Arcadie was now lost in the tidal pulses of space. A speck of sand, fighting against the current. Xan imagined him pushing his thrusters hard, trying desperately to wade through the rip with a stinging barb of electricity to cause maximum damage to another ship.

Blasts from their enemies thudded into the shields rocking the hull.

"Thirty percent damage to the shields, Juniper," Lilianna warned, studying the damage holodata report.

"Shit! I know, I know I've got to work on my evasion—" Another blast of fire crackled and fizzed into the shield followed by a frustrated screech from Juniper.

She dipped the *Attenborough's* nose, diving below at incredible speeds, evading one on their tail and one on the right.

"They've damaged the shields to sixty percent now, Juniper!" Lilianna cried. Qilin whimpered in her lap.

Xan wondered what he could possibly do to help. Out the viewport he spotted what looked like a tiny thrusting satellite.

"Swing to portside ninety degrees, Arcadie is waiting there—when we fly over him, he can punch a hole through ships tailing us," shouted Xan.

JUNIPER
24 YEARS OLD

Juniper threw a thumbs up and yelled into her comm, "You're on, Arcadie!"

"Copy that, pilot of the year," quipped the robot.

Looks like he'd learnt how to joke in the throes of a dystopia. Good on him.

"Shut up before I ram your ass out there."

"I barely have one so do your best." Arcadie chuckled over comms.

Lilianna's tone did not mimic their frivolity. "Approaching your mark in t-minus fifteen seconds."

"Shittttt." Juniper swerved around Massy who led his crew in a V formation. He flipped above at the last minute, leaving two sacrificial battering rams. Juniper pulled up hard. Part of the wing collided with the dome of one of the fighters. The *Attenborough's* wing cracked like a fissure in the earth. The dome of the enemy ship shattered, sending glittering shards of glass twinkling into the void. The pilot was sucked into space, and after seconds of flailing and floating, frost crept like pearlescent vines across their skin until they were a single serving of space sorbet.

The damage to the *Attenborough* was severe, but Juniper grabbed the shaking controls and yanked hard portside to hit the mark. She got there just in time. The cameras showed Arcadie latching onto the enemy who pursued their tail. Who knows what he actually did. She couldn't concentrate on watching him and flying properly. But one wing was severed mid-flight, so whatever he did, he caused necessary carnage. The enemy ship dropped off the pursuit and spiralled end over end until they lost sight of them for good.

Massy was the predator and Juniper was the prey.

The blooms of explosions were pale ghosts in the void. Laser fire as colourful as broken rainbows damaged the *Attenborough's* shields until they began to perforate the boronium exterior.

In the damaged ship Juniper was no match for Massy in pursuit. She danced as best as she could to the beat of an amateur percussionist, but it was a mismatch for the virtuoso talents of the Aranther with golden mallets.

Lilianna deployed final missiles, but Massy flew in arcs until the dumb hunks of explosive metal knocked into the other creating ripples in the dark. Ripples made tidal waves and the energy was like a forceful fist to the nose of the *Attenborough*, as it whined with injury restricted movements.

"Arcadie, we need you!" Juniper yelled into the comm.

Nothing but the hiss of defeat.

Where was that flying tin can?

Massy's fighter had rounded away from the missiles that fucked each other and orgasmed all over the gravity-defying tits of space. The fighter gleamed in the dark, almost winking to say, "I've got you now."

Xan yelled, "Brace yourselves."

The fighter charged, spraying lasers like streams of sperm from a sensitive shaft. Juniper limped across the starboard side, but holes had appeared in the hull now as the Solu Shield was completely damaged.

Fleurah only shot off four streams of laser turret, but one beautiful shot punctured a part of the tail. Massy lost altitude quickly but was able to fire one last shot. It fizzed toward their propulsion controls and in an instant all control was gone.

Juniper had ridden the very last of her luck. It was skill that defeated her in the end. In the air Massy was king, and she was a lowly peasant trawling through rubbish bins to survive.

Xan turned to Lilianna, yelling for her to activate the holoshield. His blazing eyes reflected the viewport, where flames latched onto the wing, where smoke trailed like the tail of a comet destined to slam into the planet's surface below. Just like they were.

Everything felt slow. She could see the spittle fly out of his mouth, spraying onto her arm. A silly thought passed through her mind: *I wish he'd spit into my mouth.*

She giggled audibly as if she was drunk on the fumes of defeat, filling the *Attenborough* and filling her, destroying her self-confidence, destroying her purpose. She was meant to protect everyone and yet here they were about to get wasted on the surface.

Sharpened claws dug into her cheek. Skin broke like the sun through departing clouds. Pain registered and the moment seized her with a jolt.

Qilin had scratched her face and her hand instinctively cradled her cheek. Xan was yelling at Juniper and Qilin had been his enforcer. "Snap out of it! We need to eject before impact."

Juniper spun around; Lilianna was strapped on top of Fleurah in one seat. Lilianna's holoshield surrounded them both.

"Protect Qilin with everything you have," Xan yelled as he ran to his seat to strap himself in.

Qilin jumped onto Juniper's lap and licked her bleeding cheek as if apologising for the harsh wake-up call. The honey eyes encased in amber shone, catching light from the burning ship. The look was of expectation as if Qilin was Juniper's cub, and in her arms, safety was warm milk on her forked tongue.

Juniper didn't have enough time to mount an argument against being the keeper of such precious cargo.

The MPD gleamed on her wrist, and she typed in the commands for the holo. It spluttered like a rusty propulsion jet then surrounded Qilin and her in motherly arms. If she happened to let go of Qilin during the ejection, it meant that the protection was devoid. She tightened her grip.

The colours of Gemarine rushed by the viewport. The curvature of the planet dipped away. Debris flew, the outside world blurred on by. It was making her sick now. The descent was a flurry of everything and nothing.

"Now," Xan yelled.

The top of the *Attenborough* burst apart in a shower of metallic shards, and Xan was gone in a flash. She heard a sharp scream from Lilianna behind her. It faded to nothing, sucked out into the void.

Juniper was now the only one left in the shell of their ship. The ground was rising to meet her. She swallowed the last of saliva that had gathered inside her mouth. She pointed the yoke to ensure the final flight of the *Attenborough* would end at the gates of Topaz. What a fitting conclusion to the *Attenborough's* rich life.

Within those walls its captain had met its last pilot—all those years ago. Xan on a med bed looking haggard and afraid, Juniper swanning in with too much swagger, wanting to corrupt this grubby little nerd. Unexpectedly, images of her and Xan featured in the cinema of her mind. It was as if she were at the end of *her* road. Her life's most memorable moments flickered by in a beautiful, soppy montage.

She smiled, though.

The last thing Xan had said was to protect Qilin with everything she had. Juniper's confidence had been warped by the torch of humility, but she was more than ego. She was summer rain on starving crops, she was love finally reaching back, she was the rusted weapon discarded on a killing field, she was a black rose, petals of hate dripping like tar. She was all those things when she chose to be, and ego would not clip her wings. As she pushed the ejection switch, she chose to let all equal parts of her take the wheel. Soaring through the air, she knew that when she hit the ground the final battle would soon begin. A battle where she would fight with everything that she ever was and ever could be.

I will die before I let her take anything from me. I have never been more than what I am in this moment. And this moment isn't ready for all that I am.

MASSY
25 YEARS OLD

Massy watched as the *Attenborough* nosedived to the ground. A ship he'd lovingly guided through so many different corners of the galaxy. It was almost poetic that it was him that sent it on its final journey.

A missile quivered in its casing, eager for release. He could feel its excitement leech through the controls into his hand, and finally into his poised thumbs moments from pressing down on that sexy little red button.

There would be no survivors. No holoshield would stem that blast.

But of course, the Valkors showed up. Huge ships for the huge assholes of the galaxy. Just like his clan leaders interrupting his alone time, he was startled and took his thumb off the button. Instead, he backed off, and got the fuck out of range so that the Valkor ships didn't shoot him down.

If his former crew survived the crash, it would be fine and fucking dandy. It meant he could laugh in the face of all those assholes when his dagger bit deep into their tasty flesh. Spit into their face as they fell to the sand. Dance on their corpse while singing a funky little ditty.

That image gave him a nice little idea. Something that he could taunt Juniper with.

If there is one thing I like more than fucking, it's fucking WITH someone. Juniper in particular is a nasty little bitch and deserves to be stricken with all types of trauma.

I'll always have the last laugh.

CHAPTER 57

LOCATION: GEMARINE
YEAR: 118
LILIANNA – 22 YEARS OLD

The force of the ejection was beyond what Lilianna expected. She and Fleurah were meant to cling desperately to one another and plummet to the ground in the relative safety of the holoshield.

Instead, Fleurah was instantly ripped from her arms by gravity's muscley physique.

Who, for once, was a bit of an asshole, let's face it. What happened to gravity's mutual attraction to me?

Lilianna spun inside the holoshield, trying desperately to orient herself. She needed to figure out a way to propel herself toward Fleurah. But upon steadying, she was too dizzy to lock on to her sister's location.

The sound of the wind was deafening, which made it harder to discern the direction of Fleurah's shrill screams. After darting eyes finally settled on her falling sister, she was a speck in the distance.

She is too far away!

Much further than the ground below who greeted them like shifting tectonic plates rising in a mega quake.

Directing her kinetic energy toward the falling star, she flew through the air, graceless like a tumbling piece of space wreckage. But she carried on, pinning her shoulders back, turning her face away from the wind. *The wind could howl like a wolf at times, and slash with needle claws in the throes of descent.*

The ground was approaching too fast. From distant rolling dunes to discernible scattered boulders, she tried to push further toward her sister, but despair was approaching faster. There was no way to reach her. After years of being lost to one another they had only just swept a fine, sedimentary layer of dust from the buried ruin of their former bond. Now, they wouldn't be able to use the ruins as a new foundation, strengthening it with a new environment in the neighbourhood of chaos.

Lilianna screamed into the wind. Her mouth was instantly dry, the sound swallowed by a larger threat. If tears fell, they were snatched from her eyes by the greedy clouds banished for subsequent downpours.

Fleurah had metres until her death when their robot brother swooped in an arc like some capeless superhero, seizing her in his jangly arms. Lilianna sighed with relief. The holoshield protected her as she slammed into the ground in an explosion of sand. Millions of years before, that red sand was a seabed, flowing in and out with a flexing current. It naturally remembered the movements, mimicking a tidal wave from years ago, spraying across the shore of time.

Lilianna lay on the ground panting, the holoshield spluttering to nothing. In the distance the city gates had been obliterated. Caved in by the *Attenborough* in its last heroic descent. Flames licked the surrounding walls like a final sensual expression after a roaring climax.

Arcadie had flown back down and placed Fleurah on shaky legs beside Lilianna. Her sister helped her up and they embraced, the emotion of the moment spilling over with heavy sobs that made their shoulders shake violently, and their chests heave.

Arcadie stood beside them awkwardly, but Lilianna grabbed the robot's arm and aggressively pulled him into their embrace.

"You brilliant and brave little robot. I love you."

Arcadie's faceplate flashed with gold lights for the first time, and he seemed confused. Lilianna considered that although he'd been around a long time, he might not have experienced that surge of love yet, jolting him through the wire capillaries, through bolts of lightning inside data clouds.

Xan limped over to them; a fog of rusty dirt enveloped him. "Get to the caves!" he yelled.

Ships screamed overhead. Valkors rushed against the small defences of the downed Gemarinian craft.

Massy was as agile as ever, darting in and out of cascading pulse beams. It was as if he was walking on the sidewalk, sidestepping the droplets of rain pelting the concrete; each movement graceful and each evasion, calculated. It was a dance to be admired. But at some point, the curtains must close and lights must dim. The dance was over when Massy opted for self-preservation over spectacle and zoomed off in the direction of the army base, as the Valkor ships steadied themselves in a defensive line, waiting for more.

"Did you hear me Lilianna? Go to the caves—I'm going to look for Juniper and Qilin." She saw him give Arcadie an unspoken directive that the robot acknowledged. The spark of electricity was gone, replaced by blinking eyes intent on the cave.

"Let's go guys, come now!" His voice tweaked as he yelled. Lilianna turned back to look at Xan, but he was now running—no, stumbling— onward to the destroyed *Attenborough*.

Fleurah yelled at Lilianna and pointed at the caves. "Up ahead!" Lilianna spun around, catching distant figures coming toward them.

XAN
24 YEARS OLD

There was nothing discernible left of the *Attenborough*. It was a collection of twisted metal frames, strut beams strewn like fallen trees. Bioplastic and glass crunched underfoot, mixed with the crumbling concrete of the heavy gates to the city.

Xan's gaze was upon the larger blocks of concrete, trying to catch a glimpse of anyone alive beneath the rubble. Out of the corner of his eye, a Mika Tikaani, *his* Mika Tikaani, pounced on top of him like he was a *flabber* hopping in the long grass.

He locked his feet in place and braced himself so that he didn't tumble into the wreckage and impale himself on iron struts weaponised by the destruction of the wall.

Xan stumbled only slightly, steadying himself with an arm against a giant concrete block, Qilin clinging to his torso.

"Shit Qilin, you could've knocked me into that pit of waiting death."

Qilin responded by licking his face. Xan's annoyance disappeared immediately.

"Where's Juniper, girl?" Xan cocked his head to the side.

Qilin motioned her head toward the city and Xan looked up. Juniper stood atop the rubble of the gates staring out at the city ahead of her. Smoke cushioned her like nubile clouds to an angel of death.

Xan approached his best friend from behind and stood beside her. The only constant position he held in Gemarine. If they survived the final sprint, he'd remain there until his last breath.

"How's the view?"

She didn't turn to face Xan, but spoke as if speaking to the city, where she forged her first connection with something. "We'll never be the same again."

Xan's MPD buzzed on his wrist, and he answered the holo call in haste.

Ryker was there, looking dishevelled, his raven hair strewn like retired fishing nets littering the shore.

"Ryker it's so good to see—" Xan began.

"Xan, I'm at the biobase. You need to get here immediately."

"What happened?"

"Just come right now—I don't know how but find a way." Ryker breathed in deep, brushing his fringe out of his left eye. "It's not good Xan, get here now."

The transmission ended, and Xan felt the fear squall swelling within. He was fearful of what might have occurred, but also of what it might evoke in him.

Juniper had turned to action and was climbing down the rubble onto the other side.

"Look, there are some hoverboards over there." Juniper stopped, noticing Xan's clenched fists at his sides. She took his hand gently.

"Whatever it is, we will make them pay."

Xan steadied his breath, but the hammering in his heart had risen to the trunk of his neck. Qilin brushed against his leg, and her big eyes told him not to lose it yet. The biobase needed him; whatever had happened, it was time to face it.

CHAPTER 58

LOCATION: GEMARINE
YEAR: 118
RYKER – 21 YEARS OLD

Ryker sat on the floor with his legs crossed, silent. He was soaked from the sprinkler, and he still shook from the physical altercation. Not to mention his long-lost flame was alive and well, leaning against the wall, casually talking with his, let's face it, current infatuation.

What is life?

Ranjit paced the floor. The poor guy had never known the intensity of what had just occurred in the last hour. After this whole saga ended, he wouldn't dare even consider experiencing anything similar again.

Xan burst through the door, his arms flexed by his sides, pupils dilated, jaw tight.

Ranjit with shaking hands dropped to his knees, tears licking the dusty boots. "I tried to save them, I'm sorry, I'm sorry," he wailed.

Ryker stood up and walked forward to Xan ignoring Ranjit in a puddle of his own sadness. "Listen, I—"

"Tell me everything, Ryker. What the fuck happened?" He spoke quietly and calmly. It was lava beneath the smoke. Daunting.

Ryker hesitated. He was aware that if he uttered the tale of the burning biobase, then Xan might conjure hell to rise up and scorch the ground they stood upon.

"We managed to contain this section of the biobase, however we have lost the *Tigress Aflexas, Rymbulas* and the *Goi-lang Gekkos.*" Ryker jumped as Xan slammed his fist into the wall, prompting Ranjit to wail louder. Juniper had bent down and was helping the doctor try to gather himself. Qilin sniffed his boots, doing absolutely nothing to assist them.

"And Duffington..." Ryker's voice started to break, recalling the manager of the biobase dying slowly. "...is dead." He pointed to the ashen corpse, mouth jarred and twisted in a deathly scream, solidified in tar.

Xan walked forward slowly, his hand across his mouth.

"But we," Ryker breathed in deep before continuing, knowing Xan's repressed monster in the pit of his shame would snarl and roar and melt iron bars with wrath alone. "We have captured one of them."

Xan stopped and turned to Ryker with a hunger in his eyes he'd never seen before. The monster needed to be fed.

"Where are they?" Xan's voice rumbled like a straining engine.

"I don't think you should..."

"Where are they?" he roared.

Dallis stepped in front of Ryker. "C'mon, Xan I'll take you to them."

Ryker watched them leave feeling sick. Xan was not only going to maim and torture the prisoner; he would slice his own soul with the rusted scalpel of revenge.

Qilin nestled against Ryker's leg and he looked down at her. She licked his hand as if to say sorry on her brother's behalf.

"Yeah, girl, I know."

Juniper stood up; her Ranjit consolation shift appeared to have ended. She sidled into the other side of Ryker and squeezed his waist.

"It's nice to see you, kid." She turned briefly to face him and put a finger and thumb on his chin, inspecting his face. "Looks like you've got some fresh battle wounds. It suits you." She smiled, clearly impressed. Behind her words and gestures there was concern and care. Something overt that he hadn't seen in her before. Maybe it wasn't just Xan that respected him anymore. Maybe all of them did in their own various ways.

"Thanks, I guess I'm not cool enough to get my arm ripped off, though."

Her neck jerked back and her mouth opened, and she laughed. "Was that—was that a joke? Fuck me, I'm gone for…well…what felt like three years, and I come back to this." She grabbed the back of his hair and tugged it toward her in a bizarre type of hug or display of affection. "I'm proud of you, buddy."

Ryker let himself be held by her. He didn't put his arms around her. It just wasn't him. But admittedly, when she wasn't around there was a gaping void in the group as if she were gravity, ensuring they stayed in tight to one another.

His thoughts were disturbed by a sickening scream coming from down the hall. He sucked in a startled breath.

Juniper let him go and elbowed him in the stomach. "Ahhhh torture. If it didn't hurt so much it would be a sexy little delight."

He wanted to say, "what the fuck is wrong with you," but instead recalled the last time he was at Fusion. He lay chained face down on a table, waiting for masochists and sadists to whip him, mark him and then get off all over him.

Ryker held a wry smile. "If it didn't hurt just a little, then I wouldn't count it as sexy."

Juniper held a finger to the corner of her eye, and her voice choked on fake tears. "I couldn't be prouder."

Even as they shared a laugh, Ryker's thoughts strayed to Xan's revenge monster, wondering what kind of hell was being unleashed behind closed doors.

XAN
24 YEARS OLD

The forefinger snapped back with a sickening crunch like rocks on a cliff edge splitting into the sea below. The victim was tied to a smouldering tree trunk, arms wrapped behind them so Xan couldn't see the pain in their eyes but could hear the shrill pierce of the scream. Xan yelled at the Sytheract tied to a tree trunk revelling in the cries of agony. Dallis watched the macabre scene play out, not daring to interfere in the display of rage.

"Do you enjoy pain?" Xan hissed.

The second finger snapped back, followed by another screech.

"Because the *rymbulas* didn't enjoy the pain as they were burnt alive."

The third finger snapped back, reverberating in the ruined exhibit of the biobase. Water still trickled down the bioplastic walls from the spray of the sprinkler system. The crispy leaves of burnt ferns crunched under Xan's boots as he walked to face the Gemarinian in his autumn surrender.

He balled his fist and pounded into the right cheek, crunching underneath the eye socket. A left uppercut struck flush under the nostrils. The bone splintered and cracked beneath his blow, and the neck went limp, head rolling onto their chest.

Xan screamed, "Wake up!" Mere centimetres from their face. They didn't move. Xan spat in their face and stormed off to a corner of the exhibit where a plant lay. An *azaliah* flower, apricot petals dangled innocently. Xan plucked the flower unceremoniously and walked to the unconscious victim, yanked open his jaw and forced the flower down his throat. They woke up instantly, spluttering, but Xan held the mouth closed and forced them to swallow.

The *azaliah* flower was a potent natural resistance to sleep, shock or fatigue. In ensuring the consumption of the entire flower, Xan sentenced this Gemarinian to feeling every moment of torture. The body wouldn't go into shock. The prisoner's entire existence would be pain, and Xan would be the tyrannical ruler of his nerve receptors.

Tears were acid droplets, bubbling down the cauldron of the prisoner's cheeks. He wailed, the siren song of melancholy in the exhibit where extinction came and conquered.

"Stop your fucking crying. Do you think these creatures didn't cry for help while you were burning them alive?" Xan pointed a twisted finger into the man's face.

"I was following orders," he managed between sobs. Strings of saliva vibrated like a mute violin.

"Everybody has a line etched ahead of them. A line that personal ethos forbids them from crossing. There's always a choice." Xan swallowed, every word laced in coarse sand. "You chose wrong."

The prisoner shifted against the ropes, the bark of the burnt tree flaking around his feet. "You know what Madame Bleu would have done to me. You know!"

"Is it any worse than your current predicament?"

The tears continued to burn. "Do you not feel pity?"

"A person with no regard for innocent creatures deserves no pity. In fact, you're alive right now for one reason." Xan adjusted his bruised knuckles, smoothing them over. "You need to tell us what Madame Bleu is planning."

"How am I supposed to know that? I'm no one."

"That's a shame." Xan turned to the next enclosure, one that had not been damaged. "That's a *real* shame."

He coughed as Xan opened the door and walked through the adjacent enclosure. "What are you doing?" The Sytheract's voice broke.

Xan held a serpent-like creature upside down. "This is the *Xeniph Serpent*. Right now it's in a catatonic state. I put it there by holding it upside down and pushing its pressure point."

"Why are you telling me this?"

"Oh, I'm not done yet." Xan's voice had sarcasm in every cadence, and it was all the more unsettling. "You know when a *Xeniph Serpent* strikes at a Human, their venom delivers paralysis in less than thirty seconds. But that's not all." He held a finger out. "The serpent is carnivorous and insatiably addicted to bone marrow." Xan came to the side of the prisoner and pointed to his back. "Human bone marrow can be difficult to get, and there is a nice little cache stored in your vertebrae. Once it sniffs it out, you can only sit there as it gorges upon you."

"I'll be paralysed so I won't feel anything."

"That's where you're wrong. This serpent is quite sadistic. It releases an enzyme through its saliva whilst feeding that enhances all nerve receptors associated with the feasting area. So, all your pain will be focused on that one zone, and thanks to the *azaliah* flower you will be fully conscious for all of it."

"You wouldn't do this to someone. I know you, I've grown up thinking you were a decent guy."

"Let me just tie this tourniquet around your upper thigh." Xan nodded. "Yep, that looks great. I am a decent guy when you don't fuck with things I love or kill innocent creatures who can't defend themselves!" The last few words were bellowed so loudly that even Dallis, who sat calmly in the face of this hideously vengeful display, jumped in his chair.

Without another word, Xan released the awakened serpent to the soundtrack of screams.

"No! Don't do this!" The prisoner screamed.

The serpent slithered around the trunk of the tree, curious to see what meat stick was attached.

It latched onto the ankle burying fangs, distributing the venom into the Sytheract's jerking body.

"Okay, so right now you're feeling a little nauseous." The screams persisted, and they shook the serpent from his ankle. It slithered purposefully up his leg now, flicking a tongue out as it did.

"Five to ten seconds in, your head will start pounding."

"I'll tell you something," they shouted, blinking through the pain in their temples.

"Go on then," Xan knelt down right in front of him. "Looks like little serpent is becoming a junior chiropractor. Best hurry."

"She has Solu Shields. Solu Shields on the army."

"Explain."

"She has rigged them up to replace the holoshields so they'll be more potent. If you attack, you'll need to hit dem wiv moe pow. Eh, eh, derp."

"Oh no, it looks like you're getting to the point where you can't speak anymore."

He groaned, saliva pooling beneath the tree.

The serpent bit down hard, and the groans turned shrill. Flowers of flesh blossomed, tended to by the fangs of spring. Scarlet rivers coursed down the canyons of his legs.

"Now, I can turn the serpent catatonic once more for your best bit of info. Blink twice if you can handle that."

He blinked frantically, more than twice.

Xan tended to the serpent with care. Blood still flowed from the open wound, but the serpent was turned upside down in Xan's arms.

"Dallis, can you please pass me that bunch of leaves next to you on the table?"

Dallis looked around, seized the turmeric-coloured leaves and went to hand them to Xan.

"I've got this big old serpent, can you crush the leaves in front of his nose? That will give him a kick of adrenalin for about maybe forty-five seconds." Xan nodded at Dallis, who still seemed unsure. But in his new exohand he crunched the leaves under the nostril. After a moment, the vapour entered their system. The neck straightened and the screams, the pleading, the begging overpowered everything.

Xan let it all play out. "You wasted twenty seconds, tell me what I want to hear."

"You'll spare me, right? Please sir, spare me, spare me."

"Stop begging and tell me what I want to hear."

"Okay, okay, she…ah…Madame Bleu has a mech suit for herself. She wants to be on the front line but this mech suit is stacked with weapons."

Xan narrowed his eyes. Another problem to solve. It was time to talk to the underground and see what kind of tech they had lying around that could even the playing field. At least they wouldn't be blindsided on the battlefield.

"Thank you for your cooperation."

"Will you l-l-let me l-l-live?" The slurring was returning.

Xan watched their head start to droop. The eyes fluttered in resignation. Xan placed the serpent on the ground still upturned, then placed an open palm on the prisoner's battered cheek. "You know, I never asked for your name. Do you know why that is?" He loosed a finger to caress a developing bruise.

"Because you are no one and you mean nothing to me." Tears streamed onto Xan's fingers now as his caress turned sinister, nails scraping the haunted face. "The *Tigress Aflexas*, *Rymbulas* and the *Goi-lang Gekkos* meant something to me. But you killed them."

Xan took his hand off the prisoner's cheek and backed away, tears flashing in his own eyes. This man probably didn't deserve such evil, such a cruel and spiteful death. Madame Bleu was the true object of rage, and the need to inflict his will upon her was taken by someone else. Luck had not been kind, and he chose to kneel upon the ground and conjure a flame. It appeared he was Bleu's reflection after all. Xan hated wearing the hideous evil mask that seemed to override the beauty in him.

But there is beauty in fighting for something. It's a type of beauty that is often ignored, but if tangible, would take its place alongside sunsets over the ocean.

That's why he loved Juniper, and where her influence upon him would never die.

Xan carefully turned the serpent over and it flicked its tongue, showing it was awake.

"Are you sure this is what you want, Xan?" Dallis asked. "There is no turning back."

Xan sighed, remembering what he did to the Valkors. They didn't deserve his wrath either, but had no choice but to absorb it. *That* was a disgusting act that he regretted every day, but this was different. He was the extinction exterminator, the King of the Wilds, and if he didn't speak for the creatures, then who would?

"I am the voice of the voiceless, and sometimes the language of violence is the only way the perpetrators will hear."

He turned and walked out the door of the ruined exhibit. Ruined by thugs and ruined by torture. Dallis followed him and put his new exohand on Xan's shoulder. Despite the very triggering scene, Dallis was an ally.

Every creature I meet gets a piece of my heart. When they walk the path of extinction like a plank out at sea, I'm forlorn. When we can save a species, when we can give them a voice where otherwise there is silence—it repairs the broken threads of the heart that I gave the others. Maybe in this case the healing will come from the screams of a dying Sytheract behind a locked door.

CHAPTER 59

LOCATION: GEMARINE
YEAR: 118
MASSY – 25 YEARS OLD

Massy couldn't believe he'd dodged the Valkor laser fire. He knew he was good, but that kind of piloting deserved not only a movie made about it, but a trilogy titled *Lord of the Skies*.

He opened the hatch to his fighter jet and jumped down with a metallic thump onto the ship hangar. The setting sun spilled gold throughout the large space, usually a dark dungeon filled with discarded tools and mechanics.

Sweat glistened across the birthmarks on his forehead, and he breathed out with relief. Other pompous fighter jets with sharp noses were being tended by extra weedy mechanics like Ryker, making sure people who mattered, would be dominant in the air. Several members of the last defence run had just landed and were buzzing around him, throwing congratulations and trying to touch the almighty pilot.

Massy was exhausted and not interested in dealing with fans trying to shove their tongue in his ass—not now anyway. "Get the fuck away from me you peasants." He shoved most of them, like swatting away carnivorous insects. "Someone take me to Madame Bleu, now!"

Flashes of welding light cast stars in Massy's vision while he looked around for someone useful amongst the crowd of useless drones.

A squad member he didn't know volunteered, grabbing him by the arm to escort him to Madame Bleu.

The doors creaked and he was thrust inside unceremoniously by one of Bleu's security detail. The heavy door slammed shut and his eyes strained to adjust in the darkness.

What the fuck is going on? Am I in a goddamn cave?

He noticed the large table, nodded in acknowledgment of its presence. A single candle at the opposite end drew his gaze, haphazardly throwing ghastly figures on the walls. Ritualistic dancers calling for intervention.

Madame Bleu sat calmly in shadow. Her bony fingers massaged her temples in rhythmic pulses.

"Madame, is that…you?" Massy inched forward.

"I saw your little show out there." Her voice was emotionless. "I don't think I've ever seen a greater display of piloting if I'm honest." She clasped her hands together, resting on the table. It made a dull sound that echoed in the large dining hall like fading footsteps.

Massy puffed out his chest and scratched his cheek to hide the emerging smile. "I appreciate that, it was nothing really."

"Did I ever tell you my father was a pilot?"

"Um, no, actually." Massy stopped walking forward and leant on the table. When the plaudits about his skills ceased, he was much less interested.

"He had grace that not many pilots do," Madame Bleu continued. "It's all about the destination for them. But he had the heart of an explorer, the vision of a true king and the strength to carry others on his back."

Where is she going with this? I don't need a picnic under a family tree.

The gnawing guilt of not knowing whether the crew on the *Attenborough* had survived was playing on him. He was worried about what she would say when he didn't have an answer. When he had to admit that although he flew like a legend, he failed at his task of killing them before they stepped back onto Gemarine.

"He was the one who took the first steps onto this planet. He was the one who told me what needed to be done." She rose and the chair creaked as it slid across the floor. A banshee shriek in a quiet forest glen.

"On his deathbed, he made sure that I would continue his legacy, continue building something greater than a homeworld with restrictions, surveyed by the eye of tyranny. Something greater than a bunch of mindless beings fighting over ideals, the size of a grain of sand or destroying their planetary home with neglect."

Massy's own footfall reminded him of a steady heartbeat as he approached Madame Bleu. Closer now, he saw the tears that welled in her eyes, the emotion so bare at the surface of someone he thought was cold.

Scars are a mask over bleeding wounds and grimacing faces, just the same as when one conjures frost that covers the heart, stemming emotions when it gets too much. Time makes a mockery of us all.

Madame Bleu had allowed time to harden her. Nostalgia, though, was a tarnished key to the locked box of her emotions. They flowed now as if dam walls collapsed with all but a gentle nudge.

I'm not made for this. I've built my own dam so I didn't have to face any of this. Why is she breaking around me?

"Listen Madame, you shouldn't have to justify your actions to anyone. Let alone me. We all do what we can to survive. If you strip everything back, leave it raw—that's what this is. Survival."

Her voice found its strength. "I'm not asking to be forgiven by you, of all Gemarinians." Flecks of saliva danced in the air, coating the varnished table upon their descent. "But I know this is survival. Just not the self-preserving kind *you* so desperately cling to. It's the survival of memory, of expectation, of fulfilment, of truth and belief."

Massy didn't have that much depth, enough to discern each of those survival traits in amongst the need to obliterate planets and commit genocide. He wasn't concerned with the survival of an ideal. He was happy walking arm in arm with self-preservation. It had gotten him that far.

"Listen, let me take you away somewhere safe. There are Valkor ships amassing, and I think this will get ugly real qui—" He reached for her arm, and she swatted him away violently.

"You've never had anything to fight for...you wouldn't know what it takes to stand up and die for what you've built and what you believe in."

Massy laughed pitifully. "I believe in winning. So I'll be fighting, but I'll be fighting to make all those fools dead. I don't care what happens to Gemarine or even you...I want to be the one standing on the bodies of the fallen because I'm better...because I'm the best."

"Were you the best when you failed to check your kill?" The quiet monotony in her voice chilled Massy. "It's all well and good to shoot the ship down, but the holoshield would've protected them. The one thing I asked of you, you couldn't do." The motherly disappointment stung more than anger.

"I didn't anticipate the Valkor ships, I was lucky enough to get out alive! They were—"

She raised a frail hand to cut him off, "Save it." She leant on the table to stand. "You did me a favour."

"What do you mean?"

Madame Bleu cracked her neck, moving from side to side, the candle throwing light on her from below. Her face was ghoulish, as close to evil as in any nightmare Massy had ever had. "I mean, I have the chance to meet them on the battlefield. To see the terror in their eyes when fate sides with me."

Massy swallowed. "I'll be right next to you."

"I don't know why I didn't have you in the inner circle this whole time. You would've been…well…quite loyal." She bowed for the first time at a civilian, and then those dead eyes returned as she looked far into the future where he didn't care to follow. "Farewell Massy, may you stand atop the fallen when this day turns black."

He returned the bow. Then silence hung awkwardly in the air. Madame Bleu erupted, "Get the fuck out of here, you fucking idiot!"

Massy put his hands up submissively and backed out toward the door, realising that this was her place, and he should have made the move to leave. He took one last glance at Madame Bleu. She had positioned her MPD in front of her, switching on a broadcast signal that would most likely go out to every MPD on Gemarine.

I wonder how this is going to play out.

The door slammed for the last time. He looked toward the motitube at the end of the hall ready to ferry him to the headquarters of the army. He needed to know what had actually happened to the *Attenborough* Assholes, and then plan his victory dance. Which piece of music would accompany it? Which finger point or leg shuffle would be most appropriate?

He wasn't running away this time, instead, he would dance into the fray. The taste for victory was stronger than self-preservation, and he was going to feel it on his tongue.

CHAPTER 60

LOCATION: GEMARINE
YEAR: 118
XAN – 24 YEARS OLD

The cave was toasty with the glow of fire. Projections of familial warmth flickered on the rock walls courtesy of the crackling flames. All of them sat in various clumps of weariness—Ryker, Dallis, Ranjit, Lilianna, Fleurah, Arcadie, Juniper, Qilin, Xan and Lambastian. It was a reunion of sorts, filled with long hugs, some timid tears and relieved smiles. But war was on the horizon. War was the moment after the setting sun dipped behind the clouds, where it hid beneath the covers fearing what darkness brings.

Xan had fresh blood on his knuckles. The scent of the burning logs on his nose and tongue. Dallis and Juniper had steadied him as they made their way back to the cave to reunite with the underground after the torture. Torture for *information,* he told himself. But in truth, it was mainly for revenge. Xan cried not for what he lost within himself, but for the creatures now lost to the universe. Extinction had won and everything that he'd done to prevent the inevitable felt worthless.

But once he breathed in the smoke around him, saw timid smiles from friends new and old, he knew that these forays into other timelines, other worlds with the task of uniting crystals, uniting their purpose showed him that it was *never* worthless. As long as someone was left to care, extinction itself would fall to ruin.

It wasn't long before Madame Bleu's message was broadcast on every MPD, urging citizens to fight against the approaching threats, to protect their liberty and to conserve their way of life. Driving home the whole, "Contentment through unity. Protection through peace" bullshit.

It was a rousing speech. To the masses, she appeared genuinely vulnerable and caring. As a leader of the "rebel group," it was important for Xan to consider a way in which to reply. The Gemarine community needed to know that the rebels were not the enemy.

"Arcadie, I think you'll need to step up."

"He doesn't have any legs." Dallis protested, but before Xan needed to say anything Ryker began explaining its meaning to him. Lambastian looked on with an amused expression on his actual face after shedding the Maraudar mask.

Xan resumed. "We need to broadcast a message to the public and level the playing field. I think Juniper needs to be the one to deliver it."

"Me? Um, why?" Juniper tilted her head. Some of the spark had returned to her following the *Attenborough* crash.

"Because you're the unofficial leader of the army," Xan said. "You're certainly the most famous warrior. You could galvanise the masses. If there's a chance they'd listen to you to fight against Madame Bleu, we have to take it."

Miami grunted in agreement as she rocked in an old wooden chair, biting her dirty fingernails. Ranjit eyed her warily.

"I hate being in the spotlight with cameras or holos. It's not my thing," Juniper protested.

Ryker stepped forward. "What if it's both you *and* Xan?"

Xan knew where he was going with it before the explanation escaped his lips. Xan was the most famous and influential person on Gemarine. He was used to being streamed across MPD's ever since he entered the city from the Wilds, sporting a Mika Tikaani at his side.

Xan knew the ghost of rage still bubbled in his eyes, and the blood from his torture victim would be an inappropriate image to cast onto the world. Miami walked uneasily with a cane made from a branch of a blackened twisted tree and linked arms with Xan. "Why don't we clean 'im up first, give 'im a bit of a massage and then he'll be right to go."

Lilianna stood up and followed awkwardly behind as if she wanted desperately to help but didn't quite know where to start.

Juniper leant against a chair beside Ryker, with Fleurah and Arcadie congregating near the far wall of the cave. "Miami," Juniper called out harshly. "I think Lilianna can handle this one. Can you make sure *I* look semi decent—enough to appear on holo feeds?"

Miami smirked a little but disengaged from Xan's arm and backed away, her knotted grey hair swaying as she used the cane to hobble toward Juniper. "I look like a pile of rhinovader shit, girl; I dunno dick all 'bout lookin' decent. But sure, if ya want some of my creams on ya face then let's party."

"I've had way worse stuff all over my face. Lather me up, honey bunch."

LILIANNA
22 YEARS OLD

Lilianna led Xan deeper into the cave. There were two small partitions that separated a shower with a small regen basin and a restroom.

She switched on the shower. It was basic, from the early colonial days and it spluttered its discontent at being awoken from slumber. A steady stream of river water flowed through pipes fastened to the ceiling. She tested the temperature.

Lukewarm but satisfactory.

She faced Xan and saw the pain in his eyes, the exhaustion in his slackened stance, shoulders drooping, almost begging to be cared for. He was usually the one who did the caring. Juniper, in her wisdom, had let Lilianna be there for him this time to make up for the Valkor incident.

Lilianna was upset with news of the biobase, more upset than most of the attendees in the cave, but no one took this burden on quite like Xan. No one stood upon the cliff edge using a forceful voice for the voiceless like Xan. When someone you speak for is suddenly eradicated, an emptiness remains like the torment of losing a child.

Lilianna unzipped Xan's suit to his navel. Though his hair hung over his eyes, she felt his chest rise and fall, shaking with hurt. She moved closer to him, and his head flopped onto her right shoulder. The coarse hairs of his beard scratched against her neck. She felt timid tears tiptoe down her chest. Lilianna's right hand came up and grasped the back of his head. She held him tight. She absorbed his darkness, his self-hatred, his regret, his vengeful exhale and she let it flow through her as if they were one. Bonded by experience, by reality, by truth. Bonded by love.

The connection was more than something activated within her DNA, like a soulbond. This was earned. This was a choice.

Love was more than an idealistic picture of happiness, more than a symbolic heart plastered above smiling faces like a halo of perfection. Love was also the darkness, the shadows that prowled when tears came fast. Love was a perpetual storm hunting a rainbow. Love was the mending of a broken soul, as long as you had the strength to build again.

She knew now that it was more than a facade. And she embraced it just like she embraced Xan, giving a piece of herself to repair his broken spirit.

The blood swirled in the drain as she ran hands over his cheeks, caressed the new scars on his biceps and tried her best to ignore anything below the waistline.

The time was not for them to engage in anything other than loving and sensual touch without the pursuit of something more. Not yet, anyway.

XAN
24 YEARS OLD

Arcadie gave the literal green light. It flashed on his faceplate replacing his eyes. It was the sign that he'd hacked into the network and was broadcasting the message to every MPD on Gemarine.

Xan took a deep breath and steadied himself. "To all the Gemarinians watching, I apologise for the intrusive nature of this broadcast. It is imperative that you hear our version of events, which will in turn give you an informed choice. Either join our cause or continue to fight for someone who has lied to you your entire lives."

Juniper began. "I fought for Gemarine harder than anyone. If you look at the data scrolls my name appears countless times, paired with words like 'hero,' 'warrior,' 'captain.' These words are not thrown around haphazardly. These words remain like an extension of myself, a tattoo of pride that I wear as part of me. I will never regret defending Gemarine and keeping all of you safe. But I had no idea what I was doing. I contributed to the genocide of worlds across space and time."

The camera switched back to Xan. "Madame Bleu destroyed entire planets, entire family trees, entire generations, entire ecosystems to ensure that Gemarine could function. Within just one standard month, we found ways to power Gemarine in the future without *any* genocidal acts—a peaceful procurement of a valuable energy source from Sytheria. The Valkors, the Cryptoborgs, who had been our enemies for years, were only trying to ensure the sanctity and strength of the entire galaxy. We, as

Gemarinians, have been completely unaware that we were contributing to the death of the galaxy just by living every day."

Juniper nodded. "What we ask you is going to be different. If you are able to fight, fight with us against Madame Bleu. If you cannot fight, then remain safe and secure in your levels. Stay with your clan, do not engage with anyone at all."

"If you are fit to fight, meet us on the wild side of the former city gates. We will repay your trust with a bond that won't be broken by tyranny and lies. The new Gemarine will be built on unity of not just this beautiful planet, but unity with the galaxy, with others in the universe. Allies who will stand with us and who we will stand with when the time comes," Xan said.

"Madame Bleu and all those who walk with her—see you on the battlefield. May your death be swift," Juniper concluded.

The transmission was cut. The cave was now silent with only the afternoon wind whispering from dry, cracked lips.

There wasn't a cause to cheer.

Even though hope was a mirage shimmering on the horizon, they would follow a trail of blood to get there. War was not a pleasant walk into a sunset stained with golden tears. Xan knew from being there for Juniper that it changed you both physically and mentally.

If you were lucky enough to survive the battle, then the war inside your head might just get you in the end.

CHAPTER 61

LOCATION: GEMARINE
YEAR: 118
JUNIPER – 24 YEARS OLD

Juniper watched thousands stream over the rubble of the gates, crossing the rusted soil to greet her. She'd never felt this level of importance before, or at least she'd never read into the hype surrounding her feats on the battlefield. Shrugging off fame, she concentrated on building her squad away from the spotlight. This time, Gemarine really needed her. The only time in her life when she would be truly fighting for unity, for a stake in a galaxy united.

Humans, Sytheracts, Aranthers bowed to her, embraced her, kissed her lips, as they funnelled through. Some wore masks of stoic resistance, while others openly wept at the fight that was to come.

Some brought word of Gemarinians too afraid to fight. Locked inside their levels, holding onto clan members, hiding in closets, blackening the windows and hunkering down. Children and babies wrenched from nurseries and creches now waited in darkness, not knowing what would come. Not contemplating that their lives would soon be changed no matter what the result.

Juniper knew that some of the Gemarinians that would stand on the other side with Madame Bleu were only doing so because of their resistance to change. What the rebels offered was unknown.

Too often fear of the unknown kept curious hearts docile, accepting a fate much less than what was deserved. Had they just dared to bury caution and stand atop its coffin, then maybe greater feats would come.

Valkor ships had landed on the ground and warriors gathered in one section, spoken to by General Heronicus standing on a rock wavering his arms around like a baboon in heat. She smirked, remembering their interaction when he stepped onto Gemarine several hours ago.

"Miss Juniper, fate keeps pulling us toward one another." His voice was like the narrator of a children's film, deep and melodious.

She shivered in disgust. Turning around, she made sure to frame the look of contempt on her face. "Fate can get fucked then."

Heronicus walked toward her, arms outstretched. A hearty smile weighed down the drooping cheeks. "C'mon, dear child, bygones be gone. We must start afresh in this new Gemarine."

The exoblades flew from her fingers, sticking into the sand just in front of his left foot. "Move another inch and I will cut off your dick and old man balls and clog your mouth with them until you suffocate."

General Heronicus started to laugh, looking at the other Valkors who had gathered around their commander. But Juniper rolled across the sand and sprang up, pressing a rusted dagger against his groin.

She heard him wince. "Dare you to laugh again and I'll make a nice little cunt for you. It'll match your personality."

Droplets of sweat trickled down his cheeks. She imagined his testicles contracting away from the blade. He held his breath with pursed lips.

Shaking hands came up in surrender and he whispered, "I'll back away then."

Juniper pressed the dagger just a tiny bit further in. His sharp intake of breath and small whimper marked him as her bitch in front of those who bore witness. "You can fight beside me. But you'll never get away with what you did to my crew, my clan and to me," she hissed, pulling back the dagger. "Watch your fucking back." Juniper started walking away, then turned quickly to correct. "I meant, watch your balls. They might just become a beautiful necklace one day." The middle finger salute was the last thing he saw before she walked back to greeting new members of their army.

Xan and Qilin stood beside Juniper, having missed the interaction with her and Heronicus. Qilin had growled ferociously as if wanting to maim the same parts on him as Juniper, while Xan just stared with the ol' evil eye. Unfortunately, he just looked like a male model—all pensive with that chiselled jaw. It was almost laughable. Instead of stewing in their hatred though, both Xan and Qilin helped welcome civilians into the fray. Fleurah practised close combat with Arcadie further behind while defected teenage army cadets watched the most sophisticated robot they'd known spar better than any of them could.

Juniper searched for Lilianna. She was sitting next to Ryker, both looking terrified. Lambastian had that battle-ready hardness about him at least, checking the charge in the Cranston ray gun and sheathing a rusted metal dagger. But standing next to those two highlighted that Ryker and Lilianna didn't belong. Despite Juniper teaching them both combat training a handful of times on the ship and on Earth with Lilianna, it wasn't enough.

But their hearts were big, swelling with courage, just enough to quiet the fear. Unified ideals were often potent enough to disguise meek skill. In a crowd of soldiers, unity could just see them through.

The first signs of their enemy emerging over the rubble occurred about an hour after the last civilian had joined their cohort.

There was no comparison to the mishmash of aliens and Gemarinians that stood behind Juniper, gazing out with wide eyes at the scene of their impending demise. They were *easily* outnumbered.

Special army issued Solu Shields glowed around each individual soldier as they trundled forward. There was a standard issued MPD version that emitted a shield, but the Solu Shield was often used to protect spaceships. The information that Xan had extracted from Bleu's captured goon ensured they were prepared for this. Juniper knew that they could withstand at least several rounds of heavy fire before giving way. She needed the soldiers to continue to believe they would be invincible with the Solu Shields, give them confidence beyond their true fighting capabilities.

The underground had tricks up their sleeves.

When the fighting began, they would find out if those tricks could change the game.

The army poured over the wreckage of the wall like insects scoping neighbouring territory. A figure strode ahead of them, golden armour gleaming under the dying sun.

That is a bit much. Reminds me of—

Her thoughts paused as she realised who donned the golden armour of her fallen comrade Boorak. It was a signal to her. A final "fuck you" screamed from a distance.

He will be out of his depth on the battlefield. This isn't like the skies, zooming away and shooting from a distance. This is skin to skin, blood on blood.

She sneered, waiting for a chance to finally slay Massy the Betrayer.

Without warning the ground rumbled, deep and resonant. The shuffling of nervous feet and the tinny clanking of body armour ceased. A muted silence fell upon the rebel army. The wind was a whisper from the cracked lips of the world. But the beat remained. A large hollow skin drum tuned low, with vibrations of horror that scattered shivering pebbles.

Then it came into view. The arm cannons first, raised high like monumental spires drawing energy from the sun, followed by the mechanical body wound tight in threads of knotted boronium armour.

The chest cavity contained the genocidal queen of Gemarine herself, Madame Bleu.

The audio duplicator blared across the empty space separating the two sides,

"We are the true Gemarine and anyone who stands against us deserves exile." The army under her command roared. "Exile is death." Her voice dangled on the precipice of lunacy.

Madame Bleu was no longer disguised as a mountain with magma bubbling within. Sky blue streams and bubbling brooks had done their best for years to hide the scalding waters surrounding a vicious volcano. But she roared now, with flowing tears of molten lava surrounding her like a moat, chaotic blasts of fury spewed forth in an eruption of intent.

Juniper raised her exohand high into the air, a fist unfurled. She felt Xan stiffen beside her, Qilin arch her back, the horde of defenders shifting behind her, readying their bodies for an injection of bravery.

She rid her mind of individuals. She focused in on the love that had grown, and let it fuse with the malevolence of her former self. Droplets of oil sailing on turbulent waters.

Juniper closed her hand into a fist.

CHAPTER 62

After her warrior lover formed that boronium fist, the scene altered. From the smell of sweat to the sound of scraping boots on mounds of dirt, pinging lasers finding supple flesh to cook, rapid, stale breaths quelled anxiety.

Grav bombs sailed overhead until explosions howled in the distance. Shockwaves rocked the planet like a cradle in the sky. Even if Lilianna anticipated the force, it still sent her sprawling across the serpent-like ripples in the sand. Heart hammering, hands trembling, she steadied herself on one knee holding a Cranston ray gun. Could she replicate what she did on Earth to save Juniper not so long ago?

The Valkors launched bombs into the opposing army, bodies scattered, dissolving in plumes of smoke and flame. Missiles were returned by the Gemarine army, disrupting the formation the rebels had formed. Scared citizens fled the fire and the chaos.

A missile detonated, and the force launched Lilianna into the air. She landed on her shoulder, cushioned by the remaining charge on her holoshield.

Members of the rebel horde charged toward Madame Bleu's army, who charged back. Lilianna flicked the hair from her face with a swipe of the neck and peered at the scene, horrified as she noticed Arcadie flying above the Gemarine army ready to unleash the underground's weapon under their Solu Shields.

Arcadie soared majestically, dodging laser fire and missiles. She thought she just made out faint squeals of delight.

Inconspicuously, Arcadie dropped the weapon like a bird releasing a seed pod. As soon as it hit the ground, the detonation occurred. There wasn't a huge explosion—it was an electromagnetic pulse that took out the Solu Shields' high velocity output. As soon as the charge was released, the Solu Shields surrounding the soldiers spluttered and exhaled a crackling dying breath. The entirety of Madame Bleu's army was unprotected. Valkors fired upon them instantly. This time bodies went flying, limbs cartwheeling, heads rolling.

Through the carnage, Bleu's Gemarinian soldiers came fast, their eyes glazed over with rage. Without the protection of their Solu Shields the inner wild surfaced, the heat of the battle prompted the reveal of the true monster within. They came quick. Way too quick. She fumbled with the ray gun, fingers slipping on the trigger as her jaw clenched.

Lilianna fired off a burst of laser pulses, knocking down one rabid soldier, while another came screaming toward her dodging the stream of her loose aim. The Sytheract male had a pulse whip that burnt with blue electric charges. The whip whirred and smashed into her holoshield. It hummed its discontent, barely deflecting the strength of the whip. It startled Lilianna, and she turned, stumbling around a member of the exiles on their knees with a cauterised wound across their neck, clutching at it, struggling to breathe. A ray gun blast struck the exile through the eye. Smoke sizzled from the wound. They dropped to the ground motionless. Lilianna squealed in horror.

The Sytheract male's whip flayed across her back, and the holoshield hummed a deep lullaby of death. She fell onto red sand. The attacker leered down at her, the whip poised above his shoulder.

A storm was in his eyes, and she was nothing but a bedraggled bird blighted by the severity of the rain. Whimpering, she held up her palms in submission. If the clouds could be summoned, they would carry the storm away and she would fly to the radiant sun.

The fatal blow was a moment away. Lilianna's muscles tensed. Her eyes snapped shut.

"Big sis has come to save you!" Fleurah roared, appearing over the Sytheract's right shoulder. Her bare hands seized the barb, and it cackled with a sparkling laugh. Fleurah's scream tore into the air. Her flesh tore from her palm, but she quickly wrapped the barb around the attacker's neck from behind. Letting go, her palms offered wisps of smoke, and the sand welcomed her spent body. The whip fizzed with excitement as it sent electricity through the Sytheract's body, turning rigid and jerking backwards. Smoke sizzled. Charred skin mixed with the salt of sweat and sharp tang of boiled blood wafted in the air.

Fleurah crawled on the ground to the body and stupidly sent her rusted sword through his chest. The electric current zapped through Fleurah's holoshield, destroying any protection she had left. The metal of her sword was an electrical conductor. Hands released the sword, and the electricity threw her back. The whip still fizzed after death had claimed the Sytheract.

Fleurah got to her knees and crawled to Lilianna, extending her undamaged hand. "C'mon sis!" she yelled.

Lilianna was beyond thankful. She was clearly out of her depth on the battlefield, so Fleurah would need to do a tad more saving by the time the battle was done.

Arcadie zoomed down to join them. "New hairstyle?" he quipped at Fleurah, who had her dreadlocks levitating from the electrocution.

"Didn't see you helpin', dickless."

"I was too busy knocking out the Solu Shields and giving you half a chance. Thank you very much!" His gangly arms folded across his chest.

"Yeah, yeah, Mr HeroBot."

"Oh, I condone that nickname."

Lilianna had enough of their quips, bombs were sounding left and right. Her stress levels were peaking. "Are you two mental—let's get the fuck out of here!"

Fleurah and Arcadie looked at each other and smiled, united by their little slice of crazy.

Arcadie took off ahead of Fleurah, deflecting stray laser bolts and felling soldiers like trees in the battlefield forest.

Lilianna ran, legs splayed, yelling for them to wait for her.

RYKER
21 YEARS OLD

The sun was low in the sky now, scarlet rays thrown across the horizon. Smoke wafted like comforting clouds amidst the chaos. The stench of burning rubber made Ryker's eyes water. It could have been flesh, roasting on the coals of war. He didn't want to know.

Dallis was with the cohort of Valkors, unseen. Lambastian had fled into the path of the galloping soldier steeds kicking up tornados of dust. His eyes glazed with past trauma, hard lines on that beautiful face signified intent. A need to rectify past injustices burnt brighter than the desire to love and hide, stroke Ryker's cheeks or soothe him as war played out around them both. It was the heat of the fight that he sought. If they both made it out alive, maybe Ryker could teach him to love again. To smile without sadness that stung the eyes.

In this battle for Gemarine, Ryker was alone.

And scared.

The only reason why he chose to fight was for his family, his crew. The same crew who was in the throes of battle, all around him but nowhere to be seen. Ryker was not only alone but he had no clue what was happening to them.

Something caught his eye to the right. Through the dust that rose like a fog in the valley, he spotted Arcadie—the floating assassin creating a free path for Fleurah and Lilianna who trailed behind.

Ryker spotted a problem.

They were hugging the eastern wall.

Upon the eastern wall a troupe of soldiers had gathered, scaling the heights for a vantage point.

The faux leather belt that held makeshift weapons jiggled as Ryker ran after them. Spindly legs making him look like a mutant spider skating across ice.

But he needed to save them.

His family.

CHAPTER 63

LOCATION: GEMARINE
YEAR: 118
MASSY – 25 YEARS OLD

It was fucking mayhem. But it was much more fun like this.

Massy had never been in a battle on the ground. Blood never touched the sand. Eyes with killing intent never saw an enemy's retinas streaked with red hot tears. From the piloting chair in the ship, battle was always a dot on a radar or a hunk of metal on a camera. There was intimacy in a blade sliding through flesh, skewering an organ or two, tasting the ionised blood flecks that settled on his tongue. His body shook with fear, sure, and in nanosecond bursts he wanted to run, wrap himself inside a cocoon until at least he was a beautiful *flutterfly* with rainbow wings that sparkled in dappled light.

But he chose to flex his newfound lust for death.

It didn't matter that the Solu Shields went down; he put confidence in his desire to win and sometimes that was enough.

The golden armour protected him, but he also wore it to spit in Juniper's face. Boorak was buried in the same armour. His rank in the

Gemarine army allowed him the accolades. It wasn't so ceremonious when Massy had wrenched his ivory skull and bones from the armour, throwing them in the tomb like pruned branches.

But why respect the dead? They were gone for a reason. Because they weren't good enough to live.

JUNIPER
24 YEARS OLD

Juniper cut her way through the surging army like a pass the parcel of flesh on her way to the ultimate prize.

Madame Bleu's mechsuit fired off laser turrets into the distance. Restless fighters that gathered behind Juniper fell quickly as bursts of projectile tore bodies apart.

General Heronicus had the same idea, wanting to take the prize for himself: slay the killer of his people and complete the cycle of revenge. With long strides he floated beside Juniper like a stray feather in her wingspan. But feathers shed and fall away, and she could only hope to shake him loose when the time was right.

Massy was out of eyesight but she wasn't concerned with him yet. After she cut off the head, the rest of the little minions would scatter.

Juniper moved like reflected light glinting on glass: sharp, bold and damaging. Her exoblades were venomous in their sting; the long, seasoned sword collected scalps like a youthful dagger. The occasional flurry from her Cranston ray gun struck purposefully at intended targets.

Juniper's ecstatic dance of war reinvigorated her. She felt deeply connected to the other dancers who she severed from life in freeing twirls. Killing was meditation for her. To reach the promised land, she bathed in blood until the pearly gates were ripped open before her and Madame Bleu stood there.

The large turrets were shaking with fury, as lasers burst forth into the crowded battlefield. There was no care for who or what she shot, only psychosis in the screeching rounds pumping through flesh like jelly. Juniper watched Bleu's elongated face, tucked inside the chest plate, mouth agape, teeth bared, the vocal replicator blasting out her shrill, manic screeches.

Just as Juniper had her sights set on obliterating the chest plate and piercing through Madame Bleu's eyes with her exoblade fingers, General Heronicus aka General Fucknut launched himself at Madame Mech, deflecting fire with a rusty shield. He hitched a ride on the left turret and latched onto the chestplate like an affectionate spider. Face to face with Madame Bleu, albeit separated by a bioplastic laser proof shield, he produced a predatory snarl. Madame Bleu registered him in his attempted cuddle. Before crushing him to a pulp, she saw past him to Juniper, then to Xan, then Qilin. And things turned ugly.

The turret swatted away Heronicus like the hapless fly he was, and he toppled across the dirt.

Congrats, your manoeuvre worked really well, you brainless hack.

The turret turned on Juniper first. Although she was certain Bleu wanted Xan's scalp more than any other, she didn't let the emotions of a kill cloud her judgement. The biggest threat was Juniper, so she needed to nullify her first.

Juniper ran four steps to gather momentum, then somersaulted as lasers punched through the air, following her like a shark on a trail of blood. The holoshield held on while a few sharp teeth nearly punctured her lower leg. Landing on her shoulder, sand sprayed across her vision she was already firing ray gun shots toward the chest plate. Bleu crossed the turrets shielding her her chest and in doing so gave Juniper the second she needed to aim her exoblades. The beautiful little blades buzzed like hornets, wings beating as they fixated on a target. The flight path was straight into the right turret laser chambers. Each exoblade plugged the chamber cannon, and the next moment that Bleu tried to fire off a catastrophic round, the right arm exploded and shards of boronium burst like glitter into the air. Shrapnel rain kissed the skin with blood. Bleu's unstable mech stumbled backwards.

"My arm, my arm!" came the screams from inside the chest plate.

Juniper had probably said those exact words in that exact inflection years ago. But this time she didn't simmer with a desire for revenge; she smiled with rancid empathy.

There was a golden flash across the foreground of Bleu's mech, but as Qilin and Xan turned inward to take advantage of her surprise, they were ambushed by Massy.

MASSY
25 YEARS OLD

Massy heard Juniper yell out, "You right with him, Xan?" and he smiled, thinking how wonderful the moment would be when her heart broke, standing over Xan's dead body.

Her tears would moisten fallow land.

In rigid lines, seedlings of sadness would grow.

He would harvest the bounty, let the fuel of its fragrance diffuse. Until he, imbued by a widow's woe, would declare himself King of the Wastelands.

"I got this," Xan called back, vengeance simmering in his gaze.

He held himself well, but Massy was going to end his reign. King of the Wastelands he would become. The land of the heart, where all emotion would be ravaged and plundered.

CHAPTER 64

LOCATION: GEMARINE
YEAR: 118
JUNIPER – 24 YEARS OLD

Madame Bleu seemed to regain herself at the sight of Heronicus making a second play for glory. He was covered in the powdered blood of the sand, but his will would not waver. It was a will born from a cruel displacement, the genocide of his people and transformation of a planet into lonely orbiting rocks. A will like that was eternal.

Bleu swatted with the left turret and missed the general, so instead of looking to exploit an area of weakness on the mech he went for force. Clearly, too much testosterone. A fist was made, the elbow pulled back, triggering the punch and the idiot general let loose on the remaining turret cannon. It made as much damage as a bee trying to fuck a buffalo. Juniper grimaced at the way his knuckles seemed to crunch and depress as he made contact with the immoveable surface.

The fight between two old enemies was blocked by the sudden appearance of Thaspina. Her legs stood apart; her bold blue eyes narrowed. A long, newly forged sword glinted in the light of the twin moons, watching the battle unfold.

"Bitch, please just get out of here before you break a nail." Juniper shooed her away.

"You forget, I served in battles before I was part of the inner circle."

"Oh, you *served* in battles, did you? I fucking *owned* battles single-handedly. Walk away and you might just see another day."

Thaspina crouched low, her sword pointed toward Juniper. She flicked her plaited hair, and it bounced off her shoulders. Gravbombs glinted on her belt. Juniper foresaw an ending so brutal and cosy she would let it make love to her, rather than fuck her.

"Let's dance, baby girl," Juniper snarled.

Thaspina charged with the pointed sword. Juniper sucked in a breath, moving with ease to let the blade pierce the fine air ahead of her. Thaspina retracted and stabbed at Juniper once more, but Juniper twirled in a leaping movement, and the blade missed everything. Upon straightening, Juniper faced Thaspina with a swipe of exoblades that stung her cheek.

Thaspina stumbled backwards, looking at the fresh blood dripping onto the palm of her left hand. A groan of hatred followed a lunging thrust of the sword. This time Juniper used her own weapon to block the strike from one side to the next, then in the following movement pressed up against Thaspina with both blades rubbing in front of her eyes. Thaspina grunted, while Juniper smiled sweetly and planted a kiss on her nose. The last remaining member of the inner circle pulled back, immediately spitting out in disgust.

"You're a diseased little whore. Don't you dare touch me."

Juniper watched the fight between Heronicus and Bleu over Thaspina's shoulder and had battle envy. She needed to stop playing with this frigid amateur bitch and get to the main show.

"You're not even a grain of sand to me. I am a tsunami and you'll soon be washed away. No one will remember you. No one will mourn you." Juniper nodded. "You will have your legacy, though."

"Huh? What legacy?" Thaspina said.

"The death of Madame Bleu—caused by you."

Confusion slithered across Thaspina's face like a worm.

Juniper strode forward. Playtime had ended.

This was the melody of life and death. The whistle sounded—a meek overture before the battle opera. The diaphragm tightened, readying her shrill soprano. The spotlight wavered in the darkness of the stage, but it was a magnet to her. She craved its electrical whispers, the sheen of sweat it lathered on her brow and the complete focus it gave her.

It was time to sing.

Her exoblades flew high and lodged into Thaspina's pupils to a dissonant, wrenching scream. On a galloping run Juniper dropped to her knees sweeping the sword just below the kneecaps. Thaspina's body toppled over onto the sand. The scream turned shrill; spurts of arterial lifeforce fizzed across the scarlet sand. The blood was more sinister. Dark and grimy.

Juniper rose and strode to the flailing body, letting the blood coat her. Licking her lips, she tasted the sweet ironised death on her tongue. Lathered in the thick, painted strokes of gore, she was a mural of war. She was a resplendent warrior masterpiece.

Juniper closed her eyes and turned her palms to the sky until the screams had softened to whimpers and the puddles of sanguine were absorbed into the thirsty sand.

"Your legacy lives," she whispered, as she pierced Thaspina's chest with her exoblade fingers and wrenched out her beating heart. It quivered. It twitched as if fighting for a second chance, as if savouring its final fight. Juniper squeezed the heart into sloppy mush that she discarded like rotten fruit.

The warrior princess took a deep breath in and gave thanks to her time on Dracia. She could see the way that each soul was connected now. Thaspina, so desperately wanting to protect her master, would be the one to contribute so wholesomely to her death. It was almost perfect. And although this was a violent exploration of interconnectedness, she had to remember that the duality of everything needed to be appreciated.

The universe was made from violence, from chaos, from anarchy. It was okay for her to embrace the beautiful disaster within and rewrite this story so that it would end with joy.

But first, the rain before the rainbow.

Juniper snatched a gravbomb hanging on the twitching Thaspina's belt.

It's not pretty, it's not something to be proud of, but sometimes you have to play dirty to win.

Juniper charged at the fighting match between Bleu and Heronicus. She would make her mark in the theatre of the psychopaths.

Bleu was correct to assume Juniper was the biggest threat, but when the lion had a chunky pile of stinky meat in front of its eyes, it wasn't concerned with the antelope sharpening its antlers from behind.

Her sword was drawn outwards, a sharpened skewer ready for dissection. Heronicus and Bleu were so entwined in their battle that they didn't notice Juniper loping toward them. She rammed the sword up through a gap in the Valkor armour, through the back of Heronicus, erupting through his chest. His heart most likely haemorrhaged in an instant. The sword exited and locked into the collarbone turret of Madame Bleu's mech armour as Juniper drove upwards.

She had made a skewer of fuckwits. It was delicious.

Juniper used her momentum to vault over the mech suit. In the cinematic slow-motion arc, floating above the two war torn enemies, Madame Bleu was the one who looked up at her. She wished Heronicus could've given her a final look of annoyance, the white flag look of defeat. But he was too busy with his ruptured heart, crumpling into submission. The maniac's eyes widened in terror and Juniper's heart soared just as she soared. Bleu's look that she could plaster in the halls of her mind like some propaganda pathway, always drawing her back to this moment when Bleu knew that her reign of terror was at its end. When her wayward dreams would be locked in a basement sheathed in shadow. When her Gemarine became the rebel's Gemarine.

Juniper dropped the grav bomb, lodging into the small gap between Heronicus and Bleu's armour. Nestled right above the space where Heronicus's old man testicles would be, shrivelling as Juniper continued to float in the air about to complete the semi-circle routine and seal her finest hour. Juniper blew a kiss to Madame Bleu and the last emotion in her was equal parts shock and acceptance. It was a bizarre look.

Juniper landed on her feet and stumbled briefly only to merge into a desperate run. Straining muscles in her neck with a grimace. She wanted to be nowhere near that grav bomb when it detonated.

Turning her head, she caught the flash of the explosion. Pieces of mech, flesh and bone flying high—a winged beast darting toward the sun. It was beautiful until the shockwave threw her metres across the battlefield, falling face first into the ground. She took a load of sand in her mouth.

She fought the blindfold of unconsciousness wrapping around her eyes.

XAN
24 YEARS OLD

"So this is your glorious Gemarine is it?"

Xan looked around. Qilin perched beside him growling, spittle dripping down the bottom half of her half-open jaw. He had to admit it was a scene he never expected nor dreamed of for his home. A civil war on Gemarine. Rebel fighters rising up against the army.

"If you can't see from your vantage point, I'll give you a clue as to how your side is doin'." Massy scanned the horizon. "Hmmm pretty terribly actually…and I'm fucking loving it."

Despite a detonation that took out Madame Bleu's mech, Xan had to admit the outlook wasn't great. An explosion sounded off toward the eastern wall and an avalanche of rock crumbled down.

They each held Cranston ray guns directed at one another in a muted standoff.

"Why don't we let the true fighting spirit determine who wins here, shall we?" Massy proposed.

Xan shifted uneasily, lifting sand that trailed down his boots. "What do you mean?"

"Discard the gun and let's fight properly." Massy dangled the Cranston ray gun on his forefinger holding it up to him.

Xan looked at the ray gun with distaste. He never liked guns. It wasn't a true extension of his rage. When he killed the Valkors it was all emotion; that was what fuelled him. He also felt more confident with his hands, especially against Massy, who was unschooled in the art of combat. Maybe this would be the way to take him down. "Sure. You first."

"Always the smart boy."

Massy tossed the gun. Xan followed suit.

As soon as the ray gun hit the sand, Massy took his cue and launched at Xan, face set with determination and hunger. Predictably, Qilin pounced, wrapping her jaws around his armoured arm. Bolts of electricity surged through her as she ripped the control panel from his wrist. Qilin went limp, like a deflating balloon, and Massy discarded her across the sand.

"Predictable," he sneered, shaking his head. "Isn't it great having all these armour enhancements when you're a member of Bleu's inner circle?" Massy narrowed his eyes at the bulky control panel. "Although my fun has deteriorated considerably."

Massy—part of the inner circle. Madame Bleu must have been desperate if that was the case. But the control panel on Massy's armoured suit was a concern. It appeared to have activated various enhancements, as Qilin had now fallen victim to.

It wasn't just Massy versus Xan, Aranther versus Man, skin to skin, which meant it wasn't a fair fight.

Xan cursed. Why would he have thought it would be any different? He had been loyal to Massy for years, defended him, welcomed him into his family. Yet Massy gripped the arm that had given so much and yanked it from its socket. It changed Xan. It meant that he would be more guarded in the future. That in itself was cause for anger. When good intentions were sullied by the insolence of another.

Xan flared with rage. He pitched forward into a heated exchange of punches, taken, deflected, absorbed, delivered. It was a nasty brawl of bruises and blood. Fists that were once open palms of companionship found fury on swelling skin.

Xan's fury shone like a splendid supernova. In the brutality of their swinging fists, who would wear the winning crown of a champion?

Xan's chest sagged with exhaustion, the dance of the fight enough to leave him struggling for oxygen, let alone have the awareness to deflect and redeploy the attacking blows. A black halo surrounded Xan's left eye, a gash opened like a fissure in the terrain of his weathered face.

Massy's gold helmet was cracked asunder, exposing half of his face. Mischievous eyes were now flecked in scarlet sparks. Blood and sweat dripped like tears, as if physical pain was the heart that bore emotional weight. But there was no emotion in him, just the primal desire to best an opponent. To serve his own agenda.

Massy blew hard. "I forgot you learnt how to fight with Crazy Bitch McGee." He had backed away and ripped off the rest of the ruined helmet. The knotted hair fell across his shoulder, the charming smile on show. He spat blood on the sand. "But I don't fight fair, Xan."

Xan fought the urge to rest on his haunches. He stood tall, adjusting his boots on the ground, "Doesn't surprise me. You never had honour."

"You climb upon the backs of others and push them into the corner taking their glory. That is not honourable. Honour is intrinsic. When you value the deep desire within, finding contentment through that, that is honour." Massy shouted.

Out of the corner of Xan's eye he saw Qilin stirring. Her paws trembled as she tried to stand. It was a mistake to look at her, to let love invade his heart amid a fight against his nemesis. Xan should've known that Qilin could look after herself. The momentary lapse in judgement changed everything.

MASSY
25 YEARS OLD

It wasn't a fair way to go for Xan, but then again what was a good way to die? Did it really matter if you had your head sawn off by an alien terrorist or bitten by a little insect with enough venom to make you shit blood for a week. Death was an end that was common ground for all.

Far too many times in life, I have been shunned or cast aside or dismissed as a clown. Xan was lauded for dumb luck, for tethering himself to a creature that helped him survive in the wilderness. The moment he was untethered from the Mika Tikaani, he would be nothing.

Some might say bitter is my pill and I swallowed it hungrily. But if I'm soaked in bitterness, then I'm just fighting against monotony. I wanted change. I wanted the world to recognise the worth in all and not glorify the demigods. Maybe it won't feel as victorious as I had hoped. Maybe when my final moment comes, I'll meet the weathered face of regret. But there is comfort in knowing I came first. I was the strongest. I won.

I made myself. Luck had nothing to do with it. Even if glory lasts for just a second, it is a glorious moment earned.

CHAPTER 65

LOCATION: GEMARINE
YEAR: 118
RYKER – 21 YEARS OLD

Ryker ran to the eastern wall ahead of where Lilianna, Fleurah and Arcadie were. He threw armed gelbomb charges every ten metres. They stuck to the cliff wall, waiting for the moment of detonation causing it all to collapse. The higher ground neutralised.

Ryker called to Arcadie on the MPD. "Move away from the wall, it's not safe."

He vaulted over dead bodies, stumbling as he ran. He saw skulls cracked like barrels, the mashed butter of brains leaking from within. Entrails streamed across the sand like engorged serpents fleeing to hibernation. Ryker could never desensitise himself when it came to the sight of so many ruined bodies. Still, he charged onwards. He didn't want any of the trio up ahead to be in any danger of becoming just another scar on the innocence of his mind.

Peering over the top of the smoke, the flying sand, and the swarm of soldiers, he had lost sight of where they were.

Arcadie came through on the comms, but he was muffled by the wind in Ryker's ears, "They're boxing us in I can't—"

Ryker collided with Fleurah, grunting as they both hit the sand. Ryker lay sprawled on the ground, resenting the mocking smiles of the twin moons appraising him. The silhouetted soldiers standing atop the cliff peered down at them, Cranston ray guns poised.

Lilianna, still standing, bent down to pull Ryker up by the wrist. "Where did you come from?"

She smiled warmly. It was an emerging seedling through a crack in the concrete. Ryker's gaze turned back to the soldiers. It was only a matter of time now before they would let loose the laser rain. He slapped a spare MPD on Lilianna's wrist, flicking on the holoshield. It coated her in a protective sheen stronger than his own arms could, a shield more stoic than skin. He rose quickly and pushed Lilianna away from him and the wall. She reeled back, stunned, her face contorting in annoyance. On his other wrist, a detonator gleamed. He pushed it. Lilianna seemed to realise what it meant, even before the gigantic split in the wall cracked like the first words of thunder.

"Run," Ryker whispered.

Arcadie took flight, grabbing both the sisters.

No shots came from above. The eastern wall was coming down. The soldiers would fall to their deaths, entombed in the remnants of their higher ground.

Granite blocks tumbled like wheels down a mountain side. Rocky tumours of the planet grew like wildfire in its cancerous desecration of life. They were swallowing the ground around Ryker, and he, too, would soon be consumed.

But Ryker breathed deep and smiled.

I have found purpose. And with my death it is fulfilled.

The fear was lost. And despite being alone when the end came, he had never felt so much a part of something, more than he ever had before.

LILIANNA
22 YEARS OLD

Lilianna begged Arcadie to stop and would not relent until he put the two sisters down so they could look amongst the rubble for their saviour. Lilianna turned stones, and shifted as many fallen rocks as could, all the while crying out for Ryker through the guilty tears that obfuscated her vision.

Eventually Fleurah wrenched Lilianna away. "He gave you freedom, so take it, you fool!"

As Lilianna was led by a hand clenched in desperation, she resisted each step away from Ryker, buried alive by the barbs she threw at him, by the stones of judgement she cast so many times. Frustrated by his apathy, irked by his overzealous introversion. But through observing the small feats of courage he produced with his back to the wall or the smaller tasks of brilliance just to keep their ship flying and functioning, it was a wonder she didn't appreciate his value before.

Bright and bold are the stars that burn quickly into oblivion. While the unassuming ones twinkle with knowing winks, shining long into the night.

Lilianna knew that Ryker's light would be shining within her now, ensuring she survived this hideous battle.

The trio sped off to the west, seeking refuge. As they flew across the battlefield, dodging fire, Lilianna felt vertebrae crack when she stomped upon half-dead bodies. Furious cries of agony rang out but she couldn't stop and apologise. Her dark boots splashed into a puddle of mud, but it wasn't raining. Flecks of bodily ooze trailed down her pants as she realised it was not mud at all, just a sickening soup of spent anatomy.

Writhing limbs were worms burying into the sand, searching for a host. But amongst all the carnage, the only host was the reaper.

Such loss confronted her. Where there were once souls attached to these hunks of flesh, now remained only food for the land and folly for the living.

Many of the bodies were poor citizens roped into their cause by a plea of hope. But there was no hope for them left. It had abandoned them all just as Lilianna was, running over nails that clawed the sand for a treasure of salvation beneath. Their side was losing, and it had never felt so hopeless.

As if on cue, the sky opened up and hundreds of ships crashed through the atmosphere. Lilianna stopped, craning her eyes to figure out who was coming through.

The Cryptoborgs were coming to their aid. The skies were alight with bursts of combat fire—auroras painted in pastel colours. It was almost beautiful from the ground.

Funny how chaos and beauty are so interchangeable.

Some small ships seemed to break away from the pack, intent on landing toward the Valkor congregation at the southern end of the territory. Lilianna just made out the Cryptoborgs climbing from their ships, mauve skin lit by fire, sheened in sweat as they stalked forward to aid ground fighters in combat with Bleu's Gemarinian Army. The sheer number of the army was the issue but with the Cryptoborgs joining the fight the odds were changing.

An explosion detonated not far away; pieces of mech were scattered across the blast zone. Arcadie screamed, "That was Madame Bleu!"

Lilianna scoffed. "You're joking?"

"Certainly not in a situation like this!"

Her eyes were peeled, looking for any confirmation, but instead she saw golden armour flashing under moonlight. Massy and Xan exchanging blows.

Massy spat blood out the side of his mouth. He threw his damaged helmet away.

Lilianna didn't wait; she ran forward. She didn't know how she would help but the sight of Massy was enough to encourage momentum. She wanted to watch the moment that Xan let him have the final furious burst of punches to his throat, leaving him gasping and bloodied on the ground. Lilianna spotted Qilin twitch in the corner of the battle ground. Xan's focus wavered and he looked at her, too. Massy pulled out something fixed to the back of his boot. It glinted like a star born out of the dusk. Lilianna foresaw it all, but she was powerless to stop it. The pint-sized metallic *immobigun* was levelled at Xan. Massy wasted no time. A bright red bubble beamed out of the barrel.

Lilianna was too far away to do anything but scream. It was from the pit of her soul, hoping that its intended target would hear her, would stir and would save him.

"Juniper!"

JUNIPER
24 YEARS OLD

Juniper sat up gingerly, rubbing her head, vague shapes starting to take focus.

A terrible scream that held her name rang out across the battlefield. Louder than the other cries of terror around her. Was it because she knew whose scream it was? Was that the reason it incited a strong instinct within?

She turned and saw Lilianna stumbling across the sand. A horror-stricken face caused a sudden sinking of her stomach. Following her direction, she immediately understood the source of concern.

Xan was frozen in an immobilisation field. Massy stalked forward with a dagger gleaming under the iridescent aurora explosions the ships caused in the sky.

Juniper was up and running in an instant. "No!"

Qilin appeared from the corner of Juniper's vision. She moved slowly from a sedentary state. But was the realisation too late? Could she save him before Juniper intervened? Would Juniper make it before Massy plunged the dagger into Xan?

Juniper strained with everything she had to make it in time. Thigh muscles shook with lactic acid, calves cramped, but her arms pumped to push her forward. Exofingers were set free long ago, catapulting through the air, locked onto Massy. They whistled as they flew, like rabid baby birds with razor beaks.

But the blade of the dagger disappeared into Xan before they reached Massy. Fist against the hilt. The heart gushed with scarlet tears. The immobilisation field phased out. Xan's body buckled and collapsed backwards.

CHAPTER 66

LOCATION: GEMARINE
YEAR: 118
LILIANNA – 22 YEARS OLD

Xan crumpled onto the powered sands. Lilianna heard nothing but her own heart hammering in her ears. Felt nothing but the bile lurch from her gut and clog her throat. She dove the last few metres onto him, tears streaking her dirty cheeks. Shaking hands found his heart, pushing down to stem the flow of blood. It gushed through the gaps in her fingers, as fervently as his passion, like a stream after a torrent.

"No," she heard herself saying, first a whisper growing into a demonic scream. "No." The vibration of her terror wracked her entire body.

Massy dropped to his knees in front of her, blood bubbling out of his mouth.

He smiled at her. Lilianna did not register if it was a smile of truce or a mocking smile at her pain.

Juniper was behind him, her face contorted in rage, nostrils flaring, eyes smouldering a bright emerald. Her sword had been thrust with so much force through his back, it burst out his chest cavity in cascades of crimson.

The smile faded. Those wooden eyes that shone like varnish when he used to utter a joke, now they were vacant and soulless. His body fell forward. Juniper did not let him off with a peaceful descent. Lilianna watched her drag him by his knotted hair, tossing him onto the sand under the mournful gaze of both moons. She clawed at his eyes, screamed obscenities, ripped the flesh from his jugular with exoblades, crunching his windpipe in a macabre desecration of a corpse. Fleurah tried to pry her away from the mutilated body, but she returned like a hungry vulture, tearing into the being who ruined everything.

Lilianna hung her head and sobbed. Wept with all the love left inside of her, letting it trickle away down into the fresh wound of the punctured heart in front of her. The only heart she ever truly desired. Her grief cauterised the open wound of love.

Something wet and coarse slid across her cheek and a paw rested on her hand. Trembling arms clutched at Qilin's neck, and she sobbed with everything she had. After the last tear fell, she would be nothing.

JUNIPER
24 YEARS OLD

Juniper fell onto her knees and crawled over to the body. She wailed. No words could describe the pain she felt. Without meaning it to, it escaped her in a sound she had never made, never wanted to make ever again. It was putrid but it was the only exhale she could manage.

Lilianna wrapped an arm around her, and she fell from the cliff of shock, into the only two people who would hold her up. Qilin whimpered with a deep sorrow that harmonised with her own cries. The song of grief was dissonant, haunting, and spoke to the pessimist in all sentient beings.

The wind began to pick up. Grains of sand quivered and rose like a levitating God. Droplets of sweat loosened from Juniper's brow, gathered into a floating pool and twirled in the swirling wind.

She looked at Lilianna, dumbstruck, and they both turned to Qilin.

Her eyes were red, her paw rested on Xan's wound.

Lilianna regained herself as the clouds emerged across the night sky and the trees in the distance swayed under the might of the wind. "No, Qilin, he wouldn't want this!"

Qilin flicked her tail, spikes concealed, and knocked Lilianna away. Juniper watched Lilianna roll across the sand but did not reach for her. She was transfixed by the Mika Tikaani. A force within Qilin was connecting to Juniper's mind, opened by the Aranthers on Dracia. Something stirred, a beauty, a depth, a wordless divinity. The eyes glowed brighter, turning to flames in the Mika Tikaani's sockets.

A flash of bright white light ripped consciousness from Juniper.

Numb. Silence. Darkness.

CHAPTER 67

LOCATION: NOWHERE LAND
YEAR: INFINITY
XAN – 24 YEARS OLD

Xan awoke confused. He lay in the same field where he was born: the Wilds of Gemarine, where he had first come face to face with Qilin. An impenetrable fog had settled upon the clearing, but it didn't shift or sway with the wind. In fact, the song of the wind was no more. Time did not move here. Only he moved.

Leaves crunched under foot behind him, rustling in long grass.

He spun around and she was there.

Qilin but not Qilin. In a composite form of Mika Tikaani and humanoid, walking on two feet. She had a Human nose but Mika Tikaani ears, patches of skin in amongst the fur. But her amber eyes were the same.

She spoke with calm affinity. "You will have so many questions, I know, but Xan, dear child of Gemarine, let me just say it has been a pleasure to be your companion all these years."

Xan didn't know how to respond. He stumbled and stared, then ran forward to draw her close to him. Eager tears fell on her shoulder, robed in a light garment of dark blue and the night sky without the stars.

Xan pulled back and noticed the blood spilled across his own chest. The moments before his…summoning came into focus in short bursts of flickering projections. The immobilisation field, the dagger sinking into his chest, the draining of breath, the blood that poured like manic tears, the screams of loved ones fading, fading.

"I'm…dead," he said coldly, as if the memories confirmed the mind's delusion. "But how am I here? How are you here, like…this?"

Qilin shifted; ripples of movement radiated briefly. The wilderness behind him was still.

"There's much to tell, and I knew you'd have questions." Xan looked around and blinked. The twisted tree forest in the distance seemed to glow with the mocking laughter of both moons. "Time is infinite in this place, so we can be as we are in this form for what might feel like decades, if you wish." She gestured with her hands, fingernails long and sharp, reminiscent of her former claws.

This form? What is this form? Where are we?

Xan looked around at the lifeless environment and tried to acknowledge what he felt. But the feeling of being here was strange. He likened it to a dream state. Vivid enough to believe what he saw. But did sight mean it was real? Real was now a figment—a causation of the wandering mind. But far off something pulled him to reality. He avoided the feeling because he somehow knew it was an expiry for him.

"I know you must be concerned about where you are but try to conjure the calm within. I am still Qilin, and I would never let you flounder in this space without a tether." Her hand grasped for his and he took it. Their wispy exhales were the only sounds that permeated the space. Looking down at their clasped hands, a feeling of mild comfort swelled in his chest. At least he wasn't going to be alone here, wherever here was.

They began to walk toward the distant forest. Their manipulation of the material around them occurred but the other senses weren't activated without their touch.

"You would know, the Mika Tikaani were fierce and loyal creatures that bound themselves to the Celestials of the galaxy. We watched everything unfold for a long, long time. The moment arrived when we thought it would be best to leave the galaxy in the hands of sentient lifeforms who would evolve and spread and endure. That was all part of the plan." Her amber eyes were drawn to the unblinking stars. "All our powers—magic or however it's appropriate to label them—were placed into crystals among the stars. Star propulsion would take them elsewhere throughout the years, we knew this, but we were content to have a safeguard out there to repair any breakages that may occur."

Boots chirped on broken grass. Her other hand touched her chest. "My own power—elemental manipulation—was extracted and placed into the Mika Tikaani who had been tethered to me. Along with my own essence, we became one. We travelled the world for years before we were valued in the way *you* valued us. And you didn't even understand what we truly were. Loyalty is often born from the strength of blind dedication, of unconditional altruism. And once loyalty is bestowed, it prevails and endures."

Xan nodded. As he inhaled, he realised all scents were absent in this place too.

Loyalty was a quality he evoked in others as often as he gave it to them. Thinking of his crew made him feel light headed, as if the absence of them reduced his sense of self.

"You studied our power. The elemental manipulations," Qilin continued. "The power began to wane, something I had not foreseen. It did so because a celestial body had integrated with a true living creature. It meant an expiry date was approaching, one which you understood would eventually come."

Xan realised with a start that all the answers he'd been searching for over the years were now flowing toward him in thick bursts. All the frustrations at not being able to verbally communicate directly with Qilin were dashed. "But why was the power not used for self-preservation? It was always protecting others, about protecting…me."

Qilin nodded with a curt smile, as if sensing that all these revelations would formulate a large part of the closure Xan would need. "As you well know, love is the driving force behind many of the chaotic decisions we make. Love is more than a feeling. It is the energy that propels us into the fire despite knowing the consequence of getting burnt. To answer your question, a Celestial is never concerned with the self—everything was constructed for others to enjoy. It stands to reason that our powers were there to protect, not preserve."

The twisted tree forest loomed closer, and Xan was taken back into distant memories feathered with cobwebs. He walked with a different version of her now and where there were once pawprints—footprints replaced them. The past entwined with the present like a reflection in frosted glass, "So, you are one of the Celestials?"

"My name in your tongue is Chimera. One of four who seeded this galaxy." She smiled. "It was beautiful. The diversity. The spawn of life sharing the same spark." The smile flipped to a frown. "That's why it's so troubling to think that one species would want to eradicate another. These considerations were unfathomable to us, yet life evidently evolves in unexpected ways. So as we departed our 'workshop.' Marvelling at what we created, our fail-safe was enacted. Messages went to various worlds as rumours or ancient texts—as you discovered—so that at the right time these murmurs would reach ears with a desire to listen."

Xan brushed a hand against a branch of a twisted tree. Their boots cracked small twigs in two. "Did you know it would be me? That I would be the one that found you, that found Periah?"

"No." It was the first time she showed signs of patronisation. "This isn't a 'chosen one' scenario. You are here because you recognised a threat."

"But you and I found one another—is that not fate?" Xan had begun to weigh the idea of fate interventions in his mind for some time now.

Was it Sythkin's influence? Or just the accumulation of coincidences stacking up? With a mind that usually stuck to the safe path of logic and form, he found himself straying onto rough terrain.

"Well, I may have been the instigator of fate. I was the one who made my way back to Gemarine because of Bleu. I knew that I needed to intervene and find someone that would help collect the crystals and try to make things right again."

"How did you make your way to Gemarine, though?"

"I can manipulate the elements and I'm like a god. You do the math." She smirked playfully and for the first time really looked like how Qilin used to look when she chased him through grassy fields, or when she kicked up dirt as he lagged behind exploration missions, or when she'd snatch the last bite of stir fry eating dinner in front of the holofeed.

He fought back tears in the melting crevice of memories. Xan breathed in deep, needing to focus on the answers. They were his salvation, his pit stop on the way to crushing grief. "Okay so what have you brought me here for? This sort of afterlife?"

"It's more like purgatory. I think that's what you'd call it."

"Oh, wonderful—are you going to judge me because I forgot to brush the knots out of your coat on a weekly basis?" Xan chuckled nervously.

She laughed along with him. "You judge yourself harshly enough; you don't need me for that." Qilin stopped in a glade, the sun beaming through the gaps in the gnarled branches of the trees. "You'll be glad or horrified to know that the afterlife isn't a thing."

The revelation felt like it held gravitas, but Xan had already guessed as much. "I brought you here because I used the last of my essence to save you. This is like a regen chamber for the soul. Once I've let you know everything you need to know, I can give you your life back."

"What, why?" Xan felt like he should have been more grateful, but this was the confirmation he had dreaded. Her eyes would have gone red for the last time.

"There are many reasons, but you know my time in this form was coming to an end. To protect you, my brother, with my final act—there is nothing more fitting for me." Her hand smoothed over his shoulder and she faced him, her amber eyes showing nothing but strength and conviction. "You are a bridge that will connect planets in this galaxy. You truly savour life." Her arm extended across his back, and she brought him into a side embrace. He started to feel the weight of his emotion burst behind his eyes. "You find vulnerable creatures and save them. You have taken on our work without having any *real* celestial power. But…" She squeezed tighter as Xan buried his face into her shoulder, hiding his tears. "I'd like to think that my love is bigger than all of that, and love doesn't require validation or evidence. I choose to sacrifice myself simply because I love you."

Now she faced him, kneeling in the mud. Xan smiled, reaching for her hands, clasping them, feeling his bottom lip quiver. Xan heard the words but the true, overwhelming sadness didn't come. He knew that when he would wake, the emotions would flood him. Qilin would be gone, and untethered, he would drift far away, far from the beauty of who he was into the dark sea of apathy.

It doesn't matter if you have an opportunity to say goodbye. It doesn't soothe the heart as it silently breaks. No matter how much time you spend side by side—sharing scars that tether two souls—it is never enough. Forever is never enough.

"I…can't…lose you. I just can't. You're my sister."

"And you, my brother."

Xan squeezed her hand, which morphed into the paw he had always known. Suddenly her entire body had transformed, and he pressed his forehead against hers as a Mika Tikaani.

"I don't want you to leave me." His eyes were closed tight, but he could feel a breeze around him now. A tear slid down his cheek. His chest pounded with physical pain, and with the ache of love for Qilin. Already grief bit down with the locking jaws of a frightful beast. The wind picked up and Qilin melted into the air, like weary petals over the edge of the world.

CHAPTER 68

Xan opened his eyes and immediately felt no pain. His breaths were ragged. Lungs fought for oxygen like it was a priceless commodity. Moments ago death had claimed him.

Midnight blue and grey tufts of fur were carried on the breeze toward the sky, darkened into evening after dappling sunset colours.

Qilin wasn't beside him any longer, and she never would be again.

The pain of that sentiment was worse than the dagger that pierced him. Without noticing anything else around him, he punched a fist into the sand. His chest depressed with sorrowful sobs. A weak, husky voice rasped, "No," on repeat while tears that polished dusty cheeks came slowly. The rain became a hailstorm and the windowpane of his emotions were shattered by boulders of ice. Saliva dribbled from the side of his mouth as he sobbed, entrenched in the pits of dolour.

Xan relented to opening his bloodshot eyes. Feeling rapid breaths begin to ease, he gazed out across the dunes. Bodies were strewn over sand metres from where he lay.

He recognised Juniper and Lilianna, then further back Fleurah and Arcadie, straining to open their eyes as if blinded moments before.

Xan felt a swarm of heartbeats thrum in his ears. He rose shakily, one arm rooted in the sand. Squinting as the cacophony of noise swelled inside his ears.

Squeezing his eyes tight, he tried desperately to absorb this new feeling, a bizarre awareness of more than himself. It trickled through his veins at first, connecting his body to all life in close vicinity. He felt a *Gem moth* beat its wings as it searched for flame. An innate need for illumination in the same way that Humans might have searched for the touch of a hand. The connection crested on a wave searching for more, sweeping across sandhills, climbing over rubble, crunching over glass for more, more, more life.

Far in the distance, the serpent he released for torture weaved through the long grass in its biosphere, belly full. In the biosphere next door, a cluster of *vampiras vectra* hung from branches, craving the taste of blood. It was as if he identified with that craving, like he would accept the flowing crimson on his tongue as a part of a primal need.

Xan felt the words on his tongue instead. Could he feed them with commands? In the spark of life across the planet, he felt them all look toward him, wondering after so long why there was a way through the dark webs of communication.

I think…I can speak to them.

He reached out and he felt them there, waiting for him. Xan tried a command to the *vampiras vectra*.

Fly to the other side of the sphere.

The *vampiras vectra* did as Xan asked. It was not coercion; it was a respectful agreement. They spoke the same language now and knew

Xan's heart, understanding that any command or request of them was not harmful and would not bring harm to them.

Before he could explore anything further, he heard Juniper's raspy voice call out. It brought him back into the moment, as if following a command himself to rejoin this world once more.

"Xan, what in the zombie fuck is this? How?" Juniper walked forward tentatively at first. Tears streaked her cheeks, hands shaking. Breaking into a run, she stumbled until she had her arms wrapped around him. The impact sent them both flat onto the sand. Her cries were deep and mournful, stained with incoherent phrases of joy. He couldn't imagine watching someone he loved die, then moments later respawn into the world.

Xan felt another body join them; he winced out as he was crushed by love. Strands of blonde hair were caught in the field of his vision. A barrage of kisses slapped against his face from two sets of lips, from two of his true clan.

Lilianna pulled back suddenly. Red strands of pain burnt her cheeks. "Where is Qilin?" she asked.

Xan's face suddenly changed. "I…" He was lost for words. It was too raw to go back to that feeling. He needed to push it down, push it away until it was safe to truly let go. Lilianna looked as though she already understood what Qilin had done. Words were not uttered, yet the message was conveyed.

Fleurah and Arcadie appeared in front of them, deflecting a blast of laser fire, then Fleurah spun forward, throwing a sword through the guts of a Gemarinian soldier just over Xan's shoulder, while Arcadie shot through another.

"We're kind of in the middle of a battle guys!" Fleurah said.

"This trio can engage in intercourse at a more opportune time," Arcadie agreed.

"Arcadie, never call it intercourse again," Juniper chastened.

Dallis burst through a boulder like a wrecking ball, caked in blood. "Why are you participating in coitus at this time? This is war!" he bellowed.

Juniper started to rise, shaking off her tears and the momentary emotional paralysis. "Can we just agree to say fuck, holy shit."

Dallis helped Xan up. "What did I miss?"

"A hell of a lot." Xan grimaced as he found his feet, Dallis helping to steady him with immense concern.

"We need to get out of here. There are too many advancements. Quick, follow me," Dallis said.

They started to retreat, allowing Dallis to lead the way. Xan was still shaky on his feet.

Dallis looked behind as if suddenly remembering that he forgot something. "Where is Ryker?"

Xan realised he hadn't seen Ryker since the battle commenced.

Arcadie began to speak, "He was—"

Fleurah interrupted, "—back closer to the cave near the underground base. Let's just get you to safety and we'll figure out where he is after that."

Her wide eyes were a warning to Arcadie. This made Xan incredibly anxious. What happened to the kid?

He understood the nuance of Fleurah's concern. Get everyone to safety and then the truth would be revealed. But it did not sit well with him; if something had happened to Ryker he wanted to know.

CHAPTER 69

LOCATION: GEMARINE
YEAR: 118
XAN – 24 YEARS OLD

They reached higher ground to the west and surveyed the damaged lands. The rock they stood upon, stained in red, mirrored the ground below. Bodies were strewn amongst metallic debris. Beads of ammunition were strung across the jugular of the planet like polished dog tags. Vapour trails of smoke were nomads skimming the air for lodging.

Dallis pointed toward the battlefield below, Xan and Juniper beside him while Fleurah, Arcadie and Lilianna explored the surrounding area. The new exoarm glowed with confidence as moonlight highlighted its polished onyx design, fit with bright blue LED buttons. "When the Solu Shields were disrupted it evened things for a while. But the brutality of Bleu's army has been too much for some of the citizens. We've sent the wounded to the caves and some poor souls scared out of their wits were ferried off too. It was too much to ask of them," Dallis said.

Juniper nodded solemnly as if she understood that regular civilians might *show* a desire to help, but when it came to the crunch of the battle, desires turned rather quickly when confronted by true violence. Xan knew that firsthand, as he thought back to Dracia and his uselessness there.

Two birds landed on Xan's shoulder; feathers of glowing gold and hardened steel fluttered to the ground. He didn't recognise what species of bird they were, and it frustrated him. He enjoyed playing that game with himself. The moth had followed him and pinned itself to his suit next to the hole in the chest. The hole that had killed him.

There was no wind on the top of the small cliff. Arcadie buzzed around behind them like a dog sniffing out a buried bone.

Dallis continued. "The addition of Cryptoborg warriors have helped, but the Gemarinians have remote mechs and they are causing a lot of damage without much loss of life. It's looking dire—"

Several things happened all at once.

The sound of metal clanging rang out atop the cliff. Everyone spun around.

Arcadie had knocked into something invisible and dropped onto the ground in a daze. Fleurah ran forward to check on him. Lilianna tentatively started moving to their aid, head craned in confusion.

Juniper's face contorted in anguish, and Dallis returned her look of concern.

She yelled "Go!" at Dallis as she lunged at Xan, tackling him off the cliff.

LILIANNA
22 YEARS OLD

Juniper yelled and Lilianna whipped her head around, blonde hair flicking the back of her neck. Dallis charged toward her like a Marillidor in heat. His Cranston ray gun was drawn, and he was shooting at nothing.

Wasn't he?

She spun around to see a ramp lowering from nowhere. It was like a universal gateway materialising out of thin air.

But what was inside? She strained her eyes.

The ramp slowly came down, revealing the inside of a ship, soldiers stacked to the hilt. Ray guns pointed at Lilianna. She sucked in a breath. Belief took a long time to shake her into action. But Fleurah was always the brave one; she was always the one with heightened adrenalin. And as she saw the ramp come down, packed to the brim with enemy soldiers there wasn't a second wasted. Fleurah rose immediately from Arcadie's body on the ground, dragging her heel back and kicking him across the crumbling stones.

The ramp inched toward the ground. Fleurah leapt onto the metallic struts; her strawberry-blonde hair was the last exhale of sunset desecrating the spotless sky.

She cushioned the first laser shot with her stomach. Instead of it catching Lilianna in the face, it penetrated her sister's flesh, careened off Fleurah's ribcage and diverted into Lilianna's shin above the ankle. Blinding pain ripped through Lilianna's left foot, and she toppled to the ground. Pain reared at the base of her leg; her scream tore shreds from the fabric of the world. Dallis swooped down under a barrage of laser fire that smashed against his armour and in gigantic strides scooped Lilianna up and tore across the cliff face.

Lilianna bobbed in his grasp and through squinted eyes watched Fleurah on her knees on the ramp facing the soldiers. There was a hole the size of a fist where her left side used to be.

A grav bomb glinted in her right hand. She held it up for the soldiers to see.

Lilianna's voice was a grain of sand caught in a gale. "No."

Fleurah spluttered out, "Sisters are always there for one another."

Dallis leapt off the side of the cliff and gripped the edge of the rock with his exohand as the explosion billowed outwards, blinding white curtains rippling at an open window. The ship's cloaking was gone. Pieces of flesh, metal, bone and glass fell slowly around Lilianna, as she rocked in the cradle of Dallis's arms.

The brilliance of light was fading, and darkness lay claim to it as she passed out, a sister no longer.

CHAPTER 70

LOCATION: GEMARINE
YEAR: 118
XAN – 24 YEARS OLD

A *philix* flapped their wings in front of Xan's face then calmly took residence upon his head. Dangling off Juniper's belt, he willed a swap of the *philix's* wings for his arms.

The explosion above shifted the stones around them, some pebbles pitter patting their way down the cliff walls, tickling them as they went. Juniper's boronium exofingers gripped the edge and she held fast. The same could not be said for Xan.

"Hold on Xan, don't fucking slip," she warned through gritted teeth.

Another *philix* landed on his left shoulder. The extra weight was minute, but it added to his stress.

A large *topaz eagle*, five times the size of anything he'd ever seen on earth, appeared beneath him, soaring down from the blinking stars.

What is happening? Why are all these creatures flocking to me like I've built an ark?

Slick sweat sabotaged his palms. He felt himself sliding down Juniper's belt.

"Xan, don't you fucking let go!"

The fear gripped him. His mouth went dry, and he closed his eyes, wishing for not just a second chance, but a third. How many times would he be saved? How were they getting out of this one?

Tingles radiated throughout his fingers, crawling up his arms like lice.

Instead of helplessness and fear closing in, Xan began to feel things rippling around him. The physical presence of the flying creatures crowded him like the tree of life, hollowing itself out for critter dens and nurturing nests. Their lifeforce flowing through him now like roots nestled in soil, feasting on nutrients. The symbiosis was more than observation; he was a part of the cycle, and it was a part of him.

Juniper's voice trailed into nothingness. The buzz of the insects took over, the bird song lulled.

Xan knew what he needed to do. He had faith in what he could now sense from the creatures around him.

They wanted to save him. Just like he would save them.

He let go.

JUNIPER
24 YEARS OLD

The idiot actually let go. Actually decided—hey, falling off a cliff sounds great.

Juniper was horrified. A silent scream contorted her face as she watched Xan fall. But a word that had never dared venture near the jungle of her mind, took a machete and hacked its way inside.

Miracle.

A miracle. A full blown, hard as a donkey dick miracle.

The big-ass eagle swooped, capturing Xan's tattered suit in its beastly talons. It squawked some majestic call into the night, dominating the soundscape above the cries of all the minions dying below. A boast of grand proportions. It rounded in an arc above Juniper, dangling as precariously on the cliff face in the same way that her open mouth dangled. The eagle planted Xan's feet firmly on solid ground. Xan scrambled to the edge and pulled Juniper up.

Juniper dusted herself off, looked at the eagle, the small *philixes* buzzing around Xan and then finally at Xan himself.

Her voice was low, monotone. "The only time I'm ever speechless is when I've got duelling dicks in my mouth, but I don't even know what to make of…whatever the fuck that was."

Dr Dolittle looked just as bewildered as Juniper. He tried to formulate a response, but Dallis called out instead, "Help us."

Juniper hadn't realised the scene of total destruction laid out before her until she turned to look at the top of the cliff. Body parts like fallen fruit steamed in the sun. A blackened carcass of a ship, twisted in agony, lay inert and hapless.

They helped Dallis up, with Lilianna laid out on the rocks, passed out from shock. Her left foot was gone. The wound was cauterised, but she was paler than usual, and Juniper felt sick looking at her there. Regen gel couldn't fix this. She would be a worthy addition to the limbless crew.

"Where is Fleurah?" Juniper asked Dallis, who looked worse for wear himself.

He shook his head, eyes retreating in despair.

Juniper looked at the wreckage of the ship around them and understood. "A grav bomb." She shook her head, "She didn't deserve an end like that."

Dallis breathed in deep. "She saved Lilianna. She saved all of us."

Juniper noticed something glowing under crumpled boronium sheets. She ran to the wreckage, flipping over debris until unveiling Arcadie's faceplate blinking between pixels and fuzzy lines. She picked him up, cradling him like her metallic child.

Buzzing sounds came from his speakers.

"Hey buddy?" Juniper inquired, lightly tapping on his head.

The faceplate flickered, and complete pixelated eyes stared back at her.

"I have…malfunctioned." He sounded disorientated, as if his system was adjusting after being switched back on.

"Can you see me? Do you know who I am?"

"Miss…Juniper."

"That's it. You're okay," she exhaled. "I'm going to place you onto the ground, don't try to fly just yet." Juniper set him down next to large stones, cracked and worn.

"Where is Fleurah? Where did she go—"

MPDs started blaring warnings. "Troops have locked sights on the Western cliff tops after the blast!" Miami was desperate. "Are you fuckers there? We'll 'old 'em off as long as we—" Explosions, terror-stricken screams and then the line went dead.

XAN
24 YEARS OLD

Xan walked forward to the edge of the cliff and saw the troops converge on them. It all seemed hopeless. The dream of revolution was dead. Lilianna lying on the rocks passed out, Ryker lost, Fleurah dead, Arcadie rebooting his system.

A *drogan* crept up Xan's leg, claws embedded in his tensed muscle, but he didn't feel pain. Only felt its connection to him, a connection that transcended physicality.

He looked out under the largest moon and didn't just *see* the flocks of birds or notice the *philixes* still buzzing from shoulder to shoulder, or the *topaz eagle* perched on the edge of the cliff watching him expectantly—he *felt* all of them. Felt their purpose, their migration toward him.

Why?

It was his time of need. The man who dedicated his life to helping lost creatures. They could help him now. The way was etched onto his soul, reborn from the ashes of a Celestial being.

The MPD glowed bright on his right hand, connected to the biobase remotely.

Open all containment fields with atmospheric similarities to Gemarine.

From afar, he sensed the creatures turn to the western cliff tops. Something had awoken in him, a sight that flowed over mountains, valleys, and battlefields strewn with corpses. He reached for them—the *vampirus vectra, xeniph serpents, torpian raptors* and the *gruellers.*

Come. Help us defend our home.

They came.

Xan felt the flapping of wings moving branches, scales sliding through underground tunnels, claws flexing, tree branches cracking under the weight.

Xan sensed the *vampirus vectra* beat their wings impatiently in a slow build up. Out the open doors they faced the stars and with fangs bared, they prepared to feast.

A pair of *rhinovaders* gathered a kilometre away, turning to him. *Come.* He whispered on the wind. *Lend us your strength.*

The ground trembled with their answer.

"What the fuck is going on, Xan?" Juniper asked. "And why are these creatures flocking to you like you're…some kind of…"

"King of the Wilds!" Dallis shouted.

Juniper breathed in deep, shaking her head, but she stopped suddenly, and her features softened. "It was Qilin, wasn't it?"

It wasn't only his life that she gave back to him, but the thing he had always wanted. A way to truly be a voice for the voiceless.

"Yes," Xan said, nodding slowly, tears brimming once more.

Rhinovaders galloped onto the battlefield. They were like glorious beasts of old, rampaging across the sand, squashing soldiers underfoot. Mechs were paper in their path as they trampled them flat. The *vampirus vectra* dove down from heights, fangs exposed, salivating for a meal. They dined on flesh until organs were the last thing left on the menu. The army ran as fast as their tired legs would allow, climbing over the crumbling walls of the city gates into the mass of secure buildings to hide. *Torpian raptors* tore limbs, splattering curved arcs of blood across the ground. *Gruellers* burrowed into the sand, emerging with sharpened teeth, wrenching troops down into the depths like ground sharks.

In less than an hour Gemarine was Xan's. Not only was he King of the Wilds, he was a king of an entire planet.

CHAPTER 71

It was a sorry sight to behold, as the creatures turned from the battlefield satisfied with their defence of Gemarine. Winning was one thing, but to win drenched in crimson stains, arms outstretched atop a mountain of corpses…it wasn't noble. It wasn't a moment to celebrate.

The damage sustained tainted whatever glory there was to be had. But what is glory without a cunning plan to obtain it? What is triumph without the desolation of the conquered?

Even the wisps of smoke lacked energy, like the long grey hairs of an oracle waiting for the apocalypse to finally claim her.

Slain bodies were desert flora, sprouting from the ground in gruesome groves. The red sand held the last moments of many soldiers, and Gemarine would keep them there so that Xan and the others could at least build upon hearts that wanted the best for the world, regardless of what side they were on.

After Arcadie finally revealed Ryker's fate, Dallis bolted down the slope of the western wall like a rampant beast. Xan yelled for Arcadie and Juniper to take Lilianna back to the caves for treatment while he chased after Dallis. Having just resurrected from the dead, Xan was justifiably sluggish.

Resurrection was a feat so incredibly unbelievable not even the Bible had managed to convince more than a couple of billion people on Earth of its truth. But there he was in the flesh, running through canyons like a sloth drenched in syrup, puffing hard to catch Dallis tearing toward the wreckage of the eastern wall.

"Where are you Ryker?" he trumpeted, taking boulders the size of motorbikes and tossing them like they were balloons.

"Stop, Dallis, you don't even know where to look. Let me triangulate the signal of his MPD."

Xan opened the finda app on his MPD, navigated to the friends list and selected Ryker's address. It took a short moment but the navigation holo appeared in front of him, where two dots glowed. One was red for Ryker and the blue was for Xan.

"Over here, Dallis." Xan pointed.

They both ran to the spot and started clearing the rocks to get to Ryker's body.

RYKER
21 YEARS OLD

After complete darkness, a slither of light is like a pin puncture to the iris. Ryker recoiled from the sudden assault on his consciousness but the act of recoiling made him realise that he was alive. He sucked in deep breaths from the speck of light and squirmed to free himself from the rocks that surrounded him. Everything hurt.

There was panic now, and he tried to slow his breathing as he clawed his way toward that light. Slithers turned to holes, and the holes expanded, throwing moonlight across Ryker's broken body.

In Dallis's desperation and excitement to get him out, Ryker felt like he was once more crushed under the weight of boulders as the Valkor behemoth hugged him tight and kissed his cheeks caked in dust. Through the pain, his face swelled into a weak smile. Ryker couldn't hold it back even if he wanted to.

As if the world dared him to stop, he felt other bodies press in around him, squeezing around him and Dallis. As long as he lived there would be no reason to be alone again. He wouldn't abandon tinkering with mechanics in times of introversion, but it was a feeling of safety, of knowing that whenever he walked into the future, he would be flanked by a family he earned, not just a family he found.

CHAPTER 72

LOCATION: GEMARINE
YEAR: 118
XAN – 24 YEARS OLD

They took their time brushing the sand from dead bodies, clearing the rubble of what was and planning for what would be.

Miami wouldn't see the future she helped build or lead the exiles from the underground into the sunlight. Her final words were a warning as they stood vulnerable atop the western cliff. If she hadn't warned them, Xan might not have realised his gift, might never have reached out to the creatures which ultimately turned the tide in their favour. Her body was burnt and her ashes floated free toward the Wilds where she was queen.

Lilianna had spent three long days recuperating on the medlevels, waking with fitful screams and then falling into deep sleep once more. She had been fitted with an exo leg below her knee, with months of recovery on the horizon. Juniper ensured that she had the newest technology fitted to the leg, but also spent those three days yelling at the med staff to make her as comfortable as possible.

When Lilianna awoke, it was to a cruel reality. Finding her sister then losing her so quickly was a bitter pill to swallow. Dehydration stole her tears, but she sobbed into the dented shoulder of Arcadie while Xan and Juniper held her close.

A week later, Xan explained to them over holocall that it was time to complete the mission. The timelines remained broken, and they needed to head back to Periah to unite them.

A sense of dread came from the unknown, as it always did. When they finally flicked that switch would it all be rainbows and butterflies? Or would there be a glitch in the galaxy restoration?

Xan was captain of a brand-new ship. The memory of the *Attenborough* was strong, but a ship was just mass of hulking metal and glass; it didn't really *mean* anything. At least not as much as living things. Like Qilin. Like Fleurah. Like Miami.

Xan held out some kind of hope that once the timelines were brought together, they might find his ferocious Mika Tikaani friend wandering the Wilds of Gemarine.

But she was a secret Celestial, Xan remembered. The Celestials would operate beyond the Bounds of Time. There was just no way he would ever see her again, which struck hard at the bell of his resonant heart.

As they approached Periah, Xan scrutinised the ancient text to the point of knowing many of the pages off by heart. Juniper mocked his nerdy ways, but he felt confident about uniting the timelines and comprehended *some* of the theory behind it.

Time travel and multiverse theory was extremely difficult for anyone to grasp but what he deduced was this:

Each time they had visited the past and changed something, it created a new branch of time. Four missions meant four branches needed pruning from the galaxy tree. With the press of a button, all timelines would merge into the current one, creating a singular, dominant timeline.

Everything on Gemarine would remain unaffected by the merge. It was as if Gemarine was the anchor while the sea around the anchor could shift and change.

When the merge was complete Sytheria, Dracia and Earth would be alive once more. If they chose to, anyone on Gemarine could use the space jump technology to visit either of the planets. But each planet's time would be linear and relative to what Gemarine was experiencing. There would be no time fluctuations any longer, and they wouldn't know what year it would be until they chose to visit.

Periah was just as they'd left it. Cryptoborg bodies lay decomposing upon the surface. The whites of their bones stark on murky soil. Xan stared at the bones as he walked to the portal gate.

Beneath it all, despite our differences, we are all the same. Our bones glisten like white gravestones under tender rain. Our flesh withers like a childhood dream caught in the wrinkled fist of reality. In the beginning we are thrust into this world, scarless and unprepared.

In the end, scars are our second skin concealing the open fissures in our souls. We shovel mounds of dirt to fill the cracks, to make us whole again. But that same dirt will kiss the coffin we lie within—as we hide rather than heal.

Xan shook his head at the scene and noticed Juniper doing much the same. Although there was a look of regret in her gaze, there was a hint of determination too.

The sins of our ancestors take a long time to absolve. But if our own sins are softened by the sting of regret, maybe we learn faster; maybe we learn deeper.

Xan placed the crystal remote back into its slot. The portal hummed its approval, flickering fingers of glowing flares in anticipation of its final act. He took an inward breath, finger resting on the button, and turned to face the gathering behind him. Including himself, he started with a crew of six, and despite additions and lost souls, six remained.

Arcadie's metal claws wrapped around Lilianna's pale Sytheract fingers. The robot's face plate showed a doleful smile and flashing amber cheeks.

Dallis and Ryker had their arms linked and resting against one another. Or at least Ryker was resting against the hulking Valkor, both watching Xan with hopeful grins. It was a look that felt like a steadying hand, like a warm hug encouraging him forward.

Lilianna and Juniper stood within arm's reach of him, close enough to intervene if anything went awry. Most importantly, close enough for Xan to fade into the background after pushing the button, melting into their arms like sun kissed snow.

That is exactly what he did.

His forefinger depressed the button. A swelling crescendo, tubas and cellos duelling in harmony. Even the ground rumbled with applause. The portal's flickering violet tongue lashed out, sharp and dangerous pulses of energy. Then it roared and with a sharp snap, a glorious burst of portal beam shot out in 360 degrees—fanning out toward the horizon and beyond.

They were knocked back onto the ground, rocking gently with the planet itself.

As the pulse of energy faded across the periphery, the portal hissed. Its glow, its life was sucked away like a dying star.

Xan rose to retrieve the inert crystals, dusting himself off as he did so. He would take it upon himself to find a place so dark, so terribly uninhabitable to bury the wretched things. No light would touch them. No host of genocide and mania would touch the celestial power ever again.

Although what if the galaxy was threatened again in the future? Would he need to compose a ridiculous poem as a road map to where they were placed?

That was a problem for future Xan.

Present Xan would seek to find only what it was to be content. True contentment was often the hardest thing to find. Yet it was precious to him now at the end of Madame Bleu's reign, and at the start of something new, something good.

"Was that it?" Juniper said incredulously.

Xan's palms turned to the sky. "What do you mean?"

"I mean, in terms of seeing a whole galaxational shift of time and space all we got was a rumble and a dismal glob of energy jizz."

"Glob of energy jizz," Xan repeated, chuckling. "I'll make sure I detail that in my record for the cloud archives."

"Please do, courtesy of Professor Juniper."

"But seriously, how do we know if anything actually worked?" Her face was suddenly serious.

They decided to use the space jump technology to check that everything was in order. Cruising above each planet, they were pleased to see it teeming with life. Not wanting to disrupt any of the planet's progress, they stayed a safe distance away.

"You happy now?" Xan asked, resting his hands behind his head and reclining in his new state-of-the-art captain's chair.

"Always confirm your kill, or in this instance confirm your...time... restoration," Juniper said uneasily.

As they readied themselves for the space jump back to Gemarinian atmosphere Ryker asked, "Any ideas for the name of the new ship?"

"I was thinking—the *Attenborough II*," Xan said, crossing his arms.

"Yeah, and I was thinking of changing your name to Boring McBoringson." Juniper shook her head. "All in favour of Xan not naming his own ship, please raise your hands."

Each hand in the crew shot up without hesitation. Xan hung his head in defeat while they all broke down laughing.

Even in defeat, Xan couldn't help but smile. The song of true happiness was back inside his ship. Although it was in a different key, with a different rhythmic section, it was beautiful.

The MPD feeds didn't stop streaming the concerns of the citizens. It was to be expected after the chaos of the civil war and the demise of Madame Bleu. But it was more than that. Neutral citizens were reeling as Valkors and Cryptoborgs came to the aid of exiled Gemarinians and wondered what was in store for them.

Xan and Juniper were tasked with intermittent leadership while a final solution was devised. Aside from openly communicating their stance and reiterating their commitment to the safety of Gemarinian citizens, time needed to be taken to determine the best way forward.

Thus began the leadership of the Topaz Council. The council contained at least one representative from each of the Gemarine alien races: Human, Sytheract, Aranther, Cryptoborg and Valkor.

Juniper, Dallis and Marvest held the Human, Valkor and Aranther positions. One of Sythkin's sisters, Ouvalenti, headed up the Cryptoborg position and the final Sytheract position was held by Voilani, who had been the member of the exiles.

The council would determine all manner of concerns that were thrust the planet's way. But the pressing concern was presenting a united front so all Gemarinian citizens could live with liberty, without an undercurrent of control or secretive tyranny.

The council decided that four cities would be established across the planet. Topaz and Rosanthor existed currently and the proposed ecoamalgamated city called Forestia would be developed in the northern region of the planet, housing a second biobase as Xan sought to double conservation efforts. In the southeast, a coastal city called Kiishma would be developed as an area of sanctity and wellness post the civil war. It would also house a new underwater biobase, taking threatened sea creatures into consideration.

All clan structures were set for reviews and a special task force was deployed to work on the applications and necessary functionalities of the clans. It was initially difficult to incorporate the selected Cryptoborgs and Valkors into previous clan structures. Nothing was enforced and a consultative approach was taken to ensure proper integration. There were some differences in how Cryptoborg and Valkor family dynamics were in comparison to clan structures. Each was given the option to join a clan or forge their own to become accustomed to the new way of life or remain on the Cryptoborg home planet of Hyperonite.

Xan had decided upon separating from his former clan to develop a new one. His new clan contained Lilianna, Juniper, Arcadie, Ouvalenti, a Valkor called Wythero and the former inventor of the underground, Dryno. Dallis, Ryker, and Lambastian were in their own clan with two other Cryptoborgs.

Most of them met up at Fusion together and had opportunities to enjoy one another's company in various ways. But they all spent regular time together, huddling on levels watching holostreams, attending sporting events, dancing under the twin moons at outdoor music festivals and exploring various zones of Gemarine and other neighbouring planets.

Xan continued to work with Lilianna, Ryker and Ranjit, except the extinction extermination operation was now much larger.

Lilianna planned solo expeditions on her very own ship, the *Fleurah*. Ryker usually accompanied her on those missions to ensure that everything ran smoothly. A Valkor security detail and an Aranther pilot were part of her team. Xan still felt nervous whenever she went out by herself, but it brought her so much joy when she was able to save the creatures she had researched for a long time.

Xan continued his own expeditions with a new pilot from Earth called Steve. The new ship was called the *McBoringson* at the behest of Juniper's mutiny. Lilianna and Ryker accompanied more often than not. He loved spending time with them both while in his element. Although on multiday hike expeditions it was often Xan and Lilianna completing a cycle of research, trail camera checks, fusing, trail camera checks part two, fusing, sleeping and repeating.

Juniper was on the leadership team in the new restructure of the defence division. Arcadie had signed up as part of the mentor program so Juniper accepted his application and looked to help teach a new crew since the deaths of Serrara, Jimeny and Benius. Juniper had more to give after her dealings on Dracia and felt that the best thing for her sanity was not to necessarily hang up the battle armour for good, but to leave it on the mantle momentarily. Hopeful that she would inspire others not to conquer, but rather defend what they had. Still, she declared, "I can't wait until someone can replace me on the council. I always hate it when bad ass bitches are confined in a cage of diplomacy."

Arcadie had a side project where he used some of his own AI tech systems, combining both the Phineas program and the RC-9 cleaning module on Juniper's level. He had the means to make his very own spare part robot legion. Xan was interested to see how far he could go.

Dallis set up an integration liaison service where he assisted Valkors and Cryptoborgs with their introduction to Gemarine culture and monitored their well-being with such a significant change. He was perfect for the role because he always saw the positive, was incredibly welcoming and went above and beyond to find solutions. He humbled Xan. The Valkor who was the bridge between former enemies, who preached forgiveness in the smiles that penetrated the skin of a man who scarred his. Xan hoped that others found the second chance that he was afforded, and instead of teaching with the blade, he taught with the heart so that they might learn with love over fear.

Xan looked out of the viewport on the way to another planet, another creature. The endless sea of black spread out before him. A planet twirled on its axis, a colourful marble still spinning after a brutal collision millions of years ago. The hero inside of him didn't need any more enemies to vanquish. But extinction was a nemesis that wouldn't abate. So here he was, still tangled in fate's web, hacking at its coarse fibres before death came to feed.

It was no longer a burden; it was a privilege. And it filled him with purpose to know that by his guided hand he would right the wrongs. A purpose that meant more having been through the bowels of time and space, emerging covered in nothing more than determination.

We are the hands of fate, right the wrongs.

EPILOGUE

LOCATION: GEMARINE
YEAR: 119
XAN – 25 YEARS OLD

The bioluminescent tendrils were nocturnal, and they slept peacefully now.

As careful boots fell upon the path, he barely registered a sound. Concerned insects droned in a raspy tenor tenuto, while melodious bird song leapt toward clouds attempting to scupper the reach of the sun. Xan brushed his hands against the tops of the flaxen grass, seed pods scattering into the gentle current of the wind.

The scent of toasted wheat wafted toward him. The Wilds were welcoming Xan after a long absence. He didn't possess the mental fortitude to walk these paths again, but after a year it was time to move forward.

A commemoration of his kinship with Qilin was a way in which he could start to heal.

Xan faced the bronze statue. Peering into Qilin's lifeless eyes, he felt the surge of complete and utter woe once more. His grief was a stone that sunk to the bottomless depths, buried in a black ocean of tenacious tears. Just as the ocean spread out further than the eye could see, so too was the understanding that grief would not follow a path; would not reach an abrupt end. It was malleable and would ebb and flow as the years unfurled. The insurmountable pain would diminish like a burning candle in the distance. Grief would turn to sadness, and sadness would wilt into longing.

He would long for the Mika Tikaani's playful personality, her loyalty and fierce force. All the endearing qualities he missed. Those lifeless eyes of the statue could never replicate that glow of perception in her gaze, the echo of truth beneath the veil of her disguise—much harder to contain hidden amongst the amber, trapped like a prehistoric fly.

Xan's forehead pressed against the statue, remembering the gesture of friendship with his Mika Tikaani friend. What greeted him was cold. Colder than a memory.

Juniper and Lilianna had commissioned the statue for him, flying over the Wilds in the evening and placing it in the very spot Qilin and Xan met one another all those years ago. Xan chose not to fly, though. This was the first year of an annual solo pilgrimage he would make to honour Qilin and their friendship.

As he sat down on the grass, he unscrewed the canteen of water and sipped under the watchful bronze eyes of Qilin in statue form. He peered into the distance at the same tree he stopped at, the same tree where he turned and watched the struggle between creature and beast.

Things were considerably different now. His essence reached out with curious hands to all manner of creatures if he felt their presence nearby. They often felt inquisitive enough to approach him, lay down beside him in the evening after the long hike of the day, or flutter over his head as he trudged over difficult terrain.

The tree was another part of the memory. A reminder that turning away is the easy path and the easy path doesn't often heed rewards. To become an advocate for those in need fills the soul with pure purpose.

Taken from his thoughts, he felt it before he saw it.

A presence that crept through the grass too close to be comfortable. The intention was indiscernible. Could he nullify a predator with his gift? This was something he hadn't tried yet—a situation he hadn't yet experienced.

Rising sharply, he backed up against the statue for protection and searched the flaxen grass. A glimpse of a small, spiked tail emerged like a periscope, then fell beneath the rustling waves once more. Curious, Xan closed his eyes and sent his essence forth instead. Immediately his breath was taken from him. There was a recognition in the feeling of the creature. It was nostalgia—a gentle lullaby that gave you warmth and security, a morsel of food that gave you back the taste of childhood. It reignited him and it buoyed him in the languid sea of sorrow.

The grass parted and he bent down expecting to see her, to feel Qilin in his arms again. But it was not her.

The feeling of disappointment lasted for a short, bitter moment before the Mika Tikaani cub launched toward him.

It was so small that it barely made him stumble, but he fell back anyway as a forked blue tongue grazed against his cheek.

Xan chuckled. "Okay, okay. Who are you, little one?"

The creature spoke not with words, but with globs of wet saliva that trailed down Xan's neck. Orbs of amber gazed up at him with relief, as if a long search had ended.

Xan looked up at a sky full of stars. The stars who were the ultimate time travellers. They winked at him—a colleague in the vastness of space and time. Tears fell like empires as he crumbled from the inside first, with the rubble of his pain surrounding him.

But was it pain? Or pure happiness?

For the first time in a long time, he felt like there was hope.

Hope. That's who you are.

Xan looked for Hope's mother, but she was nowhere to be found; even reaching out for her essence returned no results. He knew when he got back to Juniper, she would most likely kick him in the junk for the new Mika Tikaani's name.

It's totally worth losing a testicle, right?

They stopped on the second night at the waterfall where Qilin had first shown her elemental manipulation. Xan made sure he checked every inch of the depths before he dove into the pool this time. Instead of flitting at the shoreline, Hope dove in after him, brazen and unafraid. Paddling her paws chaotically, startled eyes hovered above the water line like burgeoned water lilies. Xan swam to her, letting her scramble over his shoulders, clinging onto his neck like he was a submerged tree.

Afterward, they dried off under the warm sun, the bulbous tree flowers hissed, while the thieving *philixes* were busy depriving flowers of their golden centre.

Xan's thoughts drifted calmly. The brevity of life, the existential crisis too haughty to measure and the connectedness of all things.

Love is a dandelion—stoic in the sunshine of a calm day, fleeting when the zephyr speaks. It roars in its death, petals twisting and floating into the ether as if it had never existed.

He would make sure that this love was not a living thing that could be killed. It would remain inside him until he passed it on to another willing soul, another *worthy* soul. Qilin was more than a physical presence, he knew that now. She was a life force that endured.

As he nursed the little cub in his arms, stroking fluffy grey fur with bright cerulean patches, he smiled.

That same life force was a connecting thread between them all in a rough, expansive tapestry.

As long as that force persisted, extinction would be squandered because, despite the limits of the physical self, something always lives on. Nothing could ever truly be extinct.

ACKNOWLEDGEMENTS

I would advise you not to read the acknowledgments until you have finished the book.

I would like to start by acknowledging the Traditional owners, custodians and Elders of the Darug Nation, both past and present. Most of my writing occurred on Darug land and I wanted to pay respect to all Darug community members living on and off country and show my support for the Darug Nation and its people.

Firstly, thank you again for supporting my author journey. Secondly, this section is dedicated to all the people who have been helpful over the last year, specifically related to the composition of this work.

To my developmental editor and best friend, Emmie Hamilton – The more I work with great people like you, the better I become. You not only developmentally edit my books, you do everything. You fix copy, you proofread, you are a soundboard, you are a coach. The biggest influence on my writing has been from you. As always, words won't do justice here, but just know I appreciate you and everything you do.

To my editor, Lauren – thank you for your keen eye and your insights and tips to improve my writing.

To my beta readers and proof readers Natalie, Amber, Emilia and Nick - thank you for answering the call. Your feedback was phenomenal and it really helped me ensure that this colourful group of misfits got the ending they deserved (at least most of them).

To the supportive team of ARC readers, readers and friends who have made a huge difference to my confidence as a writer: Renee, Hanadi, Kate, Tanya, Miranda, Liz, Bex, Ethan, Tabi, Jarod, Jessica, Kim, Tierney,

Sinsimelia, Krystal, Leaha, Ash, Cristina, Cassandra, Lea, Corrie, Sam, Emily, Witchetty to name a few. To the Booktok community who aren't just there to share in the fun and silliness with me, but actually do their very best to read, support and encourage. To the fellow indie author community who have been kind enough to not only show support but continue to be a source of inspiration for me. I would like to name some of you who have been on another level with your cheerleading and consistent encouragement – Emmie Hamilton, Kristen Dovnik, Callan J. Mulligan, Liv Evans, Nikki Minty, Meagan Johnson, Gabriella Margo, Garrett Godsey, Qualia Ried, Danielle Hughes, Jessika Grewe Glover, Rhiannon Marina, Mika Rayne, Emilia Dashfire, Alexander Michaels.

A separate thank you to Jenna Croman. May your sweet soul rest in peace. I'm so sorry that you never got a chance to be with Qilin and the crew on their final journey, but I know you would have hyped this story like crazy.

To Boo, my Qilin – I love you, may your memory live on in her.

Thank you to the bookish businesses who have been supportive of my work thus far – Forever Lost Bookshop, Tales and Tomes, Rosey Ravelston Books, Book Addiction, No Shelf Control, Battlestar Booklactica Podcast and Lou at Bands and Literature.

To everyone in my extended family – I love you for all the opportunity you've afforded me and the constant support provided.

To my sources of writing inspiration over the last year - Pierce Brown, Ray Bradbury, Dan Simmons. Thank you for your stories. They have helped guide me with developing my own.

CONNECT WITH JP MCDONALD

Website: www.jpmcdonald.com.au
Instagram @jpmcdonaldwrites
Tiktok @jpmcdonaldwrites
Facebook @jpmcdonaldwrites
Email: jpmcdonaldwrites@gmail.com

Call to Review:

If you enjoyed this piece of work, it would lovely of you to consider leaving a review on the various review sites and/or your social media accounts to assist in reaching more hearts and minds.

www.ingramcontent.com/pod-product-compliance
Lightning Source LLC
Chambersburg PA
CBHW050108120726
47904CB00004B/1260